By The Same Author:

Fiction

> The Gwalia Triad:
> Ends and Means
> Out Of The Dark
> Legacies

Nonfiction

> Animal Communication
> Bioacoustics

LEGACIES

A NOVEL

BY

D B LEWIS

 **New Generation Publishing**

For Pam
(as always)

And

The Folk at Theakston House Farm

CONTENTS

CODA

APPENDIX I
NOTATION

APPENDIX II
SOURCES

Acknowledgements

My thanks are due again to those who keep me in line and who ensure that what I say and the information I present has a resemblance to accuracy; if after all their help and protestations, faults still remain, they are mine, not theirs and I ask their indulgence. First thanks, of course, must be to my wife who has had the Patience of Job when different moods dominated my behaviour and to whom I turned first when my computer wouldn't obey me. Then, (in alphabetical order to avoid any misunderstanding), my thanks to Malcolm Elvines (a Geologist), for having carried out his Doctoral work (some years ago now) on the London Basin and the Thames, its Geology and that of its position and relation to the North Sea and the Paris Basin, and who was prepared to let me know his thoughts. My thanks to Gwyn Jones also, (who is a Mathematician/ Statistician) who is a compatriot of mine but one who had the greater foresight as a young man, of buying the large dictionary of Welsh – Y Geiriadur Mawr – and who has used it often to save my life and to hide my ignorance. Then to Peter Waters (a real Oil-Man, who gave me some texts on oil exploration). Many others, through teaching, talk and reading and a few beers along the way, have helped immeasurably in my pursuit of the Mythology and Legends; without them, my enjoyment of the pursuit would have been much less and my knowledge and understanding even more deficient.

DBL
2013

FOREWORD

This is a work of Fiction, but I acknowledge Robert Graves' thinking when he said in the Preface to his Collected Short Stories: *"Pure fiction is beyond my imaginative range"*, and adds that, *"most of the stories are true though names and references have been altered."* But I will go further: places have been changed or redrawn and their geographical positions altered for the sake of the narrative and to protect. If anyone recognises himself or herself or believes that they recognise others, or the places, described within these pages, I hope that they will be tolerant of my deficient imagination and that none of it will be considered hurtful or as an attack; if I am at fault, I apologise for it in advance: consider the matters to be done in gratitude.

This tale was originally conceived as a continuation of the saga of the characters developed in the earlier two books of the series, now called (for my own benefit) the **Gwalia Triad**. Gwalia is a poetic, bardic name for Wales; Triad (Trioedd in Welsh) is an ancient word for prose poems, which I hope it to be. But you must judge. Though a Triad in form, each Volume may be read in isolation or in any order.

When I first drafted my further ideas for the lives of the characters of the earlier books and the 'next generation' of the two families, it was in order, particularly, to bring the story to the brink of the ending of the Twentieth Century. There were momentous enough changes to occupy the new young. Edward, the son of Charles Williams, and Anna, the adopted daughter of Will and Megan Griffiths are now grown and have graduated, he in Geology and she in Philosophy. And they have married.

Edward returned from an assignment on an oil exploration ship in the Timor Sea and is traumatised by the events he witnessed in the Indonesia of President Suharto, and has retired into solitude. Anna came to know that her life would be short because of her medical condition. She became determined in the time available to her, to seek out her biological parents, if they were still alive, and make a form of peace with them and in so doing have a greater understanding of herself. Her mother had died but she took her father to live with her and Edward. Her father, in his own life, had become immersed in the Ancient Myths and Legends of his Country, to an extent that the Tales had become his reality and his daily life had become the fiction.

Reconciliation was to have been the intended theme, but Time worked the ending to its own satisfaction. Also the Muse had Her own agenda, and She took the tale into Celtic Mythology and Legend. I did

11

not then, nor do I now, have any scholarly equipment for pursuing this discipline. What I did (and do) have, along with most Celtic children of my generation, is a sort of *'Lamb's Tales From Shakespeare'* of the stories of the Cymru – the Ancient inhabitants of the *Island of the Mighty*. Nevertheless, the Muse was adamant that the opportunity should be grasped, not missed. She gave me a great deal of reading to do. Many of the seminal books are encased in the National Libraries and not easily accessed. But I was made to persevere and slowly I found various compilations of the Tales of my land, and I came to understand a little something of my early ancestors and their *'doings'*. I thank Her for that, for I found the Tales fascinating.

What remains to be explained is the matter of structure. To have inserted even minimal fragments and summaries of the Old Tales of Gwalia into the text itself (and to have necessarily elaborated on them for the sake of explanation and relevance), would have greatly interrupted the flow of the main narrative. Therefore, I have resorted to the 'trick' used by scientists who publish their works: I have used notation, the explanations of which and notes thereof, are given in an Appendix. This does not distract the reader from this attempt at a Tale, (or not so much), while those who are, or become, interested or intrigued by these snippets may follow that interest from the Sources given in another Appendix. (This last is not a definitive list, of course – that listing would make this book something of a Thesis, and many times as long. And it would require me – and you - to learn Middle Welsh at the very least; but it is a start that can be pursued if the interest is there. But a word of warning is required: the most greatly relevant of the books listed, especially in relation to Goddesses, Gods, Ancestors and their profusion of names, is Graves' The White Goddess. A fascinating book, but not an easy one – be prepared to devote some time to it).

Now, a note on this very little usage of the Welsh Language: I can be criticised and castigated for this use of it by those who would be far more accurate and meticulous and I respect their position and greater linguistic skill without defence. My use of Cymraeg here is as a Regional Vernacular (an Oral Slang, if you like; or laziness if you will be less generous) that would have been heard in the Valleys of South Wales at the time of this modern tale. On another linguistic matter: those who read carefully will come across occasional words not listed in a Dictionary. I quote from a character in the book: *'If there isn't a word I want, I make one up!'* This sounds a little *Alice in Wonderland –* ish, but to give a particular understanding or to get across a particular realisation with a *made*-up word was great fun; see what you think of it.

I have to finish this *Apologia* with a statement of regret. In this Modern, Secular and *Real* age, a fear of Ghoullies, Ghosts and Bogeymen, the place of Tales of Knights, Giants and Maidens, and of Gardens of Light and Pits of Darkness, seem confined to Children and Old Men who are mostly of another, earlier age. That is a great pity, for they know of the truth of it all: there is much truth in the Myths and Legends of our Lands, and in the lies of fiction, if you're prepared for the pursuit. In this context, it is of interest also, that it is the *Old Men* and *Old Ladies* – the Grandparent Generation – that are the better raconteurs of these Histories. The current generations fear Reality too much, it seems, to entertain *The Old Truths*.

Now, to lay (not quite all) my cards on the table before we start, I must say something of a matter that has puzzled me for some time. Why is it, that those who print, bind and market the tales to be read and related in the dark nights of Winter (more so than Facts, though there is something akin to it there too – the need for *Gravitas* is paramount), prefer the producers of the works to *impress* people, rather than to entertain them? I wish to entertain people, myself included. At least, that is my hope – why bother otherwise?

DBL

Itchen Abbas 2013

PREFACE

Without Solitude, there can be no Understanding;
Without Understanding, there can be no Wisdom.

*

Some will take the lead
Others will faithfully follow
And some will decline.
Many of those who seek to follow
Will fall by the wayside
On the road to their own Jerusalem
Into the Poppies or the Mud.

Which will you be young acolyte
Who knows little of any as yet?

*

No man's life can be told in one tale
Too many people have made it for that.

No one tale can give up its meaning
When the moment itself has passed away.

PRELUDE

CHAPTER 1

A RESPONSE TO A CALL

It was more than four years since Edward had returned from his Company post on an oil exploration ship on the other side of the world. That time had ended in great sorrow for him and he tried to recollect it as little as possible. The pain of recollection had eased with time, but it had not gone. Some memories, more insistent than others, still intruded on this new life that he had sought to build. He had bought himself his house on a cliff in a remote part of his home country, and had withdrawn from his family and his society. This had caused his father and sister great sorrow, but he had known that if he was ever to recover, that was his surest way of doing so.

Since his repatriation, he had not driven, nor visited, anywhere without some proper purpose to it, and only then if it could not be avoided; the telephone became his surrogate when travel and contact was to be overcome: delivery of goods and chattels were less demanding of him than collection. There were 'thanks' to give and bills to be paid, but they were both more easily dispensed at a distance. In that way, time passed unremarkably and unrecorded: a doldrum with no 'highs' nor, in due course, no spectacular 'lows'; no call on his time by others and no demands on his intellect but what he offered. Of course, the whisky had helped, even though he knew, in his own defence, that *the development of a knowledgeable palate* was an inadequate excuse. However, in that way he had come, slowly, to a form of peace; or to a precarious stability at least, and so to a form of Resurrection. Then he came to recognise that this behaviour was nothing more than a continuing act of self-indulgence, a weakness, and time became increasingly heavy on his hands. He still enjoyed the solace the whisky gave him but he now understood his need of that escape.

He began to journey a little further into the land that had made him and of which he was still a part. His interest in the ancient history of the country was rekindled; he saw again the age and beauty of the land; saw how it had been fashioned into such beauty; and why it was still so much a part of his nature even though he had travelled so far.

Now, the young woman he had known since childhood had called for him, and there was no denying her, nor his need to see her. Her name was Morwenna [1] known to him and the family as Anna [2]. She was the adopted daughter of Will and Megan Griffiths, both long-term and close friends of his father. Will had died, too young and with too little promise fulfilled, and Edward's father Charles, now shared his life with Megan, his friend's widow. A love that they had shared as young students had finally been resolved and with none of the urgency of youth, each felt a comforting fulfilment in their commitment.

Years before, as children, Edward and Anna had each pledged themselves to the other and had vowed that if either of them needed the other, they had only to call, and the other would come. It had seemed a childish pledge at the time, but sincere for all that – equivalent to the mixing of blood to be *Blood Brothers* during an age without understanding. It had become more, not less important as they grew older and closer: it had never diminished, though they had followed their different careers. Also, it had become something of a crutch to him as he had come to face his solitude: he believed that she would be there for him if he called for her: he knew that he was never completely adrift.

Anna had now called on his vow and it had broken through his solitude; he could not deny her; he would meet her train and assuage something of this renewed need for her, or someone like her – a Goddess of a kind, or at least a Muse that he could try to understand again. Until recently, he had come to believe that this need, the love of a woman, was being denied to him. So the pledge he had made in all childish honesty, those years ago, he would not deny. But, as a man, he was very afraid of the consequences of its fulfilment: he was still in denial of people outside the retreat he had fashioned for himself: this meeting could mark the end of his hermitage and he feared it; he thought it a step too far and too soon. He could not say that he was yet strong enough to hasten a new responsibility: his own desires were too ambivalent; he needed more notice, more time to come to terms with his resolve.

He had woken early and was agitated that the time crept forward so slowly as he sought to fill it. He knew and understood that there was little reason to deviate from the shortest and most direct route from his house on a headland to the agreed train station; it was best to get the meeting over with; and he knew that it was a prevarication to travel considerably out of his way to go via his father's childhood valley; there was no benefit to it; it would not delay his fulfilment of the promise he had made in a world that he had inhabited a lifetime ago; he could still meet the train she would arrive on; making a longer journey of it was not denying the pledge he had made. He had also, in an earlier life, pledged to himself that he would not forget the small world that his father had been born into. Though his father had not visited his childhood house, nor the village since he had attended to acknowledge the death of his old friend and erstwhile neighbour, Dr Will Griffiths, that was no reason why he should not.

He did not drive along the 'Old Road' cut into the side of the mountain: that had been closed to through traffic long before because of the danger of landslip. Instead, he had travelled the 'Low Road' alongside the river that the traffic now used and where it served few villagers, most of whom lived higher on the mountainside; it was 'safer' they said. From his station on the valley floor he could look up to the house and land where his father had been born and had grown to a man. He took out his binoculars which he always carried and focussed on the side of the mountain. There was little still standing; the Welsh stone walls were long turned to rubble; the old sty for the Mochyn[3] that he remembered every family had built for the pig that was to be fattened for Christmas, was fully collapsed. Even when he was a child, it had fallen into disrepair: there had been no money to buy a young porker in early Spring and no inclination to maintain the sty after an 8 – 10 hours shift underground at the coal seam of the mine; but now the sty looked in better shape than the house itself: the stone bones of the building were not as stark in their exposure, at least. There had been a substantial amount of land attached to the house and it had been tilled to feed the large, tribal family, the women of which always seemed to be *carrying*. This was not from any Religious or Ecclesiastical code; nor from any prescriptive directive: there was no condemnation of birth control as for the Catholics, strong though the 'Chapel Culture' was. It was a simple *'biological imperative'*: less a *'I give you this Land; go forth and multiply'*, more of a *'I give you this woman, go ahead and multiply.'* And there was no money for contraceptive devices in any case: that was a frivolity; in a choice between a condom and a slice of bread in gravy, bread on the table was more imperative.

The land had been tilled for vegetables and had also been given over to areas of soft fruit and varieties of apples, the bruised windfalls of which would have been fed to the pigs. The trees were now old and gnarled and uncared for, but still obstinately produced small but heavy crops of apples. Nearer to hand, was the field where what they had called, *Wild Rhubarb* had grown: knotweed with a tart taste like rhubarb, the hollow stems like bamboo that drew the water from the earth and which proved almost impossible to eradicate, it being immune to all known weed-killers. It had to be kept away from the pigs for fear of bloating and poisoning them. The children had made pea-shooters from lengths of it in the season of hawthorn berries. From the midst of it in the dark evenings of Winter, the time of Ghosts and Ghoulies, the

21

children had been frightened by the appearance of the *Ladi Wen* [4] dressed appropriately in the moonlight in her white gown (in truth, a bedsheet taken from a mother's bed).

He looked further up the mountainside to where a large stone had stood on which his father and his neighbour Will, had played as children and which he remembered visiting as a small child; there was no sign of it now; it had fallen or been overgrown. The land could do with being cleared. He considered walking to the place, but his memories were intruding too much and bringing on a sense of loss for a childhood gone, and no doubt embroidered, and most improperly remembered. Besides, he could not tarry for long; he had an appointment to keep. Perhaps then, a visit another time; now that he'd made it once, it could not be so difficult next time. He raised his arm in farewell and thanks, and drove the car to the station to meet Anna.

CHAPTER 2

AN ARRIVAL

While waiting for the train he sat with a weak, milky, Railway coffee at the grimy window of the Snack Bar which gave him a distorted view of the platform. When the train had drawn to a halt he saw Anna alight and look around for him. He left his coffee and hurried towards her. Each time they met after an extended separation he thought how beautiful she was: well-dressed in the modern youthful fashion of boots, a shortish skirt, a loose, open topcoat and, of course, hatless with short hair that would not be tamed; diminutive and slightly gauche. He opened his arms as he walked towards her.

He said, "You have no right to be looking so self-assured when getting off a train at an uncertain place that you have not known, and not knowing, taking a risk that you will be met by someone who cares. In fact, you've no right to be looking so self-assured at all, when your male paramour (if that is an apt description) has been wondering whether he would even make it at such a time."

"Oh," said Anna, "I knew you'd be here if I called because you made me a promise years ago and I've never let you forget it."

"A lapdog then?"

"No, more a sheepdog under training; but showing promise I'll admit."

"I expected you to be late," said Edward. "Trains do not run to time in the Principality."

"You know that they are never late here; it's just a different time zone that's all – it's far from Greenwich and the Meridian. Everybody here knows that, but nobody else does. That's what confuses people. Time changes somewhere towards the middle of the Severn Tunnel; it must be a geological fault, a time warp, in the Bristol Channel. You're supposed to understand all that stuff or did you waste your three years studying Geology? You should make it your life's work to find it and make a fortune for yourself moving between time zones, instead of moping in that cottage of yours that you won't let anybody see. You may kiss me now that the pleasantries are over."

They held each other close until Edward broke away and said, "Why are you here anyway? Surely your Consultant wants you to have tests and things."

"He does. But he said there was no urgent need; in fact it would be better to wait just a little while."

"I don't believe that."

"It's true, and there's a reason for it which you shall learn later if you behave yourself."

Anna had been diagnosed with a condition relating to her immune system that required regular monitoring and she had to exercise some care in her exposure to any infections. She was to avoid as much contact as possible with other people, especially in confined places: London Underground and train carriages with their recycled air had been particularly identified as being least acceptable. By living now in London, this placed some restriction on her travelling.

"You came by train and, I assume, used the Underground test-bed for disease. You're too self-willed for your own good."

"I know. But I won't be bullied into living just half a life. I won't be controlled by factors beyond my control. That is *servitude.*"

"That's being irresponsible and hurting people who care for you. You must listen to your Consultant; he has to deal with you and your condition. I don't envy him the task."

"I know. I do apologise to him for my inconstancy each time I see him. He calls it my *'lack of discipline'.* I liked that, considering I studied three years of Philosophy: I could beat him in logic and discipline, but I let him think I'm appropriately contrite."

"You must do more than that. You matter to people; you need to recognise that they love you and would appreciate having your company for as long as possible."

"Huh! A road to the *Isle of Regret.*"

"Stop that nonsense and don't be so dismissive."

"What about yourself then, hermit? Don't preach to me about filial responsibilities and altruism. Sort yourself out first."

"I'm different, and you know something of my reasons for it. You also know that I don't feel confident that I'm out of the woods yet. But it's better now that you're here; please stay well for me and for once, do as you're told."

"I can't promise it all, but I will tell you that I intend that we should try. The Consultant, who is our God for the present, also said that as I seemed well at the moment, if I had any *'Matter to attend to'* I should go away, relax, and see to it, so we can have a *'clear run'* when we do get started. He talks in *'Partial Italics'*; it's quite an interesting spoken language."

" Right. I don't recommend it, but would you like a coffee before I drive you to the Trust House?"

"Have you had one?"

"I tried, but I was defeated by it. You could try tea but I think you would be hard-put to tell the difference; I think they come out of the same urn."

"Neither then," said Anna. "Just drive me more sedately to my meeting with the Lord Mostyn. I don't suppose he'll mind too much if I'm slightly late; I don't think he works to any time-zone any more: *A Day is a Year, and a Year but a Day* in the life of our Lord these days it seems."

"As you wish Madam. I shall have you there in time for tea. Let me take your case."

Edward drove out of the City along another narrow, winding valley road.

As he drove, he said, "You managed to persuade your parents to let you off the leash for a while then?"

"Yes. It wasn't easy and in the end I had to insist. I'm afraid that I invoked your good self to help. I said what you've often said: 'If I'm to get through this with the least trouble they must let me do it *my* way.' I also said that whatever happens, while I'm still able to do things, I must know more of who and what I am. I'm afraid that floored them a bit: either they understood too little or too much. So I'm afraid I took advantage and took the coward's way out: I left quickly. You'll say that was unfair, I know, and you'd be right; but it would have been worse if I'd lingered."

"I understand. I'm not saying you did right, but I understand what you thought you needed to do."

"Oh, Darling Edward, I knew you would."

"In that case, you presumed too much; you mustn't use my name in vain; I'm no authority on what's best for anyone, myself included. You take advantage, you know, that's always been a fault. And you're too devious by far."

"I know that too. But it does mean that I get my way, you'll admit," she said and smiled. "I also said that you would keep me in bounds. They were rather sceptical about that, but it partially satisfied them, especially when I told them that we had made a vow to each other."

"Did they ask what vow?"

"No. I thought that was a bit strange. Perhaps they didn't want to know."

It had not been a noticeable climb from the train station, but when the mountains fell away on both sides, it was clear that they had been climbing the whole time and were now several hundred feet above the coastal plain, with views down the valley to the sea and across to Somerset. To their right was the house called Creigiai which had been left to the Safe Haven Trust by its owner Lord Thomas Thomas when he had died without issue.

Edward drove the car to the imposing Georgian entrance and escorted Anna to Reception. She said, "Good afternoon. I'm Anna Griffiths and I have made arrangements to visit Lord Mostyn. Would you be kind enough to let him know that I have arrived?"

"Ah, yes, Miss Griffiths. Lord Mostyn apologises but he is running a little late. He has asked that you be given tea in the Library and he will join you as soon as he has completed his business. Please follow me."

"One moment please," said Anna.

Anna turned to Edward as he said, "That Greeting!"

"What about it? It was perfectly civil."

"Oh, *perfectly,* as if there could be only *one* Anna Griffiths."

"There is," she said, "And it's me."

"And it showed off your *Superior Education and Superiority, perfectly, Madam.*"

"Piss off Edward."

"Now *that's* more like the girl I know," replied Edward.

Anna laughed and asked, "Will you have some tea?"

"Thanks love, but I don't think so. I would rather get down off this mountain before dark as I don't know the road."

"What will you do with yourself now then?"

"Well, I've ventured this far for the first time, thanks to you; it would be a pity to waste the effort. I think I'll take the long way home: follow the Brecon Beacons to the Black Mountains and the High Country where there are no trees. I don't want trees to spoil the view; anyway, they close you in on yourself too much. All I want is just moors, heather, rocks and waterfalls, marshes and *Will o' the Wisp* [5] and the ancient mysteries of our country saved in the cold, clear air. When you're there, you can't help but know you're part of an Old Land; and you can see what's coming to bugger-up your life. You have (or I do, at least) a sense of awe and history and it puts your own problems in perspective. An accident of birth no doubt but I feel I belong there, and I've missed it. Then I shall turn South for home; and peace; until you call again."

"Where will you stay?"

"Oh, in a Pub or failing that, in the car for a night. I've done it before; it's no great problem; just a bit more stiffness in the legs that tells me that I'm getting older and I should behave appropriately."

"Don't turn in on yourself again, love" said Anna; "That's no way to live. You mustn't drop me again; I won't have it!"

"No, I shan't do that to you now; that need, at least, is past. I will

26

tell you where I am and what I'm doing, though that probably won't take too much time to relate."

"How long will you be on this pilgrimage of yours?" asked Anna.

"It's no pilgrimage that I know."

"I would like to know what you're looking for as well; but not just now I suppose."

"What about you then?" asked Edward. "You will 'phone me when you're through with this, won't you? And certainly when you're home and you've seen your Consultant for your next check - up. I'll come at once if you need me, you know that. Promise me you'll 'phone the moment you can."

"Of course. As soon as I can pick up a handset. Now take care driving your long journey home."

Edward turned and walked out to the car without a backward glance. Anna watched him leave, and for a moment was tempted to follow. Instead, she turned and followed the Receptionist to the Library where a tea-tray had already been set on the table.

"Would you like me to pour your tea Madam?" asked the Receptionist.

"Thank you, no. I'll see to myself now."

"Good. I'm sure Lord Mostyn won't be too long; he hates over-running."

"Thank you."

The Receptionist left and it was some 20 minutes before she heard a heavy tread in the hallway and a heavy-set but frail-looking man walked towards her and said, "You've been very irritating, Queen of the Fairies; you've exploited my age unforgivably. You have taken advantage of an old man's generosity and I hope I shall not live to regret it. It's not done for the young to exploit the old: I cannot believe that you are unaware of that ancestral taboo? Young as you are, and if you are in any way perceptive, you must know that age comes to us all in the end; and with it, expectation is diminished – but all the more deserving for that. There comes a time when it catches us all unawares – age, that is. Then, continuing to ignore irritants is too problematic for one's declining will and one's desires; so it is easier to accede to the request and avoid perpetuation. I'll have some tea too. They've left me a cup, I see.

"I have called the principle, '*The Mosquito Conundrum*'," he said. "The risk of the consequences of being bitten has become less important than the energy required to swat the irritant. What do you think of that then eh? I perceive that you are of an age and are perceptive enough to take advantage of that immutable fact. The fact that you are here establishes that point beyond any doubt in my mind. That is not to say that by giving in I expect to have a greater peace of mind; far from it; the worry lingers. In my experience spanning more than 40 years of having to make judgements about requests of one form or another, and from one person or another – usually the other – one most often regrets giving in to pleas that have little substance and less interest and persons of little substance and even less interest, by the by, and one should stick with one's original gut instinct."

"Do you always talk in *Soliloquies*?"

"Don't be objectionable from the start. My answer is, '*When I need to*'. At one time our predecessors established a routine that one could follow; one that stood me in good stead more often than not. Most correspondents fell by the wayside."

"What routine was that?"

"I have called it '*Escape By Obfuscation*'. I enjoyed that word, and once upon a time I feared that I would never have the opportunity to use it in conversation. It wasn't original by any means; more a system absorbed by osmosis in the clubs: it's also been called '*prevarication*'. You understand the word *osmosis?* That is another particularly useful word when you need to impress people with your understanding of the relevance of scientific principles to social and business systems. You don't necessarily need to understand it yourself of course; you simply need to be supremely confident in its use. Much like most jargon in fact. But you do need to be wedded to the use of it. First, you get your secretary (or yourself if you can't afford one) to acknowledge receipt of a most interesting proposal which will be considered in depth in due course but which at the moment must be set aside because of some urgent, unforeseen demands on your time. You must assure your correspondent that the issues that have been raised are of crucial importance and will be addressed as soon as possible. That gives you a month or two; then, if there are follow-up letters, and there usually are, they are acknowledged with a note to the effect that the matter has not been forgotten. That gives you some more time and hopefully the end of it. If that is not the case, you refer the matter to an underling, as lowly as possible, in order to prepare a 'briefing note'. You are familiar with this system?"

"Yes. You've used it very effectively I suspect."

"I am proud that you consider that I have not entirely lost my effectiveness or flair, despite not having needed to use the ploy for some years."

"I suppose that there are some things you never forget. Like riding a bicycle, or riding itself."

"You intrigue me. I never learned to ride a bike; never needed to I suppose; couldn't afford a proper one anyway, and when I could, I never had the time and it had lost its attraction. I considered them too Victorian, and there were other things to see to. My wife did try to get me to learn to ride a horse once; she said that a man in my position should show some healthy pursuit, and Riding to Hounds would be appropriate. I suppose that they're not too different in their physical and mental demands: bikes and horses; without a proper balancing act, it's all too easy to fall off either of them and break your neck. I don't suppose that's too much fun for the horse either. In any case, it's too high a price to pay for a frivolous sport: one broken neck and a shot horse; certainly it is. But I understand some people make money out of it. To me, it's a bit like typewriting: it requires a *facility* but no great *intellect*. You understand my premise? Do you really believe that a learned complex activity like riding a bicycle can become virtually instinctive? Is it pre-wired in the brain would you say?"

"I don't think it's likely, not *specifically* anyway, but I can't be confident of that. But you didn't stop there did you?"

"What? You must forgive my smirk. You see, you do become wedded to deviousness; it is habit-forming and like all habits, too simplistic and most difficult to break. Still, contrary to what most people believe, it gives much personal satisfaction when it works and even results in a private snigger or two at times. I often got through a difficult afternoon by reminding myself of the discomfort I engendered. But only in those I did not consider worthy you understand; I was not vindictive. Worthy or not, you were not so easily diverted in your quest and I was unsure whether there were still some debts to be paid or duties still to be performed in relation to your father and mother. And so I had to resort to using my final hurdle: an agreement at short notice and, whenever possible, at a most inconvenient location. For this last indulgence I offer my apologies. I was not aware it would cause you such considerable inconvenience."

"Don't patronise me and do stop conversing in *speeches*. I've come for information you might have; and for my benefit, not to gratify your indulgence. Let me be clear: I shall be grateful for any information you can give me, but you must also be clear that any action I may take as a result of what you say will be entirely my own decision and little or nothing to do with you."

"So I understand and I'd better watch my tongue then; I must not let it run away with me. So, on those terms I must consider what, and how much, I should tell you. We shall see. But I admire you for not using the issue of your health as a lever in your requests for a meeting."

"I don't need your admiration either."

"You're all of a piece then are you? You don't need anyone else? That is most remarkable in a woman. And it begs the question of who that young gentleman was who brought you here? The one with no social graces, who left before being introduced."

"That's not your business, but he was Edward Williams, an old and very dear friend who seems to want my company, strangely. He has nothing to do with my visit to you, except for being kind in transporting me to your august presence."

"So the cub has little sharp teeth. You seem very certain of yourself at such a young age."

"I've had to be; I can't afford to think of others too much; it's all a matter of how much they intrude. In all other ways, I resolve my own life."

"Indeed? My impression was that there was some considerable uncertainty in your life, uncertainty that you would be much happier to have resolved by others. Was I right in thinking that?"

"Yes, I'll be honest; you're right. To a degree my attitude is one that I have needed to build; a wall if you like. But you haven't helped either; you are not the easiest of people to approach or understand. What's been written about you doesn't help either."

"I never intended that I should be transparent; quite the reverse in fact. There are people that I can work with and people that I can't; there are people I control and those I discount; there are people I meet and those I avoid; there are people I wish to help; there are even people I can deny preferment to; there are people I use; there are people I have to deny for friendship's sake; those are the complexities of a life and mine is no different from others. Then there are people I admire and who I wish to have as friends. I have been rather fortunate there in that most of them have reciprocated. Which one will you be?"

"It's too early to say."

"Yes. And I don't yet know what it is that you really want from me."

"Nothing more than your memory."

"What, all of it? You'll empty my head of it? You'd take away an old man's last haven of rest? His sheltered anchorage? His comfort in the dark hours? You'll leave him nowhere to hide? You'll go so far to pursue him? That could be the death of me. You ask too much of an old man."

"Perhaps. But I can only ask."

"As I can deny. I had reasons to ask you to meet here. I thought that if one of the things you were chasing was something of what I thought you were after, this would not be a bad place to meet. Lord Tom Thomas used to sit here for hours looking over the valley and watching his birds, and I believe that all his major decisions were made here. Certainly it was where he felt his ghosts were and where he felt that his family's ancestors were most immediate; they all leave a *presence* you know, when they've gone, if you're *tuned* to it. Many people of note think a great deal about their ancestors of one kind or another, you know; and of their legacies."

"And do you?" asked Anna.

"Now and again; now and again. I recommend it periodically and other souls would do well to emulate.

"His racing birds have gone now, died and not replaced and the sparrow hawk gave up the ghost as well; a battle over and done with. Or did it end in a truce, d'you think? That's an alternative outcome. Paul, the manager of the farm, never shot the raptor; he considered it to be too much part of the balance of things; I think he was right in thinking that. Do you? It's part and parcel. And I think that Tom Thomas would have been very sad if he'd dropped it as well; a bane of his life it was, but an understood one. So this has always been a place for decisions and understandings. The other reason I asked you here, rather than elsewhere, was that my age allows me to indulge myself even at the expense of others less fortunate. Also, I have, for a contribution to my Trust, taken over two rooms for my own use."

"After all you've done, all you've achieved, you're happy to end up with just two rooms?" asked Anna.

"Why not? It's two more than many people have at their disposal, and these also have a bathroom – *en suite* – in the jargon. Your grandparents would have brought up a family of several children in two rooms and no bath other than a zinc one in front of the fire at High Days and Holidays. And I have the kitchen service, this Library of rare books, a laundry service for everything except my starched collars which I send out, and no cleaning duties; if I want to trouble people, I can do that at a Trust Meeting. It's enough, and takes all my time. You might say I have my own hotel; what price that, eh? No, there's no need for extravagance; what's the point? Comfort, yes; extravagance, no. But between the two of us and the stone wall there, some of which goes back to the 15th Century by the way, they always were the best rooms; and I've had them done up a bit to my taste, you'll not be surprised to know; I have some of my paintings here: there's a Cyffin Williams no less, a study of a mining valley with Coal Tips, to remind me of my origins if I get above myself, and a photograph of Lloyd George if I don't: they face each other across my living-room. Artists both, but in different ways; so I thought it was appropriate, and it's no more than they deserve. The rooms have the best views and the bedroom used to be Tom's when he lived here. That's a comfort as well. You see, loved ones are not forgotten when they've gone; there are always stories to recall in the darker evenings. That used to be the job of the itinerant *Tellers of Tales,* of Mystery, Magic and Religion; the *Gleemen* around the fire of a Winter's night; the Poets like *Robin a' Dale,* and more strictly of course, the Eisteddfod Bards, Crowned and Chaired for their trouble."

"You're an old *Romantic* then?"

"Oh no; just a *Rememberer* with time on his hands and with no-one to curse or anyone to listen anymore. Anyway, they've all gone to the Big Eisteddfod in the sky now; some would say '*Fortunately';* so no more laments of Alun Mabon (the *fictional Welsh Hero,* some say) for your Welsh Scholarship Exam.

"More recently we've had a steady stream of academics (worthy I'm told in most cases, though I sometimes wonder); they come to visit the Family Library. I've converted the dining room from its original monkish ambience to a less monkish, more academic, guise complete with a top table, mostly so that I can have some decent conversation when old and new friends visit. Not so many of the Old Guard now I'm afraid but I refuse to regret that too much – it was another time: not as old as some of our Cymric Tales, but time is relative for most of us when it's gone; won't you agree?"

"Yes; and when it's with us for that matter."

"The young researchers can be fascinating in their earnestness. But I do miss Tom still, along with another."

"Who would that be, your Lady wife?"

"No; of course I miss her too, but I was thinking of someone else, then; you might be told who if you stay long enough and we get to talking without guard. Do you believe that two people can love each other without the drama of sex?"

"Certainly," said Anna. "Sex is often an intrusion."

"Just so. Do you mind an old man being so forthright? No, you're young and the young of today have a less constrained vocabulary – nothing is unseemly any more it seems; that's no loss, but I do detest the decline in Manners: there is a great sorrow in laxity; it shows a lack of discipline, which is unforgiveable; the young would do well to mark that.

"People do love, of whatever sex. Now that, I do think, is hard wired! For me, that too is gone for the simple reason that I am unlucky enough to be the last one alive. Which I suppose is why you have sought me out. So I intend to spend the rest of my time learning, remembering, philosophising and boring others: practices I had no time for as a youngster. But those who have gone plague me more and more now. I have taken to considering, as I sit here on such a beautiful day as this has been, whether the loss of a sexually loved one is more easily borne than the loss of a non-sexual love.

"This will all seem like the ramblings of an old man to you I dare say, because you are not yet old enough to believe that sex and its urgency was once a drive for us too. Then, you find that age brings the benefits of maturity as well as the curse of dementia. This is a taste of what you will have to sieve through, along with some red herrings, if you insist on proceeding with your Quest. It won't always be to your taste or your comfort, so are you prepared for what you may learn?"

"I think so, but until I know something of it, I can't tell. I have decided that it is something I must see to; something that needs attending to."

"You think so but you do not know so? Of course you don't. Old age is another country to you but it is also a place for reviewing decisions about the future; isn't that strange? So I have decided to ignore my original decision (call it this old man's last indulgence and a salute to youth) and lead you on your journey as far as I can. It won't be all of it but it will be something. It will take longer than you think, so on the off chance that we would be travelling together I have arranged for you to stay in one of the research rooms here for the duration, though the journey will take us away to other places.

CHAPTER 3

REPRISE

"I'm glad that you received my message before you expected to see me for breakfast. Breakfast is a very informal affair here; to an extent that it is sometimes ignored altogether by the younger chaps. I do not approve of that, it is a bad habit." He smiled and said, "If I had my way they'd be marched in single file through that door every morning at 6 am sharp, topped and tailed, and made to eat their gruel. I expect they'd then call this place of Charity and Learning, *Dootheboys Hall.* But I do accept that breakfast time is not a gathering of choice for conversation; how the Victorians kept it up over porridge, kippers, kidneys and kedgeree I'll never understand. Perhaps they were fortified by the Indian tea – God Bless Victoria! Is that why they were all so dyspeptic do you think? I can't face people much before eleven o'clock these days after which I will be 'spick – and – span' with all ablutions completed and buttons done up, but without the wing collar. You should consider yourself lucky as a woman that you were never required to wear a stiff starched collar."

"What about our high collars on dresses and our petticoats? And stays! I'd trade you those."

"Fair point. In any case, it wasn't the collar so much as the studs front and back that made you assume the bearing of a young Frankenstein. Perhaps that's where Mary Shelley and Hollywood got the idea of a bolt through the neck for her creation. They could also be the origin of the Englishman's stiff upper lip; grimace more like. Of course, a bolt could have held yet another connotation for the young, lady-like Mary Shelley. Anyway, I tend to take my small breakfast in my rooms (a personal dispensation) and you must not feel affronted if we don't speak to each other before eleven. Even then, I may not join you here in the Library if I consider it too early to be sensible. This morning I terminated my business and made an exception in order to explain my routine to you. Normally, I attempt the crossword over breakfast and my progress, they say, determines my temper for the rest of the day. I also forgot to ask you whether you needed anything for your stay here."

"No. All I need is in my case."

"You see? I am becoming more and more neglectful. You are lucky that I gave in to your persistence now; who knows, in a month or two it's likely that I would have forgotten everything and your journey and the efforts you've had to make would have been all for nothing. So you'd better prise it out of my head before it disappears for good. And much good may it do you. I thought about it in the night – there is an interval of wakefulness before dawn; it's to do with age and a weaker bladder, I'm told – and I realised that it might be an opportunity for me to actually put things in their proper order in the filing cabinet of the brain; though you would probably now call it a computer file. So you could be doing me a service – an Autumn Clearing replacing a Spring Cleaning, if you will. A final warning before we sail then: you will have to put up with an old man's ramblings as I think I have already said, and you must take from the diary of events what you need to give you…what? Comfort? Knowledge? Understanding? A home for your anger? Confirmation of your beliefs? Confidence? All of these? Or none of these? All I ask is that, in the end, you let me into the secret results of your Quest."

"Is that all? You're asking a great deal."

"Yes. Perhaps more than you know at present."

"Very well; I promise that whatever actions I take, and whatever the results, I will make sure that you know since it seems to matter to you. So, can we get on with it?"

"Yes. Now then, the rules of the game. Much of what you want to know, at least the part that I can tell you, is not recorded except dryly in Registers. I assume that you have started to follow those. You want more from me. You want the Lives more than the Births, Marriages and Deaths. In order not to waste time then, I need to know what you already know; in effect, who you think you are. We will start our reminiscences each day at 11.30 until lunch at 1 o'clock, a light affair. I will retire until I take tea at three o'clock. Then we will continue until dinner. Is that agreeable? Good. Then, as I say, if we are not to waste time, you must tell me what you already know. It is for you to start promptly at 11.30 in the Library."

"Why is it that you want me to start? Why do you want to know what I already know?"

"To avoid repetition and the wasting of my time. I do not have a surplus of it left. Less than you do I suspect, though I don't know whether that is any longer a matter of regret, pleasure or of comfort for either of us. Perhaps we shall find out as we talk to each other. Perhaps. But really, I need to know who you *are* more than anything; make a judgement of you; I'm not prepared for this to be all one-sided. I should also have told you that there may be times when I will not wish to indulge your curiosity; I may need to pause to reflect."

"On what?"

"On whether or not I should continue, of course; whether or not you should be told; there may be others to consider."

"I would be circumspect."

"No doubt you would try to be. But you might not be the best judge of the consequences of a loose tongue or partial knowledge – *A little knowledge*...etc. If we don't meet, you must not be irritated or take offence and you must not press the issue; you must avoid making it all extremely tedious; that would be ill-mannered. So, occasionally, you will have to see to your own entertainment. Will that be a problem for you? There are plenty of books in the Library here about our Ancient Land to keep you amused. I recommend the Tale of the Lady of the Lake [6] to set you on your way. It is a tale of Love and Loss and a rendering of hearts. Lakes play a big role in our Mythology, you know; I think you should learn a little more about them and you should visit some of them and see for yourself. Do you know the Welsh for 'lake'? It is *Llyn,* and this Lady of the Lake, came out of Llyn y Fan; near Myddfai, now in Camarthenshire – still there but mostly silted up now I'm told. It was near there that the Physicians of Myddfai had lived. They were the sons of the Lady of the Lake, *Vivianne II* and a Herdsman called Rhiwallon who's father had been killed fighting the Normans when they tried to conquer Wales (though Time's a bit conflated here or the Historians are wrong); but he plays no further part in the Legends – which makes me wonder why his name was ever recorded. D'you see what happens when you live your life in a Library of old books? Perhaps you will find the answer for me, in your reading. In any case, the sons became Physicians of great repute and grew their Healing Herbs – poisonous most of them - to heal the sick and relieve their suffering: perhaps the first recorded example of the Practice of Homeopathy. You can still see the place, though the more poisonous herbs have been removed for safety's sake: Accidental Death Through Stupidity seems to matter more now than it did in their time on Earth. Some also say that it was She, under the name Morgaine le Fay (Arthur's sister), who caught the sword Excalibur when Llaminawg (Sir Bedevere to the English) threw it into the lake when Arthur died. You see? We Welsh all know a bit of Mythology; and who will say it's wrong and nothing more than a Myth? What about the French for 'lake'? I will tell you: it is *du Lac* [6], the name of a family said to be descended from Mary Magdalene (and some say, Jesus) [35] of whom the best known is Lancelot du Lac (Arthur's nephew through his sister Morgaine). He, it is said, tarried in a somewhat unseemly fashion with his Aunt – In - Law, then took Gwenhwyfar [7] from Arthur, you remember."

"You're at it again."

"What would that be now then?"

"Relating tales as conversation."

"It is important that you understand the context of what you will learn: this is not an exercise in abstraction for your benefit, nor an exercise simply to pass the time. I will tell you something of great note; if you forget everything else, remember this: *For Good Or Ill, Our Ancestors Leave Us Legacies* and we live within that Heritage."

"What of the rest of our lives then? I don't believe in Predestination."

"No; nor do I: the Vagaries of our lives see to the rest of it. So, use the bequeathed (horrible word) commodity wisely.

"In any case, aren't the Tales more rewarding than your life's ending? They will be told when you are unremembered. That is as it should be: the Tales help us to reach an understanding of Human Behaviour in times of uncertainty; they tell us how to live and, more importantly, how to die. True or False, they are worth saving for that alone. Isn't that worth more than a Life? It's more enduring, certainly.

"In any case, these Myths are of interest to me and should be to you. So, to complete my rambling, in all cases this Lady must have been manifestations of the Great White Goddess.

"Our ancestors amassed more of such books than we have ever done, or do. What does that say about them, and us, do you think? We say that we don't have the time in the Modern World; though they did. It is certainly to our shame. Will the fact of your staying here for indefinite periods cause you or anyone a problem?"

"No. I have the time. At any rate, enough to see me to the end of this."

"Strangely, I'm beginning to hope so too, though that could easily change. Now, why don't you start?"

"Alright. It seems that I was born into a family that had no material worth, nothing concrete that is; but I grew up in a family of lovers. Is that a strange phrase to use? It's true in any case; all the members of the family had great love for each other and had none of the Welsh reticence of showing affection. We all kissed, often, even my brother and father. We, all of us, me included, had great joy in being with each other and despite the age gaps we played well together most of the time; parents too. No-one was ever excluded and there were never any untruths or taboo subjects; no questions we could never ask and no knowledge denied to us, even if we were too young to understand what we were asking. There were no taboo words either; my father, Will, saw to that; words were everything to him; you may remember that? He was called a wordsmith more than once. Snigger-making words brought home from school were explained and reasons given as to why they were not used in educated conversations. Did you notice there, that I gave an intellectual reason for not using *'Fuck'*? It's strange, isn't it that the word has become an imprecation when in reality is means *to Procreate*. It became so ingrained in us that to resort to expletives only showed a deficient vocabulary. That was my Father Will for you: proud of his use of language though he let his own mother tongue go. I never understood the reason for that. Perhaps it's something that will come out as we speak."

"He didn't use it, but he *knew* it."

"Well, we all realised that we were very fortunate. I had no reason to ask if I was any different; if I'd known or understood the word I would have said that it was sacrilegious and illiterate of me to even think it. We were not a religious family in reality. My Mother Megan kept up a pretence for a while by attending Sunday Morning Services while we were young but in hind-sight, I think that was more for our benefit than from any real conviction. I think that she wanted us to know, without preaching at us herself, that Society had another way of living – one based on Faith in God – from the one she and my father pursued. You will know how strong the *GOD bit* is in the Valleys; you can't escape it, so you succumb or rebel; neither is pleasant for a child. So we were washed, scrubbed and dressed, with bonnets even on most Sundays and we walked, led by my Mother, in procession to the Chapel. I once asked her why we had to endure it. She replied, *'So that you grow up to realise that living is a matter of discipline';* that was the non-conformist Welsh in her (as it is in you). I had no idea what she meant but it sounded too profound to question. I suppose it worked since much of what I had to face afterwards was not easy and without personal discipline I wonder whether I would have endured it. And isn't Learning a discipline you impose on yourself? And isn't Philosophy a Discipline of Logic?

"I'm boring you, so I'll get on.

"I was quite old when I became aware of the importance of a name. Before that, my name was my name, nothing more, nothing less; just something you were called, something people knew you by, a label, a taxon. I had got to the age of recognising boys from girls. Not anatomically, not that physical thing; I had a brother after all, and his penis was nothing new to me. No, it was the disturbing, emotionally unknown age of so-called womanhood. I was pretty and happy then and I was being asked for walks by the boys. There had never been a time when my mother took me aside and told me about the birds and the bees; as I have said, all our questions were answered and our developing bodies explained whenever we asked about them, so there was no defining moment of awareness as it were. And we were proud of the changes we noticed in ourselves; you could say we were an enlightened family. So it was not that that changed me for the first time. Suddenly, it seemed, the boys stopped asking me out and there were sniggers when I appeared. I did not understand why and asked my mother. For the first time ever, she fobbed me off with some tale of juvenile behaviour or adolescent exclusion but I knew that was not true because I had been popular and now I wasn't. I couldn't understand and I hated her for it. We had been so close and had loved so much that I felt it as a betrayal, one I didn't understand and couldn't bring myself to forgive. Eventually, when they appreciated how unhappy I had become at school and how I was neglecting my studies, they tried to explain to me the nature of emotional bullying – how the more understanding were taunted by the less - and how it was best dealt with by showing how childish and immature such behaviour was. I accepted what they told me; there was no reason not to and superficially at least, we returned to our previous relationships. But it was hard to forgive them. They tried hard to support me, I'll give them that, but I couldn't accept the rejection from my friends nor my mother's lies to me. I pretended and I worked hard at my studies. I was not the brightest of the family: my brother was better and my sister could pass us all but I was good enough to be held up as an example of what hard work could bring. But that only alienated my classmates and further isolated me; my only friends were girls in the lower classes who came to see me as something of a role model I suppose: Deputy Head Girl, good at hockey and destined for a place at University. Then, even that friendship stopped and my only consolation was that I would leave soon and enter a new world that I would make for myself with no baggage. So I endured it for the few remaining months and never told my mother or father anything of it: it was the first of my secrets. It could all have passed into my personal history book except for a row I had with one of the boy prefects; I can't even remember the substance of it; probably the smoking behind the bike sheds or something of no importance. Except for something he said to me: *'This friendship you have with the young girls; my mother says that you're only reverting to type.'* I asked him what he meant but he wouldn't explain himself. I doubt now whether he knew what he was talking about himself, but it stayed with me. I suppose you could say it was my first step towards irritating you, though none of us could have known it at the time. So I left for

University, away from home, and tried to put it all behind me. It was not easy loving my siblings while feeling betrayed by my parents, but for most of the time I didn't let it intrude: *I became 'enclosed'* as the only way to address it. I enjoyed my undergraduate years, too much perhaps, because I ended up with only a middling degree. Having had to interrupt it didn't help either. I had long before given up hockey; I had too many pains in my legs. It got worse and I was hospitalised. You don't need to know the details and I don't want to have to tell you them. The family moved to be near me as you already know and a slow, cautious reconciliation began. I don't think it could have happened earlier or under different circumstances but I was older, somewhat more mature I like to think, more understanding of the pain I knew I had given them and more aware of what I should do with the time I had left; is that what *maturity* is? An awareness of others' needs? You see, I had insisted on all the clinical details and I prevailed on anyone and everyone I thought would help, especially my brother who was doing his clinical medical training; it must have been hard for him. Eventually, my mother agreed to answer my questions once she was convinced I was not to be refused. So, I came to understand a little of them and what they'd done for me; there was no longer any reserve: Father Will was content with that; I'm not so sure of Mother Megan. However, despite everything, I became happy then and for me that was the most, the only, important thing; I hadn't been happy for so long; if anyone made me unhappy, I dropped them and moved on; so all my friendships were deliberately superficial and the only people who knew me at all were my brother and sister, and in a sense, my 'cousins'; like Edward Williams. Dear Edward, who won't take a 'No' from me; who insists on knowing me; and who wouldn't stay to meet you because of his own sadness.

"My grandfather, Megan's father, had left me a legacy from an endowment he had taken out when I was a baby, as he had done for the other children. You probably knew him and what he was like; I'm sorry that I didn't – I'd like him to know what I've done; that I've not been left far behind by the others, at least; and that I've not wasted his surety. Is that so strange? I was going to spend some time travelling the world; seek the great Philosophies: Greece first, then Nepal for Buddha; then Confucius; then, of course, Mohammed. A fantasy that only sustained me for a short while but it was exciting while it lasted and the family pretended to be optimistic. But reality returned all too soon which is why I'm here – as you said, for my *Quest*, if you want to be romantic about it. For me, who is not a Romantic in any sense, I'll be honest with you: I can't face not knowing who I am any more: that's not so strange for anyone who thinks, is it?"

"It's possible that you will not wish to, when you do know, you know."

"Yes, I appreciate that, believe me; but I will know it. Well, this, as they say, is me; or at least, all I'm prepared to show for now. What I want to know is how come? You see, I intend to be the last of my biological line; this disease will go no further in my line. But how did I come to this ending? Where did I come from? Where was the start of it? What made me what I am? Will you help me find out? Because I'm adrift; because I need to know and perhaps give something back. In return I pledge you my *secret findings* as you ask; is that enough?"

Lord Mostyn said, "We've missed lunch, for which I apologise. Unless you're desperately hungry we'll have tea soon. I must take a comfort break, which is overdue; you must be doing something right, lass, because I've never absent-mindedly missed a meal since I've been here. To say nothing of comfort breaks: most imperative they are, at my age, and not delayable. Mind you, the first steps of a new relationship have always had this effect of transporting me out of the here and now: too much curiosity I'm afraid. That was all fine when I was a young man but as I've become older it's not so easy to control. I expect it's a worry that most old people have to deal with. Wander about and look at the books here if you like and I'll see you in my room for tea."

CHAPTER 4

A SEARCH FOR THE BEGINNING

"You've mentioned your mother and father and your brother and sister. Do you find it difficult to refer to them in that way?"

"Not any more, and not at the beginning of course when I didn't know any different. I did for a while as I told you; I avoided using the words: it was him, her, he, she or them if they had to be referred to. In the end I appreciated that it was childish. Apart from my mix of genes which neither they nor I could do anything about, they were more mother and father to me than my biological ones had been; and I had no other biological brothers or sisters in any case. They all made me theirs and I think of them like that and I love them for it; I thought my brother and sister were more different from each other than either was from me."

"What did your sister study?"

"She had a facility for Languages, inherited from our Father I suppose, and she read Classics, what else? And what do you do with a good Classics Degree?"

"Become a good Civil Servant, I suppose," replied Lord Mostyn.

"Just so," said Anna. "And she has. But a Modern Language would have opened up the field for her, and she knows that. So on different postings, she has been learning different languages ever since; as a *hobby* would you believe? Currently she's in America learning Mandarin Chinese on a crash course"

"I never suspected that one could do a *crash* course in Chinese; I've always thought it took a lifetime to learn the nuances of its expression. Rather like the bow from the waist – how *low* do you go? I'm intrigued."

"I can't tell you any more about her; in any case, this is *my* story; it's what you asked for. And it seems to me that I've come to a stage in my life when I need to know my makeup; I must put it in order; I must try to understand where I've come from; and why I am. I know what a tall order that is and I shall probably fail at it – it's a lifetime's work; and a race to the finish. I've tried a little already, and not got very far; but I can't ignore it any longer and I no longer wish to, whatever it brings. You see, I think I know *what* I am; now I need to know *who* I am; and *why* I am; and *how* shall I live my life? It's too grandiose a phrase, but basically, the *meaning of it all.*"

"The *meaning* of your life, dear girl, is what you make of it. As a Philosopher you must know that."

"Well then, let's just say that at the very least it will pass the time."

"That gives me my parameters then."

"I don't understand."

"Your relationships with your parents and your siblings would inevitably have determined the approach that I would take and what I considered you should be told, or rather, how you should be told it. Not that I'm the sole keeper of secrets of any kind you know; I am not the only Guardian of the Past. What I tell you, you could hear from others though it would mean more work and more digging on your part. And each teller would have his or her own slant on the matters – that's in the nature of things and won't surprise you.

"This must be what makes the disciplines of Mythology, Archaeology and Anthropology so interesting don't you think? There is the 'detectiveness' of it all: the sorting of the fact from personal bias and not least, the Protection of Reputations; most of all the Protection of Reputations. Unlike cold science where one size is meant to fit all: the strive for the God, or Goddess, of Certainty. But He, or She, is devious and isn't that easy to persuade I'm afraid.

"I digress. But it's only since I no longer have to mind my own business that I have been able to judge the pleasure of other followings. But that takes more care than you think. You see, in relating information to which one is privy, it is as well to consider the sensitivities of the recipient. In many cases it doesn't matter: the matter may be trivial, the person of little expectation and the issue unremarkable. But it is not always the case and one must be aware of that and give it its due weighting. This is beginning to sound like a management seminar on employee relations. Forgive me if I am boring you but I did warn you that you would be required to do some work by sorting the wheat from the chaff. Also, I held your father in high regard and I regret that he no longer advises me on the steps that need to be taken in this other interest of mine.

"So be it.

"I told you I think, that dinner here is taken in something of a collegiate manner and I may have given the impression that it was my idea; I must correct that misunderstanding. I approved of it in the end, but it was part of your father's scheme of things. And initially it was not considered the correct approach to a situation which was somewhat ambivalent - partly academic: the University, the Library and the Thomas Fellowship – and quite separate from the Charitable venture: the Safe Haven Trust. But your father did not see this dichotomy: he saw the Charity as a Not-For-Profit Business, which I should have done; but he was ahead of me. In the present case, with some provisos, he convinced me: he insisted that there was a grave need for *A Knowledge Charity* and wasn't that what we should insist Universities should be about, but few were? Or indeed cared to be? He also said: '*We have a Duty to our children not to lose our knowledge of their past and a Duty to preserve it for their future*'. He said to me that the visiting academics and researchers, and our own, needed to discuss their interests and get to know each other socially and we owed it to our young high fliers to effect such introductions: rather like dinners at the Law Society. A dining table was, in his opinion, the best way of achieving that. He said that I should take the Chair at the top table but I told him that would defeat his purpose. He saw it in the end; in any case it was probably politeness in his suggestion. So now, they take turns: the last one in to dinner has to take the Chair. They hated it in the beginning and some even stayed away. Eventually they realised that they could set the topic of conversation and it became the game of the day, to be the last to enter. So we do not necessarily eat very promptly; but not too tardily; that wouldn't do. So we had to lay down some rules: those who entered after the final bell were required to take the Chair, in turn, over breakfast – that most difficult of meals; that soon put a stop to it. Some rooms in the house, paid from the University Grant and Tom's Legacy, are set aside for undergraduates writing appropriate dissertations and for young researchers chasing their Theses; others, along with some cottages on Home Farm, are occupied by those young people supported by the Charity and who work for the Charity in various ways to help with its Mission, and also by paying visitors. All these can dine in the main hall, mixed together; those who can, pay; those who can't, don't: it's not much, but it's something."

"You've done a great deal."

"No, that wasn't me; I would be *chuffed* to be so honoured. Do people still use the word *Chuffed?* Or has it gone the way of all flesh? I must look up its Etymology. Will, your father, had that vision from the beginning, as soon as he was given his head. He told me also that this mix would be the best way to ensure that the students knew what they were talking about when they came to write their Theses; they would not be too divorced from the unprivileged – the 'have nots'. He used to say to me that he regretted not having been to a Collegiate University for the benefits it gave. In any case, those supported here by the Trust, came to know their worth and made friends they never expected; and some were even mentioned in the 'Acknowledgements' of Treaties and Theses. And some came to write them for themselves, I'm proud to say.

He did that and more before he decided that he had to leave with you. He had a vision not given to most of us and sometimes I regretted that he had given up on a career in Politics.

"But while this may fill in the background, it is not your purpose in being here. You are after the Biological Imperative.

"Lord Tom would have been your more rewarding contact; my contribution is largely second-hand - Hearsay Evidence. It is what I've heard, what I've surmised and what I've gleaned from my friendship with Tom while we smoked, him with his pipe and me with my cigar. We enjoyed each other's company as we watched the pigeons dance the eight-some reel across the valley. So, first an apology: if there are gaps, it is because I have no information to give you. Be content that we have come some distance already: it is difficult for me to believe so early in our relationship, that I am apologising to you for what I cannot give you!

"The early days of your father – your biological father that is – are vague. Let me break off here because I don't want to have to qualify nomenclature every time it is used. If we do that, we shall never get to where you want to go. I suggest that we use given names; in that way there can be no confusion. So let me start again. My knowledge of the early years of Father Rhodri is vague. So for both of us it will be a search for a beginning and as in everything, the beginning is of great importance to the rest of the life and the person it makes: the *Vagaries* of the living of it. You know that and I don't need to stress it.

"He was born to a couple late in their lives when they had given up hope of a child. They ran a small shop, a newsagent, sweets and cigarettes, soft drinks, you know the sort of thing. The shop and rooms above were rented of course as were most houses in villages in those days. Very few people actually owned their own house. So the rent had to be paid every week; to the Coal Barons mostly, who got the wages they paid back through rents and the profits from the shops. Then the stock had to be bought. And the Shopkeepers were at the mercy of their customers: money was tight for everyone and any default by a customer in paying a bill meant a lean time.

"Before Rhodri came along they had managed, but now there was another mouth to feed, more clothes to buy, boots for his feet. His mother did some house cleaning, washing and ironing for some of the better-off families: the Minister, the Vicar and the Doctor for example though they too depended very much on the collection plate, and one or two of the old widowers who couldn't see to themselves any more. She was out of the shop for long hours, leaving his father to tend to the business and himself from before 6 in the morning, when the

45

newspapers arrived and the miners went on shift, until 7 or 8 at night when she came home and cooked a meal. It was virtually the only meal of the day. So, it's fair to say that they were very poor; most people in the Valleys were then, desperately poor: the money ran out by Wednesday but there was no pay-packet until Friday, when accounts and bills had to be paid; until then, you starved. You fought a cycle of increasing debt. How do you live like that, week by week, month by month through no fault of your own, and your hard work means nothing? You can't; but you must try. It's not too long ago that poverty was the fact of life for these people; it was unexceptional for most – Debtors All: *the Name of the Game* as the pundits have it. And I don't mean *Benefit Poverty* – that would have been riches for most of those people. It's a Poverty most people in this country can't contemplate now with all the money they get from the State; but it was pretty common then, so I suppose it's now a better society we live in. Where do you find some solace in conditions like that? In bed, in each other's arms, when the children are asleep. But like all the others who were struggling, your ancestors were proud people who would not take handouts; they detested any form of Means Testing as degrading. If any fell by the wayside it was hard not to forgive them. So don't be too ready to condemn those who *manufactured* a way out for themselves. It says something of their character that some got away: how some of them managed it was not pleasant nor even ethical at times; but in such circumstances, it would be unchristian to damn them; criminal, even, sometimes, when all they sought was some – stature – and pride."

"You know some of this, don't you," said Anna.

"I know of it; too much; and it still matters.

"It seems that Rhodri's was a difficult birth and the child could not be made to breathe despite all that the Doctor and Midwife tried; and, yes, they were both there; it was usual then, if it was a first birth – *a prima gravida* - and a woman neighbour wasn't available to carry the towels and the hot water; *still births* were common and it kept the population down and, in the long run, saved the family money they didn't have, though it devastated the women. The Grandmother, with the peaked cap of her dead husband over her bound hair and a woollen shawl about her shoulders came into the bedroom when she did not hear a cry; she had a bowl of very cold water from the well. She took the baby and plunged his head into the cold water so that his face was covered. When she took it out, it gave a loud cry from the shock of it and she handed him to the Midwife saying, *'You can tie the cord and clean him up now'*. He was alive but it had been several minutes when he had not drawn breath. The Doctor was now in a dilemma: he knew that many changes in the heart and circulation took place at the time of parturition and it was imperative that the baby take its first independent breath without delay if it was not to be listed as a still birth or suffer for the remainder of its life. He questioned if he should tell the mother and father that this failure of their son to breath had probably caused irreparable brain damage from the lack of blood oxygen, or should he be silent, say nothing, and in his deceit give the parents some joy in their lives, if only to have them come to terms with the reality progressively as he grew? He could not burden them with grief at such a time and justified his decision by citing the uncertainty of the degree of damage that might have been inflicted. He would return on a routine visit later, or the next morning, after a time to consider. In any case, the delay would not change matters. So he downplayed the consequences to the Midwife and said that they should leave the young couple to their happiness. He packed his 'Doctor's Case' and prepared to leave.

"Now I face, full – front, my first decision in this narrative," said Lord Mostyn. "And it's making me dyspeptic. Pour me some tea. I could leave the story there and pass on, as is my inclination: it would serve but it would not help you to understand my people, our ancestors, any of them; you would never understand the *What* nor the *Why* of their lives at that time in their corner of the world. I would like you to know that, in my defence. In any case, you need to think on it for your own sake, if you're to understand anything of yourself. Also, by agreeing to see you here, I owe you honesty or nothing; I cannot fudge, and *saying nothing* would be denying you some of what you came for. So I will tell you of the Grandmother's wisdom.

"She was sitting by the fire in a rocking chair with a high back, with the shawl over her shoulders still and that flat cap on her head and worn slippers on her feet. Her hands were clasped in the pinafore on her lap. The Doctor sat on the fender across from her.

'That's done then,' he said.
'No,' she said. 'It won't be that for a long time. Make yourself some tea.'
'No. I'd best get on,' said the Doctor.
'They'll have the worry of it in the end no doubt but he couldn't be left for dead.'
'No,' said the Doctor. 'We're not made like that.'
'Life or Death; that's for God to judge, not us,' she said.
'Yes. But sometimes I'd like a clearer guidance,' said the Doctor.
'He's given us a mind of our own to use to do His works and we should bless Him for that. Take hold of yourself boy. He's raised you

up, Dafydd Evans, so He must have thought you worth a trick or two. He saw something more in you than I did when you were in short trousers. You should thank Him for that and for His teaching through His Son, Our Lord Jesus Christ. But there will be one that won't thank me for it, or you either, if he gets to know,' said the Grandmother.

'Who will that be?' asked the Doctor. 'The boy?'

'No. He won't know nothing about it unless somebody tells him; and he won't understand it even then, I don't suppose.'

'Who then? Tell me,' said the Doctor.

'No, it's too late by now. That should have been put a stop to a year ago. Efan Efans, the Preacher with his Welsh spellings, would have seen it from his pulpit if he'd only looked up at the ferns on the mountain now and again where some of his Congregation was; perhaps he did and was jealous of what he saw and what he couldn't have. Anyway, instead of watching his flock close by, he always looked up to Heaven for Purity and Peace, always seeking The Guidance Of The Lord, for his own comfort before doing anything. It's all in the past now and all over and done with and best left there. It's just a pity there was an issue, that's all. Leave it alone Dafydd; it's too mixed up a tale and too late to mend; don't ferret about in the past and rattle the old bones; it will only make things worse in the end if you do – it will keep it in the gossips' mind without need. It will see its own end, no doubt.'"

"How do you know all this?" asked Anna.

"The Doctor who attended was a cousin of mine," said Lord Mostyn. "One of the early ones who got away to Medical School that the miners' penny a week had helped to provide, and then came back to help; another like your Grandfather Phillips – mother Megan's father. Years later, under different circumstances, he felt that I should know."

"What circumstances were those?"

Mostyn shook his head and said, "That's not for you. It's not relevant here for your search, so I will leave it, for now. So Rhodri's entry to life was delayed and that was the first of his tragedies. The second was his slow, an apposite word, his slow realisation that he did not understand much of what was happening in his little world; it was all happening too quickly to grasp. Except, he grew with a passion for medieval Welsh myths and legends. And it really was a passion; indeed you might say an obsession: acting out what he wished he could do, I suppose. Although his reading was slow and was difficult for him, he did persevere, I'll give him that. And he got other people to read to him. His general curiosity was virtually non-existent but he devoured anything he could find relating to his ancient land.

"The third tragedy of his young life was a mistake made by others. The Examination Board or the markers of the papers, or someone, somewhere, deemed that he had passed his Scholarship Examinations and should proceed to the Grammar School. God knows how it happened, but I could speculate I suppose."

"Speculate then. I need the whole story."

"The whole story you say? What's that? You'll not get that from me or from anyone else for that matter. A life lived, is not a single story; it's not that convenient an affair. I'll think about it. Now we should prepare for dinner and lighter conversation with some other people. You'll soon tire of me otherwise. We shall consider continuing the saga tomorrow."

CHAPTER 5

THE ROAD AWAY

"I didn't join you this morning because you gave me a very disturbed night last night and I have reached an age where such a disturbance to my system is debilitating, distressing, not easily ignored and can last for days. The only reason I'm here now is to tell you that I am cancelling this morning's session; as for this afternoon, we shall see. It all depends on whether I have solved, or at least, come to terms with my problem. I need to think and I do that best sitting in my old armchair with the curtains drawn."

"I'm sorry if I gave you a sleepless night and given you a problem. It was not my intention."

"Not your intention maybe, young Miss. I'll have to take your word for that. But you can't as easily dismiss the consequences of your probing. You need to learn that you may initiate effects that may not have been intended. You need to learn to divorce yourself from what you're doing – distance yourself. You'll not get far otherwise. Can you learn to do that? Can you?"

"I don't consider it a priority; I need other things more."

"That's a pity. For you that is."

"Why do I need to? Are you so sensitive that you need reassurance? At your age?"

"There you have it! At my age! You'll find out if you ever reach this age that it is not the most tranquil of periods, however much you feel you've earned some tranquillity."

"But it is not likely that I shall live to your age, is it? So I'll be relieved of that concern at least."

"One can be at Peace from a certainty as easily as Distressed by it, I suppose. In any case, long may you live to relish the fact. Now there's a conundrum for you: how can you live long enough to assess the pro's and con's of being dead? *Life after Death must be the answer; it's an argument for it: Eternity In Paradise.* What a dreadful thought; I don't think I could stand Paradise for Eternity; what the Hell would you do all day? What would there be to look forward to? At least in Hell you could keep the furnaces going; build up the heat! I'll give you another of my musings: *Is GOD an Absolute or a Construct? Is He the consequence of, or the response to, one's perceived mortality?* "

"Are they different?"

"In degree, I think. Problems should end with the death of the Causeator."

"A made-up word!"

"Oh, yes, certainly. I make up a lot of them now you know if I feel that the ones I know do not quite fit the bill; it's a new game of mine. I'm making a list – I recommend it. But it's been two thousand years and we're still burdened by made – up stories of His meddling: God's meddling I mean. But take comfort from Him if it matters to you; many do."

"This is not a good morning for you is it? Why don't you share your problem? Who knows, we might even resolve it."

"It is a matter for my resolution, no-one else's. You'll find as you grow older that some things can be sorted through discussion but others can be resolved only through contemplation; though discussion seems to comfort people more because they think that they've made some contribution to the end result. You'll find that out as you mature, and also which of them is the easier."

"Will you stop referring to my maturation. That is off-limits, I've told you. It is the one thing I will not talk about. Look, if I knew that I would reach my age of enlightenment as you put it, I probably wouldn't be here now; there wouldn't be any hurry. I wouldn't have troubled you, *'like a mosquito'* as you said, and I wouldn't have given you a single sleepless night nor, old as you are, made you question yourself, or your philosophy, if that is what you are doing. So either get on with it or go back to bed."

"So, the mosquito has a bite."

"Allright. Which is it then? Which is the easier?"

"Oh, Discussion of course, even if you lose the game; Contemplation is far too demanding; and you can't blame anyone for unpleasant outcomes. But that will not divert the mosquito from its purpose I think."

"Its purpose is not to upset you or irritate you. I need your memories but I'll not take them at any cost. Can't we just agree that there is a story I would like to know, and you have a story you can tell? After all, none of the characters are still alive."

"As far as you know. As far as you know."

"Am I wrong in that then? Are any of them still alive?"

"Perhaps; I've not kept in touch with those who have *gone over;* I'm not a Mystic, you understand. More to the point, neither have I kept in touch with all those who haven't yet; there are too many and I'm a Realist. So, we have no *'incontrovertible evidence for all cases'* as the Lawyers would say. That is the issue I have been struggling with and which kept me from my sleep. Resolve it for me if you will, by answering me this conundrum; that's if you can Miss Philosophy: *if you have knowledge or information about others that was entrusted to you in friendship or secrecy, is divulging that information less or more of a betrayal of that confidence if the people who confided in you are now dead?* Do you see what I mean? *Is the ruining of a reputation more or less despicable when the person is dead and so cannot defend himself against your statements?* You think about it and so shall I and I will see you after lunch if I have come to terms with myself. Otherwise I may end this altogether."

"Is it me that's got under your skin or is it yourself you're not at rest with?"

"You are impertinent."

"Certainly", said Anna, "Because it is of no consequence to me in the end. Besides, I wouldn't have got this far with you if I wasn't, would I? And are you beginning to think that that would have been a benefit, or might have been a loss? Who stands to gain most from this?"

"You are too forward and you take too much advantage. Beware. I will see you for tea this afternoon if I feel like it."

*

"You've decided to relent then?"

"Not entirely, but I have decided, on balance and after due consideration, that first, I will tell you only what I feel comfortable with; second, only what I think you are entitled to know; and third, I admit to being intrigued by how you will take the information I shall give you. I have a desire to know whether your façade is ever breached, my lady. That last reason, I'm afraid to admit, and perhaps to my shame, is the strongest of my motivations. You have stressed to me that you will not hide behind your situation; you will *'not take advantage of it'*, I think were your words. Or something like that, anyway. No matter. Well, we shall see. Shall we get on then?

"I think I left you with the unkind cut of Rhodri's entry to the Grammar School, the reason for which I could speculate on. *'Speculate then'*, you said. Let's put that aside for the moment; it's too soon. We may come back to it later if I think it necessary, relevant or appropriate for my story. To go on:

"Rhodri was a very attractive child. No, that's too twee: he was a *pretty* boy: blond, blue-eyed and with the sun's glow in his skin, and a smile in his step – a young God *Apollo, Divine Son of the Goddess, who came from the Sea.* Despite his 'slowness' (probably the word now is *dyslexia* or some such – another *made-up* word which doesn't really tell you anything helpful unless you're a Greek or a Roman) he was not unintelligent; far from it, as I have tried to show; he would never have got there at all if he was. Also, he was grateful for any show of friendship and was, if anything, trusting, rather gullible and easily led. Within months, the, how shall I say? The *Involvement* with the rather clever Head Boy had come to the attention of the intolerant, who considered that such relations were questionable and who were concerned about these *predations* – there are many motivations for *that disapproval,* none of which are for the benefit of the child concerned. I cannot relate the details; your Father Will may have told you, though probably not; if not, you must ask Megan who may be able to tell you more. The Head Boy was something of a *sport* and not in the physical, games sense, though he was that too. No, even judged against the high achievements of the pupils of the school, your Father Will and *Uncle* Charles among them, Doctors and Doctorands, he was of a different order of intellect. Such a fluke doesn't happen often; there's something terribly risky about it in any case (schizophrenia they tell me), so it's not all an advantage.

"Tea. And would you like a cake? We can continue talking with a cup in hand."

"Thank you, yes."

"Your Father Will came up with a clever idea for the Trust, you know. I will always maintain that his appointment as the first Thomas Fellow and first new Trust Executive was one of our finest decisions, Tom's and mine; and I'm quite proud of it. There could be no dichotomy then d'you see. Tom, unfortunately, didn't live to see it all come to fruition.

"So Will came up with this idea that small scale sponsors were well and good and of course, the bedrock of any Charity. But he also insisted that we should go after the bigger fish. We had a very desirable venue, so why not, he asked, offer big business, the Unions, the Political Parties, the national sports clubs, transport companies, anyone big enough, the opportunity to sponsor a seminar, of their own chosen duration and subject and with their own chosen key-note speaker, to be held here at Creigiau, this house and land, with accommodation for delegates, in return for a substantial and continuing donation to the Safe Haven Trust?

" *'That could make things terribly political,'* I had argued, *'And not to the taste of the Charity Commission'. 'Of course,'* he replied, *'But not Party Political (though between you and me and the Gate Post, Labour is likely to dominate). But it's where the money is. And if the*

Commission doesn't like it we can set it up as the Thomas Foundation Conference and just give the Trust the money to pay towards the use of the venue and as a donation. All you need is a clever Accountant.' Tom would have loved that. It was originally billed as an annual affair and it took off from the start so we had to make it twice a year, which it still is: *The Thomas Spring Conference*, and *The Thomas Autumn Conference* – the speeches to be published as a *Series* of course You would never believe the infighting there was for the first four proposed sessions. Especially when he managed to get the BBC interested. Apparently they felt that they owed him something. They were prepared to bill it as the 'Other Reith Lectures' or some such, would you believe? He put a stop to that; he felt it was going too far by far. It brought in a great deal of money and support and put us on a firm foundation; still does. And of course, the quality of the catering had to improve, which is why you are enjoying probably the best *Haute Cuisine* in any Charity. It cost in the beginning, but it was not all a drain. In order to supply the food, the Home Farm was expanded and so was the kitchen garden: more opportunities for work for those unfortunate people who needed the help of the Charity. We did set up the Thomas Foundation, as you know; it was administratively easier that way.

"That is enough for today. We will have dinner, talk to whoever is around and take it up again tomorrow."

"Tell me one thing though: why are you living here?"

"No, that is a step too far and too soon."

*

"Young lady, you would prefer to continue without digression, I'm sure. It's not possible."

"I would like you to stop calling me '*Young Lady*' or '*Miss Philosophy*'. I have a name: it is Morwena[1] but I will also respond to Anna [2]."

"I know your name and the meaning of it! And the diminutive as well. You would have been better called Rhiannon[8]. More appropriate by far.

"To get on or we shall never finish. I never met your grandfather, Joshua Phillips, though, as you said, I had heard of him from Will and Megan, and I made a point of getting to know of the work he did. Will told me a great deal more of him; from admiration I believe. He seemed a person less honoured. Will also tried to explain his ability, or curse as your grandfather insisted, of total recall. Not many people suffer from it, and it's difficult for the young to understand, but as I've got older, I have come to realise that age seems to bring a measure of it: one thing triggers off another and before you know it, you're in a parallel world, one you thought you'd left behind. It's what people call 'drifting' if they're being polite. Is this what *senility* is d'you think? A gradual drift into a parallel world, only real to the one who's drifting? And with less and less desire for the Present? With Death being the Final Drift.

"No, you can't have a view on that yet, as I didn't at your age: but for Old Men, there comes a time when there is more to look back on than to look forward to. But it is such thoughts that bugger-up what is supposed to be the Peace of Old Age; though whoever suggested that old age was peaceful can't have reached it or are brain-dead. *'Rage, rage, against the dying of the light',* as our Anglo-Welsh poet Dylan Thomas once wrote; and he wasn't at all old at the time and was still drinking well; but it was about his father, not himself; *'And you my father in your intricate image'.* He could turn a phrase I must admit, though I never liked him much: too abstruse for my simple mindedness.

"But this must be only a glimpse of the landscape your 'maternal grandfather through adoption' must have occupied. I don't envy him that. However, if I had that ability, this exercise would be easier for me; less demanding. But probably more rambling and interminable for you. On then, with less digression.

"We left Rhodri in the arms of the Head Boy, in the ferns on the mountainside, with a scandal brewing that could put paid to a promising career. Not Rhodri's of course. No-one saw any promise there, only a case for pity – which is a pity because he was worth more than that if they'd only looked – you should always look. The Head Boy was a different matter in any case, and steps had to be taken to ensure silence.

"Let me ask you a question – another digression, but I don't have much chance of conversation that irritates: suppose there was an individual who had performed a heinous crime, ordered an ethnic holocaust say, or a pogrom in his youth and which became known only when he had become a Leader who was now the only person who could forestall a greater act of vandalism; a nuclear holocaust say. As a prosecutor, God say, could you come to terms with the end of humanity in order to prosecute him for his earlier crime? Or would you say, 'I will work for the greater benefit and forget his past?' It's only a matter of magnitude after all. Do 10 Million matter more than 10 Thousand? If you are tempted, what Order of Magnitude would you settle for?"

"You should have studied Philosophy yourself."

"I never had the time for thinking too much – thinking too much can interfere with your daily bread: earning a crust so that you can go on living. And it only matters to me now, now that I have time to indulge myself. In any case it was a rhetorical question which you needn't answer. But it's a question that occurs often in society, though not, thankfully, to the same degree. Sir Thomas More stood against Henry VIII on the principle that God's Law was the last shield to hide behind and should not be transgressed for fear of your own life: a pretty argument but I'm not sure that I agree. Which is why he was Chancellor of England and I could never be. Things are rather different now in any case; more lax; less feared; less Religious; more secular. Perhaps all you have to do is wait for the Law to be changed and 'Bob's your uncle'.

"This brings us to the matter of lawyers. Action was taken, covertly of course, and the Head Boy went off to Oxford to read English, won some poetry prize, twice, wrote a book or two, then took a Law degree, went into Chambers and specialised in Human Rights; *Habeas Corpus* and all that. He rose to an extremely prominent position: a Law Lord and University Chancellor."

"I'm sorry to interrupt, but would I know him?"

"I've given too much away. You know *of* him most probably, but he's dead now, that *is* certain. Which brings me to the question I asked you before: how far can I denigrate his person?"

"It will go no further than here and will die with me."

"So you say. So you say. But how would you like it if I gave away some secrets of your life after you were dead? *'To the limit of the Truth'*, say."

"I have no secrets that matter so it wouldn't concern me. It would be different if I left a family, I suppose."

"Yes. Very well, you seem an honest person. The boy made a name for himself as an Advocate, became a Judge and a Law Lord as I said, and was marked to go higher. Attorney General? Master of the Rolls even. But he died."

"Of what?"

"It's of no consequence to the story you want me to tell you; he has no further part to play here, so I will say no more. But it is remarkable how easily a life can be dismissed. The important issue for you is that his future was facilitated while that of his paramour was not."

"Who facilitated it?"

"I'll come to that, perhaps. Of course, if it was not to leak, not just then but anytime later (*as I'm leaking it to you now*), something had to be done about the young boy. You probably find it difficult to understand, in these enlightened times in which you live (and far from

56

the Valley life), what a scandal the affair would have been if it had been broadcast publicly. Everyone knew it happened of course, and where, but talk of the baser instincts was only for the pub and for Cursing In The Name Of God The Father in the Chapel on Sundays; otherwise, during the week it was mostly gossip and mostly avoided. But this was an underage matter as well; Paedophile Register stuff these days I suppose; and that tears at people deeply. But actually, it rarely caused a problem in the insular Valleys under the thumb of the *Holier Than Thou* Chapel culture; the kids grew out of it once they did it with girls; it blew over if left alone; which was always best anyway. But this time it involved the very clever son of the manse with another young boy who had, to quote from the time, 'little or no future.' So the family were offered an inducement and sent away."

"That is appalling. How could anyone be so cavalier with a young life, especially one that needed help not ostracism?"

"I agree entirely. But people don't like differences d'you see; in thought or deed – it makes them uncomfortable; you must be part of the herd; you mustn't stand out; you mustn't draw attention to yourself. You must also picture the Hell and Damnation Chapel society in which they lived: *Place And Time; Place **And** Time* young Anna. And there were overtones of another kind also."

"What other overtones?"

"We must have lunch or we will miss it again today."

CHAPTER 6

THE WILDERNESS YEARS

"There's little I can tell you about the next few years because I was out of contact; not physically but my time was taken up with establishing myself and my Company: I was dashing about all over the place. I was especially single-minded in those days; I don't think that you, with your modern attitude would have liked me much; and you would certainly not have been prepared to sit and listen to the ramblings of an old autocrat; you would probably have been happier organising a demonstration against the sins of Mammon or some such."

"But you did well enough out of it, being an autocrat I mean; it got you into the Lords, Mammon or no."

"Perhaps you are more understanding now? "

"Not especially, if by understanding you mean tolerant."

"That's a pity. I meant 'understanding' as I said; I did not say 'tolerant' though that too has its place. Neither then?"

"No, not in this context. If anything, I've hardened, and you're not worth the effort of a demonstration any more; you no longer have the power despite your elevated position."

"You hurt madam, in your youth. But that is so, as you so brutally point out, but *I* have become more understanding, even tolerant; even of the doubtless young. But I was a bit ruthless then, as you have to be; I needed contacts and I needed to keep them so I was prepared to play with whoever had the ball. I made a point of getting to know the, what's the phrase? *The movers and shakers* of my world and plotted to make them indebted to me; not wildly so, but enough: a favour here, a favour there; take advantage of friendships. It's what we all do, more or less."

"No limits then?"

"Probably none that would have received your blessing. I was not, in essence, much different from others trying to make their way or consolidate their positions except perhaps in degree: grafting becomes a way of life for you. County Councillor Rees, from your father Will's and Charles' village, was one such who grafted; he was very familiar with the ploy, and he was good at it.

"You don't rationalise it; no-one does. So you excuse it all by saying that there was too much at stake (to me, meaning myself mostly, if I'm honest), too much at stake not to manipulate people for the greater good; and there were too many others trying to do the same but who would cut bigger corners and not do things so well. I was fortunate that some people stayed with me, understood, and even valued my friendship. Even Lord Thomas and I *'cut a dash'* as they say: he used his position to support my applications for Contracts, in exchange for a Directorship when I floated the Company and also for my support of his Charity – this one – in due course. Councillor Rees joined the game too."

"What was his price? He wouldn't have come cheap."

"No price but *silence,* and a little *withdrawal* shall we say."

"Silence about what? Withdrawal from what?"

"Silence about old *Consequences* and Withdrawal from *Opposition.* That's all you need to know."

"That's not enough; you promised me *all-or-nothing.*"

"Yes; that was very, very rash of me. In any case, it's all you're getting on that thread of your life; the dead deserve *some* privacy. Moving on, all I will say, is that it is something of the reason why I'm here now with you, as you wanted to know. Besides, isn't that what Politics is all about – the *Greater Good?*

"The business got bigger and available time got shorter until worthy proposals and interesting new people became sidelined. Your Father Will was one of those and he rightly castigated me for it when I finally listened to what he had to say. But even then he wouldn't have got very far with me; he seemed too vague, too academic; persuasive, but academic. To my shame I even considered him to be clever beyond the average but someone with his eye on the political main chance. You will know how wrong I was in that assessment but even there it could all have ended if Tom, Sir Thomas then, later Lord Thomas of Creigiau hadn't taken something of a shine to him and persuaded me that I had missed something in him. I admired Tom greatly and so I was prepared to take a chance on Will. I came to know him, slowly, and eventually I had to admit that - in this singular case only you understand - my early judgement of a person had been at fault; but he *was* a complex man. By the time Tom made his decisions about the disposal of his estate, I was enthusiastic in my support.

"We're running ahead of ourselves, but context is as important as motivations. How else can you judge decisions, or understand?

"The shopkeeper and family were *relocated* as they say, courtesy of County Councillor Elwyn Rees. I have mentioned him by name already in the context of your tale and he has been in the background for most of the time."

"How so?"

"It will become clear as we move on. As I say they were relocated to the edge of the docklands in the City. It was not then what it is now and I'm happy to say that I have had a hand in its development. But in those days, it was virtually a no-go area: even the Police went there in pairs. The small shop that was found for them was always a non-starter but the blandishments were such that they were eager to move. I had my first contract with the City to develop the docks at that time and I could see that there was little future for the family. It was a small Newsagent as they'd had before but this time the people in the docklands area, matelots and their families mostly, rarely read newspapers and certainly would not spend their money on magazines – a frivolity. The women would occasionally buy a bar of chocolate if the husband wasn't looking but even they preferred to spend it on a glass of Gin on a Saturday. As for the men, it was cigarettes, and that was the only regular income, and then not much at the end of the week when the wages were spent; not much for a family with rent to pay. All that was quite apart from the break-ins and theft of stock. In any case it was due to be knocked down. My development plans meant that the occupiers of the old tenements had to be moved out. It's ironic, but you could say that to a great extent the fortunes of that family failed because of my improvement contract with the City."

"Did you give much thought to that?"

"Of course not. And neither would you have done, young lady, despite your apparent high principles. I did not know the family then, nor their history. In any case, they were only one in a number of the affected."

"Was that a factor?"

"Of course not; it wasn't a factor at all. I was thinking only of the future benefit: I was rebuilding a derelict region to give people a better quality of life. The ones with the first call on the new apartments were those who would be temporarily relocated. As it turned out in the end, we were wrong on two counts: under the relocation plan, families were dispersed and the community spirit, dangerous as it was to outsiders, was lost. Then, high rise buildings were not the answer to the social problems: they never have been; nor will they be – people don't want to live *vertically!* The old populace didn't want to move back to a place that they had never known, and new people were afraid to venture out. No-one knew, or wanted to know their neighbours; the stairs and hallways became piss-pots, drug- and gang - land territories and the lifts never worked. All I can say is that it was not repeated as the docklands developed and now you'd need to be able to afford a yacht in the Marina to buy in there. So much for my altruism. We're running ahead again.

"The shop was dead from the start of course, though they tried to make a go of it while building went on around them; they weren't short of grit. But their debts mounted and they couldn't afford to buy more stock or pay the rent. I don't know the detail of it but the City Council served an eviction notice, (they wanted the land anyway), their suppliers demanded payment of outstanding debts and before the bailiffs moved in, the father disappeared. The business was declared bankrupt so nobody got any money. The mother was served a court summons; she couldn't cope with the shame of it all and committed suicide in one of the deep docks that was due for draining. Or so they said, but she could have fallen in the dark or been accosted. But there was no evidence for any of that: the Police didn't want to agitate in that neighbourhood, and the Council wanted the land as I said. So why pursue the cause of death of a failed shopkeeper whose husband had done a bunk? Rhodri understood nothing of this of course and was totally lost and having been evicted had nowhere to go. His answer was to run away; he simply disappeared and became no-one's responsibility."

"Poor child. That was our caring society at a time of prosperity."

"Yes. Now I must prepare for dinner. Tomorrow I hope will be a more rewarding day."

CHAPTER 7

OASIS

"It was a long time, getting on for six years, before young Rhodri re-surfaced. Much of this now, is hearsay, but it is important for the narrative. It was pure chance that he was then seen by Will. It was a foul evening it seems and Will was making his way home from a pub after an evening with some friends when he saw what seemed like a bundle of rags only partly hidden from the rain in a doorway. He couldn't walk past he told me; a few pence for a bed in the Salvation Army hostel and some warm soup was the least he could do: less than the price of a pint of beer. Untroubled and benevolent after his evening, he stopped and talked to the person. At first there was no response and Will turned to go. Then the person showed his face and although it was dirty and drawn, and the blond hair was matted, he recognised him as Rhodri; the boy refused to acknowledge Will and only asked for some money for a cup of tea. Eventually Will made him realise that he was offering to take him home for a hot bath and some food. Rhodri was afraid and just kept asking for money; in the end he was persuaded by the promise of money. Can you imagine such depravation?

"No," said Anna.

"No. Nor can I. And Will felt the guilt of that for the rest of their time together, despite his promise having been simply a ploy to persuade Rhodri to accompany him. You see, it made Will realise the ease by which the less fortunate could be manipulated, if he had needed to be made aware of it; it was one of the debts he felt he owed to his society for his own privilege."

"What privilege was that? asked Anna.

"The privilege of his intellect that he was born with. By the time they reached Will's flat they were soaked to the skin and Rhodri was shivering with the cold, no doubt. He fell asleep in the bath and drank two large mugs of soup. He took up the offer of a bed and slept until late the following morning. His clothes, such as they were, had dried overnight and Will caught him getting dressed and preparing to leave. He was offered a fried breakfast and was too hungry to refuse. So he stayed, for almost four years. Will found him various jobs; one was a porter at the station, mostly working nights, unloading mail and ice-boxes of fish, which he hated. Then he was taken on as filing clerk at the Safe Haven Trust and was proud that he had responsibility for all the records and proud too to contribute towards the rent of the flat, small though the contribution was. And that was how it stayed until he left.

"That is a brief, a very brief, resume of how Rhodri found an oasis. It was probably the happiest years of his life to that date. You probably know all of that; no doubt Megan will have told you about it. Your Father Will would certainly have done.

"The real matters of interest in this troubled life were known to very few people, if anybody bothered at all; Rhodri certainly never mentioned them. Why, you wonder? I don't think we shall ever know; was he ashamed of what he had been doing, how he had lived, or had he repressed them to an extent that they would seem not to have happened to him but to another? As I say, we shall never know I don't suppose. But we do know something of what happened in those six years."

"How?"

"Through persistence, persuasion, speculation and much investigation."

"*Investigation* you say, Why that?"

"For another reason."

"What other reason? He was nothing to you; or was he?"

"You may judge the *'what'* and the *'why'* when we've finished if you still want to know, not before. Now, how about some tea?"

"If you insist. I'd rather get on."

"There's no hurry. After so many years, these pauses don't matter a jot."

"They do to me."

"Impatient are you? Too fixated on the ending?"

"Yes. But not in the way you believe."

"Dismissive of detail then? That's wrong; it's always been wrong. Is that the fault of Philosophy? The people don't matter much: it's *Concepts above all? Conceptualisation; and Logic of course*, we mustn't forget that. Well, to move forward if that is your wish; and I must tread lightly here."

"Why?"

"For the protection of others as I have said; leave it for now; we'll get on. Most of the detective work was done by Tom Tom, Lord Thomas, or at least at his instigation. I helped, because he convinced me of the need for it. We had become particularly close friends by this time, so I was happy to do what I could. But if you ask me why Tom insisted on becoming so involved, I can't tell you because despite our friendship, he extracted a grave promise from me which I must honour,

God knows."

"Why? Why were you so persistent, then? Were you involved in it all?"

"It's too soon to tell you. Naturally, Will had questioned Rhodri about his life and what had happened to him over the six years or so, but all he got was that he, Rhodri, had *'walked about a lot'* before again ending up in the City. Nothing more than that it seems. As I've said, he might have repressed it completely; he wasn't guileless but I can't believe he would deliberately have avoided giving direct answers. So the information we managed to gather together necessarily came from others."

"What others?"

"It doesn't matter to you who they were; it's the information that's important. After his father left one early morning, before dawn, never to be seen again and his mother fell into the dock, the shop was repossessed of course; and I built on the land in the end. That suicide, or death at any rate, was possibly another factor that drew Will to him, he having lost his own mother similarly, I mean. The only place of any comfort the lad could think of then was back in his childhood valley. He walked the fifty miles or so, over the mountains, mostly, with only the clothes he stood in, with no money and no food. I wish we had known; the Trust could have offered him some support. But he fell through the net and I have often wondered how many more have suffered the same fate."

"You're not that much of an autocrat then?"

"This is now; that was then."

"I can't believe that there can be such a defining change in personality."

"I've said before, you're too intrusive and you're young yet. In my life I did what needed to be done when it needed to be done, that's all. I hope that, on balance at the time of my Judgement, it will come out as having benefited others as much as myself; I believe that I was not entirely selfish; so that will be my defence at the Gates of Paradise enow. Besides, it is not my life we are analysing for your benefit; my Devils you can leave alone. I don't doubt that you have enough of your own to be going on with. Leave the others to the Greater God. Or perhaps you don't recognise Devils other than your own; everyone else is untroubled, is that it?"

"No, I don't believe that. We all trouble in our own way. What matters to me is that people face them down. I have no truck with those who don't. But I have all the time in the world for those who have tried and failed."

"An admirable quality."

"Don't be flippant," said Anna.

"You're too uncomfortable a person to know – I doubt you have many intimates. But I shall tell you something of what we found after lunch."

*

"First, I have to issue a warning. I told you at the beginning that if you persisted in your ill-advised pursuit, there would be aspects of the story that you would not like to hear. Well, we have arrived at one such point. Are you convinced that you wish me to continue?"

"You can't abdicate now."

"Very well. But remember, the Tale is the Players' not the Teller's.

"There's little information about his time back in the village. One or two remembered a 'tramp' wandering about, following the children and trying to steal bread or fruit or anything that was available, even from the bins, and sometimes begging from door to door but nobody knew who he was, nor where he had come from. People forget so quickly when they do not wish to remember. And they didn't know where he slept. My guess is that he slept in one of the abandoned coal mines, far enough in to be out of the rain. Can you imagine the hunger, the cold, the sleeping in the dirt of an old coal mine drift?"

"Something of it," said Anna.

"Yes. A little of it," replied Mostyn. "So don't ever deny the pity of it, ever. The Police were told of his pilfering and they kept a watchful eye; but he was no threat, and they let it drift: another in the '*Of No Concern*' File. '*But keep An Eye On.*' Then he disappeared as quietly as he had arrived. Apparently, he drifted into the underworld of pimps, prostitutes and homosexuals; it wasn't difficult. He was offered money, not much but enough for basic food and a hostel bed. Sometimes there was some more payment for 'services' to men, young and old; mostly old: older lost souls like himself. (There are so many of them.) What would *you* do when there was no money and you had to live as a feral animal? Would you sell yourself to cheat Starvation? That's condemned of course, by the women or men who never have to consider it; have never had to face it. What would the Ladies of a Charitable Bent, with time on their hands do, do you think? They say: *No-one need go hungry; we are here to help.* But many did; and many still do no doubt. So many who can't see a way out. The *Life Force* is very strong; what *Way Out* would you seek then? Perhaps you would abrogate all responsibility and steal, maim, kill; blackmail is a

65

favourite; using your position is another ....*for your own sake?*

"He found no sanctuary in the City either. He slept in doorways and went even more hungry. He was ostracised by society, and warned off by those who had already claimed the 'pitches' and were not about to let an intruder and rival for business onto their patch. He had no knowledge, nor understanding of what the Social Services might do for him and knew nothing of how to approach them in any case. So he became lost among the homeless with the probability of eventually starving or drinking himself to death in the comfort of methylated spirits. The Social Services and Salvation Army were greatly at fault in not seeking out such people and offering support. But, like most caring professions or those with a vocation, there was always too little money, too little time and too few people.

"It was on one of these bleak periods that Will had came across him. As I said, he did not recognise Will immediately; I doubt that he recognised anyone in those days; I doubt that he ever looked at them – you need some confidence or belligerence to do that. For him at that time, there were two kinds of people: those who ignored his pleas and those who exploited him for their own gratification. So the offer of food, a bed and a bath was more than he had ever been offered for his services so it was not difficult for him to agree to go home with Will. As they walked home through the rain Rhodri realised who he was with but there was no reason to think that Will's motive was any different from all the others, especially since Will had known why he had moved away in the first place. And what he did with the 'one-night-stands' or other faceless people in alleyways and dark corners was only to earn a wage for food and living anyway, and was of no consequence beyond that. It came as a surprise to him that Will made no advances and fed him without asking for payment of any kind. It was something quite alien to him and he kept making proposals as a form of payment and only stopped when Will said that he could stay for a while until he felt well again and could look for his own small place, and a job. That was the start of an extended period of cohabitation if it can be called that without sexual connotation. In the beginning, I understand, Rhodri could not understand why Will would not take the payment that he offered, the only thing that he had to offer, and he became quite petulant.

"Well, I'm sure that you've been told of the period following the time Rhodri moved in. As I've said, Will found him some jobs, first as a Porter at the station, but he hated unloading the fish crates with the melting ice and hated the smell of fish on his clothes and hands. Fortunately, Will managed to get him the job as a filing clerk at the

Safe Haven Trust, a job he was perfectly capable of doing so long as the name of the file was written clearly on the document. He was happy there and made friends with the volunteers and even with Megan. It was only later that he became jealous of the two people he admired most: Will and Megan. He felt more and more excluded as their relationship developed and even accused Will of not wanting his company or friendship. And he retreated more and more into his mythology: a displacement activity, certainly, but I like to believe, something more than that: a plea perhaps? Will tried to reason with him but had little success and it all ended *'with a whimper'* as they say. Are you all right my dear?"

"Yes. But I'd like to stop here for a while. I shall take a short walk before it's too dark. The evening's dry and not too cold. A breath of air will do me good. I might even sit on Sir Thomas' *'Watching Seat'* for a while; I haven't really been outside since I arrived. I'm not hungry, so perhaps I'll miss dinner tonight. Can we meet tomorrow?"

"Certainly. Would you like me to come with you?"

"No, I take my time walking; that way you see more and you can think more. What other purpose is there in a walk? So I'd rather do it at my own pace without troubling you. I'll see you in the morning."

"Yes. Don't go too far. There could be another storm brewing up in the Southwest and they develop quite quickly as the wind comes up the valley. And there are no lights up there to show you the way back."

"I shan't stay too long."

CHAPTER 8

THE LURE OF INDEPENDENCE

"What about this gentleman of yours; Edward Williams by name I think. What's he up to now?

"He said that he would drive home via the Brecon Beacons and the Black Mountains. I only hope the weather holds for him. He needs some peace and quiet."

"No, I meant more than that, but we can put is aside for the present. He copes, in one way and another, I understand? I should like to know what he wants for himself. Telephone him when you're able and he's reached home. Unless he has one of these new-fangled mobile telephones that are far too intrusive: when I want to talk, I talk; when I don't want to talk, I want peace. An old man out of touch with the electronic age of course; but being irritated seems little return for billions of pounds putting a satellite up there. But I've given up trying to understand it all. I feel that not only is our World become too small, but Time is also conflated. But let us, at least, move on at our desired speed, as they say."

"Tell me something of how you know all this then," said Anna.

"A consequence of insatiable curiosity mostly; and a perverse interest in people; that's a peculiarity of the Welsh you know: they're not at all happy unless they *understand* the other fellow – it can be quite irritating. You know do you, that I was born, grew and started my business in the same valley as these other fellows, though at its higher reaches? Well, in my business life I found it an advantage for getting my own way if I knew a little more of the situation and the protagonists than others did. So, as a young man trying to make his way out, and having my eye on the main chance, I made it my business to find out what the problems and issues were, *before* I met with others. It paid to know what was going on and who was doing what, to whom and what their motives were. And, if you understand my meaning, who would pay the piper.

"I became quite good at it, though I say it myself. I learned the tactics and strategies quite quickly; another Welsh trait: intelligence. It's quite surprising that we ever lost a conflict; a quite remarkable feat. I blame it all on Henry Tudor of course; he started the rot. We were alright this side of Offa's Dyke until he came along and took us over it.

"Anyway, through a little devious preparation my path could often be eased. But I'm afraid that my tricks spilled over into my private life and it did not help matters that my closest friends were as nosy as I was. I now wonder whether that is not the difference between success and, failure is not the right word; mediocrity perhaps is better: establishing *your* game plan and not following that of others'."

"Is that all it takes?"

"Of course not. It also calls for a *concentration,* a degree of ruthlessness not given to many, as does great success in any field of endeavour. Most people are grateful for the fact; *it not being given to many* I mean. Perhaps you are? As an aside, though he entertained the prospect for some years, that is the primary reason why Father Will would never have really made in it politics: insufficiently Machiavellian, quite unlike Lloyd George for instance. You see, apart from anything else, he cared too much; is that too dreadful a thing to say about Politicians do you think? In any case, Will did not have that necessary streak of ruthlessness, though he did try. He'd have been a good second-in-command though. But that is by-the-by: an observation with hindsight only."

"But you recommend it? Ruthlessness I mean."

"It is not necessary in order for most people to live a satisfactory life. In fact, they should avoid it: it should be balanced against flippancy most of the time; which of them rules depends entirely on your aspirations. But people are acquisitive, haven't you found? And if you give any thought to what you want to be, ruthlessness is an aspect of your character that must be faced. Will did, and decided to withdraw."

"Was he wrong?"

"Who's to know? As the scientists would say, it's not a controlled experiment is it? Do you know what is meant by that? I didn't for some time until it was pointed out to me that *you cannot judge the success or failure of an action until you know the effects consequent on that action and can judge them against what the effects would have been if no action had been taken:* textbook words and phrases; jargon for the initiated; does that rigmarole make sense to you?"

"Yes."

"Then you're ahead of me. As I understand it, Scientists achieve control by splitting their subjects into two groups and treating them both the same except that one group is also subjected to the action under consideration. All nice and tidy, but not always possible, which takes us into the realms of *soft* science I suppose; like Sociology, or Politics even; or that liar Statistics. Still, it's all fodder for the Philosophers I suppose."

"Give me an example."

"I said that I didn't believe that Will had the necessary ruthless streak for a successful politician, or for a number of other jobs actually. But we can't know, because we couldn't have a Will with a ruthless streak and at the same time a Will without it in order to *scientifically* compare degrees of success."

"Pedantry."

"Most certainly."

"But," said Anna, "We can look at all those that have succeeded and compare their characters with all those that have not and come to a judgement of the necessary qualities."

"That, as I say, is the Statistical Imperative: the Art of Lying; an excuse for not being clever enough. Well, it is the basis for my judgement in any case. Some people say that it is a cold and mercenary way in which to judge your fellow man; instead, you should take each person as an individual and judge his or her behaviour on its own: Saint or Sinner? The trouble is, isn't it, that it is so rarely one or the other? And I never learned the trick of doing it; I relied too much on my experience of dealing with people, subjective though it is, and I do wonder whether it can ever be done, for the simple reason that people do *classify* other people, consciously or unconsciously, for good or ill, even on first meeting. I don't see how you can make sense of the diversity of humanity without some degree of pigeonholing; the diversity is too great to understand otherwise. Linnaeus showed us that case for life on earth and Darwin wouldn't have got anywhere without it. And I refuse to believe that behaviour, human or otherwise can be any different; more ephemeral if anything! Where do you draw the boundaries? The secret, I feel, is to know what you are doing. And to know yourself and what you believe you're worth."

"What do you believe you're worth?"

"Huh! Now there's a question. When?"

"What do you mean *'when'*?

"What am I worth now? Yesterday? Ten years ago? Twenty? I assume you don't mean fiscally?

"I wouldn't presume to ask that."

"The answer, anyway, would only be *'enough to see me out and in the meantime to follow my interests'*. For the other *'worth'*, best ask me on my deathbed when what I say I will have rehearsed for Gabriel (the Archbishop and God's Prime Minister) at the Pearly Gates and which won't come back to taunt me later.

"There was a 'Doom and Gloom Preacher' I knew once – *Fire and Brimstone* from the Pulpit: *Donner und Blitz!* There were many of them in the Valleys: they seemed to gravitate there for some reason; perhaps they saw it as helping the under-privileged to see God; to me, I think it simply gave them a Captive Audience with that inclination anyway. In any case, this particular one – Mr Moses Rowlands I seem to remember his name was; a very suitable name for someone bent on Religion (though I would bet that he knew little of the original Moses except that he crossed the Red Sea – which he didn't by the way; and I'll still wager that he didn't know that Moses the Original, was a Priest of the Sun God – not surprising since he was half Egyptian anyway). Was he given that name by forward-looking parents or did he chose it for himself later? This particular Moses always took as his final text on the Sunday Evening Service, when all the boys and girls wanted an end to it so they could proceed to their 'dates' (the Physical first, the Lord can take His chance later): *Man's Fall By The Wayside Into Poppies And The Mud.*

"A strange matter for a Minister to pursue on a wet Sunday evening. We often wondered where the text came from since he was too young to have fought in World War One. I think he made it up. But he must have thought it pretty good, because he over-used it. He didn't last long, this Moses."

"Alright then" said Anna; "Let me put it another way: what advice can you give?"

"That's even worse. How can I presume to advise? I can only know how *I* believed I needed to behave. That was difficult enough, and quite enough of a risk. I can't tell others what they should or shouldn't do, short of criminality that is. That's the problem with Government and Organised Religion – they're far too *restrictive,* and *proscriptive* and *Holier Than Thou.* You've got me on my *Hobby Horse* [9] now. We'd best move on."

"Yes, you mustn't indulge yourself. You said that we, all of us, categorise people."

"Touché. You have something of Will's facility for argument. Is that inborn do you think? It can't be of course; it must have been absorbed as you grew in that family. I would be encouraged if it was so. I'm inclined to the *nurture* side of the debate d'you see, like the Old Communists and the Catholics. In any case I was generalising; I firmly believe that I am a Genus of only one Species; in other words *unique.*"

"That's too easy."

"It is, thank God and Little Fishes; but it's all you're getting. This discussion has become too philosophical and too personal by far. I feel safer telling you a little more of your father and other people."

"Carry on then," said Anna.

"So. With the lad's short-term view of life, the arrangement with Father Will, with board, lodging and employment secured, would have come to be seen as a permanency and, knowing his attractiveness to other men, he would have considered that there was more to it than there probably was; he would have believed that, given time, intimacy would naturally follow and he would have looked forward to that; eagerly I would guess. Will's initial rejection of Megan, the clinic doctor and one, ambivalently, to be worshiped, came to be seen as part of the growing relationship between him and Will, if Will could only be made to understand it. He must have thought, if he thought about it at all, that Will's period of depression, if not almost breakdown, (following his Mother's commitment and death), was only a consequence of the fact that Will would not reject the *Woman* and recognise his love for Rhodri – your father. If he finally did and Will's love matched his own, then their future lives were intertwined and secure. Do you now see the consequences of the human weaknesses of Care and Compassion and where it leads you?"

"I see where it can."

"And love-sickness? Are you more understanding of that too?"

"I have never doubted any form of it. I am not homophobic."

"But it's been underlined?"

"It didn't need to be."

"In any case Rhodri's self-confidence increased as he came to believe that he had forged a life for himself at last. Then things changed. The Aberfan waste tip disaster that finally brought your Father Will and Mother Megan together, had ripples that no-one could have foreseen. I don't doubt for a minute that anyone who witnessed the disaster, in whatever way and in whatever place, and who had the slightest degree of sensitivity, was not unchanged by it. I don't mean those immediately involved; I mean all those who looked in from the outside: the *voyeurs* if you like, of which I was one. But they were people who did not accept the usual connotations that the word carries and they were right to do so. In any case, and not without a struggle, Will's form of isolationism, drawn upon himself you understand, passed: he and Megan resumed their courtship, due in no small part to Josh, her father. I understand from people who knew him that he was another who cared too much. In any case, he played a very clever game. I would not have liked to play Bridge against him; nor Poker. You never knew him did you? Of course not; you would have been just a child when he died. But he locked Will into the family before he did so, both emotionally and financially. Not many people could say that they *knew* Josh Philips; Will was one of the few who could claim it; Tom

Tom was another. But we're wandering too far from our purpose here; that is all by-the-by and not pertinent, as they say. The consequences are though. Time for lunch."

*

"It is difficult to know what Rhodri made of all that at the time. Not much I don't suppose. There was an increasing feeling of loss, of course and I suppose, a fear bound up with that: the fear of being alone again, of being cast adrift once more. You can imagine that I'm sure. Jealousy, certainly, of Megan, the Woman, and what he saw as the ease by which she had 'stolen' Will from him; an ambivalence of idolatry and hatred he could not resolve. He would have been difficult to handle at that time, even for someone practised in the art, or totally uninvolved; for someone who was both cause and effect, I would think it almost impossible to make any progress. There is a delicious irony to the tale at this point and it's to do with independence.

"For years, I understand from the time of his brother's death and his mother's, Will had vowed not to be dependent on any other person for the rest of his life: I suppose you could say that he took a vow of Hermitage if there is such a word in this context; of retreat in personal relations in any case. That's one way of dealing with deprivation I suppose and many people follow it; you'd know more about that than I. Anyway, it took the Disaster, Megan's persistence and Josh's conniving ways to drag Will out of it and for him to know his real self. His friend Charles, who you know as your 'uncle', he failed to do it, close as they had been when they were growing up. Perhaps that was because Will was afraid of him; afraid that he knew too much. In any case, as I said, it was the Aberfan disaster as much as Megan that breached his defences. We're not here to analyse Will but the point I'm trying to make is of interest: once he took his second chance, he embraced it completely, as completely as he had rejected it before, and he gave himself over to Megan. There was no turning back then, no third thoughts, which is just as well because Megan would not have lived any other way and all our lives would have been different. So you see how disasters have ripples that disturb the sand a long way from the sea's edge? What do the sages say? 'A butterfly fluttering its wings in the forest in Asia causes a hurricane in America' or words to that effect."

"You said that there was an irony here."

"Indeed. As I have said, Will gave up his attempt at isolationism at precisely the time that Rhodri decided to give it a go."

"What do you mean? I thought that Rhodri did not have that strong a personality. You've said yourself that he didn't live by his wits so much, as drift."

"That is true. But Megan coming back pushed Will in one direction and Rhodri in quite another. As I said, Rhodri felt that he had lost the battle for Will's devotion and had to look elsewhere. I don't believe he made a conscious decision of it, more a recognition of the way things happened in his life. All of which was a *fait accompli* if he ever knew the phrase. But there was also an element of fortuitousness about it, as there seems to be for most things in life. He used to finish his work at the Trust around 4 o'clock but often stayed on for a cup of tea. Other times he would go to the Library and slowly read books on the Legends. He became well-known to the Librarians and, apparently, they became very fond of him; they would send away to the National Library or University Library for out-of-print books for him. Not to take away, of course, but to read in the Reading Room. They say he became quite an expert and if you could get him to talk, quite entertaining. They also introduced him to someone else who used the Reading Room, though with less focus to her reading and probably more for warmth and somewhere to go than any mental exercise. But she was no lightweight; she once told the Librarians that she wanted to read 'all the Classics' and could they help her choose the order. So she too, made a goal for herself and for whatever reason they came to make a point of meeting there and eventually, when they could afford it, stopped for a small beer as they went their different ways home."

"Who was she? Was she my mother?"

"I don't know. There's nothing I can tell you about her. Nobody seems to have known her: not who she was, where she came from, where she lived. Nothing. What I can tell you is that she seemed to have disappeared from the scene when Rhodri did. He is also known to have travelled with a girl and sent postcards to Will, so she could have been your mother but it's all circumstantial; I can't take you down that road. You will have to find others to do that, if you can.

CHAPTER 9

CARAVANEER

"I have given much thought to your Quest, and it seems to me that you could be easily satisfied; all you wish, in effect, is to know who in the saga was the *Caraveneer?* Do you know that word?" asked Mostyn.

"No, I'm afraid not," replied Anna.

"Pity; it is a word dear to my heart. It establishes who is the Leader, and who are the Followers. That's probably something of what the Preacher in his versifying was after: God the Leader and us the Followers. But that is not the Leader that you are after, I think; yours is more parochial and if you learn who that is, you will probably then leave me alone. So all I have to do is 'leak' a name without giving leads or offence to others; not the easiest of actions I will admit. Still, we will consider it, you and I, and see where it takes us.

"The word 'Caravan' you will be familiar with of course, but you are probably too ready to think of something like a house on wheels pulled behind an old car that isn't quite strong enough to take the hills, so that other long-suffering drivers have to put up with it on weekends. Or perhaps you think of Gypsy caravans and fairs, which would be nearer the original mark but which are even more frustrating, moving as they do only at clod-hopping horse-pace. But perhaps you are not familiar with its derivation."

"Is this important?"

"Not especially. Diverting, but not especially important."

"Then why are you telling me? I'd rather get on."

"You are irritable this morning. Did you not have a good night?"

"That's of no consequence. My nights are my nights. Never anything special these days. I'm more concerned with seeing the next day in. Now can we get on?"

"In due course. And when I'm ready. And at my pace.

"When I retired from the rat-race I found that my language skills had suffered somewhat over the years. When I first realised this I though that I would take up a hobby. Some people find retirement from a demanding profession easy to cope with and are grateful for the chance to shut away all the files as it were, and get on with the rest of their lives. Others find that there are long hours in their days which they struggle to fill and they long for the morning rush-hours for years. I always advised those of my old employees who retired but who could not stay away from the office, to take up a hobby of some kind. It was more difficult for them, I found, if they had also lost their wives. Then I found myself retired, though by choice, but still in the second of my categories: I had lost my wife. You know that, otherwise, despite my earlier comments, why would I be living here? It was nothing special; she just died on me. But it did leave me feeling more alone than I ever thought I would be. That surprised me. Over the years I suppose I must have come to take her for granted and I have apologised to her for that, wherever she is. We humans take each other too much for granted and you must try not to fall into that trap. It was, by the way, another reason for inviting you to see me. Two reasons I suppose: I felt that I should tell you what I could about someone who had been taken for granted for too long and because I was interested in finding out how you would fill my hours; whether in fact, my investment would be worth it. A purely personal indulgence.

"But I was telling you about my hobby. Perhaps you know that when I built my own house, I found a plot of land near the golf course. I never played, finding it too much of a waste of time when I spent most of it in what they call 'the rough' – meaning where the grass hasn't been cut, I think. But my guests enjoyed the privilege; which meant I could take advantage. I could have gone back to that I suppose, but it held no attractions. Also, I was not looking for something energetic, something worthy. If I'd wanted that I could have stayed in the house and walked the dunes every day. It was the intellectual challenge I missed and so I decided that language was to be the thing; and language in itself, not as a tool for poets and authors. So, linguistics I suppose: I decided that if there was a word that interested me during the course of my reading I would seek out its meaning, its derivation and its first usage. Even though it takes me far too long to finish a text, I recommend the pursuit; it is a fascinating insight into the English language. Unfortunately, my facility in the language of my birth has quite deserted me and while I would dearly like to do the same in Welsh, it would take more time than I have at my disposal; a pity that, Early and Middle Welsh must have many interesting snippets. There is also the added advantage of contributing volumes of Dictionaries, Thesauruses, regional dialects, slang words and various other compilations, to the Library here, together with my catalogue – the *References* – so dear to the writer. Being a geriatric is not the be-all and end-all you see; it's not a slow drift into sleep by any means; no time of your life is really, unless you wish it to be. You mustn't drift off to sleep; you can still do something even if you think you don't have much time left. Will you do me the favour of accepting that?"

76

"With no reservation. And I thank you for it. You're a clever man."

"No, no. Just an old one who's looked back occasionally; and thought for a minute or two. But you can consider another thing for me. Do you think that perhaps, just perhaps, it was the sort of thing that Rhodri was trying to do without putting it into so many words? Not language itself, not linguistics, he wouldn't have known what that was, but a search for what being Welsh was for him? The meaning of his world? You see, I have an hypothesis, I would not presume to call it a theory, that he had been left with an emptiness in his life that he was trying to fill; like you, a search for what he was. I'll tell you something else, for nothing: I suspect that if it was not for the accident at his birth, he would have been an intellect to recon with, though not necessarily a different character: *who* we are, is not necessarily *what* we are, as you are having to face.

"But I digress, and it must be irritating for you, having to listen to an old man's rambles. I was asking you about the word 'Caravan'. Not a remarkable word in itself you would think. Everyone knows the tin box on wheels but not many will have taken the trouble to find out that its origin is about 1599 and meant a company of merchants, pilgrims or others, or indeed all of them, in the East and northern Africa, travelling together for the sake of security, especially through the deserts. It also came to mean a fleet of Turkish or Russian ships, especially merchant vessels with their rich pickings, in convoy (as during our Wars), and then a company in motion. Examples are too many to mention, from the covered wagons of the Wild West and Hollywood, to the Crusades and the Canterbury Tales. Nothing remarkable to it, merely a question of safety. But it's the derivations I enjoy and how we came to know them: *Caravanserai*, for example, from the Persian, and a kind of Inn where they stayed and were protected in a spacious courtyard. Then there's *Caravaneer*, the leader of the oriental caravan or the Chief Scout on a Wagon Train."

"Is there a point to this that's hidden from me?"

"In your narrow-minded view, not much, no. But it is a point of interest to me, though probably not one of any consequence. You see, while we have been talking together I've not been able, totally, to put matters aside when I've gone to bed; and when waiting for sleep, I've taken to wondering, among other things, who was the *Caravaneer* in the *Saga of Rhodri, Descendant of the Princes of Wales*? Was it him? Or was it his Lady? Or was it someone else entirely? And were the Myths and Legends of his country a Caravanserai for him? A place of safety? Or of comfort? Now there's a metaphor for you. We shall never know but I can't help hoping that he eventually shouldered a responsibility and had a degree of personal gratification and fulfilment as a leader."

"It seems that he did, at least towards the end."

"Indeed, it seems so, from what little we know. We too, shall soon be coming to an end, though not quite yet; you must stay a little longer and I shall attempt to drag the story out for as long as I can without being tedious, because, quite unexpectedly, and despite the rather tragedian slant to the tale, I find that I am enjoying your company. It is not at all what I expected when I foolishly agreed to embark on the journey with a young lady I did not know and whom I fully expected to be, not uneducated of course, but much too young, uncultured and tedious; one who required a degree of courtesy because of my involvement with her relations at one time, but which required no more than a short synopsis of the life of another, peripheral character. But it's not turned out as expected. Why is that do you think? Can you hazard a guess?"

"Perhaps it's because you've been doing most of the talking and you enjoy the sound of your own voice? Could that be it? You've missed the Board Room more than you've acknowledged perhaps?"

"You're being impertinent but I will forgive you for it, because at least you are being forthright and that's a quality I admire - in myself and in others. Will has taught you well, if ever you needed to be taught, which I somehow doubt. By the way, I've been meaning to ask you: do you or did you used to ride?"

"Horses do you mean?"

"Well I don't mean motorcycles. Don't show my analysis of your character to be wrong for God's sake. It really would be tedious to find that you're a closet *Hell's Angel*. Do you object to my invoking the Deity?"

"Invoke whoever gives you comfort or support; it's of no concern to me."

"You follow Will's path then?"

"I follow my own and I'll argue my stance if I have to."

"Not with me; you have a facility in argument, I think, and I would suffer your logic. Well, do you? Ride I mean."

"No. Like all privileged little girls, I was taken to ballet classes and the Pony Club. I gave up the discipline of ballet about the same time as hockey; and I fell off a horse. I never tried again; I have preferred to get to know *useful* people in my own way. Why do you ask?"

"Twice a year we have horse-racing here. It used to be fox-hunting by invitation but against my advice the Trustees (Tory mostly, I'm afraid) pre-empted the Government, for the sake of votes, and put a stop to that, more's the pity. You wouldn't believe the increase in the number of lambs lost to the buggers since the Spring hunting was banned. Ministers should try living on a farmer's income and suffer the loss of their lambs. The problem with every Cabinet is that they are elected as politicians to represent the people and are then given jobs to do that they know exactly nothing about but in which they feel that they are experts and have to leave a mark. They have not grasped the fact that most of the marks they leave behind are the consequence of ignorance or worse. It's an intractable problem, I'm afraid."

"You're becoming very irritable. Perhaps we should call it a day?"

"Yes. When I've told you about the horse-races. We have stables and plenty of space to park horseboxes. We don't have a racecourse, flat or over the sticks but we do have something which I consider much more exciting. We can do Point-to-Point races across the valley (to frighten the foxes) and we can charge Businesses a fabulous amount of Corporate money to watch it from the rooms of the House; complete with all necessary hospitality of course. It's the one time when the Hall is full out of term - time, and the Kitchen gets quite excited about it and does us proud. That was Will's idea too, and has been a real money-spinner for the Trust. All the Businesses set it against tax of course, but there's no shortage of them when they're out enjoying themselves and they feel that they're supporting Charity. In fact, so many want to come that I'm thinking that in this coming year we'll run over two days each time: New Year's Day and the 2nd and Easter Monday and Tuesday; with a premium for the Bank Holiday days of course: it's interesting to see when the various Businesses appear – it charts their rises and their falls you know – the *ups* and the *downs* - and it pre-empts the Stock Exchange listings by a good few months. As I've told you, my rooms overlook the valley and I invite special guests to share the day with me. I would be pleased if you would be my guest on one or two of these occasions. You could join me for the New Year, or come for the Easter meet. Would you accept?"

"I'm honoured but I'm not sure whether I would add to the pleasure of your other guests."

"I'm not asking you for the pleasure of my other guests. As I told you my guests are by my invitation and are invited to give me pleasure though most of the time they seem to enjoy each other's company also; once the wine's opened at least. But they do some business as well – the bosses have to show a return on their visit after all – but between you and me, that is by the by."

"I'm not much taken with company these days so please forgive me if I thank you, but decline."

"No, I can't accept that. You seem determined to ruin my enjoyment and I won't have it: I want to show you off; I want to show them I can still 'pull the girls'."

"You're past that surely; you'll become a 'dirty old man'."

"Aren't all the Cocks, given the chance, when there's a pretty Hen to impress?" he asked and smiled. "I will put a compromise to you: come for one meet and if you don't enjoy it you needn't come again. I will remind you however, that when we agreed to set out on this pilgrimage, you promised to tell me the secrets of your Quest."

"Alright I'll come once, but no promises beyond that."

"That will do for now. You've exhausted me with you prevarication. We'll take the story up tomorrow. Before I go, I'll let you into another secret: none of the people who come to watch the race ride either, though they may own the hunters.

"Here's another unusual little snippet for your memoirs: do you know, that when a horse dies here, we keep the skull, clean it up using maggots (that we then sell to the fishermen after trout or salmon), and store it away for Mary Lwyd [9] ? She comes around each year."

"That's very Medieval."

"No, no. Well, yes, yes, in a sense. But it's dated much earlier than that. I've said this before to people: it comes out of the Mists of the Myths of our country. I repeat myself, but I like the *alliteration* of it; and it's a guide to one's degree of drunkenness. Also, it's pleasing that it's true. You should read more of it all; it gives you a sense of perspective.

CHAPTER 10

AN ACHIEVEMENT

"Why is it that people are so often driven to make stories of their lives? You would think that the default position in anyone's life would be the living of it to the greatest personal advantage and that there was little time to make a story out of it – that's work for grandparents! Yet we all do it at some time or another and for various periods of time. Mostly I'm prepared to accept that it happens at a time of reflection; and mostly when you're old and tired, or on a 'comfort break'. It's a reviewing, a reckoning of some kind, a *settling* of the brain store; and it's mostly of short duration, soon set aside to get on with the proper business of living: the needs of the day; the need to satisfy the demands being made on the basis of one perceived duty or another - *responsibility* is the one most often cited. Well, there's no real harm in that I suppose, most of the time. Some people refuse to acknowledge responsibility of any kind, of course, and that can cause great pain and trauma to themselves and to others. And that defect of the lack of personal responsibility and its consequences has been the theme of literature since the time of Genesis: *'Lord I am thy faithful servant; instruct me as to what I should do then I will properly worship You.'* Blackmail I call that, but what do the scientists call it? 'The Study of Altruistic Behaviour'. That's not seriously correct but it has the same implications: *you scratch my back when I need it and so you can then expect me to scratch yours when you need it.* An interesting field of study it must be. But I keep forgetting that you must know all about these things. Here am I, a very mediocre amateur preaching to the expert."

"Hardly that. I studied animal behaviour very selectively and then only as a sideline. I would be the last to preach it or anthropomorphise it."

"You under-rate yourself I'm sure. But it's by-the-by and not the point I'm trying to make. I'm trying to determine why people make a fiction of their lives. No, that's not correct either; what I want to know is why people live one life, but periodically feel the need to escape to another. That's more what I'm after – like escaping to an affair. As I've said, in many cases, perhaps most, the escape is of short duration and very infrequent; but it does happen and I wonder whether such escapism is actually a means of rationalising our activity to ourselves;

or justifying our motives. Rather like dreams - for which Freud treated *the moneyed ladies who had too much time on their hands and who were subliminally looking for something sexually stimulating. Thereby he made a fortune for himself, but lost his way and his sense in the process.* Would there be any joy in pursuing that hypothesis do you think?"

"There may be. But then, any hypothesis is worth some investment of time, even if only as a philosophical exercise."

"Your justification for Philosophy? But there's the rub again d'you see: time! One does not have the time for all questions any more: when you're young, you don't know the *questions;* when you're old, you don't have the *time* to do them justice. It's very difficult being a *polyglot* in this day and age and so one must make choices. It is not a position I've ever been happy with, making choices."

"But you must have had to make several in a day in your position in the business."

"No. Decisions, yes and most often difficult ones, but not choices. I feel that there is a difference because they need not be the same: I feel that once a choice is made, at least half of the work is wasted; not so with decisions where some of the work not taken up may still contribute."

"That's pedantry again and you know it."

"Do I? I prefer to think that I have lived my life without becoming a pedant. There you are, you see, a period of reflection and assessment has come upon me again. It is also of interest that it happens more and more often as you get older. Or perhaps you have noticed the effect also? Perhaps it just comes with the recognition of one's mortality."

"That's only one reason for fictionalising one's life. Another is a consequence of the *'Why Me?'* syndrome: why is it that whatever has happened has happened to me and not to Joe Bloggs down the road? What did I do to deserve this life, the one I have to live? This retreat is usually in response to self-pity, a means of saying that it could all have been so different, if only…. It's so much easier to live the life you write for yourself than the one that's written for you I suppose," said Anna.

"You say, 'written for you'. You subscribe to predestination then? You surprise me; I wouldn't have put you in that camp."

"No, I don't," replied Anna. "It's just shorthand for the life you have to live through because of the accident of your birth, the consequences of your parentage, your own earlier activities and your response to others'."

"It's escapism then is it?"

"Oh, entirely," said Anna. "We all want to escape the consequences of what has made you, or who, and what you've done; but as we agree, there's generally no harm in that. Not if it's recognised for what it is. And it's often quite enjoyable, wouldn't you say?"

"But," said Lord Mostyn, "What if the pretence becomes the reality and the day to day life becomes the fiction? What then eh? You can act out any fantasy in that world and you can't be blamed for it in your 'real life': your *balance of mind is disturbed* as the clever lawyers say. A most convenient defence for your actions; no *blame* can be placed at your door in your real life, because it wasn't really you but your *alter ego* or some such; it's a defence to the charge of *premeditation*; it's a *mistaken identity; an alibi for the mind; an escape from the gallows!* It can happen, you know; and all too easily; many deaths are inflicted in that way. Is that madness do you think? People used to be committed for losing their grip on reality; asylums were full of such people: nothing really wrong with them and they were no danger to anyone but they were committed to languishing for the rest of their lives in their own *fantasy* world; for their own, and others' safety's sake, we say. There, others have decided for you: *'it's all in your own best interests. So you must pull yourself together; pull your socks up and behave yourself.'"*

"Yes," said Anna. "And how dreadful it must have been for those people who came to realise their predicament but could do little about it. What torture it must have been: *if you're not mad now, you soon will be'.* Are we more enlightened these days? It's not something I know anything about and I'll admit to you, I'm afraid to find out more; I couldn't have studied Psychiatry, I'd be too frightened of what I'd learn about the fragility of my own mind. I couldn't do it, any more than I could read 'A History Of Asylums'."

Lord Mostyn said, "I must get on with where I'm going before I forget it; but I do believe that's what happened to Rhodri, at least for a short while; I sincerely hope for a short while. I believe that he lived the reality of the Legends of Wales and that he was on a pilgrimage to find the players and I don't mean a geographical pilgrimage; at least, not entirely. I can't presume to know what contribution the girl or woman had on his life; as I have told you, I know nothing about her. But in one way or another, for one reason or another, Rhodri slid into this fantasy world, and left his own behind; and his girl must have complied at least."

"Has that been the purpose of this discussion on *Reality?*" asked Anna

"Not so purposeful initially; more a wandering; but it seems to have had a focus unknown to me," said Mostyn.

"But Rhodri came out of it, didn't he?" asked Anna.

"It seems so. It looked like it."

"You're positive?"

"Yes, as far as one can be."

"What brought him out of it?" asked Anna.

"No, I'm no Psychiatrist; you'll have to ask someone more qualified than I am for any convincing reason for that."

"But it would take too much time to relate his life story again, time we don't have. You wouldn't want to go through this story again would you?" asked Anna.

"No, I would not; and I will not. To tell you the truth, I'm occasionally regretting setting out on the pursuit at all. It's disturbing me. It's not the talking to you so much; in fact that has turned out to be rather satisfying on the whole; certainly more so than I expected, and even though I have noticed some prickly aspects to your character. No, it's not that; it's been the regimentation of the days that I have found unpleasant; it's like being back at work - regimentation. That's the first thing I enjoyed on my retirement: not having to keep a diary anymore. Have I told you my favourite observation of human nature? Listen to this: all your working life, you're ruled by the clock: the alarm bell in the early morning; the car to meet; the train to catch; the first meeting of the day; lunch; visits to sites; more meetings; evening attendances; papers to read; all before you can go to bed. Then you retire and leave all of that behind: your time is your own to fill as you wish. And what do your colleagues in their wisdom give you? A Clock; and usually a hideous one at that; ormolu usually."

Anna said, "Since there's no time for a psychiatric analysis, you seem to be in the best position to offer an explanation of his return - Rhodri, I mean."

"The simple answer, I think (though there's nothing simple to it), is that he could no longer ignore his *real* life and for that I suppose we have to thank his woman, you (another woman), Megan (the third of the Coven): the *Three Witches* – Midwife, Nurse and Layer-Out of souls; also, Will and oh, probably a host of others; and his tragedies too, though whether they were beneficial or not is debateable. The 'Big Question' though is this: did he ever really and securely set that fantasy aside?"

"I hope so, for his own soul's sake," replied Anna.

"So do I, you know; truly. But you know all about this conundrum – your little Degree Thesis *"The Philosophy Of Myth – The Comfort of Myth"* tells me that; you follow your father Will in dialectic (learnt) and perhaps your father Rhodri in the Myths (inborn tendency, as they say)."

"How do you know of my little Thesis?"

"I've kept a weather-eye open on the people I once knew about, that's all; especially after you continued to insist on bothering me – my *homework* again d'you see; it helped me to decide. You should expand it properly – research the Myths of our country."

"What, *all* of them?"

"Why not? Make it your *'life's work';* your own *Magnum Opus Dei.* Tell me something of interest: did you choose your Thesis on purpose or not?"

"One's choice of a time-wasting exercise is usually purposeful."

"Not so, not so. But that's another debate. However, in Rhodri's case, even his life, tragic by any criterion, drove him on. I suppose you could say that the fact of his return and his committing you into the care of Will and Megan was his short life's greatest achievement. No, for him, ACHIEVMENT should be in upper case."

"You say his 'short life'. Do you know what happened to him in the end?"

"This will seem a terrible anticlimax to you, but no, I do not. I do have some more to tell you before we finish, but tomorrow. You look tired and that's not surprising; and I need a period of contemplation before I draw to a close. Afternoon, I think, not morning."

CHAPTER 11

THE LOSS AND THE GIFT

"I talked to my mother, Megan, this morning, as you'd left me at a lose end," said Anna. "It seems that my current period of grace has to come to an end. My Consultant is concerned that I have been *'incommunicado'* as he puts it for too long. He wants to prod me about again."

"Then you must do as he wishes. And you must telephone young Edward with your plans. You must not ignore him for too long in his absence."

"I shall. But the Consultant and I, we both know the endgame and I can't see the point of it myself; I keep telling him so but he won't listen to *'my uninformed expression of an ill-considered position'* – how portentous can you get? If it was just him on my back, it wouldn't bother me but I don't want to trouble my mother. You would think, being a medic, she wouldn't personalise things so, but she does."

"That's probably why, don't you think? That, and her responsibility for you."

"More than for the others?"

"She's more conscious of it perhaps; it's more to the fore."

"The adoption factor again?"

"You must accept that it's relevant because however much she loves you, she is also conscious of the duty she owes, not only to you but to your Father Rhodri and to Will too, in his memory. After Rhodri brought you to them, I'm sure that Megan and Will felt that they owed something for the gift he gave them; what greater gift is there than your own flesh and blood? Well, for Will, that is over but that may make it more of a concern for Megan. Now the duty is hers; so don't dismiss it, or belittle it, nor be distressed by it; understand it; and understand that you've no right to do any of that."

"You understand it then?"

"Yes; the Eastern religions know far more about it than we do. They believe, for example, that if you save a person's life, you become responsible for it until either they, or you, die: they are under your Care, as it were. And Megan now knows something of that burden of the Duty Of Care; apparently her father often talked about it. It's real you see, for those who Care. What I don't understand is how anyone can deny it. When they took you, both she and Will committed themselves not only to you but to Rhodri too, don't you see? You become indebted to the giver of the gift; that's another debt to owe; it's a debt for you too. You cannot deny that, nor criticise them for it."

"Oh, I don't" said Anna. "But he had no right to abandon his own flesh and blood. You can't play dice with people's lives."

"*God does not play dice,* eh?"

"But we all do, I regret," said Anna. "But it's *wrong* and I blame him deeply for that."

"You mustn't" said Lord Mostyn. "We don't know him nor what he was. Nor what he faced. And he sought safety for you, didn't he? Also, understand that at present, Megan is likely to feel that you need her more than do her other two, I suspect."

"I'm too conscious of that also."

"When will you leave then?"

"I've asked for a few days. I'm sorry about that. I was actually looking forward to finishing our talks at leisure; do you believe that?"

"Why should I not? If you say so, then I believe you."

"Next New Year then, I shall come for the races, I promise. It's something I shall look forward to."

"Good. We shall have to move on now then if I'm to finish. Again, I'm unsure of how much you know and what you've been told already."

"Assume very little; that way you won't miss out anything you consider important."

"Very well. You had an older brother who was still born and your mother, Rhodri's Lady, nearly died from a haemorrhage when she gave birth to him. He was never registered but I came to know that they were to call him Bran[10] . Rhodri wrote to Will to tell him about the pregnancy and their intention to name him after one of the leaders of a branch of the Mabinogi [15] and an Ancient God: *Bendigeidfran; Bran the Blessed.* He was *'expected'* about the same time as your legal brother, the Doctor.

"You are not too familiar with the Welsh Legends I see, but you should be with the name you have. So I'll tell you again: read them when you have the time; they are best read *gently*. I'm sorry that I had little time for them at school; that was a mistake on my part; I took the road of *'Easy Welsh'* instead – just the language, no literature; a pity; I've been trying to catch up ever since. So address yourself to reading them; but I suggest that you do so in modern prose; learning Old or Middle Welsh would take too long and detract from the purpose. When you do so, I suggest that you start with *The Romance of Culhwch and Olwen* [11] "

"Why that?"

"It's the first of the *Arthurian Tales* and it's informative if you understand who they are."

"Tell me about it then, if it's that important to my education."

"I will tell you one thing now, and, perhaps, another thing later if you're worth it. *'Olwen'* or *Olwyn* is another name for *Rhiannon* [8] which in all sense should have been your name."

"What about *Culhwch?*"

"Perhaps later, as I said."

"Is this the hobby you took up when you retired?"

"Now why would you think that?"

"Because you have been much more 'animated' since you started talking about it: a Born-again Christian."

"I am honoured that you think me so involved – born again? Maybe. But not Christianity. My interest predates that Myth, though not the basis of it. But read the *Tales* of your land yourself and make up your own mind; and when you've done so, perhaps you'll write to me and tell me who you think the Mabinogi were and where they came from. I have often wondered how they came to play such a crucial part in the mythology of our country."

"Were they not just Gods like the Greek or Roman Gods?"

"*Just* Gods you say? Hardly *Just Gods:* they were more influential than that. I fantasise that they were the northern caravan of the Gods of Sumeria: you see, you just can't get away from Caravans. It's all down to Population Drift, the books tell me, but I don't believe them; it was more aspirational and purposeful than that. Anyway, age upon age, they spread to the land of the Celtic tribes [39]: Brittany, Cornwall, Wales and Ireland, all infiltrated from the valley of the Euphrates and the southern Black Sea. Rather like the lost tribe of Israel. Or perhaps they were the original Cymric itself? I'm not surprised that Rhodri, and many great scholars became obsessed by it all. The Sumerian Gods were not Gods in the modern sense of the word of course; they were mortals and were great sages who lived to great ages and were made Gods – not unlike the Romans in fact, as you say: all Caesars became Gods when they died. Do you think that Abraham may have been one of the Mabinogi? Or Methuselah? Or Jesus – the Last Prophet? In any case they are said to have known more of the Cosmos than we did until this century. The beauty of my fantasies, in this regard at least, is that no-one can prove me wrong: no-one really knows who they were or where they came from; Aliens perhaps? That's been suggested would you believe, and a so-called 'Religion', called Scientology has been fashioned by some megalomaniac idiot who thought he was the Angel Gabriel or somesuch. Ridiculous concept; he didn't even know what an *Angel* was; but many others followed him, so he managed to make a lot of money out of it.

"The Mabinogi (wherever they came from) are said, by some, to have spread and co-habited with our various tribes and found it good, so they stayed around. You can't blame them for that bit of biology.

"Do you think they may be related to the Grail Kings? That's what I want to know – the *Secret* – like everyone else. There seems to be little new in the legends of the different peoples – just name changes mostly. Think of the Greek God Dionysius now: he was not Hebrew, but he had a virgin birth; his father was the Sky-God Zeus; and when Dionysius was killed, he rose from the dead and ascended into Heaven with his mother the Goddess. How's that for *parallelism?* But that was before *our* God put an end to all that malarkey when He said, *'Your God is a jealous God. Thou shalt have no other God before Me.' 'Before'* you notice, not *'But'*. And then there's the Mother, a Woman. Was She the Three – fold Goddess do you think? *Mother, Bride and Layer – out to Fallen Man?* If so, which one was she? In what form? It's all so similar, it makes me think that there *must* be some Universal Truth behind it all. Perhaps Rhodri came to understand it all. I will be interested in your views when you can get around to it."

"That may not happen."

"Don't become all negative with me now. I'm enjoying this conundrum and I look forward to understanding a bit more."

"I try not to be negative; but I do have my book to do."

"I see that, but it will fit in, I'm sure; it might even add something to your conclusions: you may call it *Myths, Legends, and Heresies* so long as you acknowledge me for the title. Besides, I'm irritated; I need an answer; this could help both you and me. There's still much of interest that you can pursue. Two days then you say?

"Bran would have been the same age as your brother now, had he lived. Rhodri cast him to his ancestors on a raft in one of the lakes, they say; but that might just be wagging tongues. It was sometime later, two years I think before his lady was again pregnant with you. She suffered a haemorrhage again but this time they managed to reach a hospital. You were born safely, but your mother died. Some could make a case that *you* were the death of his *Lady* and that's why he had to give you away, though I can't believe that."

"Why not? I was a female – a *lesser person* - that he was lumbered with; someone who could not replace a *Blessed Son of the Father*. Someone he could dispense with, and not regret; someone he didn't want to be bothered with," said Anna.

"No, no. You're making too much of it; that's too concocted a tale;

too artificial: that belongs in the *Legends* or the Sunday School. Whatever his state of mind, he couldn't have thought of that. So let me finish my tale with what I know."

"Tell me what you know, then."

"Between me and God. Of course, Rhodri had *'no fixed abode'* in their jargon and they, The Decision Makers, intended keeping you for a while with the intention of fostering and adoption. But Rhodri absconded with you and sought out Will. He gave you to him and Megan and disappeared again. I don't know where he went that time and I doubt if anyone else does; he may be still alive but I doubt it."

"Why?"

"Just a feeling; he could not have been in the best of health himself after sleeping rough for some years. I spent some time once looking through the Register for Births, Marriages and Deaths but I found nothing. It's not surprising; he could have changed his name or died alone; or maybe not dead at all. I'm sorry but I can give you no more comfort than that: it must seem a great anticlimax for you. It must have comforted him though, that at least you were safe."

"Why do you say that?"

"It's natural that a parent would be comforted in such a situation," said Mostyn.

"No" replied Anna. "Usual, certainly, because most offspring are wanted; but not therefore natural; offspring are not necessarily welcome, are they? Quite often it's 'Get rid of it'. He had a tragic life, I grant you. And I owe mine to him, I suppose, and I should be grateful, I suppose. But he owed me more than that; he couldn't just dismiss the consequences of his mating. What about this Duty of Care you mentioned? Having made me he also owed me that."

"Yes. We can view it and say that."

"He never once sought me out"

"No. But he probably thought that was for the best. I don't think he could have dwelt on it too much; I don't think he made too many comparisons with others; what had he to compare? I believe that he felt it was the way things were: a *fatalist* then, but as a consequence, not a conviction. And I'm sure that he felt joy towards the end and *joy* would have been an alien emotion for him; it would have undermined his resolve. I don't think he could have lived with that: best to put it aside and forget it. I just wish that he could know you now."

"I don't know. It could be too dramatic and serve no purpose because he wouldn't know who I am any more than I know him; again, *reunion* is not necessarily joyous and I'm unsure whether it would be welcome. But it would make him face the *fact* of me: I would *exist!* I would *matter!* That would be something he would be made to face; a fact he's ignored for twenty – eight years: *'what you made in minutes stands before you'*; he couldn't dismiss me as easily then, and I couldn't let him; he would *have* to recognise me and acknowledge me as a woman and that may not be to his taste."

"You're too harsh. You're more Megan and Will's than his; he just made the raw material; they fashioned you."

"Bravo! That's a good way of putting it: Nature / Nurture resolved at a stroke. Have a Free Entry to the Communist Party," said Anna.

"Don't be flippant. I thought we'd at least come to respect each other."

"Yes. I'm sorry."

"Don't tell me you're not what I think you are."

"You must make up your own mind about that" replied Anna. "I really want to believe that what you've said is true; please believe that. But you see I can't believe your credo that I still mattered to him, once he'd dropped me off as it were; I don't think I mattered a jot to him. And I can't just dismiss the Nature factor as easily as you seem to; he gave me his genes didn't he? I've tried all the arguments, and I can't dismiss Nature: that dismissal is a falsehood conjured up by unbelievers for some purpose of their own: for their weird manifesto; for their abrogation of any responsibility; for their particular Secular God that they can blame: their *Confusion,* in short. I would be more content if I could dismiss it, I know. Perhaps then I could even dismiss him in return: Tried, Tested and Filed Away."

"It would be an easier option. For you, that is. But you won't do that, will you?"

"No; almost certainly not. Not until I find the ending anyway."

"Tell me your purpose in this search then: not revenge I hope; I can't believe it's that."

"I don't know; I wish I could tell you. Revenge is some of it I suppose; that often seeps into it just before dawn: so I can show him what he's missed and to gloat. And I know; that's cheap. Why does it matter to you anyway?"

"It tells me about you of course. And me. Conversation is an interaction, a two-way process: I tells me how much I should tell you; for your own sake; or mine."

"You can't deny me now. Perhaps it is to disprove my belief of rejection by having him welcome me back? Perhaps it's to finally dismiss him as irrelevant; an unwelcome intruder who may be responsible for my ailment; one who helped to perpetuate it in any case. I can't ever forgive that; it can never be forgiven, even if you use a pretty name as you've done – *Altruism.* You can always find a pretty name for the unpalatable can't you? Perhaps it's a more obvious, entirely selfish purpose: a question of where my condition came from (Science); and *to find the way for me at this time?* (Intellectualism). Both terribly selfish. To have an understanding of my character and its expression, is the best I can do to describe it, I think. But I don't know. Perhaps that's the real reason – I don't know the purpose of my – *Quest* - as you put it; and I want to."

"Do you know yourself any better then, as a result of what I've been able to tell you?"

"No. I still can't say that I know myself any better; and I don't know if that was really what I came for; I just don't know. And it's making me feel vulnerable. It's not what you haven't done; you've done all you could and more than I had a right to expect when I first started pestering you. Lord Mostyn, I am deeply grateful to you for all the time you've spent on me. I know more *about* my father now; but he's no more substantial a person to me now than he was before. He's still a ghost in my life and I want him to go away; I still feel no kindred. I've mentioned what I believe was his Duty; I must accept now, that there is a Duty on my part too; and a debt of a kind. I must find the ending at least, before I give it up. Even though I've known you only a short while, I feel I know you better than I know him. I suppose you have to interact with people in order to know them."

"You're an astute young lady but too introspective. I suppose that's your Philosophy training. Will you see yourself home?"

"No. I feel too tired. You see what you've done? You've drained me."

"What about young Edward Williams? Will he come?"

"He would if I asked him to."

"Then ask him to come, I should like to meet him. You have telephoned him as I suggested, I suppose?"

"No. I haven't called him, though I did promise him I would. But I need to think about him and where he fits; he's part of it all, d'you see; he's another one that's always been there. I can't ask him again just yet, I'm not ready."

"What will you do then? I could arrange to have you taken to the station, if that's of any help."

"Thank you but my mother will come and pick me up. She'll come by train and taxi."

"I'll send a car to pick her up; and to take you both back down or where you want to go; it's the least I can do to thank you for your company and for listening to my rambles – I haven't had so much fun for years. Now I have some thinking to do before we see each other again. After breakfast I think, so that you have time to yourself before you leave."

CHAPTER 12

A KNOWING

"What time will your mother arrive?"

"The train's due at the station at two o'clock."

"Then forgive me so I can arrange for a car to meet her. Take some more coffee."

"I've had enough thanks, but I'll read the paper."

*

"Well, that's done; she'll be here in time for tea. I will be pleased to see her again after all these years. You know of course that she did a great deal of voluntary work for the Trust in its early days? I don't think it would be putting it too strongly to say that she was also quite a force in persuading Will to join us."

"I think you're wrong there. He wouldn't have crossed her I'm sure, if she'd dug her heels in; he loved her too much to put such a distance between them. But she loved him too; more if that is possible. She could have made a life, and a good one with Charles but it was not enough for her, so she held out and existed on hope for a few years. So she would not have crossed him either. What he wanted for himself was her goal too and she virtually set aside her own career and worked tirelessly for him to achieve it. He was more strong-willed than you give him credit for."

"I have no doubt of that young lady: this Trust wouldn't be as successful as it is without his commitment and determination in the early years. People thought him all of a piece, but he was, *uncertain.* No, without Megan he could not have committed himself so completely."

"He had something to work with: first, Lord Thomas' bequest then your support."

"Indeed, and the University's; don't forget them. But most others would not have made such a solid job of it. It'll be a pity if you can't be here for the point-to-point; there is someone I would like you to meet and provide him with some conversation."

"Who would that be?"

"Our new Thomas Research Fellow. Interesting chap, if somewhat introspective; rather like yourself. He doesn't speak much out loud, but when he does he seems sensible enough."

"Tell me something about him."

"He's Eurasian; graduated well enough from Calcutta to be offered a year's Science scholarship to Cambridge. He's pursuing a research interest. He's only been here a few months so far."

"I thought my father said that there were restrictions on the fields of research. I don't remember him saying anything about Science. Quite the contrary: *'There's too much money sloshing about in Science'* he said. *'They don't need any help to blow us all up.'*"

Lord Mostyn laughed. "It sounds like Will, I must say. I'll tell you the changes here. The Fellowship is now limited to a maximum tenure of four years so it doesn't get bogged down. The Field of Research has been broadened since Will's day (against my advice I will tell you. It makes me feel that my position here as Tom's Executor for the Trust is redundant since they won't listen). Anyway, this present chap does his research in Molecular Chemistry and the Philosopher's Stone [24]. I thought we'd left all that rigmarole behind along with the Alchemists and the Wizards and the Witches and the Cauldron. It belongs with *The Sorcerer's Apprentice* I said - loudly, for the benefit of the deaf among them - and with the *Get Rich Quick* fellows, but it seems not, and I'm out of touch, they say.

"He does that test-tube work at the University of course, but he has his rooms here and takes dinner here. I've told him that if he manages to make Gold from base metal, I want the first ingot and the First Option on the Process. He said that it wasn't what he was after. So I asked him, again loudly, *'If you're after the Philosopher's Stone and you don't want to make Gold, what is the point?* He went off on a long explanation but I lost interest at that point.

"I don't hold with all this modification of endowments *post demise*; if a chap says *Sociology*, it should be *Sociology;* even the *Sociology of the Trobriand Islanders;* but not *Alchemy.* They're even thinking of getting a mathematician next time, God forbid; Modelling or something. For a change, they said; a Change too damn far, I said. And I also pointed out, that the trouble with Mathematics would be that no-one would be able to talk to him sensibly at dinner; the poor chap would have to sit through his dinners and equations, in silence, I shouldn't wonder. I also pointed out that X, Y, Z, is about as far as any of us can go – he'd show us up in no time and we'd all be avoiding dinner.

"I did admit one thing though: *'as a subject,'* I said, *'it's not much of an improvement on Alchemy and Magic'*. I couldn't say more than that. But you should get on well with him if you limit your talk to the

Philosophy angle and ignore the Chemistry."

"Don't be flippant."

"No. I don't pretend to understand any of it but he's very highly regarded and I'm told we're lucky to have him. '*Indeed,*' I said in devilment, '*and how long do you expect us to keep him?*' I hope that you can meet. You'll enjoy each other's company I think."

"Then I look forward to meeting him. You said last night that you had some thinking to do. Was it about this student?"

"No. More an issue relating to what we've been talking about over the last days."

"Does it trouble you that much? I thought we'd finished."

"Not entirely; probably not significantly. But it is a matter that troubles me and it's one, I now realise, that I have been avoiding since early in my brief biography of your Father Rhodri. And it's mostly the reason for this involved conversational deviation we're having about this young Fellow. It puts off facing my dilemma; but, I can't continue to avoid it any longer. Decision time: I must grasp the nettle or forget it for ever."

"Is it so momentous?"

"Maybe. You may think it most significant, but that's not why I'm prevaricating."

"Why then?"

"It's what the Lawyers call '*privileged information*' or '*insider knowledge*', for the Money Men. For me, again, the question is whether I have the right to use it."

"It is important then?"

"Possibly. It's not that I could be sued or anything because what I could tell you is the truth (at least as I know it); but it could do harm, personal harm, to the individuals concerned; and you may not welcome it. The old lady would surely tell me not to *ferret*. If they had all died it wouldn't matter, despite my earlier polemic; it would then be an episode that was closed. But I have no evidence that that is the case."

"You're being infuriating."

"I understand that."

"Then tell me. I shan't act on anything you say without your agreement, I promise you that."

"I accept that your promise is most sincere but you may feel so strongly about the information that you will wish to retract your promise."

"It's that momentous?"

"Enough."

"Then you must tell me."

"I fear so. We'll start off simply, though there's nothing simple about the outcomes of peoples' relationships. Neither of us knows what has happened to your father Rhodri, though we have an unspoken presumption that he has died: a reasonable assumption given his early life-style but not an inevitable conclusion. After all he could be in his late fifties or sixties, settled in a job or retired and with a home. He might even have married, legally, and raised a second family for all we know. You might have half - brothers or - sisters who know nothing of you as you know nothing of them. If alive, he would remember you of course but that doesn't mean that he would have talked to anyone about you and may not be best pleased to have you turn up on his doorstep – especially so if he also has a wife who knows nothing of you. He didn't want to intrude on your life either, did he, after he gave you away? Not later, but when you were younger. Perhaps he found it difficult to stay away from you – who knows? After all you were all that was left of his Lady; the one last link to his Goddess. No, I don't think that he could have set you aside entirely. So I'm prepared to believe that he died, but I can't contemplate the circumstances. I also shy away from finding anything more about his last years: if he's settled, then I wouldn't want to upset his peace; if not, then he shouldn't be disturbed then either."

"But he might just want to see me now, but can't find a way; he might feel lost, wouldn't you say?"

"It's possible of course but the least likely option after all these years, wouldn't you say? So that is one uncertainty that dogs your family saga.

"I assume also that you know something of your paternal grandparents. Will and Megan would not have kept you in the dark about them I'm sure."

"They kept nothing from me on purpose, but it was only when I needed my Birth Certificate to register at University that they told me the whole story. My fault: I had never been inquisitive enough; I hadn't needed to be. It was a shock I admit, but I loved them too much to condemn them. But I did shed tears and there were tantrums and I even left home for a while. All they asked was that I told them where I was and the door was always open for me. That didn't last long. I was home in less than a month."

"You know, I've told you, that your grandparents had a small shop: newspapers, cigarettes, soft drinks, that sort of thing. It was nothing fancy but it gave them a small income. It was an incongruous marriage: your grandfather was from a very poor family and worked for a while in a flour mill hauling sacks of grain for grinding or brewing and sacks of flour for sale. It earned him a 'bob or two' but didn't do much for his school work. His nick-name was Snowy and you can guess why. He later developed emphysema and if it wasn't for the shop I can't think what he would have done. Your grandmother on the other hand was a daughter of a primary school teacher, strict but fair and a devout Baptist. She was an attractive young woman and wanted to be a nurse. It wasn't a degree qualification in those days, but hard enough to get into and low wages, so there was a financial consideration as well. Fortunately for her, her mother, your great-grandmother – a wise woman as I've said – and you'll remember that she told the Doctor not to *ferret*; she was able to give some support and your grandmother enrolled for her training. You can imagine the disappointment and distress then when she dropped out of nursing training after less than one year."

"Why was that? Couldn't they support her any longer?"

"They certainly found it hard, but they struggled and would have found ways to keep her there as long as was necessary. It was a *step up* d'you see? It's amazing the degree of social stratification these valley Nonconformists practice; they're much worse at it than the 'Landed Gentry."

"Why did she drop out then?"

"This is where we come to the difficult bit. But having come this far I mustn't prevaricate any more. I don't like doing this, it would be better left alone; as the old lady said, it's too much in the past. But I promised you honesty and I have come to think that you deserve it. So here goes; I must bite the bullet as they say.

"Your grandmother became pregnant; that's why she had to leave."

"Who by? Who was the father?"

"In good time. You probably think that's not such an issue these days, but at that time it was very different: she was unmarried, so it was shame and condemnation and most likely spinsterhood and adoption. But your great - grandmother refused to go down that road and looked around for a husband for your grandmother before it was too obvious. Not an easy task in a village, all of whom knew, or at least suspected, the reason for haste. As I say, the field was not great, but there was that one young man who was attracted to your grandmother and when she managed to get the lease of the shop for their wedding day he was prepared to be considered the father of her child."

"Was he not my grandfather then? If it wasn't him, who was it?"

"He was accepted as such. A nice enough young man and very personable. He'd started working in the local haberdashers by then and he was happy enough; he had no great ambition except for having a shop of his own. So the offer of the lease as a wedding present clinched it as it were. It should have been a quiet and tolerant marriage. But no, he wasn't your grandfather."

"Then who was? Stop prevaricating and tell me."

"For many years I didn't know myself. I came to know only by chance. It was when your Father Will was offered the Thomas Fellowship and also joined the Trust. When Will and I talked about the possibilities here, he said that he was reminded of the two English words that his own grandmother knew and would have used: one was '*flabbergasted*' and the other was *flibbertigibbet*. Nothing remarkable in that you would think: onomatopoeic, but just expressions of Victoriana in a secluded Welsh valley village. But he also mentioned that she had no time for the, by then, influential Councillor Rees who Will had come up against. Will couldn't tell me any more because she would never gossip about it. But it intrigued me, as it did him, and so I dug a little deeper. My methods and my contacts are not important: what is important is what I found out. Your grandmother had become pregnant by Elwin Rees but he had refused to acknowledge paternity and your grandmother would never name him."

"So this Councillor Rees was my paternal grandfather. What a disgusting man he must have been; he took his pleasure and cast her off."

"Try not to be too harsh, gel. He had to make his way from nothing as well. Too many had to in our valley, and he tried, in his way, to change that. Later, when he could, he used what influence he had for the benefit of the school children who needed it and he facilitated their careers if it pleased him. His methods were not attractive certainly, nor honourable in our eyes – he made people *indebted* to him. It gave him a sense of power, I suppose and that's addictive for some characters. Yes, he did take advantage of her as he did all his life with many others and lesser people. He was certainly wrong to do so, but perhaps he lacked confidence and knew of no other way to better himself. And he could be a very charming man in his own way. So try to be a little compassionate."

"I'll try but I can't guarantee success. I understand that he wasn't very pleased with Father Will either."

"They rubbed each other the wrong way, that's all – he thought Will showed too much *Honour* and had too sharp a tongue. And I'm afraid that I used the information I'd gathered to get Councillor Rees to '*back off*' as the saying goes, when Will needed some political help; that's not too honourable either. I'm not proud of my behaviour then, but I convinced myself that it was needed, and I owed Tom Tom some support. Now, it's too long ago to go into that *(no need to ferret any more)*. It's not really your tale anyway; yours is more recent than that."

"Well is there any more?"

"Very little. Your grandmother had that difficult birth and the baby, Rhodri, your father, was born brain-damaged, as I've told you. Don't ask me any more details, I'm no medic. Your mother Megan would be more reliable on that. But it explains your great-grandmother's predictions, don't you think? Now, we've reached an ending; it's time we prepared for Megan's arrival."

"I must thank you from the bottom of my heart for your patience with me. I am greatly in your debt."

"Nonsense. I can only hope that I have a new friend. You will keep me posted, as they say in the modern jargon, with your future search and with your young life. You've promised me that. Now, I shall be sorry to see you go. Time may hang heavy again."

"I will write, of course I will. And I will not forget the Point – to – Point races. Again, thank you."

"I must do something: I shall write of the complexities of the Families, perhaps. I shall be the Caravaneer that tells the tale of the Families as I've told you of your bit of it; that should keep me going, I've no doubt."

PERFORMANCE

CHAPTER 13

SEARCHES

Megan and I had travelled down to the City from our house in London that morning. Megan had made every effort to pressgang me into accompanying her to collect Anna and had even been provocative in her entreaties: "Charles, I won't have you ignoring old and dear friends like this; to say nothing of my daughter."

I had smiled and tried to calm her, not entirely successfully. So I had arrived in the City alone; Megan had left me at an earlier station where a car had been waiting to take her to her adopted daughter. I would hear that news in due course. It would also be something of a reunion for Megan with the one-time Chairman of the Safe Haven Trust. My knowledge of that time in her life was largely second hand through her and her husband Will; that was now some years before: more years than I cared to consider. It could well be an emotional meeting with reminiscences, where I had no part to play and no desire to intrude. So I had made an excuse that I would take the opportunity to visit an old doctoral student of mine who had recently been installed as a Professor at my old University.

I had come to realise that living my life was easier if I avoided too close an attachment to the past. The years I had spent at the University here had been ones of great happiness but also of profound sorrow. Even now, so many years later, I could not view it with equanimity: my mood was too ambivalent and uncertain, and my memories surfaced unbidden and unwelcome. All my ties had been cut and with each severance, I had been grateful. I had come to realise that living my life was easier if I avoided too close an attachment to the past; I had no wish to prolong my history of the place. My presence here now was a duty that I could not shed.

Megan knew that I had promised the visit to my old student for some time, but I had made no effort; that time was past and now, having been brought to it, I could not face it, even for an hour or so. So I had stayed in our room; I had rung to cancel my visit and we had talked for a short time on the telephone; if Megan enquired, I would call on a little white lie and lay the cancellation at his door. She would not be fooled, and would guess the reason for it: but it would be easier with the little lie, at least while Anna was with us. Having made the decision, I had the afternoon and early evening to myself. That was not a pleasant prospect in my old City either; I had no desire to walk aimlessly through the once-known, busy, bustling, silent town below the hill, where no-one talked to strangers and only whispered to each other in the pedestrian precincts for fear of 'showing yourself up'; nor did I want to visit the half-remembered pubs in Vine Street; that road that had once led down to the busy docklands and the ships; the Liners, Tugs and Merchantmen, that had long ago been laid off, and where the pubs were now filled with silent, aimless, introvert, long-ago finished sailors who would never see the sea again in their lifetimes.

From the window of the hotel I could look out at the sea and across to the City where I had lived. It was breasting summer, but without a calendar you could not have been certain of it: the clouds were low and there was a bitter, strong wind amongst the dwarfed trees along the road. Young leaves were already being stripped from the branches and blown across the dunes. It was a wretched early holiday for any who had wanted the beach; but it was not-at-all unusual on this stretch of coast with its backing of a hill that curved along the shoreline. That hill contained the errant south-westerly squalls that blew in from the Atlantic, and turned them upon themselves. The sea was flecked with white horses and they were racing into the bay as if seeking shelter. The tall white tower of the Guildhall to my left had almost disappeared in the spray from the churned-up sea. The only escape from the squalls was in the lee of the Head at the other end of the sweep of the wide bay.

When I was sure of being alone, I took the opportunity to telephone my son Edward. Although he now travelled little, there was no guarantee that I would be connected: he often walked the coastal path in solitude, whatever the weather, and was often away for some hours. However, I could always leave a message on his 'answerphone' and he almost invariably returned my call. To a degree I was surprised when he did reply to my call and told me that he had met Anna when she had arrived by train and had taken her to the Safe Haven Trust house and her appointment with Lord Mostyn. He was in a short temper which surprised me; rarely were we distant with each other.

After delivering Anna, Edward had taken several days to reach home, most of which he had spent amongst the mountains and bleak moors of the Beacons and Snowdonia and the broad bay facing the Irish Sea. Then he had tired of the bleakness and sought his house as he would a sanctuary. Once home, he had hoped that there would be a message from Anna but it seemed that she had not called and he felt this new distance that had grown between them as an unexpected physical emptiness and he was not comfortable with it. In consequence, he was grateful for the information that we had arrived in the City and that Megan was in the process of collecting Anna. He asked that his disappointment in not having been contacted, after being faithfully promised a *communication,* be conveyed to the *young lady* as soon as she was visible. He also made it clear that he was now stood at the window of the cottage and looking out at the same sea.

Megan and Anna arrived in good time for dinner and I relayed Edward's comments. Anna smiled, but it was immediately clear that she would have much preferred to have headed straight for home: she had no desire to perform a post-mortem over her discussions.

"Edward didn't stay with you then?" I asked.

"No. He said that *he had some pressing matters to attend to;* you know that superior look of his; but he also said that he'd come when he was called. That sounds like your Edward doesn't it Charles?" she asked with a smile.

I nodded and fell silent; it hurt that my son had not troubled nor waited to greet me and I tried to put a benevolent gloss on it by emphasising to myself that this time was for Anna and her mother, not for me. Megan tried to ease the path but it was not until we had eaten our dinner that Anna seemed to understand that we needed to know something of her progress if we were going to be of any further help. Even then, she waited until Megan and I had our coffee and she had poured herself the last of her water.

"Mum, Charles, I've been turning things over while we've been eating, and I feel I should tell you some things, and I need to ask you some things. I don't want to go over all my talks again, it's too soon; you'll hear it all in good time anyway, I'm sure. What I can tell you now is that I have learned a lot about my Father Rhodri – what sort of a man he was. That, by the way is how we resolved our family nomenclature to be sure who we were talking about: there was Father Rhodri; Father Will; Mother Megan; and Mother who? Sorry Uncle Charles but you didn't come in to it."

"That's of no matter for now."

"As I say, I learned a lot about him, but I can't say that I know him any better for it."

"I don't think anyone could say that they knew him in that sense, except perhaps your Father Will," said Megan.

"How sad to have no-one who knows you," said Anna quietly, more to herself than to us. "I will always want someone who knows me, otherwise you might just as well not live. You'd think that with a name, anyone could call you out. That's one of the things that Lord Mostyn said about me when we argued: '*I know your name and what it means. So you are not alone young lady*'. He's wrong though, because through no fault of your own, you are alone."

"You follow your Father then? Is that your Philosophy?" I asked.

"He was right, you are alone. Most people don't accept it, don't even think about it; they avoid it because it frightens them; and they certainly can't be rational about it. All that doesn't make it false though; that's not logical."

"That's very bleak and so wrong," I replied.

"We differ," said Anna. "But this is not the time for a debate so we'll pass on."

"You're not satisfied with what you've been told then?" asked Megan.

"I've met an interesting and dear man who I would like to call a friend and to whom I now owe a debt."

"Debt? What debt?" asked Megan.

"Some of my secrets, that's all; they'll be paid when they're due," replied Anna. "I could happily spend many more hours in his company and get to know him; he was so unexpected. But no, I didn't learn much about my ancestors. Father Rhodri's was a sad life, I've learned, but the greater sadness is in not understanding why it had to be so. But then, everyone is condemned to that sadness from birth; aren't they? *Why does it have to be so?* " asked Anna.

"Will would have understood Rhodri's life; *did* I suppose ," I said. "In many ways, they had much in common, strangely: each believed, or felt, that they were fundamentally alone; their lives led them to that. It's probably why he took Rhodri in in the first place."

"No; at least, not at first," said Megan. "There were other, more historical reasons as you know; there was also some guilt. But he came to acknowledge it in another who couldn't understand why it was. What do you want to do now then?" Megan asked Anna.

"Oh, I haven't finished by a long way yet. I said that I didn't learn much and that's true; Lord Mostyn knew nothing about my genetic mother, nor her family. That's something still to follow and he suggested I ask you about her, Mum. We argued and jousted a bit as well; something we both enjoyed I think. But I did learn something: now, at least, I do know who my grandfather was."

"Who was he then?" asked Megan. "All I know is that he left your grandmother when the shop failed and she needed him most of all; he can't have been a man of much character. I hope he was seriously troubled by a conscience about it; and that's no less than he deserved."

"There sermonises a true Welsh Nonconformist. Dear Mother, don't condemn him like that; have pity; try to understand. He couldn't face the failure, I suppose, after all he had wanted for himself. He played no part of any consequence before he disappeared from my grandmother's life and left her to cope alone. And if you were a blood-and-thunder Religionist you could say that it was also her retribution. You see, he wasn't my grandfather. My real grandfather was Elwin Rees."

"The old Councillor?" I asked.

"Yes. Father Rhodri was the consequence of an illicit, swift, extramarital bonk, probably in the ferns one Easter. I suppose it could be seen as our Original Sin from which all else flowed. So, if you want to condemn anyone, include my grandmother in the list. "

"Well, I'll be damned," I said.

"You could have chosen your ancestors a bit more wisely," said Megan. "But we can't blame you for that unpleasant man."

"Mum, thank you for being your honest self."

"Well, I'm sorry but none of us ever liked the man."

"I know; but it's not Lord Mostyn's view. Which is one reason to find out more about him so I can guard against his traits when I see them. But I must seek him out, dead or alive, and he might lead me to my father Rhodri too. Then I must chase my mother. Then there's the book to get on with. I hope I can do it all."

"What do you want from us then?" asked Megan.

"Two things. First, always be here for me; please. Second, I want to start with finding my grandfather. Uncle Charles, he lived in your village didn't he?"

"He had a house there, certainly but I don't think he ever returned there when he retired. No-one knew where he'd gone."

"Let's start there then. Perhaps whoever lives there now might know something."

"Anna, darling, are you sure you want to go on with this? Is it so important for you?" asked Megan.

"Yes. For now anyway."

"It might not turn out all that pleasant for you," I said.

"I know. But I'll stop if it gets to be too rough; if I can."

"Right," I replied. "In the morning, I'll show you where I grew up. Now, I think we all need a nightcap to put us to sleep."

Later, as Megan and I lay in bed and drifted to sleep, I said, "It all does make some sense now."

"What does?"

"How Rhodri got into the Grammar school. Rees was a school Governor and on the County Education Committee. I suppose he wanted to help his boy; give him a chance without exposing himself at the same time. But he didn't do him any favours then either. It would have been better to have left them alone than do that. Having taken that first step, he then made matters worse. Well, it's a little mystery solved. Goodnight my love."

CHAPTER 14

A PILGRIMAGE

I had no idea how Anna had coped with the night; there was no doubt that she would have run and re-run her conversations with Lord Mostyn in a search for any item of information, no matter how trivial, that she might have missed. It was unlikely that there was anything of any significance but that would not have made her mind any easier. For Megan and for me, for different reasons – hers the greater concern for Anna and mine a worrying over the odd, unexpected behaviour of Rees - it was certainly an unsatisfactory night. We kept each other awake with our restless tossing and turning; so much so that we made ourselves tea at 5 am. We had no desire to return to bed but we both found it difficult to articulate why we were so restless. Megan had thought that this visit would put an end to what she saw as 'Anna's obsession' with her antecedents. Instead, Anna seemed too fired with a new determination. Although she tried to understand and tried hard to be rational, Megan could not dismiss a feeling that this pursuit of Anna's was 'unhealthy' and must come to an end. To what extent there was an element of jealousy involved I could not judge but Anna's pursuit of her genetic family did not sit comfortably on Megan's shoulders; she was fearing a new sense of relegation to a less important relationship.

My concerns were also of a personal nature but not even marginally tied to Rees' activities. I told myself that it was understandable that I was not as involved as Megan with Anna's pursuit. My relationship was significantly distant from the issue and did not strike at the roots of my emotions. What affected that family, Megan and previously Will, was important to me but there was no denying that my part was more of a supportive role than that of a protagonist. It was different in degree, only when I considered Megan's other children. I knew that because of Will, whom I had known since our childhood, I had overcompensated in my friendship with them; I was less prepared to criticise them than my own children. When they were all younger, this had sometimes caused friction, for which I hoped to be forgiven. But I could not have changed this ambivalent behaviour, even had I known how to. Consequently, I found it difficult to articulate my own concerns and gave little away to Megan. In truth, my concerns were related to my return to what I still considered my valley. I could not explain it, even to myself, but there was an underlying disquiet that would not be stilled. I feared the emotions it would resurrect.

We showered and decided on a walk on the beach which we knew would be deserted. The wind had died but the clouds still hung low and dark on the water; early Summer or not, without our topcoats we could not have strayed for long. As we walked, we were silent for some time, until Megan said, "A proper Summer morning would make this easier." She did not need to explain but she added, "It is difficult to *brood* on a proper Summer morning; it's all too easy in this weather." It was clear that she still had not reconciled her emotions; she was still torn.

I tried to lighten the mood on us and said, "I don't know. The Spaniards are terribly *broody* and they have decent weather - think of Don Quixote; and the Italians are very *volatile* – think of Mussolini. And they don't suffer from too little sun."

"They're just *Mediterranean.*"

"Perhaps you also need to eat a lot of garlic, then."

"Don't trivialise it," said Megan.

"No, I'm sorry. I don't mean to do that. But it would only seem so, you know. It's clearly something Anna feels she has to do; and it doesn't diminish her love for you – it's not an Either – Or situation; it's all separate from you and your family. If you could just consider it objectively you would know that; you probably do already. And shouldn't you applaud her for being so caring?"

"That doesn't make it any easier either; she's always been included; we made a point of that."

"Yes. And perhaps she's noticed that."

"I won't be criticised for doing what I considered to be best. I'm trying to be rational about it but it isn't easy. I have this feeling of being betrayed and I don't like it. Tell me I'm being foolish."

"You're being foolish Megan. Does that help?"

She smiled at me and said, "No. Not much."

"Look, listen to me, now. You must let her do this and you must support her gladly or not at all. For some reason or another she's come to feel that there's a vacuum in her life that she must try and fill. We don't know what's triggered it, but she's obviously come to a point when she wants to know more about herself: there are possibly some things she doesn't understand. She's probably terribly afraid of what her Consultant is going to say and wants to put her life in context. That's understandable, surely?"

"Yes it is – in the abstract. But why now? Why at this time?"

"That's always a question, isn't it? Along with, 'why me'? You should know better than I do why. Look, it's difficult for her, you know that. She's been trained to think and she's uncertain of who or what she is. Be understanding: you and Will were all her young life and she loved you both, you know that. Nothing will change that you know, except your opposition to her search. You're very dear to her but you must give her the freedom to know herself – isn't that what we all strive for: the freedom to know ourselves? Otherwise, you could drive her away and that would be such a tragedy. For all of you. Don't you see that?"

Megan was shedding tears but she smiled at me. "I do understand that; you know I do. And most of the time I can be rational but occasionally it tears at me. Some sort of maternal instinct I suppose, that I should have grown out of. I'm sorry that you've been dragged into it though."

"Now that's not a very welcome thought, Madam."

"I'm sorry again. But you know what I mean. Nothing in our two lives has been easy or straightforward for us, has it?"

"No, but I believe we're better for it. I'll tell you something else: I wouldn't change any of my people. And certainly not you. So just be yourself and let it run its course. Will you?"

"Yes. But help me."

"Always."

"Good. Now take me to breakfast. I'm starving."

We turned to walk back to the Hotel and as we approached it we saw Anna sitting alone on a dune and looking out to sea. Megan's hand tightened in mine.

"Anna, what are you doing here? Do up your coat; I know it's supposed to be Summer but you've been given the gift of common sense as well. And you should have a hat on as well."

"I couldn't sleep Mother," said Anna, "So I thought a breath of fresh air would help. Like you."

"Well, it's certainly fresh. Come on, inside. A big breakfast is called for."

"I wonder if Edward is looking at this sea," said Anna. "I hope so. I must do something for him, too. He needs something to grasp."

We took a leisurely breakfast but we did not linger; conversation seemed forced and stylised. We drove up my well-remembered valley to the village of my birth virtually in silence. Most of the coal tips had been cleared or levelled but the still-open mouths of the old drift mines reminded us of the valley's past. Still, the mountain had greened, though paradoxically that seemed to make the valley narrower. And here they had avoided the blight of densely-planted pine trees that was ruining the beauty of ancient landscape for the small profit they would bring; I despaired of the greed of my species who seemed so cavalier with its legacy. However, the river was clean again, and fast flowing, and no doubt supported large trout for the fishermen, if they still bothered. I hungered for the untroubled freedom I remembered of the walk across the school playing fields alone, to the part of the river overhung by trees, where the water undercut the bank and the oxbow pools were dark and deep and the water was always cold; and where I should see a boy reflected in the water, who was worried about what he should be when he was grown.

Megan turned to me once as I gave her directions and said, "You're not happy about this, are you?"

"I thought I'd left it all behind but I find I haven't. It's unexpected, that's all."

"I don't suppose you ever do," she said.

The constraint that we had felt over breakfast still lingered while we drove, and in the silence, my memories pressed, and would not let me rest. Soon after Elizabeth, my wife, our toddler Edward, and I had returned from our time in Melbourne, on a warm, sunny day we had climbed to a place called *Y Garreg,* named after the large stone on the flank of the mountain, to meet Megan and Will and their young family. The children had been small and had climbed the stone; and Will had been still alive. So the journey was difficult for Megan too. I could acknowledge that, and I wished that we could have talked out our emotions but that would have been wrong.

In an attempt to end our silence, I said, "Edward told me on the 'phone that he'd come here before picking you up Anna; but *'only to look up at the old house',* he said, *'there on the mountain. And I was early anyway'* he said. I wonder what he made of it now; he can't have remembered much from his childhood visits."

"I think you'd be surprised Charles," said Anna. "He has a very *'blotting – paper'* mind; he doesn't forget much; he carries *pictures* in is head, always. That's why things are hard for him; he remembers too much, too clearly; it would be easier if he could forget things; he can't and it doesn't make him 'comfortable' in himself."

It was interesting to hear another's assessment of my son and there was more that I wanted to say, but I could not when Anna was sitting behind me.

"He's your son Charles but he's too much like my Father was; his mind's too cluttered," said Megan who also, I believed, was playing the game.

I laughed and said, "We've become the 'Older Generation' too soon! We look back too much already."

Megan reached for my hand and replied, "Accept it then, and move on."

I said, "In any case, *then* was a different time; and we were different people, *then*," partly to Anna but I hoped that Megan understood my meaning as well.

I was re-assured when she said, "Water under the bridge."

I wanted to say, "Not entirely," but held my tongue.

When we arrived, it was both more and less than I had feared. The village seemed much more insular, more turned into itself, even than the last time I had visited: the stores were open and the counters and shelves seemed stocked with more expensive goods than they could have carried in my day. But there was no evidence of work and there were few people about, and no gossiping women in the doorways as there used to be; the houses of stone no longer looked substantial but seemed as if they would be cold to the touch. Perhaps I was being histrionic, but I couldn't overcome the feeling that, at last, the heart had gone: it had turned into itself for fear of being judged. I shouldn't have returned; I should have remembered the village as it had been for me. But I knew that even then, I had found it claustrophobic.

Councillor Rees had lived in a large, rendered house in the road that had run away from one of the two Village Primary Schools. This school now stood derelict, which increased my sadness: a good few able people had launched themselves from there. Clearly, the County Council had not thought it viable, and it had become too costly, to maintain two Primary Schools in the village, when the population had decreased as the young moved away for lack of local employment. So it had been closed, as the easier option. That, I thought to myself, must have happened after the reign of Councillor Rees: whatever his faults, he would not have countenanced such a move.

We stopped in the road at the bottom of a long garden path that led to the front door of the house. The garden was well tended and the house looked inhabited but there was no sign of the occupiers. Megan rang the doorbell and we waited for a response. After a few minutes a young girl who couldn't have been more than eighteen with a small baby on her hip opened the door.

"Yes?" she asked. "What do you want?"

"We're sorry to trouble you," said Megan, "But we're trying to trace a Councillor Rees who used to live here. Is he here now?"

"Nobody here with that name. It's only me, the twins, this one and my dad."

"He's not Councillor Rees by any chance?"

"No. I told you, there's nobody with that name by here. We don't know any Councillors. Are you from the Council?"

I intervened and said. "No dear, we're not from the Council. We're just trying to find a Mr Rees who used to live here some years ago."

"Don't know him then. We've only been in this backwoods of a place without even a bloody bus to take us anywhere a year and a bit; and they won't give us free travel anyway; bloody skinflints. The bus goes down the bottom road as well; that's a lot of bloody use up by here. How do you expect me, the twins and this one to walk all that way down by there to catch the bus? Tell me that. And leave my father to shift on his own, who can't walk. You haven't fixed the bloody windows yet either – we'll all catch our death when the Winter comes, see if we don't. Where will you be then, I'd like to know? Pissed off somewhere else, I bet. I've told you we want to move from this deadbeat place by here, but you don't take any bloody notice. As usual. You need a stick of dynamite up your arse to get some movement."

"I'm sorry, but it's important that we find Mr Rees."

"What's he done then? Has he bashed somebody? Are you the Police? I don't want nothing to do with the Police."

"No, we're not the Police either; just old friends of the family, trying to find him. Who was here before you came?"

"Don't know. It was empty when we moved in. Carried out, I expect they were, with the cold. The Social pays the rent and the coal and the electric. I asked them for Gas but they said no."

"Do you know who they pay the rent to?"

"No idea. Nothing to do with me, that."

"Do you know where the Social Services are?"

"In the Town, where else?"

Megan was about to intervene, but I said, "Thanks for your help anyway. We're very grateful. Goodbye."

"You could put some Central Heating in from the Range; that will keep us warm in the Winter. One like Flossie's got like."

We walked back to the car and came to terms with the feeling of anticlimax.

"Eighteen," I said, "And three kids and no husband. My God, things have changed in the Valley."

"Not much I don't suppose," said Megan. "Anyway, how do you know she's only eighteen?"

"Alright, nineteen then. Does that make it better?"

"No," replied Megan. "It's just as tragic."

Anna said, "Not much progress then."

"Oh, I don't know," I said. "We know the house is being rented. The question is, who from?"

114

"We'll go to the Social Services," said Megan. "They might tell us. And you," she said to me, "Might know how to talk to Valley people, but a Medic might get more joy out of 'The Social'. So I'll do the talking."

Anna laughed and said, "What a team! Laurel and Hardy. It's better than television." And the mood was broken.

"We can try," I said. "But don't hold out much hope; Authority is very sniffy in the Valleys you know; they think everyone's out to grab what they can before anyone else gets it. Like Central Heating. And, truthfully, they're not far wrong. Well, we don't have much time. We must get back tomorrow to arrange for Anna's appointment and I have a meeting."

"I'd rather stay and delay the appointment," said Anna.

"No," said Megan. "Your health is most important. We go home tomorrow."

"Yes," I said. "Listen to your mother. But there's something else I wanted to ask. Stay here; I shan't be a minute."

I walked up the path to the house again and rang the doorbell. I waited until the young girl had opened the door and again apologised for disturbing her. She was not at all pleased at having to answer it again and her answers to my questions were short and dismissive. I walked back to the car.

"What was that for," asked Megan.

"I wanted to know if there was still a Minister in the village."

"Why?" she asked.

"He might know something of Rees. As we were here, it was worth a try."

"And is there?"

"Yes but he now serves three Chapels apparently. He doesn't live in the old Chapel House by the Doctor's surgery any more it seems, but in a small house by the bridge. She also said he's most often not there but out 'on his rounds' she said."

"Try it," said Anna.

We drove the short distance to the house, but with repeated knocking there was no reply.

"We'd better get to the Social Services then, before they shut up shop for the day," said Anna.

It was another silent drive back to the town.

CHAPTER 15

FANTASIES AND REMEMBRANCES

We eventually found the Social Services Department in a small backstreet of the town. There were a number of tired, dejected men and women seated on small, hard, folding chairs; they looked as if they had been waiting for hours and were prepared to go on waiting to have their problems resolved and a shilling or two in their pockets. There was another small knot of people congregated around the 'Jobs' board as if wishing that more than the present three postcards would somehow appear; there seemed little hope and they continued to stand and smoke their cigarettes, their fingers stained orange from the nicotine in the smoke. When we approached the enquiry desk I left the talking to Megan.

"Good afternoon. My name is Dr Megan Griffiths and I wonder if you can help me."

The lady behind the desk was also weary as she said, "What exactly is it you require?"

"We're trying to trace a person who used to live at this address," Megan said as she handed over a note. "It does come into your area? We've come to the right place?"

"Yes, that's us. But we don't deal with missing persons; that's the Police."

"I understand. But the thing is you see, he's not *missing* exactly; we just don't know where he is."

I suppressed a laugh and Megan glared at me.

"We know that he doesn't live there any more. One of your young charges told us that they were now living there and you were paying the rent on the house."

"Just a minute," she said.

She rose and disappeared behind some screens. Megan made a face at us as if to say that she was not pulling her weight either. It was a few minutes before the Receptionist reappeared; she was accompanied by an older man. He addressed Megan and said, "Can I be of assistance to you?"

"Thank you, you're very kind." This did seem to disarm him somewhat and Megan moved quickly on. "My name is Dr Megan Griffiths and I am a Registered Paediatrician. This young lady is a descendant of the person we are trying to trace. He was, at one time a

County Councillor and lived in the house whose address you have there. It is especially important that we locate him and we visited the house. He is no longer resident, but you have the occupants under your care and they indicated that the house was rented and that the rent was paid by your Services."

"That is the case but we can't divulge any information regarding our charges or our payments. What's the point of your interest specifically?"

"I wish I was able to tell you; it would make things so much easier for us all, wouldn't it? I hate this sort of secrecy, but I'm afraid that at the moment, it is – how shall I say - privileged information? You understand that I'm sure; you must be placed in this situation quite often in your responsible position. I can tell you this, in strictest confidence of course, but you are a man who knows responsibility obviously; it concerns a young child who may, or may not, be a descendent of Councillor Rees. Paternity needs to be established d'you see. You will understand that, of course."

"I understand, yes, and I am grateful for your confidence but we cannot give out any information about our charges or our benefactors, who specifically ask for anonymity."

"Of course not; and you mustn't do so. I do not ask you to break your confidences. I don't wish for personal information. Let me put it this way: I believe that the house concerned is rented by your Social Services. Can you tell me, in general terms, as it were, if the rent is paid to a bank at all?"

"The rental on the house is not great and is paid to a firm of Solicitors in this City."

"Thank you. Would you help us with the future of this child by giving me the name of the Solicitors? That's all I ask. Then I can take the matter up with them. I would be very grateful and would mention your name for the help you gave me."

"Very well. I see no harm in that. You realise, of course that they may think otherwise. They are Lewis, Lewis & Davies of this town; a long - established legal practice here, and very well thought of. You should try to see Mr Davies if you can. He's the youngest of the partners, a son of the old Mr Davies and grandson of the original Mr Davies and he's more easily available." He looked at his watch and added, "I should think their office would be closed by now though." He returned to formality and said "As we should be."

"We will leave you to your evening then. I am most grateful to you. Your name is?"

"Stanley Mainwaring, Senior Assessment Officer here."

Megan smiled and said, "Thank you so much Mr Mainwaring," and she shook his hand.

As we left I mimed a clapping of my hands and said "Bravo! You even pronounced Mainwaring the Welsh way, every syllable enunciated clearly, you naughty girl."

"Mother, I will admit that was good. Even though you expect everyone to know what a 'Registered Paediatrician' is."

"It's a skill you must learn. Everybody has their personal fantasies. Find them, and play to them and you'll get what you want in the end."

"How mercenary is society," said Anna.

"Well, what now?" I asked.

"This Solicitors' Practice is not Elisabeth's father's old practice, is it?" Megan asked me.

I was caught off-guard and that brought back a pang which I fought hard to conceal: Elisabeth, my wife, had died when my children were very young. "No, I don't think so; not at this address in any case. But that was a long time ago. If it was, the old partners are long gone. I don't know any of the names in this firm."

Megan laid her hand on my arm and said, "That's a pity. It might have given us an entry."

Anna said, "Mr Mainwaring said they would be closed but it might be worth going there, just in case; somebody might be working late on a brief. That's the right word isn't it? What do you think?"

I said, "We've nothing to lose and there's nothing else we can do."

It was a short drive to the edge of the City. The offices occupied a substantial Edwardian house on a crescent above the County cricket ground. I had not spent much time watching the game there in my youth; there wasn't the money for the bus fare down the valley to the town and for the entry to the ground. It was only when I returned to the University that, in the summer, I used to escape for a few hours of indulgence, especially after Elisabeth had died and the children had grown. It had given me some sort of comfort in my solitude for there were no memories of the two of us at a game; we had not shared an interest and neither had the children; when I had attended, I had usually been alone. I had preferred it that way in any case. While understanding the boredom that many felt at the pace of the game, I indulged myself in its strategy and tactics, and dismissed them and it.

The houses on this Crescent had fine views across the curving bay and to our hotel. Looking out at a sea that for once, was so still, and which was catching the evening light over the headland in the West, my mood changed from my earlier disquiet at the return to my village to one that could only be described by a Welsh word: *hiraeth*. There is no

English equivalent to this word: it expresses a longing for what has been, good or bad, or for a place that may have seen great happiness or sorrow, but which is now gone forever and cannot be retrieved. The understanding of this loss brings heart-ache but also joy and a thanks for having known it before it passed. It is a farewell, and a sad one, for there is no return to that world. It is an ambivalent, complex word, as so many in my mother tongue are. It's also been said to be *a sadness of the heart.*

Megan turned to me as we walked towards the house and asked, "Are you alright?"

"Just a touch of *hiraeth* that's crept up on me," I said. "It will pass, no doubt."

"What does that mean?" asked Anna.

"A word you should know," said Megan, "I will tell you but not now."

The door was locked. We rang the bell and waited but there was no reply. Mr Mainwaring had been right, it seemed. There was no alternative but to return to our hotel. Over drinks before dinner we considered what we should do the next day. Our limitation was the need to catch an afternoon train home. It would not be possible to seek out the Minister and also beg an appointment with the Solicitor; it would have to be one or the other. There was no disagreement between us: the Solicitor was much more likely to provide us with useful information. Despite the lack of substantive progress then, we felt that something had been achieved, though we could not have identified what.

CHAPTER 16

CURIOSITY ABOUT ANOTHER

We went down for breakfast early the next day so that we could be free to approach the Solicitors at a time of their choosing during the morning. It was while Megan and I were waiting for Anna, and reading our newspapers that I said that we should have made contact, at least by phone with Roderick Samuel, the owner and Editor of the regional paper who had been a pillar of support for us in the past. I said that it had been remiss of us not to have called him already and that we couldn't leave the town without talking to him.

Megan too, was contrite and said, "Go and phone him now then; Anna won't be down for a while; she's not the earliest of risers is she?"

"Right. He's less likely to be busy at this time. I'll do it from our room."

It took longer than I had expected to talk to Roderick. He was disappointed that we were unable to dine with him before we left but insisted on seeing us; he would join us for coffee when we had breakfasted. Megan and Anna were well into their cooked breakfast by the time I returned to the dining room. I ordered my breakfast and poured my first cup of coffee.

"Did you get through to him?" asked Megan.

"Yes," I replied. "He wasn't pleased that we'd been here two days and hadn't given him the chance to treat us to dinner. I told him it had been a bit of a rush altogether, what with one thing and another. He said he'd come and join us for coffee."

"Was that all? There must have been more with the time you took."

"Yes. He acted the newspaperman and asked why we were here anyway. I couldn't not tell him." I turned to Anna and said, "I'm sorry if I've overstepped the mark my dear, but he has been good to us and I didn't feel I could avoid it; he won't release anything unless he asks us first."

"There isn't anything to release, is there."

"Nothing I don't think he knows or guesses anyway. We won't linger long; I've told him we have to leave soon anyway."

Roderick took longer than we had expected and we were on our second cup of coffee when he arrived. He kissed Megan and shook my hand. I introduced him to Anna whom he had not previously met.

"I'm sorry if I've kept you waiting. I've been making some

enquiries for you. I've got nothing immediate you can use except that ex-Councillor Rees died three years ago. His estate passed through probate and he left a significant legacy which was placed in trust. That's all I remember but there will be more in our files. Give me your current address and I'll send you what we've got, though it won't be much more that that; it seems to be an end, of sorts anyway."

Megan said, "Roderick, thank you. You've always been a great help; you know how much we thank you for it."

"It's not all been one-way you know. We go back some years anyway. I know you're anxious to move but there is one other thing: I phoned Daniel Davies the Solicitor; he'll see you as soon as you arrive. I hope that helps."

"Mr Samuel, I'd also like to thank you for all you've ever done for us," said Anna. "You've been very kind."

"I do what I can for friends but I'm grateful. Take care young lady."

Megan and Anna left us to finish their packing and Roderick walked me to Reception to pay our account. While I waited for the printout, Roderick said, "As I said, I hope that you find what you want, but be prepared that what you find may not be what you want. Anna could find some unpleasantness tucked away. You remember what Rees was like; he could be quite vindictive."

"Yes, I remember."

"Remember also that he got short shrift from the County Council in the end. There were a lot of 'heavies' who relished taking him down for 'old times' sake'. At one time he would have fought, and with his contacts, he would quite probably have won; a lot of people 'owed' him. But he went quietly, which was not like him."

"No. I should like to know why he 'bowed out'," I said.

"So would I, but I haven't found anything yet. We don't really know how he took that, nor how he coped with it. In fact, I don't really know who engineered it, nor how. It all went too quiet, too soon. I'd like to finish the story."

"Yes, I understand and I'm reluctant to rake it up again", I said. "But I have to do this for Anna's sake. I'll try to shield her as much as I can, but that may not be much," I said. "She has a strong mind of her own."

Roderick nodded. "I'll see what's in our archives. I'll address it to you so you can decide how much of it to share. And you take care too. And if you get really stuck, let me know; there must be something somewhere."

Megan and Anna arrived and we said our goodbyes. We left our cases at Reception and drove once again to the Solicitors' Offices. On arrival we were taken to a Board Room and asked to wait while Mr Davies had finished his appointment with a client. We did not have to wait long before he came to shake our hands. He was a short, portly man of middle age, clean-shaven and with a finely drawn face; his hair was already grey. I noticed his hands as he sat at the table and interlaced his fingers: they were narrow and his fingers were longer than was expected from his height and build. When he spoke his voice was soft but the words were clearly enunciated.

"I think it would be best if you told me how I can help you. It would also be best if you assumed that I know nothing of your quest. That way we won't miss anything. Do you agree?"

It seemed it was for me to make the first step; both Megan and Anna were silent. "Mr Davies, were grateful to you for agreeing to see us with no appointment. I'll try to give you a resumé so as not to take up too much of your time. Anna was adopted by Dr Megan Griffiths, here, and her husband Dr Will Griffiths when she was a baby; a very young baby. I have been a friend of the family for many years. My name is Charles Williams; I used to be at the University here until I left on medical grounds."

"I won't interrupt you more than is necessary Prof Williams but I do remember the circumstances of your departure – a dreadful business. I will ask you only if they are relevant to your enquiries?"

"No, not in the least."

"Then please carry on."

"The fact that Anna was adopted was never kept from her and at any point her questions were always answered with the truth. There has never been, nor is there any friction or secrecy. More recently, Anna has wished to know more about her biological parentage and we have tried to help in that regard. In brief, she knows who her biological father was; we have no information, even now of who her mother was."

"Let me stop you again Professor Williams." He turned to Anna and asked, "Do you find these statements distressing or difficult? Would you rather be here alone?"

"It's difficult facing it all, of course it is. But it's not the relating of it – it's what is. You should know the background to why we're here."

"I'll carry on then," I said. "We are trying to pursue the paternal line and to this end Anna has spent some time visiting Lord Mostyn at the Safe Haven Trust house. She has been told that her grandfather was not her grandmother's husband as everyone thought. She has been told that her biological grandfather was the one-time County Councillor Elwin Rees. I suspect that he was rather before your time."

"Yes, somewhat. But I can find out more if we need to."

"Well, we may need to. Anna's biological father whose name was Rhodri Morgan but who took the name of Rhodri Llewellyn, also disappeared after he had given her to Megan and Will Griffiths. We are now trying to find if he is still alive. Our first steps were to seek out Councillor Rees because he used to live in the village where I was born and grew up. We went to the house but it was occupied by a family supported by the Social Services, who, we were also told, paid rental on the property. The Social Services told us that the house was held in trust but nothing else. Whether that was because they didn't know or would not divulge any further details we don't know. They gave us your Company name, to get rid of us I think. Then Roderick Samuel was good enough to ease our search."

"Thank you," said Mr Davies. "A concise resumé. Now what do you want from me?"

"Whatever you are able to tell us."

"That can't be much I'm afraid."

"Will you tell us why?"

"Of course. It's very simple: the information is privileged."

"Is that all you can say to us?"

"I'm afraid not much more, except for generalities. The Trust was set up by the testator in such a way that it became effective on the testator's death. There were two named trustees, one of which was this Partnership. I should not reveal who the second person is without explicit authorisation from that person."

"I understand your reticence. But the Will has been made public we assume, and the names of the Trustees will be lodged legally, I assume also, and so can be made available to a descendant who can prove her legitimacy. But before we pursue that line through our Solicitors, with an unnecessary expense to us all, we would be grateful if you could determine whether his or her name can be made known to us. We can assure you that if necessary all contact will be carried out through yourselves if that is made a condition."

"I will see if that can be done. Now, is there anything else?"

"Yes. We know that the rental on the property is paid into the Trust. We can also assume that there is an expenditure for the upkeep and maintenance of the house which the Trust pays. Can you tell us whether there is any other outlay of payment that is made to a third party?"

"I can't tell you that without the agreement of other parties."

"At this time, we don't wish to know to whom any payments are made; only whether there are any such payments."

Davies shook his head. "I can make no statement."

"I see," I said. "Can you tell us then, what will happen to the Trust if any beneficiary dies?"

"I can't tell you that either. And that's not just obstruction on my part."

"Obscurantism then?" asked Anna.

"That information is particularly specified in the wording of the Trust deeds; you will need to have access to them in the first instance. To do that, you will need to prove your *bona fides* to the Trustees who hold Power of Attorney."

"Yourselves?"

"In part, yes. Also, there would be the requirements of the probate to ensure."

"I see; Legally Locked, then. It seems that we have reached an *impasse*," I said.

"I'm sorry that I cannot be of greater help to you."

"I understand. And we thank you for arranging your time to see us."

"I wish that it was possible to be of more help. I will contact the other Trustee and if you leave your contact details with my Secretary I will let you know the outcome."

We left the offices and sat in the car. "Well," said Megan, "That was rather depressing. It might have been better if we'd gone back to track down the Minister."

"It might," said Anna.

"I expected something of that nature, but not quite so much stonewalling," I said.

"Well, what now?" asked Megan.

"I don't think there's much more we can do here. We haven't got the time to be chasing the Minister now; we must get back. Time to think and re-group I suppose. I'll 'phone Roderick and put him in the picture; he might have some ideas."

"I'll write to the Minister," said Anna. "Who knows, we might be lucky."

"Yes," said Megan. "Back, then."

We drove back to the Hotel to collect our luggage. Megan telephoned the car hire company and arranged for them to collect the car we had used, from the Hotel. I telephoned Roderick and told him of our lack of progress. He sympathised but offered no consolation. The Hotel car took us to the railway station and we travelled to London in a subdued mood.

CHAPTER 17

CURIOSITY ABOUT ONESELF

I left our house early the next day to attend my meeting; I would not see them until the evening. Megan would take Anna to her Consultant's appointment, one of a series that she'd had to attend over the last two years and both Megan and I could sympathise with her reluctance to close her search in Wales for just another routine appointment. In reality, Anna understood the necessity for these monitoring consultations and tests and although she often accused Megan of behaving like a 'mother hen', it was more in jest than in any serious dismissal of Megan's care. Anna had occupied a special position in her family: no more and no less then her own children, but perhaps carrying a rather greater sense of responsibility. Whether this was because Anna was her adopted child or because of Megan's status and qualifications as a Paediatrician were factors that were difficult to untangle: there was no doubt that Anna had a serious genetic disorder, most probably inherited, which required regular monitoring and that was the end to the matter. But these clinical visits had become routine and with the best will in the world were a tolerated intrusion. Each of us understood this but it did not make the dates in the diary any easier to accept, nor any less fearful.

I arrived home in the early evening. Megan had left me a note to say that they had gone for a walk on the Heath. This was not unusual; Hampstead Heath and Parliament Hill Fields were convenient and mostly inviting. I made myself a drink and read the notes I had made during my meeting. I had switched on the evening news when I heard the key in the door. There was no conversation as they came into the sitting room. I switched off the television and said, "Well? What?"

"We have something to tell you," said Megan.

I was immediately concerned and replied, "Then tell me."

"We wanted to walk and think about things and how to tell you, which is why we weren't here when you came home." She gave a wry smile and added, "Well, that didn't help either of us much either."

"For God's sake what is it?"

Anna said, "Tell him straight. This isn't fair."

"No," said Megan, "It isn't. We've bad news. Anna's last blood tests showed a deterioration in her lymphocyte count."

"What does that mean?" I asked. "Speak English for God's sake."

"She has a worrying white blood cell level; they're the ones that protect you from disease and infection and also do some cleaning up. If the concentration in the blood falls, or rises, or if they don't mature properly, we need to find out why. We don't know if this current finding is significant or not."

"No, Mother," said Anna. "I know that you're the one who's qualified, but we mustn't delude ourselves, must we?"

"No, we mustn't," said Megan. "But, listen to me now. What I say is correct: we can't know how it is until we know the results of today's tests."

"When will we know that?" I asked.

"To be sure, not for three weeks or so. So we must try not to think the worst; it could be just a blip."

"I know you're trying to help and support me," said Anna, "You've been trying to do it all afternoon. Believe me, I'm grateful. And not knowing hurts all of us." She turned to me and said, "Charles, it's what we've been repeating to each other all afternoon. I know it matters to us all but remember I'm me, it's *my* life that could be on the line and, ultimately, *I* must decide what's to be done; I'm of age now I've been told. One can't live one's life through others' lives, especially when it's been accepted by Authority that you're old enough to make your own decisions. You'll fail anyway; you'll always fail."

"I've told you," said Megan. "That's not fair."

"Megan, darling," I said, "I'm sorry, but she's right."

Megan burst into tears and said, "Not you too? You're both closing me out."

"Nobody wants to do that; most of all to you," I said. "The three of us must be closer than ever for the next few weeks and we must give each other strength when we need it. It's terrible when there is nothing you can do, isn't it? So we'll have to wait and see, won't we? No false hopes, but also no false fears either. And we mustn't avoid the issue. Anna, if you want to talk about what you want done or what you want to do, then tell us when you're ready. Promise us that, at least."

"Of course I will but I may need to think about things first; don't be angry or upset if I'm quiet or seem withdrawn. I must think; I owe so many people. Mum, I'm not shutting you out and I may need your strength more than ever if it comes to anything, but be understanding with me: I'm seeking a way through all this."

Megan nodded her head and took our hands in hers. She tried but she was unable to stop her tears and that made Anna cry too. I rose and made them both a drink but Anna shook her head. I felt washed out, so I could guess the turmoil they were both experiencing. It was Anna that recovered some level of composure first.

"I've been giving some thought to one issue already," she said. "The boys and girls (she meant Megan's and my children) must be told the position, of course, but except for generalities, they needn't be made to worry until we finally know."

"Whatever you wish darling," said Megan. "It's probably more sensible to wait."

"Yes, I think so; until I decide what to do. But just for now, I don't think I could even tell them nothing. Richard will be impossible; he'll ask all the awkward questions. He'll ask for my lymphocyte count and guess what's up immediately."

Richard was Megan and Will's son, their eldest child; he was on secondment as a Practicing Clinician in the United States and due to return soon.

"Mum, Charles, d'you understand? Mum, I'm sorry to put it on to you, but will you do what I want?"

Megan took a deep breath and said, "Of course."

I intervened and said, "I'll speak to my kids, but would it make it any easier if I spoke to them all?"

"No," said Megan. "They'll know that as an avoiding action. We'll do it together if it comes to it, but it's my job."

"Right," I said. "We don't feel like eating I don't suppose but I'll organise a takeaway to be delivered and we can play around with that."

For the rest of the evening, little was said; we toyed with our food and ate little of it. I opened a bottle of wine, hoping that it would lift the mood but it seemed to do otherwise and it was left unfinished. Once, I tried to be rational about the situation, claiming that we knew little and that our fears could turn out to be unfounded. I extracted no response: neither of them would follow my lead; all of us knew the futility of clinging on to that belief. If it was all ultimately shown to be a false alarm, we should all be joyous and laugh at our terrors; but it would not alter the fact that one day we should have to face the same probability again. Whatever the findings of the present tests, we knew, not to put too fine a point to it, that for now, it would only be a stay of execution of a young life. Although I was unable to attribute the quotation, one repeatedly came to mind: *'We all die; the only questions are How and When'*. I didn't express it. After all it always was a truism and would be of no help to anyone.

And so the evening dragged on; at some point I suggested a walk, even while listening to the rain on the windowpanes. Megan gently smiled and shook her head. Each of us was locked in our own isolation: what Will had called, I seemed to remember, one's *'ultimate aloneness'*. At times since his death, I had come to understand what he had meant and what trauma he had endured. But that way was not for me, it was too barren; but I did understand.

Anna eventually broke the silence by saying, "I need to write a letter of thanks to Lord Mostyn. I think I'll do that now before bed." She kissed us both and said goodnight. Megan and I sat with the last of the unfinished wine until she said, "I think I'll try to phone the children."

"Hadn't you better leave it a little while?"

"No, there's no point in that."

"Be kind to yourself then; tell them only what Anna asked. Don't let Richard press you. And you must put them off visiting for a few days."

As for me, I would phone my children in due course.

CHAPTER 18

PROTECTING A NAME

During the hiatus before the results of Anna's tests became available there was little that we could do; like others before us (and no doubt many who would come after us) we tried to fill our days with activity and to a small extent we succeeded by indulging ourselves in restaurants and theatres. It was a sham that each of us understood but it did limit our brooding: Megan busied herself with her locum work, and though I had little appetite for reading, I tried to lose myself in reports and committee work. Anna took to taking long walks on the Heath alone and showed little enthusiasm for her writing. Those were our days; at night we were each alone with our fears.

Some time after our visit to South Wales, Anna received a letter from the Solicitors who were handling the Trust for the house in the valley. None of us had given a thought to pursuing them for the name of the second trustee; it had been sidelined and become of secondary interest. But, contrary to expectations it aroused Anna and she became eager to pursue it. The second trustee was the retired Head of a Teacher Training College who had been, during my time, the Headmaster of Will's and my grammar school. His name was Edward Daniel; he had been an Historian of the mining communities of our land and had played a significant part in Will's early academic life. When we knew, it was no surprise to us: the School was in the Village; Councillor Rees lived in the Village and was a School Governor and had later served on the County Education Board. Anna wrote to thank the Solicitor and immediately wrote to Daniel to ask if she could visit him sometime soon to continue her search for her antecedents. She also received a letter from Lord Mostyn reminding her of her agreement to visit for the Point-to-Point races. Together, these two letters lifted her mood and, consequently, something of Megan's and mine.

The date of Anna's appointment with the Oncologist could not be ignored however, and this time the three of us made our way to the clinic. We were not made to wait and Megan led Anna into the Consulting Room while I fretted outside. It took every bit of my rational mind not to break down: memories of such hours spent with Elisabeth that I thought had long ago been laid to rest were, in fact, as strong as ever and, it seemed, needed little to trigger them. Elisabeth's trauma and her death had left me devastated for a long time. I had withdrawn totally from all social contact and if it hadn't been for a responsibility to my son and my daughter I could not have continued. Megan knew most of it, though not all; some was too deeply embedded, but as a doctor, she could imagine the distress. At times during the past two weeks I had caught her watching me, as if looking for any sign of distress or grief. I did not challenge her for I knew that it would only make the situation worse; it was an involuntary tic; in any case it was all done in love. Now, again, I was being called upon to remember Elisabeth but this time it was with a feeling of gratitude: the *hiraeth* I had spoken of earlier. There was a sadness for this child of course, and for the things which she may never know but I also knew that I could now provide whatever was needed of me.

It seemed a long time since my introspective thoughts had surfaced and I was surprised when I looked at my watch, that so little time had passed. A nurse came towards me and took me to the Consulting Room where Megan and Anna sat in silence. The Consultant rose as I entered the room and said, "Professor Williams, my name is John Turner and I am Anna's Consultant. Both she and Doctor Griffiths wished you to be present. Please sit down."

"Thank you."

"I have already told Anna and Dr Griffiths that the results of our tests so far are not all that we could hope for. I must stress to you all that these results are for the tests that we have been able to do on the blood sample. I must also tell you that they are indicative of a progression in Anna's clinical condition. At this stage I must also stress that the results are indicative of what has been classified as Progressive Indolent Lymphoma – terminology, jargon if you like; we all hide behind it and suffer from it, but it does allow us to be accurate. But the important word for us now, is 'Progressive'. So we cannot simply ignore the data, hoping it will go away; it won't. That being the case, I must give you all the information you will need to help you to decide your course of action. It would be wrong of me to hold anything from you and you wouldn't forgive me if I did. It's best hidden for some people, but not for those who know something or at least know where to read and so find out."

"Why has it appeared now?" I asked.

"It has not suddenly appeared, I'm afraid," said the Consultant. "The early stages can go unnoticed, even by the patients, for a long time, and as there seems no cause for what's considered a minor irritation, there is no reason for troubling a busy GP. As a result the condition is significantly advanced by the time the routine tests show positive."

"What treatment regimes are there then?" I asked. I was ignoring

Anna and Megan, but in any case they seemed unable to respond.

"We shall need to consider what will be most effective in Anna's situation; I can review that with the team while more tests are being done. In any case, epidemiology has shown that there is no advantage in rushing into what will inevitably be a restrictive treatment; which is why I've given Anna some time for her own business; but that does not mean we should delay unduly, you realise. But yes, there are a number of further tests we need to do before we finally decide on the treatment regime; we want to get it right, of course, and not cause more distress than is inevitable."

In a small voice Anna asked, "What are they please?"

"Mainly an aspiration of your bone marrow and a piece of one of your lymph nodes in your axilla if needs be. Neither is particularly intrusive: a sample will be taken from your pelvic blade under local anaesthetic. From this sample we can do some chromosome studies to see if there is what's called a *translocation*. It's when a part of one chromosome (usually chromosome 14 in this case) becomes attached to another (usually 18). We shall also be able to classify the affected cell. We shall need to look at your general health as well and do some X-rays and scans."

"So what is the treatment?" asked Anna.

"Usually, Chemotherapy, oral in the first instance, or by transfusion; and targeted Radiotherapy. But as I've said we will review the options following these next test results."

"And the success rate?" I asked.

"Overall, 75% remission."

"Permanent?" asked Anna.

"No, we're not that good yet I'm afraid; but some research with stem cells is promising. For up to ten years. There is another drawback. If the disease relapses, it may do so as a further episode of what you have now, Progressive Indolent Non-Hodgkin Lymphoma; or it may undergo transformation and become aggressive."

"Towards the end?" asked Megan.

"No. At any time following treatment; but later rather than sooner."

Anna gave a deep sigh and said, "Given the caveats, the odds don't attract a heavy bet, then."

"The odds on life are always worth the bet," replied the Consultant.

"So you say, so you say," said Anna. "My Mother here would agree with you; it's why you're in Medicine of course. I'm in Philosophy, so tell me, what is so rewarding about Life?"

"Why, the living of it."

"Ah, *the great get out clause*. Whatever the quality of it would that be?" asked Anna. "Well, I'll tell you, I wouldn't take you to the Races with *my* money."

I closed my eyes and I was re-running Elizabeth's last days – the crying and the pain that broke through the morphine barrier; her pleading for an end to it; and not finding anyone who would answer. I could easily acknowledge Anna's stance – I had faced it myself; I did not know, now it had come to this, if I could indeed cope with it again. I thought once more that it is one thing to cope with fear in the abstract but quite another to face it in reality.

"But why do I have it?" asked Anna.

"A viral infection probably; EB virus is the most common one and we've all had that at some time or another, mostly as glandular fever; AIDS virus is another, picked up by an ancestor in Africa or the Caribbean; or even the Human T-cell Lymphoma virus (HTLV-1). This virus was first identified in Japan and has subsequently also been shown to be present in a significant percentage of the Caribbean population. But potentially any virus can interfere with cell growth and stability. There is a strong genetic link as well; perhaps it's the most important factor here but we just don't know yet; however, I feel it's likely."

We all sat quietly trying to come to terms with this information in our own way, and also with the thought of our fragile mortality.

"Is there anything else you'd like to know?" asked the Consultant.

Anna shook her head and I said, "I think we have enough for now. Thank you for making things clear for us. I'm sure you'll understand that we would like some time to digest what you've told us."

"Of course you do. As I've told you we will not rush into treatment until we have the full profile of the disease. We need to consider our options, in particular, our treatment regime – which regime we consider will be most effective. But that mustn't stop us from proceeding with the tests. We need those in any case. I'll get my Secretary to organise a date." He turned to Anna and said, "You'll only be here for a morning so long as you don't exercise too much for a day or two afterwards."

"I don't intend to aim for next year's Centre Court you'll understand," said Anna. "And I shan't watch Point – to – Point Races either, unfortunately; it would become much too intrusive."

We rose and shook hands and left very subdued. The short journey home seemed interminable and we could not give way to our emotions until we were safely indoors.

CHAPTER 19

THE FORMALITY OF LIVING

Anna's medical tests were carried out during the following two weeks and, again, we had to wait for the results. It was Anna who showed the greatest fortitude but throughout she refused to discuss the possible outcomes. She spent a great deal of time in her own room and this time rarely left the house. She wrote letters to both of the Trustees explaining that, for personal reasons she was currently unable to visit them. She asked them, in the meantime, if there was any information concerning the house left for the use of the Social Services by ex-Councillor Rees, or his bequest, or the administration of the Trust and any beneficiaries of the remainder of the Estate, that they could tell her without breaking any conditions of the Trust she would be very grateful. She also explained that her concern was not directly with Councillor Rees but with tracing her antecedents and in particular her biological father, whose name was Rhodri Morgan. Any help in that direction would also be very welcome. At this time she also initiated a legal consideration of her position as the grandchild of the Councillor. She wrote to Lord Mostyn saying that there were doubts about her future visit for the Point- To – Point Races and expressed regrets. She would visit him as soon as she could, if only briefly.

At that time, there was no justifiable reason for keeping the news from the other children. There were telephone calls from all of them which she took with little sign of distress; with each she took a formal stance and at the suggestion of a visit she said that it would be more welcome following any treatment she would need to undergo; it was probably then that she would be most restricted and bored and would welcome some decent conversation. She would not relent and when they telephoned Megan and myself we had something of a task of smoothing feathers; it was only concern and anxiety on the part of her family; and they came to understand that it was Anna's way of dealing with her worry and they reluctantly acceded. Nevertheless, their telephone calls increased and became more insistent until Anna told them that they would be told of any news as soon as it was known but at the moment it was best for all of us to be patient.

One morning at breakfast Anna said that she would be out for most of the day but would be back in time for dinner.

"Where are you going?" asked Megan.

"I want to go to the University Library. I've decided to try and extend my little Thesis Book on the Myths, as Lord Mostyn has suggested. I want to immerse myself. So I want to see if I can have access to the Library's books and journals without hindrance."

At that time in the morning the traffic would be heavy descending the hill and there would be a queue waiting at the bus-stop, no doubt considering the low cloud cover and the dampness in the air. Once again Anna thought that the absence of an Underground Station was a disadvantage in living in this part of London, but the proximity of the fields and the sense of being part of a village with views over London more than compensated for the occasional sense of isolation. In any case, there were few occasions now when time mattered. It had not always been the case: during her undergraduate days time had always seemed to be an issue and 'running late' seemed to be an inevitable consequence of life. Nine o'clock lectures seemed unreasonably early and had no regard to the needs of the general working population. Time had also to be set aside for the inevitable rush-hour traffic crawl. It had just started to rain when the bus arrived for her journey to her University buildings.

Anna told us over dinner that evening that she was considering enrolling on a Master's degree programme on Mythology and insisted that she would not expect opposition: her decision was final, she said. In the event, no opposition was expressed but there were clearly degrees of acceptance. Megan believed it to be a positive action and one which could only mean that Anna would also commit herself to the prescribed treatment for her condition. So Megan felt that she could prepare for her role of support for whatever needs her daughter would require. Therefore, she was as content as the situation allowed.

"Anna, darling, your father would be proud and happy with you," she said.

"I hope so," replied Anna. "I also hope that he'd understand that I'm doing it for my own sanity."

I thought that a strange phraseology to have used but I did not comment; Megan seemed to have missed it entirely. Instead, she said, "We must get you moving on then, as soon as we can. We must concentrate on this challenge for you and put some of the other things aside."

Anna did not directly respond to the implication of Megan's words. She turned the conversation back to her proposal by saying, "I just hope that I can do it justice."

"I have no doubt about that," said Megan.

"Then you're more confident than I am," replied Anna. "It will take more than just my Philosophy, you know. Won't it Charles?"

"Yes, it will. You'll move into areas and disciplines you're not familiar with. You'll have your work cut out. Myths and Legends are not only a philosophical issue you know. In fact I'd say that they're not principally philosophical."

"What then?" asked Anna.

"It's only my view, of course, but I'd argue that they are more of almost any other discipline that you care to mention: early history, of course, but selective; theology, again selective; sociology and economics, economics mostly perhaps – relating to the Gods of the Harvest and that; it's why there are so many wars involved – Rape and Pillage. Then behaviour, psychology, especially megalomania; all of these and more. But I suppose you'd argue that all of these contribute to Philosophy anyway."

"Of course. From the Greeks onwards – most of their Myths are on Wars and Women: their Gods are Warriors and their Goddesses do the ruling. People are wrong to think that it's all abstract and intellectual – tales to frighten children - and I intend to argue the point, with Goddesses as well as Gods; with Goddesses mostly I think. Is that the Heresy of our Modern Patriarchal Christian age do you think? Feminism? I suppose that my thesis really is *Why did our Church turn from the Mother to the Father?* I'd like an answer."

"Well I wish you luck with it," I said. "But it will take you longer than you think to think your way through. If there's anything I can do to help, you won't need to ask."

"I know. And I also know it will take time; perhaps more than I've got, but I can't opt out. And Mum, I know that it would be easier for you, perhaps for all of us, if I forgot about other things, but that's part of it all, d'you see? I need to know matters. There can't be one without the other."

"It will only side-track you and stop you getting on with it."

Before Anna could reply I said, "Megan, leave it for now."

"But we need to do it now," said Megan.

"Leave it," I said.

"Yes," said Anna.

For a few seconds there was an awkward silence and it was clear that each of us was searching for a way out of the possible conflict. It was on the verge of a hurtful argument that none of us wanted and which would cause all of us great distress, but none of us could see a way to avoid it. It was Anna who broke the tension.

"We don't need demonstrations of conflict," she said, "good or bad, it will be my fault and I don't want that. Let me do what I believe is

135

best for me; let me use my time as is best for *me*. I want your help and I certainly need your support and that of the rest of the family. Which reminds me; I want to write to them too."

She kissed us both and went to her room and her own thoughts. As soon as we were alone, Megan started to revive the conflict.

"Best if we leave it for now," I said.

"I can't leave it hanging," she replied.

"It will be better if we do. It will only hurt."

"D'you think this way won't?"

"No, of course I don't but it will be easier if we hold off for a while."

"It's easy for you to say; she's not yours to worry about."

It was on the tip of my tongue to point out that neither was she Megan's. That would have been insensitive of me and unforgivably hurtful; for all of her young life, except for biology, she was indeed Megan's child. Although biology was not the driving issue, Megan's attitude was a consequence of her non-maternal status and, perhaps, there was a sublimated guilt that she had not done more to avoid such situations as this. I truly believed that Anna's condition and decision was no more or no less for Megan than would have been the case with any of her own offspring; but there was a difference: in this instance she felt the need to analyse and justify her responses, even subconsciously, which would not have been the case with her own children. It was understandable also, that she should feel isolated without her husband. It had been he who was the closest friend and protector of Anna's biological father and now, he wasn't there to be called upon. All this was understandable but it was in hindsight; and I felt the greatest exclusion. So my tongue was sharper that it should have been.

"It's best that we leave it now," I repeated.

"I'm sorry. I shouldn't have said that. I'm sorry. I shouldn't take it out on you; you've done more than you should already."

"That's not the most gracious of apologies. But leave it."

"I'm making it all worse. Sincerely, I'm sorry."

"Right, then leave it there."

Megan nodded, but it was obvious that she was not convinced. She would continue to worry the issue but in private, not in conversation. As so often happens when arguments or disagreements are consciously avoided, neither of us could call on other topics to talk about. Most of the time, conversation was never a problem for us; if nothing else, we would talk of the books we were reading and even our silences were by choice. I searched for a topic to re-establish some semblance of peace.

136

"Do you remember the first time we all got together? Yourself, Will, Elisabeth and me and the children?"

"Yes. It was at the Stone; why do I always think that should take a capital 'S'? You were not long back from Australia. The children were climbing the Stone and I was afraid they'd fall and hurt themselves."

"You and Elisabeth were both pregnant, you with Gwen and Elizabeth with Nia; and it was a warm day."

"Yes, I remember. It was a happy time for us; for all of us I think. What's made you think of that?"

"You and Elisabeth walked ahead and the children ran after you. Will and I tarried, catching some emotions from our youths I suppose."

"Why do you remember that? And why now?"

"As Will and I walked down to the road, we talked about the children and what they would do with their lives. We, him and I and others, had been the 'unknown' generation in our village: our futures were inconceivable in any detail to our parents' generation. But their hopes were sharp, if unfocussed; they believed that somehow or other we would make things better. We rebelled against them of course; too much of their hopes rested on us and we could not let them live their lives vicariously through us; we refused the responsibility. I understand all that now, of course, but I didn't then, though I believe Will knew something of it.

"Anyway, as we walked behind you, we watched the children and I said something along the lines that we would be able to help them chose their futures, where nobody had been able to help us: we had been vague about what the options were, and vaguer still about what they were about. He said, *'No, if they have anything about them, I don't think they'll want it any more than we wanted to be told what to do. They'll make their own choices and their own mistakes; we can't, and mustn't do it for them. All we can do is be there when they stumble, or fall. Or rise and achieve joy'.* He was so right you know, as in many things, even then; and it's still true for our children, though they're a bit older now of course. You cannot and mustn't regiment people; nor should you try. We've been made aware of it again now, haven't we? They must make their own lives."

"He was so insightful," said Megan. "And you're clever. God help us if you were one. I'll try to do what you ask."

CHAPTER 20

MOVING ON

That night, neither Megan nor I found sleep easy and we each tried to avoid disturbing the other; it was becoming routine. I rose soon after the dawn light framed the window-curtains and made myself some strong coffee in the kitchen. I tried to read but could not become engrossed in my book. Megan soon followed me and sat at the table.

"I smelt the coffee," she said.

"I did shut the door."

"I know; it wasn't really that; I was awake already but I didn't want to disturb you."

"I suppose some people would say that we're too damned caring! Would you like some?"

"Yes, but Instant will do."

"No, I'll make a fresh pot. We won't want to go back to bed."

We sat across the table from each other in silence. Neither of us felt that we could sustain a conversation: we felt talked out after the previous night. I was conscious of the fact that the silence was dragged out (prolonged was the wrong word). Occasionally, one or other of us would ask a question and again lapse into silence. There was only one point when our introspection might have been broken: it was when Megan said, "I suppose this is another instance of what my father meant by 'Duty of Care'."

Her father, a Family Doctor had often used that expression for a parent's responsibility for his or her child, but I was too distant to take advantage of her gambit.

Somehow the time passed without our noticing it, until we heard the newspapers being delivered. The sound and the evidence of a continuing world broke the mood and I rose to get the papers: reading them would give us some semblance of normality. I read but Megan rose and said, "I think we need some breakfast."

"That would be welcome. No dietary restrictions."

"The whole bit then? A full Welsh?"

"Yes, as much as you can manage. And tea, strong with sugar and milk."

"Right, but no laver bread [12], I'm afraid; I'm not going to Harrods to get it this time of day. Anyway, I'm not dressed for the West End, so you'll have to do without that little delicacy."

"You're not dressed at all. I don't suppose there's any cockles either."

"You know I don't keep those; you know I don't like them and they smell the fridge out. So, no. But you can have the salty bacon."

"I know it's early for Anna, but I'll bet you that she'll smell the breakfast cooking and will be through that door before it's on the table."

"I won't bet against you and you'd better put the brown sauce out. Set the table then."

Anna appeared as predicted and drank a large glass of fruit juice while waiting to be served. "What's this in aid of then? It's usually cereal and a piece of toast if you're lucky."

"We just felt like it for ourselves for a change."

"You've been up early haven't you? You didn't sleep much, did you?"

"No, we didn't sleep well, and yes we were up early. So, we felt like a treat," I said.

"Was it me? I won't have you worrying about me. If it's going to upset you and come between you, I'll move out. I swear it."

"I won't lie," said Megan. "Yes, of course we're upset and worried, there's nothing surprising about that, is there? We'd be a sorry lot if we weren't. But you've not come between us, so you mustn't think that. Besides, your moving out would make it worse. So help us out and stay."

I smiled and said, "United we stand. But you must accept that our focus on you has shifted somewhat."

"Yes. But there are two ways of looking at this, aren't there? There's the road you two seem to be taking, one of grief and sorrow, and the other road."

"What do you mean?" asked Megan.

"It's a philosophical problem. I've been thinking about it in the night. Let me explain it to you: everybody dies - *fact;* then there's grief for some, sorrow for others, but for most, nothing much, and easily dismissed. But Death *is* a FACT. The only unknowns, we've agreed are *How* and *When*. If you were asked whether you would like to know the answers to these questions in advance, how would you answer? Would you say 'Yes', or would you say 'No'? Neither answer can change the '*fact*' of course. So which one would it be Mum?"

"Certainly not. I would always be in dread of the time's approach. It would be alright in the beginning I suppose, if it was far enough ahead but it would get worse with the passing of the years; or months."

"Or days?" asked Anna.

"Stop it," said Megan. "No, I don't want to know."

"The issue intrudes anyway as you age, doesn't it? You inevitably think more about it; when there's less time left than you've had. So what's the difference? Charles, what about you?"

"The difference, Anna, is one of 'Specifics'. For the other question, a considered *'No'*, though I think I could accept it if I had no choice. My biggest problem would be coming to terms with the belief that the time still available to me was still worth pursuing – and finding a good way of filling it – what you're trying to do, I think."

"So," said Anna, "A *'Doer'* and a *'Thinker'*. Just as I thought. You're both very predictable you know. But that's a comfort, most of the time," and she smiled.

"What about you then?" asked Megan.

"I've not been asked to chose, have I," replied Anna.

"But if you had been?" I asked.

"I think I would probably go along with my mother and the crowd, but I would accept being with you, Charles. And truth to tell, a bit of me, let's call it the irrational bit, would have little problem saying *'Yes'*, just out of academic interest you understand. You see Mum, you can't opt out, or retire, because you won't see the end of the game – *'That's just not hockey!'* as they say. You just have to do more in the time – the things you would normally put off for another, later time maybe; you must bring everything forward, pack in more when you can; see to your affairs, if you like. Now do you see why I need to do these things?"

"No," said Megan.

"Mum," said Anna. "Can I try to explain myself to you? Please listen and try to understand: I have been very lucky in the family who have given themselves to me without pause; I could not have hoped for better and I love them all. But most people know their parents: they may love them, they may hate them, they may admire them but not like them much, they may dismiss them as of no account, or think nothing of them, or they may be totally ambivalent about them; those are their choices. But however they judge, they will know them and through them and their own attitude, come to know something of themselves. I can't be blamed for that unknown and I can't be blamed for thinking and wondering about it. And you and my dear Father Will must take some of the blame for it too, you know: you insisted on me being *Educated*; you shouldn't now dismiss the consequences of your foolishness."

Megan was quietly sobbing and shaking her head, not in dismissal I believed, because she also had a half-smile on her face, but in some wonderment at this clear-headed woman that she did not know.

"You're too literate," said Megan. "Your father taught you well."

"Yes. What about you then Charles?" asked Anna. "Do you see the truth of it?"

"Yes," I said.

"Thank you. I know it's distressing, but you must be logical about what you need to face; and to face down. It's an interesting state for another reason as well. Lord Mostyn said to me that studying the discipline of Philosophy was the greatest possible act of self-indulgence because you're only looking to understand yourself. He was right, too; it's too introspective a pursuit. He's a clever man is our Lord.

"There's a terrible irresponsibility in having to face yourself as well, you know; an invitation to be irresponsible: *You cannot condemn me for this! I am my father's daughter*! That's always there in the back of your mind; you don't need to think about it; and you must do something physical to get you off the roundabout. *Murder or Martyrdom! Death or Glory!* Once you realise that, it's strange, but you become more *benevolent.*"

Megan rose and almost shouted, "Stop it! This is too much: it's *morbid!*"

She busied herself with the dishes in the sink and turned her back on us. Anna reached out her hand to take mine. She started to say something but changed her mind and took up the tea-towel to dry the cutlery. I walked to the lounge and left them together to cry or to compose themselves. We had lain awake during the night in sorrow for Anna and in wondering whether we could provide the support and comfort that she would need. I had also been uncertain of whether I could provide the steadfastness – awkward word – that I knew Megan would need. But I realised now that we didn't know this young woman at all: it was she that was most untroubled amongst us and the one most certain of her purpose, and her will, whatever she would turn it to be; and I envied her clarity of mind. I hoped that it was not morbid nor exploitative of me, and I hoped that my almost spiritual interest in the intellectual progress of Anna's sickness, would be understood by her, and if unhidden, be forgiven by Megan.

I showered and shaved and decided to try and spend some time over my papers. I believed that however difficult it might be for each of us, we should try to move on with our interlocking lives.

CHAPTER 21

NO COMPLIANCE

The next few weeks were disruptive on many fronts. On the face of it, Megan continued trying to be stalwart, but she could not bring herself to an understanding of Anna's stand nor of Anna's acceptance of the inevitability of the final outcome: to her, that seemed an abdication from living – a surrender - and no discussion would ease her trauma. It was deeper than sadness, more like an emptiness of the heart which she could find no way of filling. At times it seemed to dominate her life and no amount of sympathy or understanding could assuage the feeling of doom that she was experiencing. It was only when I said that she should give some thought to the effect of her attitude on Anna's need to come to terms with the possible finality of her young life, that Megan nodded and withdrew. But that was equally distressing: there were times when her maternal or medical concern would have been helpful and supportive but it was not offered. It seemed that only by distancing herself sufficiently from the prognosis, as much as would be expected of a medical practitioner with no blood ties, was she able to come to terms with the situation and Anna's objectivity. It was distressful for me to follow the widening gap between Anna and her mother but neither of them could take a position that would have eased the distress of the other: if Anna could have shown a little of what her mother wanted, a sorrow or fear of the ending of her life, then Megan would so easily have softened her stance; and if Megan could acknowledge Anna's need for withdrawal, Anna would have sought to close the gap; but neither could comply without losing all semblance of control. I tried to explain to both of them the inevitability of over-reaction by a loved and loving person and although Anna understood my words, I did not believe that she accepted my meanings; I became sure that she had her own rationale and was plotting the course of the remainder of her life. As for Megan, for a short while, out of fear I believed, she was the most distant.

It was a difficult period for our relationships: mood swings, sometimes violent, became an expected part of our daily lives to be forgiven with apologies, tears and demonstrations of love; and subsequently, in private, coped with by each of us apart, in our own idiosyncratic ways. As the time moved on and a greater realisation dawned, there was some comfort in that the outbursts diminished. We came to understand that we were all wasting the time that should be the most precious for us; our responsibility and love for each other should be paramount and the loss of it became the greatest tragedy. It was like a bereavement: the greatest sorrow and distress was not for the dead or afflicted but for oneself who has to endure both the loss and that guilt. I understood again the worm of self-pity that was occasioned by the misfortune of those one loved.

This understanding was forced upon us when the other children visited and showed such an easy and uncomplicated love for each other. The prognosis was not avoided in conversation and no demands were made of each other; Anna was treated as each of them had always been treated: an equal and precious part of the family.

I also realised, and tried to make Megan accept it, that through our children's unconditional love and uncomplicated understanding, this would be remembered also as a beautiful time in all our lives: our children knew more of living than their parents did. To impress upon her, I made Megan realise that it was through the benevolence of our children, and in no small part Anna and her noncompliance, that we had been given the *'knowing of the beauty of it'*: some would say, and would no doubt insist on calling it, a Religious Awareness of the Glory of God and His Love of Man; indeed many had gone to a Nunnery or Monastery for less. I knew it as more than that; there was no need to invoke any Deity – it was Human and I was grateful for the recognition of it, though I felt it as a *hiraeth of the heart*.

Not all the children had been able to visit; they were too scattered across the world by this time: Richard, Megan's son, was coming to the end of his sabbatical clinical position in Arizona and we now knew that he would be home to a Consultancy in Edinburgh in a month. Gwen, her daughter, had entered the Civil Service and was currently at the British Embassy in Washington DC but took leave and flew home; my own daughter Nia was plying her trade with her husband in Canada but had assured Anna that, if needed, she would drop everything and be on the next plane out of the prairies with her daughter and with or without her husband in tow; Edward, my son, was of course the nearest, in his somewhat remote house in Wales. He did not even reply to Anna's letter and instead arrived at our house within days of having received it. He apologised to Anna for not coming sooner and accused her of ignoring him; but he had shut up his house, re-directed his mail and informed all who needed to know that he would now, until further notice, be contactable through us. Anna kissed him, rather more physically than as family members who had grown up together. While he stayed with us, they talked late into the nights and gave us no intimation of the subject of their conversations. Eventually, he said that through his contacts at his Company, he had found a small flat to rent on a short term basis while the owner was abroad. It would give Anna a 'change of scene' if at any time she felt constrained or needed to get away from her books. That was all we were told but Anna soon came to spend more and more time with him. None of the other children overlapped by more than a day or two but their comings and goings gave the house more of a Central Train Station atmosphere than if they had arranged their transit accommodation *en bloc* with sleeping-bags on the floor. But that time was gone: the bones and the joints weren't up to the demands any more.

During their visits, the children also spent most of their days at Edward's borrowed flat, returning to us for dinner and the evening; we were beginning to feel what could only be called 'a generational exclusion'. It was understandable, but for Megan it was hard to take. However, when it ended and only Edward remained, the house seemed depressingly empty and quiet and our minds turned inwards again to the progressive stages of Anna's treatment. The year was moving on and we discussed whether we should repair to Spain for Christmas and New Year and forget our 'Open House', but at no time was it a serious consideration. Anna and Megan attended a final consultation with her Oncologist. I had to be away at the time and learned the detailed outcome only a few days later. Edward had been on hand throughout the extended appointment and was the first to be made aware of the decisions that had been agreed. Anna had been told that there was evidence of the appearance of her lymphoma in her bone marrow and that the prognosis of her condition was not good; the outcome was confirmed to be a duration of a maximum of ten years; even then there were caveats as had been explained. Arrangements would be made for her course of treatment. They were still debating the options, but whichever treatment they finally agreed upon, it would be debilitating and she would have little energy for any other matters. Her Consultant had reiterated that research had shown that there was no advantage to an early admission and treatment of her condition: her fitness and resilience were also of importance. Therefore, she was told again, that if there we things that she wished to do before starting her treatment then she could take the time, within reason, to see to her affairs. I learnt of the confirmation that we had all expected but irrationally hoped that would be otherwise, by telephone from Megan. There was little I could do other than provide support but when Megan said that she needed me, I concluded my work and asked to be excused. I was home by the evening. Even so, I only caught the tail end of their discussions. Anna, in consultation with Edward, had drafted herself a timetable and insisted that she would take as much time as she felt she needed to pursue her intentions, which we were told, without invitation to comment were to work on the expansion of her book on Mythology and its implied Heresies, and to continue the search for her antecedents. When she had progressed those projects to a state with which she was satisfied, she would submit herself to the ministrations of the medics, but not before. She was realistic enough to appreciate that neither of her wishes could be entirely satisfactory, but she could at least hope that her interim life would contribute something worthwhile. There was no convincing her otherwise. It was clear that she had already planned whatever was to be her future and even when Edward added his voice to ours to persuade her that there was, just, an outside chance that an early treatment could improve her chances, she had reached for his hand, smiled at him and said, "We mustn't delude ourselves, must we? You should know the futility of that." Edward had shaken his head and then had remained silent. Both Megan and I finally realised that Anna had decided what she would do for the rest of the time available to her. For that time, we would be wanted for the support we could give, but, in truth, we would be spectators.

CHAPTER 22

THE OUTLAWS

At this time I received a letter from Roderick Samuel, Editor, reminding me of the death of Elwin Rees at the grand age of 81 and enclosing an Obituary Notice reviewing his career and his contribution, as Councillor, to the smaller world in which he had lived and worked. It was a fair, but not an enthusiastic report, being somewhat superficial and impersonal. I had no doubts but that all the facts were correct; the newspaper archives would have seen to that, but there was no suggestion of any warmth from the writer. It was unsigned of course so there was no way of knowing who the writer had been. However, Roderick was in the privileged position, as Editor of the newspaper to have commissioned the Obituary. He was clear enough in his letter to me to identify the author as *'a Lord, well known enough to us in this little backwater of the Principality as well as to others who would not have had the blessings of his benevolence.'* I thought that Roderick's wry turn of humour had got the better of his Editor's guard, but I could not suppress a smile. Roderick went on to say that he had remembered the obituary when we had met recently but had not wanted to rely on his memory and so had waited until after his search of the newspaper archives: Elwin Rees had died at home, in a house not too far from our old Village and still within the County he had served as Councillor, but sufficiently far to remain unobtrusive and not be readily recognised. During our youths, as I have said, I knew Rees, but unlike Will, who even then had had an interest in both 'closed' and 'open' Politics and who had pursued the players, I had never known the man in any personal sense. Roderick had sent me the notice out of supposed interest and because we had talked about his life when we had last met.

There was more to the letter. Roderick had declared an interest in the probate of the estate, which it seemed, had been substantial for that geographical location. The whole of the value of the estate, after death duties and taxes, and which included two houses had been placed in a Trust, as we knew. We also knew the administrators of the estate and the current use of one of the houses. For the other house and the financial balance, there were legal restrictions on disclosure which had been established by the benefactor and which required the written agreement of the Trustees for it to be divulged, as we also knew. However, continued Roderick, this Trust, like any other would be

146

required to present a report to Revenue and Customs. He had delayed writing until he had reviewed the last two reports. There was nothing startling: a regular expenditure towards the maintenance of the fabric of the properties, Council and Utilities payments and a regular payment for a part-time Caretaker. Roderick concluded by saying that as there were no irregularities (legal or illegal), it would be difficult to find out more and to be more helpful. He could only suggest, if we were still so inclined, that we work on convincing the Trustees of our sincerity but added that Trustees could be difficult to say the least.

I showed the letter to both Megan and Anna but it seemed that I failed to arouse an interest. I could understand this from Megan who considered this interest too consuming, even macabre, and wanted to see an end to it. But I had expected an inquisition from Anna. But she too seemed to set the matter aside and continued with her library work. That took up most of her days and with her evenings spent with Edward until late, we saw little of her. We were often in bed by the time she arrived home. They did not avoid us and Edward regularly came to dinner, but they were superficial affairs and sometimes difficult as we tried to avoid any allusion to the one major concern that had settled in all our hearts and minds. The weeks passed in this fashion until the owner of Edward's borrowed flat returned from his period overseas. He came to spend a few days with us but showed some anxiety which we took for concern for his own property. While Anna was at her studies, he took long walks across London as I had done so many years before. His discoveries, especially in the East End where I knew very little of its waves of immigration, became a topic of conversation between him and me but there was constantly a feeling that these conversations were also a means of filling time. One dark Wednesday afternoon when Megan had gone out and I was working and had drawn the curtains on the torrential raid outside, they came into the apartment, drenched. The Summer was ending as it had begun: cold, wet and blustery. It was some time before I joined them in the sitting room and saw them sitting close together; their faces seemed lit up from within and it took a while before they realised that I was present.

"You're lucky that you got home before the worst of this storm," I said.

"Yes, I suppose we are," said Edward.

"It wouldn't have mattered anyway," said Anna.

"You seem very pleased with yourselves," I said. "Is there a particular reason, or am I not to be told?"

"You are to be told," said Edward, "But we'd rather wait until Auntie Megan gets in. How long do you think she'll be?"

"Another couple of hours I should think. The underground will be dreadful and there won't be much of a chance of getting a taxi in this weather. Why?" I asked.

"No special reason," said Anna. "She'll be tired and need a drink by then, I should think. So I'll cook us something decent we've bought, to cheer us up."

I had a period of apprehension and concern; I could not prevent myself from asking, "Is there anything wrong? There's nothing wrong is there? That isn't why you're both here early?"

"Father, stop clucking," said Edward. "No, there's nothing wrong. Not at all. We just thought it would make a nice change if we cooked something good for dinner for you for once."

"Pamper you for a change," said Anna. "Now, is it too early for a drink?"

"Well it's earlier than I usually start."

"A Sherry then," said Anna. "That's not really a proper drink so it doesn't count."

"God forbid Sherry," I said, "Unless, that is, you've put a single vineyard, very dry, in the freezer. Otherwise, it's a drink you only have in for Vicars when they call. I wonder if anyone of that persuasion ever really liked it, do you think, or was it a duty to drink and pretend? There's a decent bottle of Hock in the fridge, I'll go that far. I'll get it."

"You stay where you are," said Edward. "I'll get it."

"There's something up, isn't there? You've rarely been so solicitous before. Why now?"

"Just a nice evening in," replied Edward, "With this atrocious weather and with the curtains drawn while we wait for the worker, before I say 'Goodbye for now' and go back to my hermitage. We'll have a glass and then we'll start cooking."

"Well, I suppose you'll tell me what it's all about when you're ready."

"Father, you're becoming a grumpy old man."

"Well I suppose it's something if you feel that I haven't quite got there yet."

"It's an inevitability, of course, but there's still hope."

The wine was nicely chilled and we sat making small talk while we enjoyed it. We were on our second glass with just one left for Megan when she arrived and hung her coat in the hallway.

"What a foul night. What's all this then, boozing in the afternoon while I'm not here to keep you in line."

"They've got something they are refusing to tell me but it seems we're celebrating with my best Hock anyway. Perhaps you can get some sense out of them. I can't," I said.

"Mum, we've saved you a glass. We're cooking tonight as a treat for you before Edward goes home, that's all," said Anna.

"And I don't believe a word of it," I said.

"What is it Anna?" asked Megan. "Is it something I should know about? You've not heard anything have you?"

"Nothing for you to be concerned about. Now relax while we prepare dinner. If you're too fussed, you can set the table," said Anna. "But stay out of the kitchen."

They left us alone and Megan looked at me, obviously concerned. All I could do was shrug my shoulders and say, "I have no more idea than you have. They'll tell us in their own good time I suppose."

"I don't like this secrecy; they must have heard something."

"It's possible, but I can't think what; there's no point in speculating. Tell me about your day."

Megan made to rise as she said, "I'm going to have it out with her. I refuse to be put in this position; I don't like it and she knows that."

"No my dear, don't. They'd tell us if it was something serious; they wouldn't let us worry, you know that. Anyway, they seemed happy when they came in and very buoyant, so there can't be bad news. Perhaps they've just decided to treat us, or say thanks, before Edward goes home as they say. Don't read anything more into it."

We passed the time in small talk and gossip until Anna came back and said, "Dinner will be served at seven thirty so if you want a proper pre-dinner drink you'd better have it now. We won't have one and to stop you wandering about, Edward will set the table."

It was clear that we were not welcome outside the sitting-room. As I poured our drinks, Megan said, "I wonder what they're going to surprise us with?"

We did not have long to wait until Edward called us to the dining room. I noticed a decent bottle of Margaux on the tray on the sideboard and that our first tastes had been poured in my finest glasses. When we were seated, Anna came in carrying our large serving plate and was followed by Edward with a vegetable tray. I looked at Megan and raised my eyebrows.

Anna said, "*Tournedos Rossini* with Field Mushrooms and Marrowbone sauce, *Dauphanoise* Potatoes and Baby Leeks, how's that? You may now taste the wine while Edward serves."

"Anna," said Megan, "I refuse to stay silent any longer. There's something up and I insist on knowing what it is."

"Mum, there's nothing. Just thanks for everything. So be patient and just enjoy yourselves. What shall we drink to? I know: the family as one. How's that?"

"The family then, but what's this *'as one'*?" I asked.

"Just as we've always been, that's all," said Edward. "True, isn't it?"

I could only nod my head and Megan stayed silent. As we ate and enjoyed our dinner, Anna told us of the progress she was making on her writing project. She said that she was finding it difficult drafting the path she wanted to follow as she wanted to introduce the heretical factor early in the work, but she was talking too fast and making too much of it all.

"I don't want a straight, flat, repetitive account of our Old Land – *The Land Of The Mighty Who Crossed The Sea And Vanquished The Irish* – nor about the beauty of it -- a *landscape* book with Old People in it to be carried on walks in our high mountains and narrow valleys where the people speak a strange language. Many others have done that, some good, some not so good, some bad; none has much meaning. I want to find the *meaning* of the tales for the people who heard them then – in their own time and in the place they knew. I want people to think that they are sitting around a fire, cold and tired and hungry perhaps – with a storm outside say - and imagine them looking to the arrival, when the weather's turned, at Easter or Harvest Time say, of the Troubadours and Gleemen who sang and spoke their verses on the *meaning* of the lives they had to live; and of the *other* Life, the one outside them, that had a different, secret, eternal meaning known only to the Gods and Goddesses whom they had to worship, *for their Souls' sake*. What did it mean to them? Were the stories then, and are they still, just an *escape*, or a *parable* and to be read as such? A *Commentary* on their lives, as in the Torah. Or was it just an *escapade* around the fire, to pass a harsh Winter's night? Nothing more than that; like our tales of Ghosts and Ghoullies in Midwinter. What was it like for *them?* I can't believe it was forgotten in the morning. I have to do much more reading; I can't see my way through."

"Your father had the same problem on his book: he couldn't see his way through either," said Megan. "I think that it's why he let it drift. He didn't work on it much towards the end, I think he got a bit tired of the whole thing".

"I can understand that; it must have been frustrating," said Anna. "I've felt it as well, so I talked it through with Edward." She turned to face him. You said, didn't you, that the Myths were based on devout Religious Belief, not especially Christian, often much older, which is why the Established Church held them to be heretical. You said, 'work on the conflict then: Good and Evil; Light and Dark; God and

150

Goddess'.

I noticed that Anna reached out to take Edward's hand and there were smiles on both their faces which could not be ignored. "Is that why you're so happy?" asked Megan.

"Yes, that too."

Megan was about to continue but Anna quickly said, "There's some more news."

Edward rose and collected our plates. "Let me get the desert first."

"Desert as well? I asked.

"Yes," said Edward, "But this one's bought prepared I'm afraid, though from a very good store in Piccadilly."

When he had cleared the table and brought in a *Pavlova* and a small bottle of Sauterne, a *Chateau D'Yquem* no less, Megan said, "Now I know there's something wrong. Don't pretend; I won't have it."

I already thought I knew what this charade was about but I addressed Megan and said, "Eat your desert first."

Megan tried but soon laid down her desert spoon. "I can't eat anymore, I'm too wrought up. You're wasting all this lovely food; you've brought on indigestion, the two of you. I don't know what game you think you're playing but you've gone too far. I want to know what you're up to."

Anna turned to Edward and said, "I suppose it's enough. You were right; this way doesn't work either. Bring it in then."

Edward went into the kitchen and returned with a bottle of champagne and four glasses, which he set on the table. He then took Anna's hand and said, "Megan, Dad, we must tell you that we were married this morning and we want you to be happy for us."

We were silent for several seconds until Megan gave a long cry and rose so quickly that she overturned her chair as she ran from the room. I understood: Anna had cut the last strand of the cord: first the search for her father and now this; all without any acknowledgement to Megan. They had each grown to independence without our realising it. Edward turned to Anna and said, "This is wrong then."

I rose and held them both close. "There's no right way unless you let your Mother plan things a year ahead. Eloping doesn't work either, it only estranges. You **must** allow the Mother time to shop for a hat. This is *'the family as one'* then. I congratulate you both, of course, and say that neither of you could have done any better; you've been lucky, both of you. Now Anna, I think you should go to your Mother; it's been a shock for her; this, on top of everything else. She'll be angry, but don't mind that; she still wants what's best for you. Take her shopping for our wedding present tomorrow and have a girls' tea or something."

Anna kissed me again and went to her mother. Edward and I were set to finish the wine.

CHAPTER 23

THE COMPLEXITY OF LIVING

The following morning was cloudy with a sharp, cold wind from the East that seemed directed at our front door from the Steppes. The cloud ceiling was low and threatening and but for the time of year would be expected to carry snow later in the day. If this was the autumn we should have, there was nothing for it but to look forward to winter. None of us was inclined to venture outside and so we lingered over breakfast, without making much of an effort at conversation. We were too drained after the drama of the previous evening: Megan and I had sat until the early hours with cups of tea, trying to support each other and resolve our thoughts and emotions; this excessive fluid intake had not helped ageing bladders either. So we had slept badly. Nothing had been resolved and Megan was still not reconciled to what she took as devious behaviour by her adopted daughter. In the early morning, she had continued to worry at what she had come to believe was her failure as a mother: *'me, a qualified Paediatrician and I don't understand my own daughter. She's cut me out of her life completely.'* I tried to reassure her and offer some support by saying that she was, nevertheless, not a child psychologist. But that seemed to make matters worse so I resisted further comments, even when, at one point she said that if Anna had been her real daughter, none of this would have happened. But this was clearly a search for comfort and not to be believed. It was not unexpected that her feelings of guilt surfaced: it was no longer what Anna had done to her, but what she had failed to do for Anna. For the few remaining, fitful hours of the night she believed herself condemned to purgatory. Nothing that I could say was of any help but I could not remain silent; she needed me to respond to her comments, so again I tried to provide the necessary reassurance but it became increasingly difficult until, at last, we both became comatose, felt drained and fell silent. But we were too restless to be still for long. We rose early, tired and heavy-eyed; we were soon followed by Edward and Anna who it seemed, had also not slept well.

Anna said, "We heard you clattering here in the kitchen and we're dying for a cup of tea too. Is there any going?"

Megan was silent but I said, "Yes. You can have tea or coffee. Then a full English if you're up to it."

"Tea first I think," said Edward, "Then we'll see."

It was a difficult breakfast; the offer of a 'full English' was declined. It seemed that not one of us could face sitting around the table while the breakfast was being cooked. At the same time, none of us wanted to be the first to rise from the table; so desultory conversation was made and I felt we were saved again by the delivery of our daily papers. I made some obvious comment such as, "Ah, there are the papers, I'll take them through to the living room," which broke the impasse and allowed me an escape. I rose from the table and Megan put the breakfast dishes into the dishwasher.

"Anna," said Megan, "We'd better get washed and dressed if we're going to make the shops early. It would be best I think, before the crowds and it will give us more time."

It had been a selfish, conscious ploy on my part but it seemed to have served the purpose of motivating Megan and Anna to pursue their arrangement to shop and that, shamefully, was a relief to me. I tried to engross myself in the newspapers but I could not focus on the news of what was happening to other people across the world. There would now be some hours when I would be alone with Edward and I wondered how we should fill the time. I could not recall any other period of our lives when I had felt such a difficulty in talking to my son. Even when his Mother had died and it had been a difficult time for us all as we struggled for some certainty in our lives, even then, in our grief and while withdrawn from all other contact, we had still been able to talk to each other without constraint; when I had suffered the consequences of an Animal Rights attack we were able to engage in banter and could converse on a serious but warmly affectionate level; and when he had had to face his own tragedy, his sister and I were the people he had considered before settling in his remote house looking out to sea.

I had drifted into this reverie with the papers strewn across the floor and I was asking myself what was so different now? Our circumstances, our time, relationships and their consequences, had wrought changes; none of them, alone, or at the time, had been weighed for their subsequent importance; living your life did not work like that; actions were taken in the present; consequences were in the future to be faced and dealt with in their own time. Some Physicists denied *Time's Arrow* believing it just a human construct, but I couldn't follow that, didn't understand it; there had to be *Cause and Effect* surely? For me, the childhood game of *Truth and Consequence* sat more easily; for me, one couldn't live in the future any more than in the past. Again I thought, would living in hindsight be an improvement, or make it any easier, or impossibly difficult? A fearful thought for any guilt-laden life. I cherished my memories, acknowledged the sorrows and accepted others without too much thought and grasped at the joys; it was no life otherwise. I had vowed that I would not live in the past nor in hindsight. I would try to embrace my son's action and rejoice for him and for Anna; but there were still some questions I wished to ask him.

I was in this pensive mood when Edward, already dressed, came into the lounge and noted the newspapers on the floor.

"Nothing of interest in the world then? It can't be all that uninteresting surely? Something must be happening. Or is something else bothering you?"

"I was just wondering, again, whether everything would be much better if we all lived our lives in hindsight."

"What a dreadful thought."

"Yes. I came to that conclusion also."

"What you need is a good walk, then a pub lunch. On me for a change."

I could so easily have cried off a walk, which I did less and less of at that time. Also the weather was not attractive but if the rain relented, it would help both of us to re-assess our lives and our relationship. It was worth that much effort at least so I said, "You've done us well enough already."

"In some ways I'll accept your judgement. But perhaps not in others?"

"No, I'll not go down that road with you; I won't live your life for you."

"Come on then, get dressed. Aunt Megan's out of the shower, I think, and she's planning the assault with Anna. So get dressed."

"Yes. Just one thing: give Megan some space and time, will you? She loves you and wants what's best for you; and Anna is a great deal in her life, in so many ways, so it's been a shock."

"I know, I understand now; it was wrong of us to do it this way. But once we'd decided to be married, we couldn't deal with having to argue a case for it: it would expose both of us again, you see. And we wanted to surprise you with something wonderful at this time."

"So long as you are both sure, nothing else matters, you know," I said. "You must remember that."

"Yes. What a conundrum: no one can believe that previous generations could possibly have loved as much as you do now; nor wanted to make love as you do. Though of course, if they hadn't, you wouldn't be here to do the wondering, would you? Nor can they be believed to have cared as much. Isn't that tragic? Now get dressed."

Megan and Anna left some time before us and as I pulled the door to I asked, "Where would you like to walk?"

"Let's go to the Fields if that's not too much."

"No, that's fine," I said. "It's not uneven, which is the worse terrain when you have to wield a stick. Come on then."

We crossed the road and walked away from the houses. Although easy underfoot the climb up the hill was trying and my hips were aching before we reached the top. We paused and sat on a bench to look down over London.

"It's quite a view from up here, isn't it?" said Edward.

"Yes. And it's always been one I've loved, whatever the weather: sometimes, you can sit in the dry here, even in sunshine, and watch the rain being driven in sheets along the line of the river. It's done a great deal for me over the years. I used to come up here quite often once you know."

"When was that?"

"When I needed to tailor my mood to the weather. I lived just down below, not far from our house in fact, and I was pushing myself to overcome an earlier mistake and get my first degree. It was a haven – if an open hillside can be said to be a haven: in any case, I could isolate myself with my thoughts and nobody bothered me. I was very reluctant to meet with anyone. As I said, I thought of it as my haven, I didn't want the intrusion of another – I was happier with my own company. It's paradoxical you know Edward, but you can guard your own solitude more surely in a city of 5 million people, say, than you can in your cottage.

"I did bring Megan here though, on her first ever visit to London, just to show her that there were views other than valleys, coal mines and tips. I thought I could bring her out of our past so she should not succumb to *parochialism*. Snobbishness, of course, and very foolish."

"Didn't she appreciate it then?"

"The view, she did, yes. At least she was kind enough to say so. I was wrong, I know now; and she was right to respond by showing me Cardiff Docks. In any case, she was more interested in the poor souls who spent their evenings in the shrubbery, with nowhere to go, no money and often cold and wet; just hoping to find some comfort and love for a few hours in another's arms. I tried to help if I had a few coppers but most of the time I was pretty short myself, with rent to pay and books to buy.

"It all seems so long ago now; it's another world I lived in then. But I can't dismiss it. It's still imperative.

"I suppose they still congregate here, but I'm out of touch now; I wouldn't recognise any of them, wouldn't want to and nor would they I dare say, if they're still alive; I don't suppose they are, given the lives

156

they led. Here's an interesting piece of Human Behaviour for you: if you're down and out (shorthand words), you never look at faces; you seem to accept that you're *diminished,* and you may become belligerent as a reaction. The converse is true too; and that's a *diminishing* action – asserting your confidence and dominance. And it makes the difference very considerable.

"So while I used to sit here, I came to understand something of Will's care of Rhodri, Anna's biological father: his commitment to another less endowed. Laudable of course, but it's difficult not to also read a domination into it. Inevitable I suppose. Will and I had drifted apart at that time, for no good reason I can remember other than intolerance and indolence, but I missed him then; still do, very much; especially his dry appraisal of events; and I miss his *irreverence.* There's too much of that now, so it means too little. Then, it mattered. He's left me a gap that's not been filled.

"Anyway I don't walk as much as I used to."

"Well you can't can you, with that stick?"

"It doesn't help, certainly. I could do more than I do but that time has gone and we're not the same people now as we were then; our world has moved on, as they say, and brought its changes. Sometimes I think that's a pity: we leave too much behind; *baggage* they call it, don't they? I would call it 'lives'. But I won't have it any other way; I find, more and more, that I wouldn't want to go back to it. The worst question of all is, '*If you had your time over again... ...?*'"

"Hindsight too dominant?"

"As you say."

We were silent for some minutes as the wind freshened a little. Then Edward said, "What was he really like?

"Who?"

"Uncle Will."

I paused, then said, "In a word, *'Difficult'.*"

"Is that all?"

"No, of course not. No-one can be dismissed in one word."

"What then?" Edward asked.

"He was a difficult man, not at ease with himself: few are, if they ever think about it at all, but he was rather extreme. He was cursed with too penetrating a mind, I think. He could be warm and funny one moment, and hard and uncompromising the next. He often said to me about Science: '*Knowledge, of itself, is unimportant; Understanding is*' That used to draw some blood, I tell you. If it's a summary you want, I should say that he was a very clever, insightful man who was unsure of himself and who, somewhere, lost his way. He thought he knew what he wanted, but when it was within reach he conspired to lose it. Oh, not in any deliberate way; that would have been much against his nature; but in ways that he could avoid blame for the outcome. It was ever so, even from the time he fixed his mind on editing the school magazine."

"Did he edit it?"

"No. He deliberately threw the chance away; he had a habit of doing that; especially if he thought he would not succeed or not achieve at whatever project he wished to engage with. In this particular case, he used the one matter that ensured the staff would not accept his view."

"How's that?"

"Oh, like a callow youth he denigrated all that had gone before and said that he intended to oversee a more adult and mature production."

"By which I assume he meant 'sex'?"

"Yes; mostly. He said that he would *determine the female view,* a la Kinsey. He had already been called to task over that.

"I remember asking him why he had taken up the banner for the female. He said, 'because *She*'s much older than *He* is.' He wouldn't elaborate, though I asked him many times. I thought it was all part of how he had worked hard at playing the intellectual bohemian caught in a waste-land."

"Tell me about it. I never felt I knew him."

"He was not ever an easy man to know. I like to think that I was one of his closest friends − from childhood anyway, but there were times when he shut me out too. Megan, I think, was his nemesis in that sense; she broke through; but perhaps her father even more so − he was held in high regard I do know. It's a long story, for another time perhaps, but there was a particular case that involved our Society's hypocrisy − he abhorred that in anyone. In this case, it concerned the damnation of some juvenile practices in the ferns on the mountain. Or at least, that was one of the triggers he used. In more than one sense, he was his own worst enemy."

"But clever?"

"Oh yes; very clever. But more than that, very insightful."

"There's much of that in Anna," said Edward. "She detests hypocrisy."

We both fell silent. I had no idea what he was thinking, but for myself, I was tired of raising the dead. I turned away from the memories of Will and said, "I first met your mother down there as well, when she first visited London."

"Yes, you told me. And how you dug a hole for yourself when you asked if they were paying by the hour for their beds in Sussex Gardens."

I laughed. "An attempt at conversation from an inept 'Big City Man'. They didn't know that Sussex Gardens was a red light district; in any City you find it near a rail terminus. And I assumed that the rugby boys at home, having travelled to Twickenham for International games against the 'English Foe', would have told them; a natural assumption I believed. But no, and Megan has never let me forget it either. I've been cautious ever since about repartee, throw - away lines and aphorisms. I decided that they weren't worth the transient sense of superiority they are supposed to give."

"You learnt early on then?"

"Quite early, yes. What about you?"

"I have never been quick enough with the repartee. All the 'spur – of – the – moment responses' I think of only happen when it's all over and the audience has left."

I laughed.

"Do you think that's our scientific training?" asked Edward. *"Caution, dear boy; caution! Don't be flamboyant!"*

I smiled and said, "The trick in repartee, is to remember what you would like to have said and save it for future use when you can shock to best advantage. What do you think of this view of our capital city then?"

"It's as good as many and better than most" said Edward. "And it has a river which all great cities must have: from the Thames here to the Loire, the Ganges and the Yellow River and the Mississippi; and at the end, the Styx."

"That doesn't tell me much about you, except you've changed; you're more introspective; much more guarded."

"I've grown older, that's all. Some of the enthusiasm has gone."

"What of the view then?"

"Oh, it's fine enough but I find it difficult to relate to landscapes in the sense you'd like me to."

"What sense is that?"

"Pleasure in it for itself, I suppose: an artist's impression, whether Constable or van Gogh. I understand that stance and I can understand the pleasure it gives but I can't let it do that for me; I can't relate to it like that," he said.

"What then?" I asked.

"I call on my education and training I suppose; I retreat. These Professors don't know the damage they do to young minds."

"Explain."

"When I look at the world I live on, my questions are, 'why is it like this? What's caused these hills and valleys? What's underneath them

159

and how old are they?' It's the way I am supposed to make a living. Or was."

"You blame your Geology then?" I asked. "It's your excuse for being uncivilised?"

"No. It's just a means of escape; we all find them, don't we, one way and another? We escape through our interest in structure and function; and of course, time. You and me, both: Biology and Geology. Geology just happens to be what I'm good at it, that's all; I have a three-dimensional mind, so my escape is easier."

"You're very fortunate; I hope you understand that."

"Oh, I do. We've not talked like this for a long time, have we?" asked Edward. "It's been too long: we've both made too much time to think about other things; and we've looked back; we have thought of our lives in retrospect, if not in hindsight – I do understand the difference. So I want you to understand too; I want you to understand something of me, as I am now; it might help us, you see: you and me; we're both very similar.

"There's no lack of appreciation, Dad; there's too much, if anything – I have to guard against it. Planet Earth is so beautiful, and we don't deserve it; I don't, at least, I see that. I am easily overwhelmed by it; and I can't live on it and also deny it now, can I? Many do of course, without a thought: they exploit it for its riches and they use it as their shit-house for their waste. I can't do that and I would be less of a Man if I denied it; so I distance myself instead, in order to cope; I look for the *mechanics* of it; I go deeper, below the surface temptation – that's one way; the other is to embrace it all; so, in my way, I pretend to understand. But I envy the Painters, and the Poets who have to face it full-front. And it's your fault, Old Man, because you taught me how to look. I would love to believe in *Gaia* [13], and that She'll save us from ourselves. But I can't, because the Goddess [25] will tire of us and our profligacy, and we will ruin it, in the end, as we do most things – there's your *Female* for you, and Her age. She'll take Her Third Form then: *The Layer-Out Of Man* – one good Uppercut! Is that because our *Intellect* has evolved faster that our *Sense?* You're the Biologist, answer me that!"

"I'm afraid I can't," I said; "Not sensibly enough to satisfy either of us in any case."

"So then," said Edward, "I cope mostly because I avoid the obvious and have less involvement with the surface appearances: it's less of an argument that way. Besides, that's just one of our Preacher God's little tricks anyway; and too *superficial* for me.

"This is *Romanticism* Father, and I blame you for it. You've made

160

Romantics of your children: me *and* your daughter Nia. But, to finish, the Planet is in Her Third Age I've found. Do you know the Ages?"

"No; tell me."

"*Mother, Bride* and *Layer-out of Man.* She thinks nothing of us. So I escape to try to *understand* Her trick; I want to know *what it all means.* It's like what Anna talked about over dinner last night: *what does it all mean?* I expect you dismissed what she said, as I used to; that's a pity, because she talks sense (*most* of the time). And I, too, always want to know 'how' and 'why.'"

"That's not always bad so long as you continue to understand that there are other joys to experience," I said.

"Yes, so I've been told. We pride ourselves on our Intellect. But all that means is, that we kill things off faster. The only thing I'd *really* like to know and understand before I go, rather like you I think, is the Human Mind – is there a purpose to it? Or has it just evolved to trouble us? I don't mean the Human Brain – of course there's a purpose to that; but what about the Mind? I guess you have to be a *Committed Religionist* to know that, and I don't have the tools for it: your neglect again, Father. The *Religionists* say '*It's not for us to know God's Purpose*'. My reply to that is, '*What nonsense. We should know the* Construct *we've Created.*' That's the only Creation in Town in any case.

"All this confession is too florid; forget it please."

"Tell me how you see this view then," I said.

"You bring us back to Earth. It's a large syncline," said Edward. "Do you know what a syncline is?"

"No. Educate me."

"It's a U-shaped dip in the rock strata usually because the rocks around it have been upraised by geological forces deep in the earth's crust. The Earth was very violent at one time to give us our seas, rivers, and lakes – and our landmass. The original rock formations may be exposed by rain, winds or rivers but in synclines are usually covered by deposits like chalk (which can turn to marble) or clay (which can turn to slate). Here in the London Basin we have clay which overlies the chalk of the North and South Downs, and it actually stretches from Marlborough in the West into the North Sea in the East where it joins the Paris Basin. It dates from the Cretaceous Period, about 40 to 60 million years ago, about when the Alps were being lifted and Dinosaurs were holding on. It was originally all tidal, hence the chalk, until the sea retreated with the Ice Age and the Thames moved south. Enough, or do you want more."

"Enough for now. I'll stay with my view."

"But doesn't its age give you a feeling of Earth's permanence; and our individual transience? "

"Of course it does, but for me the present intrudes too much."

"The surface changes," said Edward, "And things change. Everyone knows it as Evolution, thanks to Darwin. It's inevitable, in any case as things cool down: you don't need a *Choir Master*."

We were silent for a while again, each with his thoughts. Then I said, "Don't isolate yourself; that's not the way out."

"No. I've come to know that," he replied.

"What about Anna's work; will she pursue it?" I asked.

"Most certainly, one way or another."

"Yes. She's a very determined woman," I said.

"She's more than that; she's intellectually stronger than I am - her discipline I suppose. But I'm not concerned about that. What worries me more is how focussed she can be, how exclusive. She gives the impression of having no views, fixed or otherwise, but all the time she's analysing her options. Once she's decided, you won't change her mind. And there's no point in arguing with her; she's already rehearsed all the arguments and far more cogently than you could. Yes, she'll work on the book, if she's given the time; if not, then she'll leave an outline for somebody else. And she'll take her treatment, more for our benefit than her own I believe. I have a strange feeling that she thinks the outcome is of little consequence, though she won't admit it to anyone."

"Not even to you?"

"Least of all to me. Dad, I do love her very much. I did, even as a child. I looked up to her: the kids saw it and teased me. So, it's not escapism, nor rebound. I have recognised that danger of course, but I'm sure that it isn't."

"And her? Does she love you?"

"I believe so. I don't know all about her yet, but for me it is different, and different from my last time. People say that they fall in love. Well we, we fell in *need* with each other a long time ago, as children; each was the other's half. What there is now came after. I don't know if you can understand that; I hope you understand and I hope Aunt Megan will, if we give her some time."

"Oh, Megan will be happy, once she gets over the fact that you presented her with a *fait accompli*. You were rather foolish there."

"I know, and I'm sorry about that. But we were happy and we wanted to give you what we thought would be a wonderful surprise. Bad move. But Megan'll find it harder still unless she knows that you welcome it."

"What do you mean?" I asked.

"You don't much like Anna, do you?"

"That's nonsense. She's your wife and she's part of those I've loved."

"Yes. But it doesn't therefore follow that you *like* her, does it? She's not your style, too hard for your taste I think."

I could not engage and I said, "I think we've sat for long enough. We should move, and I don't know about you but I'm getting slightly cold."

"Don't avoid me Father; you have a habit of doing that – putting up walls when you don't wish to be engaged, when you wish to avoid a confrontation. Is it a Welsh trait? I've heard that Will seemed wedded to the gambit. Well I'm not going to let you do it to me any more. Father, I'm grown now and I've chosen a wife. I'm no longer going to let you shield me like a child, nor set yourself up as an *eminence grise* who is my father, but not for engagement. You don't like her and I want to understand why."

"Old age I expect; inflexibility again."

"No, not you, you can't get away with that glib comment. You pride yourself on understanding people, but you sometimes seem too blind; you shut your eyes to them too much. In any case you won't engage with others and explain yourself unless it suits you. Dad, you're my father, and I love you; I always have, but sometimes I can't *like* you. You pin out people like specimens for dissection but you insist that you yourself are 'off limits'. *Nolle me tangere* [14]. I'm sorry; I've said too much but I hope you understand why: people want to understand you too. Especially those who love you. So be honest with me: tell me the truth. I can cope with that, if *you* tell me."

"Can you? That's often a dangerous assumption, lad. One can't guarantee that the truth is palatable you see. You could be mistaken, you know. It's possible."

"I understand that too, but it will be *my* mistake. In any case, if I'm to be told the truth, I'll take it from someone I love, before I take it from others."

I nodded. We were silent for some time. I wondered at his train of thought. For myself, I was confused: I did not want this distance between us, nor would I risk estrangement; I did not want to wound with my truth; I blamed him for noticing my wounds and my defences, the barriers I had imposed on myself many years ago, as everyone does; now they were showing and I did not want to be analysed by anyone, certainly not by my son. It would be easy enough to engage the pretences of childhood, the little white lies we had used, for convenience's sake; or simply lie as an adult would for an easier life; or just prevaricate; but it would be seen for what it was: social cowardice, an avoidance of the intimacy that I had always professed to hold dear: to him and to his sister. But more than that, I would not have been honest to myself and he would never forgive that: the truth is what he had asked for and what I would have refused to give him. I loved him too much to fail him in that.

He was right: I felt no warmth toward Anna; I found a thick carapace every time I tried to get close, one that I found I couldn't breach. In all probability, the fault was mine; I was becoming too old to analyse my likes and dislikes and these days I made little effort; it was so much easier to stay within the comfort of those I knew well, with an occasional foray to acquaintances. But Anna was now part of my family and deserved my efforts to understand her: there seemed to be nothing between us, no recognition, no warmth, no sign of future friendship, not even dislike. There was an emptiness that I was unused to. And having been made to face it by my son, I felt a chill for him.

"You're asking a great deal of me," I said. "Perhaps more than you know."

"I do know that; but it's what you taught us."

I nodded. We stayed silent until he said, "I still want to know."

"Let's walk around the ponds then and back to the pub. I'll try to explain as we walk."

We rose and started downhill. I could have made my feelings known with just a few words: *for all of her abilities, she's too cold for you.* But that would have been too harsh.

164

CHAPTER 24

INTIMACIES

As we walked, the air turned colder and there was a dampness which seemed to seek out my bones. Because of the mood I was in, I recognised that creep of age. It did not often happen these days, but each time it did, the realisation of mortality was less welcome. Edward walked bareheaded in the fashion of the young (even in the rain) and with his jacket open. He did not prompt me further but I recognised the barrenness of my conversation and I sought for a way to relate my feelings and explain to my son, who or what his father was, so that he should know me and take my words as they were meant.

"You know, none better I suspect, that among the most imperative of my traits, I have been blessed – or cursed, the jury's still out trying to resolve that problem (as they were with Megan's father all his life) – with some measure of insight into the human character. You never knew Megan's father. Well, nor did I, but I've heard a great deal about him at one time and another. He had the gift of total recall: things that had happened to him many years before were as clear as the things that happened yesterday; and he could tell you the day of the week, the time of day, the date and what the weather had been like. He held that it was a curse he had to bear and he came to acknowledge it and accept it. I sometimes wish that I had his fortitude, but we live within our own skins."

So we walked in silence as I tried to frame my answer. Edward must have thought that I was attempting to avoid confronting the issue for he said, "We love each other, believe me, and have, ever since we were children; you must believe that Dad. But now we recognise there's a greater *need* too; for each of us. That's the difference between *now* and *then*. It makes it a very much stronger binding."

"'Need' is not a good basis for a life together: it can break too easily. But, I concede, it may be a necessary factor in human relations; *yes* I do understand; I've had the experience too. From what you know of me, you'd expect that, wouldn't you?"

Edward replied, "Yes. But there's truth too: sometimes I feel that I will never really know Anna – she's too *ethereal* at times. Is that a funny word for her? A different plane, anyway – more *abstract;* her Philosophy, I expect. Much of her is a mystery to me."

"Much always will be, son, but you'll come to know enough of each other in time I expect. I hope that it'll be what you expect and what you hope for."

"I hope so. She's extremely clever too. I don't think I'm a slouch, but she often leaves me standing."

"Perhaps just a different intellect," I replied.

"Perhaps. Did you know her father?"

"You don't mean Will of course. No, I can't say that I did; he never intruded in my life. I must have seen him at school when we were kids, when Will stood up for him when he was being bullied. But I have no recollection of him at all."

"Was he clever?"

"He could well have been for all I know. Will believed he was; but he was what the mothers and grandmothers and Chapel Deacons called 'very slow witted'; a consequence of a difficult birth it seems. There was also a scandal, some childish male bonding and the family moved away from our village. Megan can tell you more, I'm sure, if you really want to know; but she may not want to resurrect matters just at this time. I don't know if Anna knows anything of it or not. Lord Mostyn may have told her something of him, but I'd advise letting it rest as well. She may come across something in her searches; if she does, then would be the time to say what you can."

"I would feel I'm living a lie."

"I understand that but there's no great advantage in raising it before then. You see, we all do keep our secrets; it eases the journey."

"And the mother? Anna's mother?"

"There, I know even less – which is nothing. I don't know if anyone does; perhaps Megan does, I don't know. In any case as I say, best to let it rest."

"Anna would not agree."

"No, I dare say she wouldn't. Whatever she finds out, I just hope that it doesn't hurt. Her or you."

"That would not be her criterion for judging."

"No. I can believe that."

We walked a little further towards the road and the pub. I was looking forward to a beer and a sandwich and sitting away from the cold for a while.

"But all this is of little consequence anyway," he said. "You see, I've come to feel that I've been solitary long enough; apart from anything else, I'm lonely now and I need her. I don't know, but probably more than she needs me. So why can't you like her?"

I did not reply; I could understand him all too easily. I had suffered all that he had suffered when his mother had died; and I, too, had had to find my way through it. There was even a residual guilt that my actions had led to consequences for others I had held dear at the time; but it mattered not a jot. I could not counsel him in his affairs; such relations are too personal, too fundamental, to try to explain to others. I could only hope that he would have a rewarding period of comfort. But he had asked a question and I could not refuse an answer.

"For all her ability, I think that she is too *empty* for you," I said.

Edward was silent for a while, then said, "It's difficult to believe that people swim in those ponds on Christmas Day. But I suppose that they get some satisfaction from their masochistic activities; after all, we're all masochists at heart."

CHAPTER 25

THE WAY FORWARD

We knew that Megan and Anna would make a day of it, shopping with determination, so Edward and I had a leisurely lunch. It was warm in the pub and at last we were easier with each other. We ordered our drinks and each had a Ploughman's. A few people I knew or recognised, retired people mostly, passed through and gave a greeting, but we were not disturbed. I asked Edward what his and Anna's intentions were since her treatment could not be postponed indefinitely if there was to be any chance of benefit; or at least of moderating the progress of her condition.

"We're aware that we don't have all the time we would like, so any honeymoon will be short. Anna has suggested that we have another day or two with you if you can put up with us and then go down to my house in Wales for a while."

"Stay as long as you like, you're welcome, you know that. Under normal circumstances we'd be going to Spain now anyway and you could have a run of the place. But things are not normal, are they? Megan won't hear of Spain until things are settled, I'm sure."

"No. We must move forward one way or another."

"Go to Spain then; it'll be warmer than here at least."

"Thank you, but no. We did think of it but Anna fancies the Atlantic gales and the wild sea; it more suits her mood at present she says. She says she has things to do, though she can't, or won't, tell me what."

"Is her writing on her mind?"

"No, not that. Yes, that of course but there's something else she's after. She's taken to using the word *'maelstrom'* though I don't know what it refers to. And she wants to run the house, clean it up and set it to rights. She's convinced it will be a hovel."

I smiled and said, "And is it?"

"It's not that bad. But I expect it could do with a bit of a tidy, because I'm not obsessed by it; she'll find enough to do. She wants to see us there together and I do too. Understandable I suppose."

"Perfectly understandable. What about after that?"

"Things are fluid but obviously can't stay like that. She must have a deadline to work to and she's arranged to see her Consultant tomorrow to fix some dates. Then we'll go."

I was immediately on my guard. "Does Megan know this? You must stop shutting her out."

"I expect she's being told today. It's the main reason Anna agreed to go shopping. I've told you she works everything out."

"And you were deputed to tell me. This is not the way to do it you know. Megan will hate being excluded and won't thank either of you for it."

"Neither of us is enjoying this secrecy either. But it's Anna's way of coping; you can understand that, surely?"

I nodded, but he would not leave the matter and continued, "But what about *her* then Dad? Why is it you're against her?"

"That's much too strong. But you'll want me to be honest: it's just that I find it very difficult to know her. My fault I expect; I should like to be closer but I feel a difference I can't cross. And I would like to, so it's frustrating. No doubt it will pass with time."

"I hope so, and soon."

"Yes. So do I."

"Truly?"

"Of course. I don't like a distance from people any more than the next chap."

"I'm glad. But know this, Dad: it must be us two first now, for us, mustn't it? You accept that? Both of you? We want you close with us, especially now, but we also need some isolation. No, that's not the right word; we need 'a separateness', not distance, so Anna and I can come to know each other. Do you understand?"

Again I nodded. He continued, "We shan't be far away; you and Megan must understand; and you must believe us; even believe *in* us. You Dad of all people, must understand what we're facing together; what we're trying to do for each other."

For a moment I was angry with him for again calling up the traumas of my own life but that was being unfair: he did it because he loved me and wanted me to know that he was living through something of what I had had to face: the loss of a love and the search for another. I felt a great love for him then, as flesh of my flesh. It was not often any more, that I wondered what his mother would have understood of him; but much as I could relate to his decisions, I also feared for him – such is the burden of parenthood. So I replied in a more distant fashion than I intended.

"Besides all that, you're not being honest or open with us."

He smiled broadly and said, "Guilty on all counts of course. But forgive us our failures; we've not lived as long as you have."

"There is no need to invoke the generational differences."

"Look Dad, you will know of any decisions we make, as soon as they are made. That's fair surely; we're not children any more."

"No, indeed, as you keep saying. But you can't use that escape with your parents: they have a right to know how you see your future."

"You mustn't over-egg it Dad; rationally, you know that you have no right at all other than what you're given. You gave us life, but it's *our* life so don't be too much of a tribal elder. It shall not be like it was for me last time."

In the end I said, "So, you were deputed to talk to me. Is that also the real reason behind this walk?"

"Yes, and no. I was to take the opportunity to talk to you but I could have done that at home."

"Machinations again. Anna's idea or yours?"

"Mine, mostly. I hoped that we could enjoy a walk and talk as we used to; we haven't done it for such a long time. My fault really, but I excused it all by saying that we all had lives to live and things to do. But now I've committed to Anna I wanted to come back to you too. I feel that I've been away from you too long. I'm sorry if I'm being – what was the word Uncle Will used to use when he thought people were behaving badly?"

"Untutored."

"Right then – untutored. I'm sorry if I've distressed you."

"Thank you, but it's waiting on Megan that disturbs me more at the moment."

"Anna will bring her round I'm sure."

"Of course she will, in the end; and she will be happy for you and Anna. But I think I'll have a stiff drink before I'm alone with her."

"Have you finished your drink? Do you want another?"

"No more thanks. We'd better get back; with luck they will have spent enough and be at home waiting for us."

"I doubt that."

CHAPTER 26

SHORT ODDS

We left the pub and as we turned towards home, he said, "Would you mind retracing our steps a little? Or is it too much for you?"

"Round the ponds again and back will be far enough, if you insist."

It was clear that there were other things on his mind; the slate was not yet clean but I could not anticipate whatever matters he still wished to say. We walked in silence for some minutes until he said, "I've been trying to think of the best way of telling you this."

"Whatever it is, straight out is best; there's no other way really. Prevarication is always unhelpful."

"Yes. Well then, here goes. Anna and I will not give you grandchildren. I'm sorry to be the bearer of bad news."

"I think I understand why but you'd better tell me I suppose."

"I've no doubt you can guess. There will be no children because Anna will not risk passing on her genetic condition."

"I thought as much. It is a risk but it's not inevitable, you know."

"We know that, but as far as Anna is concerned, the chances are less than even and she says that those odds are too high. She is not prepared to condemn our descendants and future generations to the possibility. I told you that she works out all the odds."

He tried to lighten the news. "She's quite a Mathematician. She'd make a successful Bookmaker at the races."

"And you?"

"I'm sorry for you and Megan; we know how disappointed you'll be. Especially Megan."

For no apparent reason, I said, "Christmas will be the worst time."

"Well then, the other children will have to fill the gaps," he said, trying to make light of it again.

"No. I meant what about you?"

"It's not as I would choose of course; I should like a child; for the coming together of the families as well. Our toast: *The Families As One*. But I'll take Anna on her terms and she's adamant. I've agreed with her, naturally."

"You may have agreed and I can understand that for any number of reasons. But how do you feel about it?"

"I've told you; I've agreed."

"That's not an answer to my question."

171

"It's my answer to your question. I'll say no more. I won't be unfaithful."

"You can keep the answer to yourself, of course, but I believed that we had more than a father – son relationship, even though it's slipped a bit. If you don't wish to confide, then there's not much more to be said. We can cut back to the house through here. I'm a little tired anyway."

"There's a seat over there. I must tell you some more things."

"If it's of you and Anna, it's not necessary. You must enjoy each other in your fashion, for the time you have."

"We shall. But it's not about us; at least not about Anna and me."

"What then?"

"You only know a little of my life when I worked for the oil company. I wrote to you about the searches and the breaks in Indonesia. When you were recovering in hospital after that bomb attack from the Animal Rights people, and we thought we'd lost you, I told you about Jacqueline."

"Yes. You needn't go over it again. It can't help."

"You'd have liked her." He smiled and said, "She was warm and open. Much more your type. Mine too; then, at least. I've changed since then, and she may be the reason for it. In any case, she's there all the time for me; my life works around her memory."

"I wish I'd known her, then."

"So do I."

"Does Anna know this?"

"Some of it. Enough anyhow. She knows what Jacqueline meant to me and there's no jealousy."

I wondered to what extent that was true: one could be jealous of the living and that was resolvable; to be jealous of the dead took you into another dimension. I thought of the Blessing for the War Dead: '*For they will not grow old as we grow old*'. That is a terrible memory to overcome.

Edward continued with tears in his eyes: "How much do you know of Indonesia?"

"Very little; that too seems to have passed me by, by and large."

"Then let me tell you something about it; this seems a time for tales. I told you I was at sea when we heard of the new troubles on her island and the slaughter of so many people. President Suharto came to power in a military coup in 1965 when between half a million and a million Indonesians were wiped out within a year. But he was a darling of the West, offering support against the spread of the 'Red Devil' from the North, and building a huge market for arms sales as well as being a massive source of profits from the exploitation of the country's natural resources. But Suharto was not so popular at home; his rule over 200 million people was maintained by brutal repression. The economy expanded with the help of the Multinational Companies, which he courted, but it was too much, too quickly. It couldn't last; economic slump was gradually approaching.

"This is sounding like a 'Foreign Affairs' tutorial that Civil Servant Gwen would understand. But I have read about it because it mattered to me. And no less so with the passage of time. The findings of the UN Development Programme were embargoed; they were not reported at the time, because they showed that nearly 15% of the population would not reach their 41st birthday; 38% lacked access to safe water; 15% lived on less than a dollar a day – Malaysian equivalent dollars, not American; and half a million children would die before their first birthday. The people were starving; can you imagine a *regime* that starves children to death? It is easy to see that a people who were suffering so much repression and exploitation would explode in anger."

"You do know a great deal about it."

"No, not really; some, that's all – but enough to matter. When I first knew that I was going to drill for oil in Oceania, I started to read about it; I wasn't sure that I wanted to perpetuate the exploitation."

"But you did."

"Yes. I believed that the exploration rights were fair in the end, and they would help their economy."

"Has that happened?"

"Some. Not enough yet but it might come. And there's more. Even before the world knew of the riots and the fall of President Suharto who had ruled his people without mercy for 32 years, Indonesia was a lost country: the currency, the Rupiah had effectively collapsed and the costs of basic foods had rocketed. Early on I tried to get Jacqueline to persuade her parents to leave, at least temporarily; you can understand why. But they wouldn't hear of it; they were needed even more then they said, and that was undeniably true. And Jacqueline wouldn't leave them behind. The unrest spread to Solo, Medan, Surabaya and eventually the capital Jakarta. The people were starving, as I said, literally so, and students and young people took to the streets. It escalated into riots when four students from the University of Trisakti were shot dead by Suharto's thugs. There was no controlling it after that: there was a blood lust that had to be satisfied. It became a pogrom directed principally against the ethnic Chinese – they were easily identified after all; they were ostensibly integrated and not allowed Chinese signs and the language was frowned on – but in reality they lived separate lives. But the pogrom became more general, against anyone who looked or seemed different or behaved differently or were of an 'unacceptable religion' in a Moslem world, meaning Christianity in general and Catholicism in particular – the Devil's creed, as they believed; or at least professed to believe. And I have to go along with them: Religion has caused more deaths, more sorrow and destruction and hidden behind more home-grown 'Martyrs' made into Saints than the whole of Birth, Death, Sex and Politics put together. And has caused more wars. I can't help feeling that Religious Dogma is the most invidious and evil of Humanity's edifices; and Rome is one of the greater murderers. And I ask myself, *Why?*

"Anyway, that's for another time. The men were butchered and the women gang raped, mostly by the military, and left for dead. The rape cases were under-reported, in the belief that the knowledge would further inflame the situation and lead to continuing instability. There was also the legal fact that the Criminal Code would only consider penetration by a male sexual organ as constituting rape: the use of other sharp or blunt objects were not regulated by the Criminal Code. Also, the Indonesian Criminal Code specifically stated that a rape victim had to provide witnesses and evidence for the accusation, however traumatised the victim. It would have been better to be dead. All pregnant ladies were killed horrifically: I won't embellish, but more horrifically than I hope you can imagine. But one or two young women – would-be mothers – actually survived; and wished they were indeed dead. And no babies were born in the populace for two years."

"Leave it son. This serves no purpose now."

He nodded, but still continued, his face set in a determination I had not seen before, such that I felt excluded and dared not intrude on his memories. It was as if now that he had started he was unable to stop. I doubted he had spoken of it before: it seemed a necessary form of catharsis and it did not matter if I was there or not.

"Well, all that was the legacy of Suharto, and you can't *'Just Leave It'*. At the time, I tried to fly there but it was impossible; there were no flights available, in or out. So I flew to Singapore and from there went by sea. A round-about route so it was four days before I managed to reach the hospital where Jacqueline's father had been based and the compound where they had lived. The 'Western –style' houses had been razed, and it was deserted. All the patients and all the staff at the Hospital had been butchered and there were corpses everywhere, rotting and covered in flies. This was blood-lust on an uncontrolled scale. Paramedics had arrived and were trying to do what they could but it wasn't much other than burial. For a while I wandered about feeling lost. Then somehow, someone, a Malay, recognised me and took me to

174

shelter. He told me that the family and the other hospital staff had been taken into the jungle and shot for helping the Chinese. There were few survivors. Those spared for some whim had tried to dig shallow graves as best they could but there were so many and no-one could tell who had been buried or where. Jacqueline's family, especially her father, were revered for the work they had done but there was no indication if they had been buried properly. He took me to a grave which he said might have been theirs; the people had fashioned a primitive cross; I wondered how it had lasted in such a Muslim country. But there were no names. I wrote them on, along with the cause of death: *MASSACRE*. I stayed in what was left of their old house and tried to give some help, but I was more in the way than helpful. I tried to find out how Jacqueline had died but they pretended not to know. I persisted for a while and even threatened to dig up her body, but they wouldn't tell me. Then I, too, pretended they didn't know; the alternative was too horrific to contemplate, you see. So eventually, I let it go because I was afraid of what I would find. The time passed; I was told later that I was there for at least three weeks, but I don't remember. I went back to the ship, as the one place I knew, and tried to put it aside. That wasn't possible of course but I kept trying and lasted another year. Then, as you know, I had a breakdown and the company sent me home. They were very good to me and they still have me on their books as a consultant in gratitude for the two fields I found for them, but I don't do much for them."

"Edward, I'm so sorry for you my son; you've had too much to bear. I have been afraid for you also, all of your life. Now you must try for some happiness."

"Yes; I've come to feel that too. You knew some of all that but I had to tell you again, because there's something else I must say. There's one other thing which you didn't know about; nobody did, except Jacqueline and myself; now, only myself. You see, she was one of the pregnant women who was raped and killed. When I say *'raped'* it was not just the erect male penis that was forced into the vagina: so was a *Kris* the local spiritually-revered dagger with a wide wavy blade; and then turned. The pregnancy had just been confirmed and we were making wedding plans. We wanted each other so much."

I took him into my arms as I had done when he was a child and said, "I am more sorry than I can ever say. I have rarely wished to live another's life for him but I wish I could have spared you that."

"I know; but you can't, can you? No one can, ever. But no more tears, they've all been spilt; there's emptiness still of course, and loneliness and anger; and it's the living of that that's the bugger. I never realised how different they are from 'Solitude': it's the way I coped, and that's strange. I shall never forget, of course, and as I've said, my life is lived around it with whatever gives me some pause."

"You must try for some peace then."

"Yes. That would be welcome. Now do you understand me and what I am? I've told you this so that you understand a little of why I want Anna. And why I'm not too disturbed by not having children; you see, it wouldn't be Jacqueline's, but it would remind me of her. But I do need Anna and her strength, and I believe in her way she needs me."

"I'm sure she does if what you say about her is true. And, do you know, I'm not afraid for either of you any more. Come, let's get back home and the warm."

CHAPTER 27

IN EXPECTANCY OF RIGHT

Unsurprisingly, Megan and Anna were not at home when we let ourselves in. On the hall floor there were some letters that had arrived after we had left on our walk. I started to sort them as I said, "The Postal Service is not what it used to be; deliveries seem to be later and later."

"Was it ever what it used to be?"

"Oh yes. There was a time when you had two deliveries a day. Now you're lucky if they get around to one before tea, and you never know whether it's yesterday's post late, or tomorrow's post early. And it was cheaper as well."

"Well, not many people send letters any more; e-mails are easier and you don't have to pay for stamps."

"True enough but I regret the passing of the art of letter writing; it seems more 'caring' than a satellite. Most of this stuff goes straight into the bin. Would you like some tea?"

"Yes. I'll make it."

"China then; in the cupboard. And there are some biscuits if you'd like some."

Most of the correspondence did find its way to the bin, but there were two letters for Megan which I put on the sitting room table and some larger post for myself which I also put aside for later. There was one letter addressed to me with the logo of my old local newspaper. I was intrigued but had no sense of concern. I had given Roderick my address so that he could write to us should he come into possession of information about Anna's biological family. But that had been more of a courtesy and for the benefit of Anna. I had not expected any further communication and had dismissed the matter almost as soon as we had left the City. Although Anna had continued to worry it for a short time she too seemed to have set the episode aside. If I had come to know her as Edward had described her, then I might have been less cavalier in my attitude. Edward brought in the tea tray as I slit open the letter at my desk. There were two closely-typed sheets under the newspaper masthead. He sat on the settee as I read.

When I'd finished, I said, "You'd better read this."

Roderick had apologised for the delay in writing but I would appreciate, that in view of the information he had obtained, he hoped I would understand his need to confirm his information and check his sources. He had then set out what information he had before coming to ask us, Megan and I, whether he should continue his investigations.

Edward read the letter in silence. He set it down and said, "Anna will need to see this."

"It would be proper," I replied. "But would it be right?"

"It would not be right to withhold it. It's about her family after all."

"Oh, believe me, I'm fully aware of that. If it wasn't, I should not be so concerned. I don't have to tell her, nor Megan either. They both already have enough to deal with. But you probably feel that you do."

"If you really believed that was your only course you wouldn't have shown it to me either. You know you can't keep it to yourself, you know that."

"Yes."

"After all, your involvement is only second order."

"Yes."

"Way behind Megan and Anna."

"I said, 'Yes'."

"And certainly behind Uncle Will."

"I've said 'Yes'. What more do you want?"

I was becoming angry with myself for the doubts that I harboured. "And you needn't have brought in Will. That was unnecessary."

"Is that what you can't swallow? What would have been his distress in your actions? Your weakness? Your fall from grace? Is that why you feel guilty?"

"That's enough."

"It is, isn't it? We all know that you hate hurting people and you go to great trouble to avoid that. And we love you for it. But you try to do the same to yourself – you try to avoid hurting, and all the time you know that you can't do that. You could no more burn that letter than destroy someone; it's not in your character."

"Stop it now. It's enough."

I understood that his comments, with their implied criticism, were a counterbalance to his earlier, unguarded account of the loss he had endured on the other side of the world: he had been too raw, too naked, and I, his father, had witnessed it. He had made it public, and he blamed me for it. But it was no easier to take for all that. I was angry too, and for some seconds I wished that my son had less insight than he did. Then I acknowledged that he coped with his character in ways that I was coming to understand more and more and which were not too far distant from my own: we both hid within ourselves too much for fear of being called out; that was the trigger for his choice of Solitude, as it had been mine.

"They must know of course," I said. "But I hate the thought of doing it."

"We both do, but that is no reason to avoid the duty."

I could do no more than nod my agreement.

We were sitting in silence when we heard voices from the hall.

"We're home," shouted Megan, "And dying for a cup of tea. Where are you?"

Her voice sounded so untroubled that for a moment I forgot all that Edward had told me and indeed it felt as if the letter had not arrived to break the tranquillity. But it was a short-lived illusion that Megan grasped as soon as she saw us.

"What's the matter? What's happened?"

"Edward and I went for a walk and we talked a little. Have you two talked?" I asked.

"We've not stopped to take a breath. Make us a cup of tea please."

"I'll make it," said Edward.

"No," I said. "I'll make it. You need to be here."

"What for?" asked Megan. "What have you two been cooking up? I swear that you men can't be left alone for two minutes. You'd better tell us."

"A cup of tea first. Then we'll talk."

"Bugger the tea," said Megan who rarely swore.

Although she appeared to others as calm and sensible, there was a depth to her; I had been a target of her emotions at one time soon after we met. She was holding herself together, but only just; beneath the surface, I could see that she was not as peaceful as she appeared.

I spoke directly to her, acknowledging neither Anna nor Edward. "You said that you'd talked. You know something of their plans then."

"Yes," she said.

"How much of them?"

"I know that Anna's seeing her Consultant tomorrow." She turned and took Anna's hand. "And despite my pleading, she won't let me be there. She just wants Edward." She smiled and added, "There's gratitude for you – we're considered redundant."

Anna said, "It's not like that and you know it; I explained to you. So don't provoke, it's unhelpful."

Edward moved to sit beside Anna as I said, "Well, they are husband and wife now you realise."

"Of course they are and about time too."

"I want to be there with my husband," said Anna.

"We'll meet up with you afterwards," said Edward quickly. "In a

179

suitable venue. I can't arrange for a Nightingale to sing in Berkeley Square, but what about tea at the Ritz?

> *'De dum..... De dum....*
> *De dum..... De dum...*
> *There was magic abroad in the air*
> *The time we were dining at the Ritz........*
> *And a Nightingale sang in Berkeley Square.'"*

I admired my son's attempt to lighten the mood; and he had a rich voice, and sufficiently off-key to be listened to.

I said, "I don't suppose the moneyed families in that Square have seen nor heard a Nightingale since before your time," and looked at Megan.

"They wouldn't know one even if they heard one, I don't suppose," she replied. "Too much urban sprawl now. – You wouldn't hear it above the sound of Rolls - Rhoyces and Bentleys. "

"I prefer the magic of *'London by night'* said Anna. "Sung by a warm crooning voice: *'Down by the Thames,'* with the lights on the water. I can't remember how it goes on but there's something about *'A girl and her beau.'"*

The mood was becoming sorrowful. "We'll meet you for High Tea then," I said, "After which I hope that you won't expect to be fed again tomorrow." I turned to Megan and asked, "What else do you know?"

"You're pressing me."

"Yes, but for a reason."

"If you mean that they are not going to have any children, I know about that, too. That's their choice; I think they're wrong, but I understand. Anna just won't take an argument for an answer; she's always been the same; she makes up her own mind and that's it. Edward, you'd better bear that in mind and make some allowances for her attitudes. Anyway, as I say, I understand. No, I don't: In the abstract, yes; but not in reality: you can't just dismiss the love that a child brings with it; that's inhuman; it's worth far more than any problems it might bring, however long they last." She turned to me and said, "And I know what you think, so don't start; I could make your argument for you and I wouldn't be far wrong. You take the *sensible* option: you're the ultimate rationalist. But you won't accept, any of you, that love runs both ways. But I won't ever persuade you that it's selfish to opt out."

"But Mum," said Anna, "We think that it would be totally irresponsible of us, Edward and me. Not just for us, but for our

180

descendants to have to face this unnecessary risk. Don't condemn us for that."

"Playing God then are you? My God, you're worse than the Pope," said Megan. "Leave it now; we've had this argument. We shall only say things to hurt and where's the love in that? So we'll accept it and set it aside. It's important to us, of course it is, but it's not earth-shattering for anyone else."

I leant across and took Megan's hand, and saw tears in her eyes. "Tea now, I think," I said.

CHAPTER 28

SOME RESOLUTIONS

While I busied myself in the kitchen, I knew that I was prolonging the making of the tea so that I could postpone having to move back to our consideration of the letter which I still had in my pocket. But that was placing too much of a burden on Edward who was holding the fort.

I took the tea tray into the silent room. "I didn't ask what tea you preferred, so I made a decision; I thought some Earl Grey would be best – full of drugs."

"What do you mean? What drugs?" asked Anna.

"Bergamot, amongst others," I replied. "But they say it's good for the heart in low doses. Like the rat poison, Warfarin."

As I poured out their tea, Megan said, "Edward's been the strong, silent type while you've been out there. There's more, isn't there? That you haven't told us?"

"Yes, I'm afraid so."

"You'd better tell us then."

I took out the letter and said, "I've wondered about that but this was addressed to both of us. You and Anna had better read it together."

"Who's it from?"

"Roderick."

"What's he writing about?"

"Just read it," I said.

Edward and I sat in silence while they read. Their tea had not been touched and was growing cold in their cups, the milk they both liked forming a skin on the surface. They read without once raising their eyes to either Edward or me. I had virtually committed the letter to memory:

Dear Megan and Charles,

As I offered when we last met, I have made some enquiries about our erstwhile County Councillor Rees and it has also brought up some more information about Rhodri Llewellyn (born Morgan). I initially gave the job of searching our archives to an aspiring young journalist but in view of what he found, I took the matter in hand myself and farmed out the field work in small sections to others. There is little likelihood of any one of them putting the sections of the story together but if it should happen, I shall put an end to it. If that is your wish. Let me know what, if anything, you would now like done; my view, even as a reporter, is that it should be left to rest; there's no advantage in resurrection – not in the **'Public Interest'** *– I feel. Nor Private Comfort, come to that. But, for whatever you make of it, here it is.*

As you already know, Rees resigned his position as County Councillor some years back without giving a reason other than 'family matters'. I am able to tell you that pressure was put upon him to do so by the Lord Mostyn and the then Sir, later Lord, Thomas Thomas of Creigiau. I needn't elaborate on these Lords – Megan will tell you more than I can of 'personallia' I'm sure – but the action they took, at that time, was related to Will's consideration of a life in Politics. Quite what pressure was brought to bear on Rees is known, with any certainty, only to the protagonists and I fear that we shall never know for certain, what with two of them dead and one in his dotage who is unlikely to 'unbutton' as the Americans have a habit of saying. You may know otherwise, but the indications are that the issues were truly 'familial' and reputation-destroying. For such a proud man, that was too much.

Rees moved away from your home village, as you know, but not too far away. He bought another house (without selling his 'family' home, so it did not attract attention) and settled again in another of our valleys – we have an abundance of them, after all. That is of little interest in itself. What is of interest is that he set up house with a young lad who, when Rees died five years ago,- of what cause I cannot determine, which is strange - was willed the bulk of his not inconsiderable estate, even after taxes. At the reading of a Will, unless the deceased died intestate of course, the beneficiaries must be listed. Apart from small amounts, the beneficiary in this case was named as Rhodri Morgan (also known as Llewellyn) who was his unacknowledged son. The gift carried a blessing, (too late, of course) 'In Sorrow And A Hope Of Forgiveness' and a caveat that when Morgan died, the estate should fall to his issue; if there was no issue alive, the balance of the estate should pass to the charity Safe Haven Trust, again for personal reasons. If there was issue and he, or she, then died without issue, the estate would then pass to the next of kin if legally proper or to that Trust, if not. You must make what you will of this legalese; I've précised it all, for brevity; perhaps you are able to fill in some details. It seems that Rees is a more interesting person in **Death** *than he ever was in* **Life**.

All this is not especially unusual but there is a somewhat more distressing continuation. The current house, (not the one in your old village by the way which still forms part of the estate, and is overseen by our Social Services) is at the foot of a small mountain and somewhat remote. No surprise. As you know, our roads wind around the bottoms of the valleys and rarely go over the top. Morgan, or Llewellyn as he preferred to be known, carried on living there after the death of Rees and is still there it seems, though he is seldom seen. According to the Health Visitors who call on him, he keeps the house and himself clean enough and tidy; someone arranged for his provisions to be delivered so he never needed to go hungry. Things drifted rather over time: the Social Services attended less often; he refused to have a live-in carer, though he could have afforded it, and he started to 'let himself go' as the saying goes. But, d'you see, he was nobody's particular concern and it was believed that he had money if he needed it; though he always denied it and he may well have believed that, for it never passed through his hands (Rees again?). He was recognised and quietly tolerated in the village when he did appear. The children, as they will, avoided the house because he made 'spells'- probably burnt his bacon or something. Then, for whatever reason – perhaps he became lonely - he started walking alone on the mountain; he could be found sitting out of the wind for hours, talking to himself. The children found him first and would tease him but as he always smiled they slowly came to sit with him and he told them stories of Cardiff and, according to the children at least, his mate Dr Will and his friend Dr Megan. The kids didn't believe him of course but it didn't matter. Then he started telling them the Legends and how he and his girl had made babies called Bendigeidfran [10] and Morwenna [11] who had gone to live with the Mabinogi [15]. All this is background so that you understand what happened.

Writing about it now, it all seems inevitable, but played out by the day it could seem either nonsense, trivial, and a simple search for friendship, or as threatening; such is the time we have come to live in. Whatever, some of the children's mothers started gossiping, as they will, and word got around that his 'friendship' with the children was rather unhealthy. For a short time nothing happened and the children continued to seek him out. Then one of the mothers called in the Police because her daughter had told her that Morgan had told the child how to make babies. You can imagine the consequences in a Welsh valley and the Baptist Chapel: the Police were told of his 'interference' with minors, he was questioned, as were the children, and he was sent before a Magistrate and told he would be placed on a paedophile list and shut away for a long time, and that he was not allowed to talk to the children any more. I imagine that he understood little of all this except the consequences of his being found alone with the children. He *continued his walks for a while and the children would follow him as before. One suspects that their mothers would have read them the riot act, so, no doubt, they would have called him names, but it's not likely that they would have understood much: it would have seemed another dare-devil thing to do. He used to shout at them apparently but they would not go away and, to them, it became the game. But he became so distressed that he was hospitalised for a while. When he came home, he shut himself away completely. Now, he never leaves the house and hides away; the local Minister visits him and, periodically, the Social Services.*

Well, that's it. I have the newspaper reports and I have attached his address if you wish to pursue it further. For what it's worth, I think it's probably best to close the book on it. But your families may not agree. In any case let me know.

Roderick

Eventually, they both stopped reading and Megan let the pages fall to the floor.

"I'm sorry," I said. "I wish I could have held it from you. But that wouldn't have been fair."

Anna said, "No, you had you tell us."

I retrieved the pages from the floor as Edward took Anna in his arms. They sat like that, in silence while I opened my arms to Megan but she did not move. Roderick had sent the letter but he must have wondered whether his final decision was justified, wondered whether it would not have been best to have left the information in the archives. But that would have constituted a lie that I believed he would not have been able to accept. The silence became extended with no-one sure of how to break it, or how to proceed. Because something needed to be done, I collected the teacups and took the tray back to the kitchen. When I returned, Edward was already making drinks and I took them to Megan and Anna. I poured myself a whisky and sat in my chair.

I said, "What do you want me to do? Shall I reply to him? Or do you want to think about it for a while? I can easily delay things, if that's what you want."

Megan said, "Just thank him. Then leave it."

"No," said Anna, "He deserves more than that for all his trouble. Something must be done but I need a little time to think. And then there's the estate to think about, we mustn't forget that: I shall have to see a Solicitor." She took Edward's hand and said to him, "We must think. It won't matter if we take a couple of days over it and we're

185

going down anyway. We'll be in a better position to know what to do then."

Megan said, "You're seeing your Consultant tomorrow. You can't be thinking of this as well. It's come at quite the wrong time."

"Mum, don't things always happen at inconvenient moments?"

"You must sort your own problems out first."

"There's no first and second, you know as well as I do: both matters need attention. Ed and I will decide for the best."

It was strange to hear her refer to my son as 'Ed'. Although many of his friends must have used the diminutive, his family never had and I had never before heard him called by it. For me, it gave an unreal context to our conversation.

"It will do no harm to leave it all for a while," said Megan.

"Possibly not, but my time's compressed as we said. So, *we* must decide, Edward and I. Mummy, Charles, I'm not excluding you, but he is *my* father, and I must see if he needs me; if he does, I must go to him. But most of all at the moment, I must think." She turned again to Edward and said, "If you can bear it again, I'd like another walk."

Despite Anna's assurances I knew that Megan felt ignored and cast adrift. I could see that she was retiring into herself and had turned her head away from me so as not to catch my eye.

"It's getting dark and there's some rain in the air," I said. "It might not be pleasant."

"We'll take our coats and we shan't be long," said Edward.

After they had left us alone, neither Megan nor I spoke much; she started to speculate about their intensions and decisions and these became more and more wild until I became irritated by them and pointed out the futility of her exercise. She rose and, walking out of the room, said, "How can you understand? She's not yours to worry over."

I was forced into a reply and said, "No, she's not of my blood, nor yours for that matter; but in all but biology she's yours. So that's unfair of you. Do you think that biology makes a difference to me? It takes more than *Biology* to make a woman. Do you think that I hold her less dear and love you the less because of that? You must hold a lower opinion of me than I credited."

"You use words like Will did; with no thought."

I dismissed that response and said, "In any case, she's married to my son and that does mean a lot to me and you should have the courtesy of at least acknowledging that. In my heart she is yours and Will's and has been from the start. I wish to God you would stop treating me as a Visitor in your life."

She paused at the door and said, "If Will was here, you wouldn't say these things."

"If Will was here I wouldn't need to."

I had said more than I should, or had intended, and I regretted my indiscipline; to say that I had felt provoked into my response because of what I had been told of Edward's traumas was not an excuse. For many years I had believed that I had my temper under control and that I no longer needed to guard against the outbursts that at one time had come too easily to me; nor, I thought, did I now feel that I needed to control my tongue. Thus, I was saddened also by the fact my character was still volatile and I needed little to provoke a hurtful response. I was also jealous of the fact that Megan should still call on Will for support even some years after his death and in her life with me. It also distressed me that I had used him to put her down. All - in – all, I was too angry with myself to follow her to the bedroom, even though I knew that we needed to seek forgiveness in each other's company; our sense of distance from each other would only increase if we gave it more time.

I poured myself another drink and tried to read some papers that were long overdue for return. They returned home before the rain.

CHAPTER 29

THE GAMBIT

We never came to know the directions that their discussions had taken while they walked; Anna at least, seemed resolved on their return, but to what was unclear to us. Neither were we told the details of their visit to her Consultant the next day. Our intended meeting at the Ritz for tea had no longer seemed appropriate: none of us would have appreciated the irony of it. But they did appreciate that we would be distressed until we knew something of what had transpired and what arrangements had been made regarding Anna's clinical condition and if there was a timetable for her admittance for treatment. So we arranged to meet in a pub near the hospital that was a 'watering hole' for University students and junior doctors waiting for their residencies. I believed that they had chosen it with care: it would be busy; not so much that it would curtail our conversation, but busy enough to avoid too detailed a probing. I understood, and acknowledged, their reasoning but not to an extent that meant having to struggle for a table in the bar, particularly if they were delayed, for whatever reason. I insisted on arriving ahead of time and Megan did not demure.

It had always been at such times as this that I wished that I could avoid contact with other people and the closer they were to me, the greater the need I felt to distance myself and be alone: I wished that decisions were solely mine without having to consider the concerns, sensitivities, susceptibilities or involvement of others. I knew it was protectionist and how entirely selfish an attitude it was; and I had grown to realise how hurtful it could be. I knew the shame of it, but I could never ignore it; and now I saw this same phenomenon displayed in my son.

I had exercised that desire a few times in my youth, sometimes to my own cost and that of others dear to me, but now, I could not indulge my wish for such singularity. No-one had held his beliefs more clearly and certainly than Will and I remembered that he had once said to me: *'You, like us all, will come to have your own credo, and will want to follow it; but sometimes you must behave otherwise, for others' sakes; if only for their peace of mind'*. I had come, slowly, to know the truth of it, and at this time, I had to acknowledge the sorrow that Megan, who had been his wife and was a love of mine, was having to confront.

Of course, we arrived ridiculously early for our meeting, even though we had both made every effort to moderate our haste. The advantage however was that we were able to chose our table in the saloon bar. Megan was characteristically worried that we would not be seen and that they would miss us as the pub filled up with customers. In contrast to my previous response to her worries, I found that amusing and teased her for being a mother hen. She smiled in understanding even though each of us was on edge; we were not easy with each other and made little effort at conversation. It was fortunate, then, that as I rose to get us another drink, they arrived and came to our table. They sat and I searched their faces for some indication of what had happened. But their faces were set and I could read nothing from them. I ordered drinks at the bar and brought them to our table.

We were momentarily silent with the silence that comes from over – expectation and uncertainty of how to behave: how *do you* behave when you don't know the context? Then Anna said, "I expect that you've been sitting here worrying about things. We'd better tell you then hadn't we?"

"Yes," said Megan.

"It would save some palpitations," I added.

"You mustn't be too sure of that," said Anna. "But best to confront it none the less." She took Edward's hand and said, "We've agreed to start treatment no later than four weeks from tomorrow, and earlier if possible. Until then we have been advised to get away and try to forget about it while preparations are made."

"I said that was asking a great deal," said Edward, "And there was a distinct possibility that we wouldn't come up to scratch."

I smiled at his gambit, for I knew it well. He saw me smile and acknowledged it with a nod.

"What treatment then?" asked Megan. "Have they decided?"

"Yes," said Edward. "At least, they've offered what they consider best in this situation."

"What is it?" asked Megan.

"Stem Cell transplant," said Anna. "You'll know Mum, that it's new, and it's not without risk either. But they seem to think it the best regime."

"Oh, God," said Megan. "It's after my time, but if anyone knows about it, the Oncologists will. What I do know, is that there is also a risk of rejection, like any tissue transplant. They'll need to suppress your antibody reaction."

"Yes, he said that, but they're intending to use my own cells," said Anna. "An autologous transplant."

I had not spoken, because the clinical details meant little to me. Now

I asked, "Megan, explain to me please?"

" It's where they separate your own Stem Cells from your blood. They'll take your blood from one arm, harvest the stem cells then drip your blood back through the other arm. It takes time but if it works it reduces the chance of rejection to a minimum."

"Thank you," I said. "They'll harvest enough will they?"

"No, they don't think so as matters stand," said Edward. "They'll need a great number of cells. That's why they've given us 4 weeks."

Anna said, "They've told me to go and have a holiday and come back in 4 weeks. If there was something we particularly wanted to do or see, we should do it, because it could be a little while before we had another chance. In the meantime I'm to inject myself with hormones to increase the rate of Stem Cell production."

"What then?" I asked.

"Then we set sail," answered Anna. "If there are enough cells, I go into isolation because I shall need a high dose of Chemotherapy to cleanse my own bone marrow before the new cells are transplanted back. I won't have any resistance to infection for a while, hence the isolation. And there'll be side-effects. I'll be able to wave to you, but there'll be no hugging and kissing. It will be a very lonely time, so we had better do all that before hand."

"But remember Anna," said Edward, "The end result will be worth it."

"So they insist on telling me; repeatedly," replied Anna. "I'll judge that for myself, when the time comes, and I have full control of my functions again, which could take a long time; two years maybe. I don't know if I really want that – it's a high cost for a restricted life. I'll do a cost-benefit analysis, but that will be the goal – no tiredness, no more vomiting, giddiness or diarrhoea. But that's the colour of the future; in the present, it's stop thinking and take a break."

"Go to Spain then," said Megan. "We'll come with you."

"Or not, if you prefer," I added.

Anna looked at me and said, "Thank you, Charles; you do understand. We have thought about that, of course. Part of our walk yesterday was talking about that, but I don't want it. I should do nothing but think about this hanging over my head and that would be sad for us all; for you and for my husband. So 'no' to Spain."

"Where then?" asked Megan who still seemed to be hoping to be involved, though she must have appreciated that they wanted the time to themselves. "Will you go to Edward's house?"

"For a day or two perhaps but there too we'd just be waiting for the time to pass. We'll stay for longer later, when it's over. I have come to a decision, and Edward has agreed, that we need to do something to fill the time. But it should be something worthwhile, but not too strenuous," continued Anna.

Apart from a first taste, none of us had drunk from our glasses, nor made any effort to do so. Again remembering Edward's understanding of Anna's character, I said, "I expect that you have something in mind?"

"Yes," said Edward. "Anna would like to try to see her father."

There was a cry from Megan that drew attention from a few people in the bar. "With your connivance I suppose! I expect you suggested it! I wouldn't put it past you to take her away from me."

It was a feral cry of loss and rejection, only half suppressed as if the ache was too overwhelming. I reached for her, as did Anna, but she shook off both our attempts. "Get away from me, all of you. Leave me alone to myself."

She rose and made for the Ladies Toilet knocking over her chair in her haste to escape. Anna followed her as Edward righted the chair. Some of the people seemed embarrassed by the display and tried to avoid looking at us but neither Edward nor I could give them any attention. I too, was distressed, but for a different reason: during the conversation I had become convinced not only that they had decided on their actions before that morning's appointment, but that they had even choreographed the breaking of the news of their intentions as they had walked to meet us. I did not agree with Megan's understanding of it: it was not in Edward's character to try to control others – all his life he had believed that people should live by their own counsel - and Anna would not have accepted his control in any case; this was Anna's decision and Edward, in loving her, had agreed to her proposals. I was not unused to tactics in personal relationships, nor in closed or open politics, but I appreciated that all too easily it could evolve to manipulation, and so I was saddened to see it in my family. I then wondered at their marriage: who had proposed to whom, and why? Who had led and who had followed? I drained my Scotch quickly to give me time to compose myself.

Edward asked, "Would you like another?"

I paused and said, "Yes, but a small one and topped with a little water."

We sat in silence for a while and I longed for Megan to return. Edward also kept looking at the toilet door. Young ladies emerged and gave us some concerned looks and then looked quickly away; their thoughts would have been of tragic news from the University Hospital, which they would have seen often enough in this venue.

Eventually, Edward said, "I hope you'll believe me when I tell you that this decision is as much mine as it is Anna's."

"If you say it is, it must be so; why should I not believe you?"

"It might help Megan to cope if you could assure her of that."

I became very angry with him and said, "Now, at last, you give some thought to her mother. You should have thought of her before you even got married in your fashion. Do you have much say in this relationship of yours? Are you behaving in character? Do you ever consider others? What right have you to play God with people's lives? What right have you to say how others must behave? How dare you? Well I won't be a puppet to your ventriloquist and I won't let you treat Megan like that either."

"Dad, it's not like that; it's not what I meant. We wouldn't do that to either of you."

"Go. As soon as you can, just go."

"We would be hurt if that was the way of it."

"Hurt? What do you know of *hurt?* Talk to me when you find yourself in Megan's position: when you've lost your love, when your children have gone and the only one you have close to you now was somebody else's but who you've looked after and grown to love over twenty-odd years, because she also meant something to the one you loved and lost; but she has turned her back on you and thinks that you don't need to be bothered with any more."

"It's not like that; the reverse if anything."

It was unfair of me of course, especially after what he had told me of his life; it was a *'lashing out in distress'* and I was ashamed of it. But it was said and couldn't be retracted. "Say no more. Go. Just leave us alone."

"You're closing us out then?" he asked, with tears in his voice.

"We'll all benefit from some distance as you said," I replied. "I will see Megan through it, if she'll let me." Now I also understood his urge for solitude: he had sublimated his own *hurt* but he feared it still; and he did not wish to have to face it again.

I rose and walked to the pub door and stood outside. I watched the young people entering and leaving the bookshop across the road. Many generations before them had used it to buy the needed course texts; others had used the University Libraries until turned out into the night. Theirs could be a time such as I remembered having to live: everything set aside against one purpose; there seemed so little change with the years. But that was baggage from the past; there was no escape in reverie this time, my emotions were too bare. It was one of the very few times now, that I wished for a cigarette.

I had no sense of time passing, but I felt a hand on my arm. I turned and looked at Anna.

"Charles, come back in, Mum needs you."

I sighed deeply; there was nothing for it but to carry on. I nodded and followed her back to the table. As we walked in Anna said, "We've had a crying *fest*; I think Mum won by a tear. What about you and Edward?"

"I think we both lost something," I replied.

She stopped and took my arm and said, "You mustn't blame him; please don't. He's very dear but like you, people matter to him too much and his defences are not as strong as yours yet; he's too open; he can't bury things; he worries them; and he hurts too easily. It's why he turns away and won't engage; it's because he cares too much. It's terrible to care too much, isn't it? When you know it and there's no escaping it? I know his story, you know, and I don't think he's really come to terms with it, whatever he says; I don't know if he ever will. He's *naked* d'you see? And he will let no-one see that but himself; it's why he hides; it's his way of escaping. And he'll do it again, of course, if he has to; or needs to."

I nearly broke confidence and told her of our talk on the seat in the Fields; but it was not mine to tell; it was for Edward to confide, not me. Instead, I asked, "Doesn't that ghost matter to you?"

She shook her head and said, "He's better when he's with me and I'm not giving him a hard time of it." She smiled, and for the first time with me, her gaze was open and understanding. "Is that what *love* is – making things better?"

"One always hopes so; sometimes though, it's just *being there*."

"It's such a pity then, when it can't be like that."

We had reached our table and Megan held out her hand to me. I said, "These drinks are stale. What will it be, a fresh round or home?"

Anna said, "A fresh round, then home."

She was more astute than the rest of us: she knew that another drink would delay the possibility of any further confrontation, but more than that, such a public place would call for a civilised attempt at conversation and in that way would go some distance towards defusing our antagonism. She was a clever girl this adopted daughter of Megan's.

It was to be a difficult remainder of that day and there had seemed no immediate prospect of an improvement. We did not refer to Anna's intentions again, nor did Megan and I voice more than polite objections to their proposals to leave for Edward's house the next day. I was asked to telephone Roderick at his office, which I did when we arrived home, but I was grateful that he was unavailable and that I could avoid the need to explain matters to him. I left a message that Edward and Anna would call at his newspaper offices the next or subsequent day and they would appreciate it if he would leave what information he had concerning Rhodri Morgan at the front desk. I added that if he would be kind enough to let me have a copy of his information, it would be greatly appreciated.

And, there it was.

It seemed a final link severed. Once their decision was made, I knew that it was best implemented sooner rather than later. As we lay in bed waiting for sleep, I asked Megan whether what Anna had said about her treatment and its outcome was true.

Megan replied, "Not false; but it was glossed. It will be more difficult than she believes to cope with it, strong as her mind is; but there's no alternative that I can see. And Edward will need support too; perhaps more than Anna. In situations like this, it's more difficult to be the onlooker, isn't it?"

Both Megan and I needed a pause and time to acknowledge our changed positions. Besides, any healing of the rifts would be more likely and happen more quickly over some distance. I grew to regret this way of thinking, but at the time, it seemed so sensible.

CHAPTER 30

THE PURSUIT

Edward and Anna left to take an early train the next morning. I tried to think of somehow occupying Megan's and my time after they left. I wanted to avoid the places where we had all been together recently and we ended up walking unexceptional streets looking at the lights of houses and shops of that part of London and wondering about the lives being played out behind the curtains of the houses: we became extravagant in our creativity.

A cold, soft drizzle set in that would last for days and seem unending. The disappointing Autumn would soon be over; the gutters were already filling with the leaves of the London plane trees and even hoping for a change in the weather and a warmer period seemed futile.

We both tired of the forced walks and the damp and stayed home and wondered. We were not left completely adrift; they telephoned regularly but did not offer news other than where they were and something of their immediate intentions. Such calls seemed to impose a greater distance than the geographical one and I came to dread them and their interruption of whatever peace Megan and I tried to fashion: she was torn between relying on the contact, however tenuous, and its re-enforcement of the ache of her loss. We had become the audience in this tale and could do little now but listen, watch and wait.

They had broken their journey to Edward's house to collect Roderick's information. He had not been available but had left his material. They checked into an hotel near the sea as we had done previously and as we did whenever we visited the City. They made something of a honeymoon of it: they breakfasted early each day and walked along the beach through the wind and the low, damp clouds brushing the flecked sea, or though the parkland on the hill behind them, complete with its ruined castle that caught the wind and made it sigh. Autumn had long grasped the coast, and was succeeding in disengaging it from the dregs of Summer.

Anna held Edward's arm tightly to her breast.

"I love the sea, don't you?" she asked. "There's so much mystery in its colours."

"Of course," he answered. "It's why I bought my house on a cliff-top so that I could always see it, and I always miss it if I don't see it for a few days." He paused and then asked, "What's your favourite time of year?"

"Anytime. All the time."

"That's not good enough. You must have your favourite time or season. Tell me."

"Time is easy. Sunset, with dawn running it a close second. And really that's only because I've been awake at sunset more often than I have been at dawn. I don't know though: Dawn is always a *new* Dawn – a *renewal,* a *rebirth*; a *new God – Cronos* - from the *Cauldron of Rebirth* [10] in the East. It is so full of promise. Sunset is when the Sun, the Old God, Zeus, goes to be sacrificed before being reborn: a *little death* each day until Midwinter, when a new Sun is crowned and starts, again, to grow old. So Sunset is an ending, an obeisance to something that can never again be captured and that's sad – a *hiraeth,* as you say. *The Sun is Born in the East and Dies in the West.* Who said that?"

"Apart from you, I don't know. Mine was not a Classical Education," replied Edward.

"No matter," said Anna; "he – or she – is acknowledged. The Ancient Myths are so right, aren't they? And they make much more sense once you understand them. They are less Myths then; more *a Guide to the Living and the Dying.* In any case, so much more preferable than the old Hollywood film ending of *'And they sailed off into the sunset to live happily ever after.'* That never worked for me; that's an ending, not a beginning. So I'd like to change my mind if that is allowed. My favourite time then is Dawn even if it turns out to be a foul day like this. You can always hope that it will *'Turn out nice again Missus'.* At Sunset, you've had it I'm afraid. I even think that if I ever did have a child and it was a girl, I would call it 'Dawn'."

"Strike one then."

"What do you mean?"

"Dawn is my time too," said Edward. "When I'm at home I make a point of sometimes getting up before dawn to watch the Sun rise, even if it's cloudy, perhaps particularly when it's cloudy; there's a different light then."

"Or you believe there is."

"Yes. I like to believe so."

They turned to walk back to the Hotel.

"Come on," said Edward. "What about the time of year?"

"That's too difficult."

"Try."

"I can't make a choice. But I'll tell you this: Summer for the peace, the ease, the *unhurriedness* of the long, hot days; then the colour of the sea, the smell of the Bladderwrack drying on the rocks at low tide, and

196

the warmth of the sand between your toes – it's a *Mañana* time. Then, Winter for the anger, the wildness and the torn seaweed smell of the sea, the White Horses – the *Goddesses Maidens* - racing for shelter in the bays, and the spray in your face and the taste of salt – it's *Sirens* time then. Then the warming cup when you get home."

She turned to kiss him and saw that there were tears on his face.

"Edward! What is it?"

"Damned foolishness, that's all."

"No. Don't close yourself off again. Tell me!"

"Too much sensitivity: it's enough just to live out your life; thinking about it as well is nothing but trouble; it makes too many demands - I don't know if it's worth the contemplation. I couldn't have studied your Philosophy; it would be too *raw*. And I've upset my father again because he expects too much and cares too much about his children. I should learn to guard my tongue. That's all."

"What's brought this on then? Now?"

"Me, with my question – and – answer session. But I was curious; I wanted to know what you felt about this time we have to live in. But I'll tell you the consequence of my loose tongue: I could use what you've said for myself; but I'd strengthen the Winter: more *Jason and the Argonauts* along with their problems. I chose my house here for a reason that's become a purpose. I wanted the loneliness and to be away from people. I wanted the world entirely as *I* fashioned it: *me,* not others; nothing to do with others. I've not allowed anyone to visit me at the house; I've always found some excuse to avoid them; this was for me: the Land, the Cliffs and especially, the Sea in its moods; and the Solitude of it. Now you've showed me the futility of that and made me stop that foolishness and I love you for it."

"I'm glad. But it's not foolishness, just sensible if you need your solitude. And you mustn't think of me too much as a crutch. You mustn't. I can't be that."

"You'll be the first person to come inside my house then. I wonder how the house will like that?"

"I shall say 'Hello house' and introduce myself as Anna Williams; or perhaps it would understand *Morwenna* [1] better. It won't reject me then. I won't let it."

"I'm sure it will love you as I do. Come on then, let's get back for some fresh coffee, then we'll get on."

They ordered coffee and prepared the car to drive to Rhodri's house. Edward considered that they were probably still too early, but Anna fidgeted with her cup and became disagreeable so they did not delay for too long.

The drive to the house address they had been given was not far in distance, but they had forgotten the tortuous nature of the roads through the valleys. The roads had not changed over the years of their absence, but the villages and the houses gave note that they had enjoyed better days: there was a sense of 'age', of neglect and loss of pride that neither of them had known as children. They parked the car in the centre of the village to ask for directions for the last mile or so to the house. Neither of the two village pubs was open, probably because there was not much trade during the day; if you wanted a drink, no doubt you went to the backdoor and asked (as had always been the case when the pub was shut) and you were asked inside to sit by the fire in the kitchen. They walked to the small Village Stores and Post Office. There was a small old lady bowed over a handbag that was far too large for her talking to the Post Mistress in Welsh while she waited to have her Pension Book stamped, and her money counted. She then turned and with a gesture walked slowly to the door where she stood and looked at them.

The lady behind the grill turned and asked them, again in Welsh, if she could be of help: *"Gellai neid rhiwbeth i ch'i?"*

Anna smiled and said, "I'm sorry but we don't speak Cymraeg. We did, a little, both of us as children but we've been away so long that we've forgotten most of it; we struggle with it now. We've become the ignorant Sais."

Edward noticed that as soon as they had spoken in English, the lady with her handbag and week's pension walked into the street. It was salutary to realise that for an older generation, at least, English was as foreign as Chinese.

"Oh. Been away then have you? To Lloeger, sorry, England is it then?"

"There mostly," said Anna, while Edward moved from one foot to another and fretted in his embarrassment.

"Nothing wrong with that, so I'm told, if you fancy it like. For me, Cardiff is the furthest I've been and that's far enough. Too far, really. I'm in no hurry to go back there mind, once is enough – too *hoity-toity* for me and not a spare minute for a chat to catch up with the news – and did you see the prices for a Bed - and – Breakfast? I could cook for a rugby team for that. Did you come from by here originally then?"

"Born here, yes: me in the North and him in the South."

"Oh, the North is it? Funny people up there they are if you don't mind me saying so. Present company excepted. Different Tribe they are it seems to me: they think they're better than anybody; but they have to come down by here for their coal. Except for *Point of Ayr Colliery* of course; but that's as much the Isle of Man colliery as much as theirs being so far out under the sea, so they're welcome. And you can't understand a word they say with that accent they've got up there: cut it with a knife you can – *cut glass* they like to think. I'm sure they put it on on purpose up there; not like us down by here; you wouldn't catch me up there and no mistake. Do them the world of good to go down a proper pit by here for a shift or two; then they'd know what *living's* about. Good job you got away in time it seems to me. I expect you know the lakes they've got up there then?"

"Not really. I grew up mostly in London. But our parents were all Welsh."

"Oh, London is it? You'll know the London Welsh then? Good Male Voice Choir they've got, I'll admit that. They come to sing in the Brangwyn Hall in Swansea once a year or so; but I've not managed to get there, with the shop and Post Office and all. And it's too far without the bus. I suppose it was your job that took you away was it? There's not much opportunity for nurses round by here; not if you're any good, anyway."

"No, I can see that," said Anna.

"Never mind. You've come back here now then have you? Looking for a nice place perhaps?"

Edward broke into an interrogation that he could see would continue until everything that defined them had been explored.

"We're just on a visit now. Actually we've come to try and see someone. We'd just like some directions. The valley roads can be very confusing."

"Only when you don't know them; once you know them, they're no trouble. If you lived here for a while, you'd soon get to grips with them."

"It would take us a while, I think," said Anna.

"No doubt about that. There's nothing like growing up in a place to know it. I know everyone here and I could tell you a tale or two if I had a mind to. But that's by the way of the bath-water and you'll be wanting to get on I dare say."

"Yes, thank you," said Anna. "We are short of time. I hope you can help us."

"Rush, rush, rush. That's half the trouble with England: everyone wants everything by yesterday. It doesn't do for me I'm afraid; day after tomorrow is alright for me, and sometimes that's too soon, make no mistake. No, I'm more of a slowcoach, me, and that's no bad thing seems to me. If they took their time for a chat now and then, you wouldn't have these Wars and Strikes and things."

"I'm sure you're right," said Edward. "People have become too frantic. But we'd like to get back to our Hotel before dark, if we can. What with the Valley roads and all? So if you can just help us, we'd be very grateful. We're looking for the house of Rhodri Morgan."

"There's no one by that name by here."

"He used to live here with an older gentleman called Elwin Rees."

"You mean the old Councillor? He died a few years ago now."

"Yes, we know," said Anna. "But it wasn't him we came to see. It was Rhodri Morgan."

"Oh, you mean Rhodri Llewellyn; that's his name: Llewellyn, not Morgan; I don't know where you got Morgan from; the only Morgan we've got here is the Preacher, God bless him and he's eighty three now; a good age I call that. Can't preach much now but he likes to try when he can get to his pulpit; but he only lasts for a minute or two with 'Bless the Lord God and His Son Jesus Christ', and then we sing the hymns. He runs out of breath see. Sometimes when he says '*Jesus Christ*' it sounds like he's swearing about something; it's difficult to keep a straight face, I promise you. Of course the small boys and girls giggle until their mothers give them a clip round the head. But it's only in devilment; they don't mean no disrespect."

"Rhodri Llewellyn then?" asked Edward.

"Oh, yes. He lives in the old Vicarage. On his own. I don't know how he copes with the big old place. It must take him all his time keeping it clean and tidy, though I've never been inside, nobody has, except the Social now and again. Keeps himself to himself like the old Councillor did before he died."

"But he's still there though?" Edward asked.

"As far as anyone knows he is; nobody's seen him go – walking or feet first like. Nobody sees him, full-stop, from one day to the next. He doesn't get any post, not from me anyway and he gets all his groceries delivered by van once a week, like the crachach. He never comes into the village; doesn't spend a penny in the shop here, convenient or not as they say: doesn't spend a penny in this Convenience. His rubbish is left outside for the Council. And I don't know what he does about his washing; there's never anything hanging on the line."

"Perhaps he sends it out to someone," said Anna.

"Perhaps so but I've never seen anything like that being collected that's all I'm saying. He can't be living in the same clothes day after day after all; not for all these years. And he can't be sleeping in the same sheets either. Come to think of it, you never saw the Old Councillor's Long Johns either. Perhaps he dries them inside; perhaps he's got a washing machine with a tumble drier that's all the rage. That's not good for them, time after time. They need a good blow once in a while, and a bit of sun to blue them up and save on the *Reckit's Blue*."

"But he is still there? Edward asked.

"Oh, I'm sure he is; or as sure as anyone can be anyway; he's not been carried out anyway, not by the Hospital or John James the Burial. And his food is always taken in so it doesn't attract the rats from the old gully where the Signal Box used to be; they've got worse in the last few months too; more adventurous. The weather I expect. I've told the Council about them time and time again but you can't get them to do anything: too busy talking and not enough doing they are, like all of them. I don't know what they get paid for – money for old rope, if you ask me. They should work in this shop for a change: eight ours a day on your feet, chilblains or no chilblains.

"But it's about the lad you've come for and here's me going on about my chilblains. You haven't got them I hope?"

"No, thank goodness," said Anna.

"Well, I wouldn't wish them on anybody. Walking in the snow without shoes and socks is best for them; you get a bit of peace then. They used to beat them with holly once upon a time, for some peace. I've asked the Social about him, to help like – I like to help when I can, see, but they won't tell you anything. Not the Police either, after that last incident."

"What incident was that?" asked Edward.

"Oh, it's more than a year ago now. The kids were throwing stones and smashed all his windows. The Police got on to that quick enough, fair dos, and took some of them to the Juvenile with their mothers. But they said they couldn't *prove* anyone in particular had done it. So they were let off with a good talking - to. Not enough, I said; a good thrashing across the bum they should have had I said, all of them, whoever did it, so they wouldn't do it again; across the bum with the buckle end of the father's strap so they couldn't sit down for a week; but they're too soft now. You watch – *spare the rod and spoil the child* - I said at the time; if they didn't do it this time, what about the next time I said; put some of God's fear in them is best. The people have been keeping an eye on them since then to see it doesn't happen again. Not much point anyway as he's had them boarded up. He could have had them repaired; I don't think he's been left short after the Councillor died."

Edward saw that Anna was becoming distressed and he was concerned to get her away. "Perhaps you could tell us where the Vicarage is, and we'll leave you in peace," he said.

"Yes, of course. You'll be anxious. It's the other end of the village.

It's a bit stretched out, so carry on until you come to the railway bridge, though the trains don't run any more, more's the pity; too many cars now they say, but not for the old people and those that can't drive, I say."

"The railway bridge, you said?"

"Yes. It's not so far. The road does an S-bend to go under it. Buses can only just get through – not Double Deckers mind; there's no chance there, the bridge is too low see; I don't know why they don't knock it down, it's not doing any good without the trains: what's the point of having a railway bridge if you don't have a railway? Anyway, you go left there and it's at the end of the lane. You can't miss it with the windows boarded up. I hope you find him well; we all do."

"Thank you. You're very kind."

"Oh, it's no trouble. It's been nice to chat to you. I like a good chat now and again. Come back again soon."

"We'll be off now then," said Edward and ushered Anna outside and across the road to the car.

"Well, that's a relief," said Anna.

"Yes," said Edward. "For a moment there I wondered whether we'd ever get out or whether we'd suffer the fate of visitors for an eternity: we were talked to death, Your Honour."

"A bit of a gossip."

"I wouldn't call this a one-horse town, but a bit hillbilly would you say?" asked Edward.

"She was only trying to help," replied Anna, "And it can't be often that she has a chance to talk to some strange people from London. But mark my words we'll be all round the Village long before we leave; they'll all be out to see these funny people from Lloeger."

"Yes," said Edward, "But unfortunately there'll also be a new interest in Rhodri to wag their tongues."

"Yes. Perhaps we shouldn't have come," replied Anna.

"Too late now. It will be even worse if we just turn around and leave."

They had reached the railway bridge. The chicane in the road was indeed tight and a small bus would have passed through to the other side only with difficulty. Beyond the bridge the road rose steeply up the mountainside. There was a pub on the other side of the road but that too was shuttered and in decay. At one time it would have been busy, as people changed transport and rested and refreshed themselves before the long climb. Now, with the loss of the railway and with limited public transport this part of the valley had become even more isolated. Was that why Rees had chosen this house for himself and Rhodri, it

202

being the only form of escape he knew?

To the left of the bridge, an unmade track, ran parallel to the railway embankment. There were deep ruts in the lane with grass growing between them, which made driving difficult. The house was at the far end of the lane and, as they had been told, the windows were heavily shuttered. Edward stopped the car near the front door.

"It must be pretty dark inside," said Edward, "And it must be costing him a fortune in electricity."

"Yes," replied Anna. "But perhaps he doesn't switch the lights on. It must have been pretty noisy too, when the train ran."

"Perhaps the Vicar was deaf," said Edward.

"He'd have needed to be; and possibly blind as well."

They walked to the front door and rang the bell; they could hear nothing and they knocked on the door. There was still no response and indeed no sign of habitation. Anna, crouched at the letterbox and shouted, "Hello? Hello, Mr Morgan? Is it possible that we could speak with you please? Just for a moment?"

The house remained silent. "Mr Morgan? My name is Anna Williams but it used to be Anna Griffiths before I was married. Perhaps you remember the name? Griffiths? Will Griffiths? Can I talk to you please?"

"Let me try," said Edward. "Mr Llewellyn, my name is Edward Williams. My father, Charles Williams was a very close friend of Will Griffiths and Megan Phillips who you must remember. They were married when you left your daughter in their care and they adopted her as their own. Well she's married now and she's here and would like to speak to you."

Anna said, "I am your daughter Morwena who you called Anna. Please open the door and talk to me."

They waited, but there was no sound from inside the house. Edward said, "This is too difficult for you and it seems like he doesn't want to be disturbed. We'd better leave it."

"I've come a long way for this; 28 years it's taken me; and that's a long journey. I can't just forget him now."

"I understand, of course I do, but you'll end up tearing yourself apart. Leave it love."

"No. I'll leave a note and we'll come back tomorrow." She tore a sheet from her diary and wrote that they would return the next day. She also rummaged in her bag and took out two photographs. One was of a small child and the other a more recent photograph of herself.

"Where did you find those?" asked Edward.

"I thought this might happen so I took them out of my album. They might help," replied Anna. "At least I hope so."

She folded her note around them, pushed them through the letter box and shouted, "We'll come back to see you tomorrow."

They drove back through the village and, indeed, there were more people on their doorsteps and no doubt many more behind their curtains.

CHAPTER 31

AN ERONEOUS UNDERSTANDING

They drove back to the hotel, took dinner and retired early. Over breakfast the next morning they considered the advantage of again driving the length of the valley early, but there was no benefit in arranging their visit to arrive at any particular time. It seemed there was no particular routine that Rhodri followed from day to day; or rather, whatever routine he had established for himself was pursued within the walls of his house. They were reluctant to return to the Post Office and have to face the Post Mistress again so soon: long explanations would be expected, and they had nothing to say; neither did they wish to face an 'I told you so' stance. However, they acknowledged that there were some further questions to be asked and some additional information that they might gather such as when any deliveries were made; and were the gas and electricity meters ever read? Neither of them could believe that the information was not known in such a small community, nor that any activity relating to that house and its occupant would not renew an interest and become a topic of conversation again, to be considered, discussed and gossiped over for as long as speculation could be entertained. Besides, as Anna suggested, if they got no response in the morning, they could seek a pub for lunch and try again in the afternoon.

For Anna, the path was laid out over which the search was to be made and she would not accept any doubts as to its need. But for Edward, the pursuit was vicarious: of course he wished for an outcome, for Anna's sake, but it was more a case of laying the matter to rest so that they could take up their own lives, as for any responsibility or care for the life of the man who dwelt alone of his own choice. Edward also knew the emptiness of a life that had to be lived: he had struggled with it and initially failed. Then he too had searched for a haven away from the intrusion of others and slowly, the emptiness had eased. But it had not gone away nor become less of a heartache; he knew it never would. He now had the support of a woman he loved: a stronger woman than he was a man, but one with traumas of her own to face, and fears of her own mortality to confront. All this he knew and understood; but he also knew that when that choice of life-style has been made, it must be acknowledged and respected. He knew the selfishness of that and the pain it brought to others but he could not protect them by diminishing himself: and he still nursed the fear of being cast back to his own darkness; and the fear that, this time, he would not emerge. So, though he loved his woman, he also longed to turn his back on this insular, claustrophobic valley and all the others he had known, and seek his own haven on the cliff facing the sea, to hope that the wind would set fair and blow his memories away: a florid thought, maybe, but true enough.

But now, was now, and there were matters to try to resolve before they could depart. So they left soon after breakfast and drove again to the end of the valley.

There were more people on the streets than there had been the day before and they all turned away from their gossip to watch this strange car as it made its way to the far end of the village.

"Golgotha," said Anna.

"What do you mean?" asked Edward.

"All these people have gathered on the Mountain of the Skulls in the hope of witnessing a Crucifixion or a Resurrection."

"You have too vivid an imagination," said Edward. "It'll be the death of you if you don't give it up."

"How do you explain all this then? You can't say it's the Garden of Gethsemane now, can you? Even with rose-coloured spectacles for your native land."

They had expected the news of yesterday to have produced some concrete and obvious change in the pursuit of the village life; however irrational the thought, it was tempting to believe that the increased numbers of people was a consequence of yesterday's disturbance, rather than that it was a shopping day like any other each week.

In the lane, nothing had changed and for a while this seemed in strange contrast to the main road, but then, this lane was largely unvisited and travelled only for the purpose of delivery and by the tormenting children whose voices were borne from the playground of the village school.

They parked the car and again walked to the door of the boarded house, and knocked. There was still no sight nor sound from inside the house. Edward bent to the letterbox and said, "Mr Llewellyn? We've come back to see you as we told you yesterday. We hope that you found the photographs we pushed through the door. As I told you I'm Edward Williams; my father is Charles Williams who was a close friend of Will Griffiths and Dr Megan. You must remember them. And your daughter Morwena is here with me and would like to speak to you. Is that possible? Will you open the door to us please? We've come a long way to see you. We won't stay long if you don't want us to but

Anna very much wants to talk to you. Just to say *'Hello'* like."

There was no response from inside. Edward turned to Anna and said, "This is futile. He obviously doesn't want to be bothered. We'll get no joy from this. Just leave another note and we'll go."

"You're right of course; we should just leave and forget it. It's unlikely to be any good anyway after all these years. It would probably be very harrowing for him and that's very selfish of me."

"Harrowing for you too I expect. And I can't see the advantage."

"Well, you wouldn't, would you? It's not your father you're searching for – you know yours and what he's like. But you're right. We should leave; and leave a sad old man to his loneliness, if that is what he wants."

"Come then," said Edward.

"No. Every rational thought tells me to go. But I can't. I want to know my history; that which most people dismiss too easily; it's why we cling to our Legends, isn't it? Those of us who think too much? Or wonder too much? To know *who we are.*

"I want to see what he's like, hear his voice talking to me and try to see what he feels about his life. I would like to hear *my father's voice,* don't you understand? I think this is what the religiously devout mean when they say in prayer, *'I want to hear My Father's voice'.* No, I can't expect you to understand why I want this, but I can't simply turn away, harden my heart and go and forget it, as my mother wants me to do. I have a life to acknowledge, and a debt to clear for what he did – the debt of My Life, and the *shape* of my life, *such as it is,* do you understand? And whatever it's worth. I want to *untangle it.* Please Edward, understand me on this."

"Yes. But you understand also: it won't change the past."

"I don't want to *change* the past; that's done. But there are consequences of what he did, and I want him to know them; all of them. I feel that there's a hole in my life; and there may not be a lot of time available to fill it. This is one thing I must do and I must find a way of doing it."

"There's no more to be said in that case" said Edward. "But remember, you never knew that past, it isn't yours to know now, so don't try to worship what you've never known; and don't make a haven of it: that's Religion, and there's no comfort in that, only sorrow."

"I know that. But what's to be done now? How can I get at him?"

"I don't know; if he doesn't want to answer the door, there's not much more we can do. There's just one thing: I remember that nobody uses the front door in the Valleys except for the Preacher or Vicar, the Police and the Insurance Salesman for his penny- a- week. Everyone else uses the backdoor or the kitchen door. We could try our luck there; it may be less frightening for him; more usual. Come on."

For such a substantial house, the pathway to the kitchen door was narrow, dark and slick with moss, and overhung by large trees. There was a stone wall defining the adjacent field where the knotweed, brambles and ferns were held at bay. Beyond the kitchen door the wall had collapsed and the field was already growing over the stones. Beyond that again there was what looked like a small pond but was only a shallow puddle formed from the water seeping from the wall and held back by the fallen stones and debris. Then the ground rose steeply over shale to the defunct railway line above. Over it all was a dampness of neglect; it seemed that rarely did the sun penetrate to this gable end of the house. The kitchen door was showing some signs of rot and the paint was peeling away from it and from the kitchen window. Under this was a waste bin whose lid caught a steady stream of water from an overflow pipe higher on the house wall, which the lid sprayed onto the pebble-dash rendering of the house. This overflow was clearly of some duration for the wall was green with algae over a large area and at some time the frost had got behind the pebble-dash and lifted it away. There was little doubt that the water would have seeped through the walls and that the inside of the house too, would be suffering from dampness and mould.

It seemed unlikely that there would ever be future occupiers of this house, built substantially, and to last, for the Vicar and paid for by contributions from his parishioners for the glory of God and the fear for their souls. It had been built of the local stone at a time when there had been work aplenty in the surrounding coal mines and when the railway had run, carrying the people and the spoils away to the market town and the docklands at the mouth of the valley. Now, the village and its life was inconveniently located at the far end of a valley which was no different from most, with no work and little aspiration, no transportation to effect an easy escape and no money for cars. Signs of deprivation like these where everywhere, from each house like this one, to whole villages that epitomised insularity. None of the present generation wanted to take on the job of saving these houses, and by doing so, consciously deprive themselves of the pleasures and entertainments taken as of right by others, while they lived out their lives in poverty. The house would follow the course of the others: decaying along with the village, as the older generation died and the new one moved away.

Edward pulled the bin away from the direct fall of water. It was surprisingly heavy; he looked inside and saw that it was filled with cardboard boxes, food tins and wasted food. However, there was no litter that was not contained and which would have attracted the mice or rats; there was some understanding of hygiene and health that seemed incongruous in the particular circumstances.

It was causing Anna some distress which seemed to increase her resolve to see her father. The kitchen curtains were drawn tightly and the door was also shut. Edwards knocked but there was no response from inside. Anna turned the door-knob and the door opened easily.

"Well, it's not locked up, at least. But we can't just go in," said Edward.

"No," replied Anna. "We have no right to go that far."

She called again through the open door and this time a head appeared from inside. It was difficult to see for the inside of the house was very dark and the head seemed insubstantial. The top of the head was bald but above the ears was what looked like a tonsure; the hair looked clean but was very long and seemed not to have been properly cut for some time. A short, stooped figure appeared in the kitchen. The face, now that it could be seen, showed a grey pallor and the cheeks were sunken and the mouth pinched. The clothes on the body looked sizes too big but could once have covered a solid frame; now, it had gone to seed and the person shuffled in carpet slippers towards the kitchen table.

"Did you bring my fags? I haven't had one for two days and I'm gasping."

His voice was low and quiet and across the kitchen it was difficult to understand what he was saying. He gave the impression of talking to himself as he probably did through his waking hours. He ignored Edward and Anna and embarked on a monologue to himself as he shuffled back and forth across the width of the kitchen, his slippers slapping the stone flags of the floor.

"In normal circumstances I could have gone to the Post Office to get some but I've got a bit of a cough see; it wouldn't do to go out and give it to everybody else. And I haven't got any money from the buggers as usual. The boyos are at school, so that'd be alright, I wouldn't pass it on to them. They've got some good fags at the Post Office, that's what I need for this cough. I remember they told me the fags were from Turkey but I don't believe them; it's a long way to go to get a fag. I wouldn't fancy it with all the Tribes and the Sheiks of Arraby, and Errol Flynn riding a camel and waving his sword like the Prince of Bloody Baghdad; and that woman from the Hareem and that; too bloody dangerous in the circumstances. I wouldn't enjoy a fag at all in those circumstances. Chop your head off with a cutlass, soon as look at you; and your balls too no doubt – one more Eunuch for the Hareem, your Greatness. Your head would end up speaking in a high voice. And the bloody sand in your sandwiches all the time: Sand – Witches; too bloody right. Pashas they are, the fags. They smell like shit that's been left to dry but they're good and strong; just as I like them. They must have good lungs, the Turkeys – all that Yodelling I expect – gobble, gobble, gobble. I could have sent Vera but I don't know where she's gone now; it would do her good to get out and about a bit. She's never around when you want her; always flitting off when I'm not looking; and she never comes home now. I'll have to put a stop to it one of these days, show her who's boss. So it isn't normal circumstances and I haven't been able to find my shoes, and I can't go out in these slippers. Anyway I haven't got any money; they won't give me any. Bloody old skinflints they are, all of them. I'd like to shoot the bloody lot; waste of bloody space they are, all of them. Anyway, they said, the buggers, that I mustn't go out."

He turned to Edward as if seeing him for the first time and said, "How can I get some fags if I can't go out, tell me that, Sunny Jim, whoever you think you are? So it's me that has to suffer, not them. Shoot the fucking lot of them for peace and quiet and a packet of fags."

He turned, shuffled very slowly towards them again as he continued his monologue, and close-to, his eyes were clouded and rheumy. It was clear that he saw little at any distance and in all probability knew his way about the house more as a consequence of usage than sight.

"You're not my delivery. You're not Winford. I thought I didn't recognise you. What you doing here? You're not Daly's. Winford usually comes today with my fags; if he's late I run out. So he must be late because I've run out. I ran out yesterday too if you really want to know. Who are you then? What you doing here? What do you want? Have you come instead of Winford? You shouldn't be coming here, I don't like change. The Police promised me nobody would bother me if I didn't bother them. Where the bloody hell's Winford?"

"Mr Llewellyn," said Edward. "We've come to visit you."

"I don't want none of your visiting; I didn't ask for it and I don't want it; too bloody dangerous it is; nothing but trouble; go and visit somebody else for a change. I haven't got no money and I don't want no trouble. So you won't get anything from me. Go away or I'll be in trouble again; I don't want that; I've had enough of that thanks be to God; I've got enough for a day-and-a-half. Go away now and leave me alone or I'll call the Police. It's the only bloody thing they're any good for, the buggers. Are you sure you didn't bring me any fags? Perhaps you've got some in your pockets if you have a look."

"Mr Llewellyn, I'm sorry but we don't have any fags. We don't smoke see," said Edward.

"Missing a treat you are then boyo. You can have one of my Pashas if the lazy bugger Winford ever brings them. Good they are; the best; I only buy the best so you'd think you'd get some service. Not everybody buys the best so you'd think they'd be grateful to serve somebody who knows what's what and pays for the privilege. You'd think that they'd make sure of the delivery on time in the circumstances. They get their money too easy now that's their trouble; not like in the War, by God: you had to be on all-fours then, everybody was on short rations then, ha, ha, and no mistake."

He pulled a single kitchen chair from the corner of the room and sat at the table. "Have you tried Bananas? You didn't have them then, boyo, only Ration Books and Pension Books and Penny – a –Week books; except the 'Spivs' of course, they had a bob or two for the girls I'm told; like the Americans with their nylons: *'One for a feel, two for a fuck missus. I've just flown in from Holl – I – Wood and I'm looking for A Star.'* And the girls fell over with their legs in the air. What did they say about them, those Yanks?

Over sexed, over paid and over here.
Easy come, easy go.
Have some gum, chum.

Stuck in my mind that did, the bastards; the girls thought they could go to America for dropping their knickers. Fat Chance. I'll tell you something for nothing boy *bach* and it won't cost you a penny: there are more children speaking Chicago in London than in the whole bloody United States put together. What did you say you wanted?"

"This is Anna; she wanted to talk to you."

"Talking's easy; doing's hard. Better with a fag though, both of them. Are you sure you haven't got one tucked away? It doesn't have to be Pashas. But they're good fags I must say. Champion. You get a good cough from them in the morning. I look forward to that. There's only one thing better than a good fag and I bet you can't guess what that is."

"No," said Edward. "What?"

Rhodri had lapsed into silence again. Anna too had been silent and was clearly struggling with her emotions. "Mr Llewellyn," she said. "We'd like to talk to you if we can. Can we come in and sit down?"

"No sitting; no talking. Sitting's the first step to trouble and talking to a woman's nothing but trouble. Always has been, always will be. Till the End Of Days."

"We won't stay long if you don't want us to but we would like to sit down; we've come a long way."

"That's your own look-out. I didn't ask you to come in the first place. I didn't send invitations out to Tom, Dick and Harry Missus. So that's your look-out."

"We came to see you yesterday," said Anna. "We knocked and called through the front door but perhaps you didn't hear us. Did you hear us?"

"I never answer the front door. Don't use it. Some people would miss it, I suppose, especially the people over the mountain in Pontrhydyfen – do you know what the name means? I'll tell you anyway: *The Bridge Over the River Fen'*. There. Now tell me I'm daft. They think they're *crachach* over there they do, those people: God's gift to the Valleys; His Chosen People after the Jews made a mess of things; the rest of us are leftovers – Adam's unwanted rib, like women."

"Mr Llewellyn."

"Don't interrupt! It's rude that is. I could do without the bloody door all together if truth be told, which it isn't often. Waste of space it is; something else to worry about. Who the Hell needs two doors anyway? The crachach want one to come in and one to go out I suppose. Best to live in a tent I say, like the Pashas and the Sheiks, and smoke the Pipe Of Peace. No bloody doors to worry about."

"We put a note and some photos through the front letter box yesterday. Did you find it?" asked Anna.

"No. I haven't been to that door for years; no reason to. Everything I want comes 'round the back. Too bloody draughty it is as well if you take the pillow away. And I took the bloody bell out too. I suppose the Pontrhydyfen people with two doors want it; they're welcome to it and they can have mine if they're short. Too bloody loud it was, day in day out. 'Specially when the children started ringing it day in day out; four or five times a day in the holidays. They didn't mean no harm I expect, but they wouldn't leave me alone to get on. I felt like telling their mothers but I didn't want to go out in my slippers in the rain."

"Can I get us a couple of chairs?" asked Edward. "I'll put them back later, when we leave."

"No, no chairs. You'll stay too long if you sit down. You can leave now if you're tired, it's no odds or evens to me. I didn't ask you here. I don't know what you want or who you are. Are you from the Social?"

"We thought we'd given you notice yesterday. That's why we left the note," said Edward.

"Notice is it? Notice for what? I'm not moving out anywhere if you're after this house. I know your name – *'Stealer'*! I'm not doolaly. I've got my wits about me. It's this girl I don't know; did I ask your name Missus? And what you're doing here, disturbing peaceful folk who only want peace and quiet?"

"No, you haven't."

"Haven't what? Stop talking in riddles – I've got enough Riddles on my plate already, thank you very much."

"You haven't asked my name. It's Morwena and I'm called Anna for short as you wished."

"I haven't wished anything; not for ages; only for a fag now and then if it's not asking too bloody much of bloody Winford Better-Never-Late. I don't know anyone by that name, that's a fact. That's a name from the Legends if ever there was one: *Morwenna Of The Fairies; Saint Morwenna* [1]. A name to be proud of. Not many have a right to it. It comes from the Ancients and you must be descended from them to be allowed a name like that. Of course, you're a woman, so you'd have a priority when the names were given out. *She* would have seen to that. They last you a lifetime you know."

"I know. And I am proud of it. And you gave it to me."

"When?"

"When I was born. You told Dr Will and Dr Megan it was my name when you asked them to look after me."

"When would that be then?"

"When I was born and my mother died."

"No, no. You're wrong there, Missus. I remember Dr Will and Dr Megan of course; of course I do; I wouldn't forget them of all people: *wouldn't want to, wouldn't do*. But they went away in the end. I didn't see them again after Father Rees came."

"Don't you remember the baby girl you had?"

"No girl. There was a boy once. Bendigeidfran [10] his name was. Another great Celtic name not given to many; it was the name of a God you know – a *Duw* in the exact same place as the Pashas come from. But a bit too long in the name, and a bugger to spell all the time: no two times the same. And what if you wanted to call him home for his dinner eh? Tell me that? If you shouted Bendigeidfran every time, his bloody dinner would be stone cold before he arrived. Poor sod would starve and you'd have to give the food to the whippet who couldn't beat a fart in a race to the shithouse. So we called him 'Bran' for short. He waded across the Sea to Ireland to tear them off a strip for being too forward; as they are, the Irish, *begorra*. But the Ancients called him home and we didn't see him again either. Pity that. But no girl, no company for my lady."

213

"Mr Llewellyn," said Edward. "Is that how you like to be called?"

"Great name. He was a Prince you know. I'm proud of that."

"Quite right too."

"Or Llew Llaw Gyffes [16] . I'll answer to that too."

"We can explain it all but it would be much easier if we all sat down."

"Are you deaf or something, boyo? No, I said, and No I meant: *no sitting, no shitting.* One's too forward and the other's all behind."

"It will be easier with the photographs," said Anna. "Mr Llewellyn, can I go and get them from the front door? Would you mind?"

"It's *Come si, Come sah* to me. I don't want the bloody door anyway. You can brick it up and take it with you when you go if you fancy it. It's Bob's Little Fishes to me."

Anna walked out of the kitchen and along the hallway towards the front door. She was longer in returning than Edward expected, and when she appeared she was drying her eyes. She put the note and the photographs on the table and turned away.

"You found them then? Bloody miracle if you ask me. I expect there's lots of things there if you only looked; I never do, see. I found a New Testament there once; from the Mormons or the Seven Day people or somebody. I've kept it in case they come back for it but I haven't looked since; you don't want to encourage. Never mind, Father Rees will see to it when he comes back I expect. Only one miracle left to ask for and that's bloody Winford with my Pashas. But that's too bloody much to ask even Aladdin and his magic lantern for. You didn't notice any fags by the door, did you?"

"No, sorry," said Anna.

"He does that sometimes. Too tired to walk to the back. If you'd brought some fags, we could all be sitting down enjoying ourselves now."

Edward passed the two photographs to Rhodri and said, "These are what we wanted you to see. You can tell that the big girl is Anna here. It was taken only last year on holiday."

"On holiday was it then? Where would that be? Barmouth?"

"No. A bit further. South of France."

"Oh, I wouldn't want to go there. They eat Frogs there, you know. I don't know how they can stomach that – cold and slimy. Because of the war I expect; bit short they'd be no doubt with the Germans and no rations. And snails. You're lucky you got away safe and sound. They make some good fags though. I'm happy to try those. No, Porthcall and Pasha cigarettes is all I ask for on my deathbed, given the chance. I'd be happy to call God my uncle then. In the circumstances like. Is it alright to say that to you? Are you religious?"

"No, that's alright."

"Well you can't never tell these days. You can upset people easy as burying them and a damn sight more expensive too. Who's this other one then?"

"That's Anna too."

"Got a tongue girl? Is this you?"

"Yes. I was four then and just starting school."

"You, is it? Four you say? You look a bit young for four; more like three – and – a – bit it seems to me and that's a fact. Are you sure it's you?"

"Yes, I'm sure."

"Why?"

"Why what?"

"Why are you sure? Get a grip for Christ's sake and be a bit of help. Remember it do you?"

"Not exactly. It's a long time ago now."

"It would be if you were really three – and – a - bit and it really was you. I'm not convinced; you don't look a bit like yourself. You could be anybody as far as I can see. Goldilocks! Red Riding Hood! Hansel-and-Gretel! Snow White! Not Sleeping Beauty though, you're not pretty enough for that."

"No. It's me."

"Well if it's you I'll go to the bottom of my stairs. I'd never have guessed it if I'd been tested. I suppose everybody has to be four some time; or three – and – a - bit even. What are you doing here now then?"

"We've come to visit you," said Anna.

"I can bloody well see that, can't I? You wouldn't be standing there without a pinafore on if you hadn't come to visit, would you? Bloody obvious that is. Think I'm doolaly or something? Well think again. I'm all there. Where the bloody hell's that Winford? What day is it today?"

"It's Thursday," said Edward.

"Thor's day. A Great God; one of seven you know, one for each day of the week. He was always throwing thunderbolts about he was. I wouldn't mind that job if it came up. One straight at bloody Winford without telling him it's coming. He was Welsh you know."

"Who? Winford?"

"Don't be bloody dafter than you are: Thor was, until the foreigners took him. He always comes on Thor's day. I bet the bugger's forgotten. Needs a thunderbolt up his arse, he does and no mistake. That'd shift him a bit more than a laxative. Do you mind me swearing, you posh people with two doors and a bell? It's up to you; you don't have to

215

listen. I only get enough Pashas to last a week and I smoked the last one yesterday, expecting him to be here by now. Lazy sod."

"Perhaps you should cut down on your smokes," said Edward.

"Why?"

"Why what?"

"There you go again; get a bloody grip. Why should I cut down on my smokes? We've got two *Penstiffs* [17] here and that's a fact. I'll say it slow like so you understand the English tongue: Why should I cut down on my smokes?"

"Better for your health; you wouldn't cough so much," said Edward.

"My cough's my own look-out and enjoyment, thank you very much and how's your father if he's not kicking up the daisies. You need a cough of your own in life; it's a good start to the day is cleaning out the tubes. And don't worry about my health either. It will see me out and no mistake, thank you very much, and a bit left over for God if He's fast enough. Don't you worry about that boyo.

"What do you want then, with your visiting? I haven't got any money. No good asking for money, I haven't got any. Handouts is all I get. And no bloody fags when I need them. What do you want then if it isn't money?"

"We came to see you," said Anna. "I found out that you're my father and I found out where you lived, so we came."

"Shouldn't have bloody bothered. I'm nobody's father any more, so you can't expect any money from me."

"You're my father. And I learned that I had a brother, who died. My mother died as well, though I don't know who she was. I was hoping you would tell me. You were on your own then, and you left me in the care of Dr Will and Dr Megan and they brought me up. Don't you remember any of that? Now I wanted to see you."

"Took your bloody time then didn't you Miss three – and – a – bit if that's bloody true. Nobody could call you Speedy Gonzales the Bandit of Mexico, could they? You're a damn sight more than four now, that's obvious. Have you got a television? Answer me girl, when I'm talking to you."

"Yes, we have."

"You want to watch a bit more of it then; like what I do. Then you'd know about Speedy Gonzales - *Eh, Hombre!* and Road Runner - *Beep – Beep!* and that lot. *'What's Up Doc?'* is my favourite, with that Rabbit and his carrots. That and a Pasha. You had a half-sister too so my Lady said, did you know?"

"No. What was her name? What happened to her?"

"She died sometime or other – went away. Everybody dies around

216

...ave. A very good cliff, high and open to the Welsh Sea, where ...wind blows through your hair and the sun shines through the ...d the yellow Gorse Flowers [20] are at your command. You ...nd there and be known."

...ome with us," said Anna. "You owe it to yourself."

...do it, it won't be for me; but for all the sons of Gwalia lost ...the ages."

...it for them then," said Anna.

...s, you've persuaded me of my destiny. Shall we go now?"

...omorrow," said Edward. "We've got some preparations to do ...We must prepare things."

...ike St John the Baptist: Prophet he was who washed away sins in ...ame of God. *Prepare thy table before me.*"

...Exactly. We'll come for you tomorrow afternoon. You can pack ...case and be ready."

...Are you sure you've got shoes," said Anna.

...'I've told you once, of course I've got bloody shoes; and boots as ...ll. What do you think I am, a bloody hobo or something? I just don't ...ow where they are at the moment, that's all. I haven't used them for a ..., that's all"

"Try and find them by tomorrow then, will you?" she asked.

"I'll find them, don't you worry your head; they can't be far away ...an they? This isn't a bloody mansion now is it? Not like Buckingham ...Palace or the other one. Shoes don't walk on their bloody own now do ...they Missus three – and – a - bit? They need a foot or two in them to ...walk. I can't stand on the cliff in bare feet now, can I? That wouldn't be ...respect now would it? You go now and prepare the way and make sure ...that you give it your full attention. Do it properly. No slacking. And if ...you see Winford, tell the bugger to hurry up or I'll be to hell and gone ...by the time he gets here. Go on. Off you go, and don't be late for the ...blessing. Double quick now."

They were ushered out somewhat unceremoniously. "You see? It's a ...good job I didn't let you sit down. You'd have been here forever. And ...then where would we be? Tell me that now. Up shit's creek, lantern or ...no lantern, that's where. Go on. Do your preparations. If you do them ...good, I'll let you sit down for a bit next time."

As they reached the car, a young lad cycled up to the gate with a ...cardboard box of provisions and carried it to the kitchen door. Edward ...said, "I would guess that's Winford about to have his ears pinned ...back."

As they sat in the car, Anna cried silently. "What is it love?" asked ...Edward.

me, so you'd better not stay too long. Though when you're dead it's neither here nor there I suppose. It's all God's will and Bob's your uncle, then."

"What was her name?"

"Whose name are we talking about?"

"My half-sister."

"I don't know, it was before my time, but my Lady told me."

"Your Lady? Was that my mother?"

"Who else are we talking about here? Think I'm made of girls? Think I've got a bloody Hareem like Errol bloody Flynn?"

"Sorry. What was her name?"

"I told you, I don't know. 'Day' or something."

"No, my mother's name, I meant."

"That's easy. Her mother, whoever *she* was from Pirate - Land, called her Vera. Not a very good name; not a Welsh name at all. Never trust your mother to give you a name; but it was alright for her. She was very clever; she could read the Legends in no time at all. She knew all the families of the *Mabinogi* [15]. You'd have liked her when she was well. Everybody liked her. But nobody could take advantage; I wouldn't let them get away with that."

"I'm sure. Father, we'd like to ask you something."

"*Asking's easy; doing's hard.*"

"We'd like you to come on holiday with us. Would you like that? Get away for a change?"

"I'm not going anywhere near bloody Frenchies for a start; no chance. I can't eat frogs and snails; I'd starve to death first. I've got a weak stomach, see. No, not for me, thank you very much. I'll stay here and wait for my Pashas."

"No, not to France. Just to our house by the sea; just for a few days, or until you want to come home."

"I don't like the sands. It gets in all your sandwiches: you've got a choice of *Eggs and Sand, Bacon and Sand, Egg and Bacon and Sand, Lettuce and Tomato and Sand or just Bread and Sand.*"

"No sand," said Edward. "The house is on the top of the cliff and looks out to sea. You can see boats in the distance quite often."

"Ilfracombe then is it? Lloeger?"

"No. Nearer than that. It won't take long to get there and we could get you home in two shakes if that's what you wanted. What do you say?" asked Edward.

"I expect it's alright for you posh people who like two doors and a bell, but it wouldn't do for me. Too many people on the beach. No, you go; I'll stay here and watch Popeye – *it's only me, from over the sea -*

and wait for my Pashas. I couldn't do without my Pashas, see: they clean the tubes and settle the stomach. You go and enjoy yourselves. I'll be alright here."

"We could pick up your fags on the way and we'd make sure that you had enough of them. You'd never run out."

"No. I wouldn't want to put bloody Winford to any trouble. I don't want him to come all that way. He's a nice boy. P'rhaps his bike's broken down, so he can't get here. So long as he's not smoking my Pashas that's all, the bugger. I wouldn't put it past him."

"We could tell him to keep them for you until you come back. We'll buy you some more."

"I haven't got any money."

"We have. We'll get them for you."

"I don't want to get anything on tick; trouble that is. Father Rees was strict about that. No. I don't think so, not at my time of life anyway; not in the circumstances. Anyway, I'm not supposed to go out without telling them."

"We'll arrange all that. All you have to do is pack a case and enjoy yourself. Sit on the cliff-top, smoke a Pasha and watch the sea; and nobody to bother you. Then home for tea. It'll make a change for you," said Edward.

"Father Rees promised me a trip to the seaside once. But he never kept his promise; it never came off. He was a bit like that, was Father Rees – catch him when you can. He went away like the rest of them did. Nobody here but me now; me and Mister Magoo. It'll do for me now though at my time of life. 'Nough said; 'nough done."

"But wouldn't you like a little holiday? Just for a change?" asked Anna.

"No. Too old for change. Peace and quiet for me now; if the buggers leave me alone. You go; send me a postcard of Ilfracombe; see what it's like, like. I'll see you when you get back. Pity you're not going to *Pasha-Land* though. I'd go there if there was somebody else to take the strain like, and watch out for Errol Flynn and his sword. *Dessert Song;* that was the film – bloody awful it was; too many fucking women in the Harreem and not one of them ugly. I wouldn't mind a dose of that like, if it was going."

"We're going to our house, Father. We'd like you to see it."

"House, mouse, catch a louse; they're all the same, too many doors. It's just somewhere to live while we pass through."

"Mr Llewellyn," said Edward, "I've got an idea. I don't want to call you Mr Llewellyn all the time and I can't really call you Dad. I've decided that I'm going to call you 'Llew'. You know your Welsh, don't

you?"

"'Course I do; it's my tongue."

"So you know that Llew means ? Llewellyn. It's a good name for you, Lle

"Nobody's called me that before."

"Well, that's their look-out isn't it?"

"That's a good name for me that is. Lio that's you that is. But I wouldn't like too it. That wouldn't do at all. They'll think I'n and getting too big for my boots and shoes the Cowardly Lion like in the picture though;

"Certainly not. A true Lion. But we'll kee three of us, you, me and Anna I think. It will b us."

"That's a good trick that is; I like Codes an only powerful when they're kept secret; if they name, they can't dominate you. Like God's nam that once you let the cat out of the bag you can kiss die."

Edward smiled and said, "That's very true."

"Of course it is; that's why I said it, even though sayings. I've got lots of sayings in case you haven't not

"Yes, we've noticed and very sharp they are too," sai I think we should celebrate your new name, make a fuss

"It wouldn't be a secret then though would it?"

"We'll make a fuss in secret; only us three will know We will stand on the cliff and shout at the sea: 'Take notice Llew of Morgannwg [18]. You shall all know him and all his shall obey. Be still until you are called to serve him and him a

"You daft bugger! But it's good is that; but it's not the sea call to but Poseidon [19], God of the Sea and his mucker, the b the Garden Fork. I've always fancied that job. Champion. listen?"

"It's got to. You are Llew of Morgannwg, and Llew Llaw [16], a child of the Ancient Princes of Wales. It has to listen whe called out, and it will carry your name to the four corners of the Ear

"That's rubbish. The Earth is round so it doesn't have any corn That story's as bad as some of the Old Tales."

"They had to make it seem like that because they wanted to kee their secrets as well. They only wanted those in the know to know the secrets."

"That's a fact and a half, that is. Anyway, we haven't got a cliff."

Anna shook her head and said, "That poor man; my father; he's had to carry his cross all his life. I should have been here years ago. Do you know that he sleeps in the front room? I saw his unmade mattress when I went for the photographs. He can't ever go upstairs. What kind of life is that?

"One he lives as he thinks easiest and best; one that troubles him least. He probably thinks that 'upstairs' is as superfluous as 'two doors.'"

"Yes. Him and his Pashas and his *sayings* and his TV cartoons for company. How many live their lives out in that fashion? While the World and its Village outside rolls on in oblivion."

"Hardly that my love. You must understand them too: they can't keep trying to approach if they're not welcome."

"I don't wish to understand them. I have enough trouble understanding myself. I should have been with him years ago. I am at grave, unforgivable fault; I could have alleviated some of his sadness, given him succour, given him something in his life."

"You can't know that. Remember that he did what he thought was best for you. You should respect that."

"That simply compounds my guilt; it doesn't ease it."

"It should. It's what a parent must do. You didn't ask to be born. A child owes a parent nothing; it's the parent that owes the child everything."

"Sophistry. A clever argument that has no meaning at all. But I will tell you one thing: I shall not leave him again; if he won't come with me, then I shall stay with him. And it hurts to say this because we mean something to each other and, yes, we need each other too; but if I must make a choice between you and him, it will be him; for all your sorrow, you can cope; he can't. Do you understand?"

"Strangely, I think I do."

"Then you must not curse me." She dried her tears and smiled at him. "And thank you for the story to make him come with us. That was sharp of you."

"I hope that the effect lasts until tomorrow and we don't have to start all over again. Come on, we'd better get back for some food."

CHAPTER 32

PREPARATION

When they arrived back at their hotel, Anna tried to telephone the Solicitors that she had previously visited with Megan and Charles, but, as expected, there was no reply: the Partners would have closed their files for the day and gone home long before. After dinner, they took a short walk along the beach and retired early.

The next morning, Anna telephoned again while Edward was taking a shower. While he dressed and she did what little she always did with her short hair, she said that she had arranged an appointment with the young Mr Davies for 10.30.

"He was rather reluctant, citing an important tort meeting that could be delayed no longer, but I said that we were only in the City for the day and wouldn't take up too much of his time. *'In and out in two shakes'* I said. I also said that we were in desperate need of his guidance. I think that aroused his curiosity."

"You're as bad as your mother. No ethics, that's your family's trouble."

"Anyway, ethics or not, he relented; chalk up a positive result for unethical behaviour. But it's true, we won't need to take up much of his time, so long as he plays ball."

"What's with all this vernacular all of a sudden?"

"Slovenliness. But there's another thing I want to do before we pick up father Rhodri."

"What else? We shouldn't leave him too long to think about things; it could make him difficult to persuade again."

"I know. But I want to clear another debt while we're here. It won't take long either, but I owe it, and I need to clear it."

"What is it then?"

"I need to go to Creigiai again to see Lord Mostyn."

"What the hell for? That's miles out of our way. It can't be so important that we'll make problems for ourselves with Rhodri."

"It's a risk, I grant you, but I must settle it."

"Well, I don't suppose you'll be happy unless we do, but I can't think what can be so catastrophically important to take us miles and hours out of our way that can't be done by phone or a letter."

"Just trust me. Accept that it's important to me to see him."

"We'd better get our skates on then and get down to breakfast and to *young* Mr Davies. It had better be a 'Full Welsh' because God knows when we'll eat again with all this gallivanting across the Principality."

"Now you're being crabby. Time you had your laver bread and salty bacon. Salt depravation obviously makes you crabby."

After breakfast they checked out of the hotel and drove to the Solicitor's Offices in the Victorian Crescent above the wide sweep of the bay. The weather was balmy and the sea very still. The road that curved around the arc of the coast could not be seen and there was only a very distant hum of traffic. Anna said, "What an idyllic spot to spend your working life."

"If you can afford it," said Edward. "Something tells me that you need to be a lawyer to do it though; indulge yourself on other peoples' misfortunes."

"That's uncalled for and you know it."

"Yes, I suppose. True though."

They introduced themselves at the reception desk and were not kept waiting long before being taken through to the Solicitor's office. Mr Davies rose as Anna said, "We're very grateful to you for seeing us at such short notice. We appreciate that you have some pressing engagements so we'll be as brief as we possibly can."

"That would be appreciated. I have a difficult meeting to attend and I do need to do some reading before hand. So if you could be brief?"

"Yes," said Anna. "We've met before but may I introduce my husband, Edward Williams? You have met his father Prof Charles Williams."

"Indeed. I remember him well, and that distasteful occurrence at the University. I should offer you my congratulations then. Now what can I do for you?"

"Advice, principally," said Anna. "Following the guidance and advice of Lord Mostyn and others, we have been able to track down my biological father, Rhodri Morgan who calls himself Rhodri Llewellyn, and we have been to visit him and have talked to him."

"I see; I wish that you had not been so 'precipitate'. If you had discussed it with me, I would have counselled against it."

"Why?"

"Because of the implications to the requirements of the Trust. One cannot be cavalier in these matters and we must consider the goodwill of the Trustees."

"The Trustees must be secondary; this was a visit of a daughter to her estranged father. It should be welcomed not condemned."

"I will admit that you have been persistent. You will remember that through the constraints of the Trust I was unable to be of much effective help. If you have talked to Mr Morgan, then you probably know as much as we do. I must use the name Morgan you understand, because there has been no legal change of name, by deed or other method. Otherwise, there is little more that I can add."

"Well, there's the question of who pays all the bills for his needs, for a start."

"There need be no secrecy there: accounts are rendered by the providers, through an Accountant, to this Office. We discharge the debts, monthly. Everyone seems happy with that arrangement and there have been no disagreements. Was that your concern?"

"No, that is incidental at this time but thank you for telling us. I must tell you now, that I know of the Will of the late Councillor Rees; and as the biological daughter – the *issue* - of Mr Morgan, I can declare a legal interest which you will understand. But for the moment, the important issue about which we asked to see you, Mr Davies, is of a more personal nature. We have, I think, persuaded Mr Morgan to accompany my husband and I to our house in the West, for a short holiday, or, perhaps, if he will accept, permanently. We will need to determine which. A holiday in the first instance, in any case; I do not believe that he will contemplate any longer duration at this time."

"I'm pleased that you have persuaded him, naturally," said Mr Davies. "But why do you need to see me?"

"He and others, are under the impression that his movements are restricted by Order of the Police. We do not have details, but it appears to have some basis in activities with children. Whatever it is, he does not leave his house and has boarded up his windows after breakages by children."

"I was not aware of the breakages and I will see that the necessary steps are taken to repair any damage, and make the house secure if that is needed."

"Thank you. But what is most needed is your advice on this other matter: the restriction to his movement."

"There is no restriction to his movement that we are aware of I assure you. No charges of any kind, neither minor, Civil, nor Criminal have ever been brought or lodged by any person or authority to our knowledge."

"If that is the case, then why is he under the impression that he is unable to leave his house?"

"I cannot surmise, nor can I penetrate his mind in that regard. I can only speculate that he was given that impression by the Police, perhaps intentionally, in order to curtail his wanderings on the mountain at all hours - for his own safety you understand."

"Of course," said Edward. "But principally for the benefit of the Police would it be? After all, they might otherwise have been called to account by the local Worthies and the Chapel Deacons no doubt."

"I cannot comment on that, except to say that he lives in what is, after all, a very insular society; especially so in the Valleys."

"Yes, especially there," said Anna. "There can be no doubt that it is such an *insular* Society as you *surmise* Mr Davies."

"Quite. And you must appreciate that it is a matter for the Police, as they see fit, to decide on how best to pursue their duties in keeping the peace."

Anna said, "Ah, there we have it, do you see. Surely, it is not entirely for the Police to decide. 1984? A little overdue, but have we come to it at last?"

"I'm afraid that I don't follow you."

"No. I thought perhaps you wouldn't. The Orwellian Utopia Mr Davies. How sad for us all."

"Just so," said Mr Davies. "I'm afraid I have no time for speculation of that kind; I deal in the facts."

"As I deal in the Philosophy. But what are they?" asked Anna.

"I beg your pardon?"

"Your *facts* Mr Davies. What are they at present?"

"There are no charges that this Partnership is aware of. Now, if you'll excuse me, I must be moving on. I am running way behind and I do not have more time to offer you."

"Yes," said Anna, "You must be moving and so must we. You will confirm, though, that we shall be able to take him with us to our house? Without any form of restraint or hindrance or objection?"

"Certainly. Though it might be courteous to inform the local Constabulary of your intention."

Anna smiled wryly and said, "Yes. We mustn't forget to inform the Uniform. Well, thank you for your time. Please send your account through to Dr Megan Griffiths; you have her address I believe. Good bye."

She left without offering her hand. As they walked back to the car, Anna could not restrain her repetition of "Pedantry!"

"''Don't upset yourself, love; we've got the information you wanted. Just leave it now."

"Leave it? It's *'leaving it'* as you say that brings the ends no one wants. I will wager that that pedant has never in his life doubted anything he's ever said or done. God, how I hate the *'Walking Certainties'* on this earth."

"I agree. Give me a Doubting Thomas anytime. But we don't need to see him again, so set it aside. Now, shall we go to your father?"

"No. To Roderick Samuel, the Editor first, then to Creigiai, then to my father."

"Samuel won't see us on speck. He'll be far too busy."

"I've phoned him too. He'll see us."

"Why didn't you tell me you were going to do this? You can't behave like this Anna. Besides, if we see him and then go to Creigiai we'll be far too late going to your father."

"Not if we miss lunch; you ate more than enough breakfast anyway. We shan't spend any time with either of them, and I don't want to have to retrace our steps."

"Why should we have to retrace our steps? What is it you want?"

"Information, if there is any, and the discharge of a debt, as I've told you. That's all."

"I think we'd better get going then, if Madam allows."

They drove back into the centre of the City and spent some time finding a parking space near the covered market. From there, they walked to the newspaper offices and their appointment.

When they were seated in his office, Roderick Samuel said, "Congratulations are in order, I understand. I wish you had let me know; I would have run a column for the daughter of Will and Megan Griffiths and the son of Charles and Elizabeth Williams. *'Families United.'* Many of our readers would remember your parents. But perhaps that's why you kept it so clandestine?"

"We decided, and we did it," said Anna. "It would have been no big deal to anyone else."

"You under-estimate people's nosiness. A bad fault in journalism, I must tell you. But too late now. Well, what is it I can do for you?"

"Information," said Anna. "Or rather, more information. From what you wrote to Charles and my mother, for which our thanks, we have traced my biological father and we visited him at his house yesterday. It seems that he has been subjected to some persecution by the children of his village and has been virtually incarcerated in his house. Apparently, he doesn't leave and relies on the arrangements that have been made by others for the delivery of his needs. They are reimbursed from a Trust apparently. We have persuaded him to come with us to our house but he insists that he has been forbidden to leave his village. According to the Trust Solicitor, this is not the case but it seems that he has been - 'misled to that conclusion'- shall we say, to be charitable, by the Police because of some previous activity. We should like to know whether that is true and we would like your advice as to whether anything should be done about it."

"A very precise précis. You are easily answered. A few years ago, there were reports in the National Press of the deaths of young girls in particular but also of small boys, some of whose bodies have never been found. You will remember, as the older generation do, the case of Rosemary West and her husband when children were subjected to unspecified practices, killed and buried somewhere on Cannock Moor; not all have been recovered to this day. Then, the spectre appeared again and the word 'Paedophilia' became writ large in people's vocabulary and I have to admit that the 'Fourth Estate' was much to blame. So, any new occurrence of that nature immediately generated the expected response and it seems that every village should have a Paedophile. Many an unfortunate suffered as a consequence, particularly, or especially, in isolated communities: men, and it is always men, of a rather retarded nature for whatever reason, were somewhat 'hounded'. They, who were once considered to be as a child, who played with children and were known to do so, who were treated with benevolence and understanding, became targets for the frustrations and venom of unfulfilled women, and it is usually women, who pressed their husbands to take some action to protect the children and their way of life. Fortunately, not many were prosecuted and the Police, in their fashion, acted with some common sense. That is your situation: Rhodri Morgan, as the next best thing to a retarded adult that could be identified, was targeted and the Police put a stop to it. Their method might be questioned, but their action did prevent bigotry from becoming a vendetta. So to answer your questions: there is no reason why you cannot take Rhodri Morgan to your house; you need take no action with regard to the Police, though for the safety of the property, you should cancel all deliveries and removals. As for taking any further action, against the Police or anyone else, I would counsel against it; there is no case to prosecute and anyway it would be counterproductive. I hope that this satisfies your concerns?"

"Once again Mr Samuel we are greatly in your debt. We will take up no more of your time," said Anna.

"Thank you," said Edward. "This is greatly appreciated; we want you to know that. I cannot think of anything, but if there is anything we can do in return, you have only to mention it."

"There is one thing: visit me some time and tell me your stories; I'm very 'nosey' d'you see," he said with a smile. "Oh, and give my best wishes to Megan and to Charles and tell them that they too owe me a visit."

"Certainly. Goodbye, and thank you again," said Anna.

They walked back to the car through the market and bought

provisions for their kitchen. "These smells are making me hungry," said Edward.

"After that breakfast? You'll put on weight, you know."

"I know, but not just yet."

"Buy some Welsh Cakes then. And get some for my father. I don't suppose he's had those fresh for some time. It'll be a treat for him and better than cigarettes."

"I have a feeling that it's not 'either/or.' We'll get him his Pashas on the way back, and cancel his deliveries. I wish you'd put off going to Creigiai."

"I can't do that."

"Why not? What's so pressing?"

"Promises. I must tell Lord Mostyn that I can't attend his New Year Point-to-Point Races; and I want to help him finish his story as I told him I would."

The distance to the Safe Haven Charity house of Creigiai was not great, though it occupied the commanding heights at the head of another valley. They both knew the history of the house: the last of a once large estate given to the family of Tomos ap Tomos of Benfro by Henry Tudor for raising an army in his support; the gradual decline in acreage as daughters were married off with land as a dowry, and the childlessness of the last of the of the line; his gift of the house and remaining land to a charity for single mothers and parentless children; and his gift of the library to the University together with sufficient income to support a Research Studentship and Research Fellowship. It had been this last position that Will, Megan's husband had occupied. The Charity was now on a firm foundation and the house had also become the home of Lord Mostyn, Chairman of the Safe Haven Trust and one-time Chairman and Chief Executive of a large building and aggregates company floated on the Stock Market.

"I'll tell you what I'd like you to do for me," said Anna.

With ill grace Edward said, "What now? This is becoming too much of a duty trip, and I'm not happy with it."

"I know; and I'm sorry but it's something I have to do. And it's not a 'duty trip' as you call it. It's rather more than that."

"What then? Why do you want to drive all that way to see an old man who lives alone in a large house surrounded by unmarried mothers and children?"

"Don't be angry with me. I need to talk to him; he's the one who told me of my father Rhodri, who my grandfather was and who helped my father Will. Now I must talk to him again, tell him what's happened; and what we intend to do. I owe him that before he dies."

"Alright. What do you want me to do?"

"We'll drive to my father's first; you can stay with him and I'll go on to Creigiai."

"Why?"

"That way, he won't feel forgotten."

"No, why go on your own?"

"Because I don't think he'll talk to me, if you're there. Oh, he'll be polite and make conversation of course, because that's how he is and it's what he's done all his life but he won't talk to me, he won't tell me what I want to know."

"Which is what precisely? Or can't you tell me either? I'm beginning to feel like a super-numary; it would be better if I was not here at all."

"Now you're being childish, and it's not like you. I just want to pump him a bit more about my ancestry, that's all. He's reluctant to do that in any case – a matter of honour or some such nonsense – but whatever it is he won't do it if you're there. So please, for me, do this my way."

"Well you mustn't drag this out for too long; just remember that I shall be with your father and we should get home sooner rather than later."

"I know. But trust me. I'm asking for your trust a great deal at the moment but I hope you'll understand why."

"Well I'm not best pleased, but I suppose I'll have to accept it for now."

Anna leaned over and kissed him and said, "Who's a good husband then? I shan't be any time before I'm back, you'll see, and then we can go on our way. How's that?"

"Second best, but it will have to do. I'd like to get home before dark."

"Come on then. *Chop, Chop the Chinese Cook* as my father would say. Stop dawdling."

They stopped to cancel Rhodri's deliveries until further notice and bought him a pack of 200 cigarettes. They then drove on into the village and to the house. There was no sign of Rhodri as they opened the kitchen door. Edward called, "Llew? We're here. Where are you?"

There was no reply. "Llew, we've come for you as we said. Are you packed ready?"

There was still no reply. "I'll go and look for him," said Edward. "He must be in somewhere."

"We'll look in the front room first," said Anna.

"If he's there, he must have heard us," said Edward. "Perhaps he's gone outside."

"Not likely, would you think?"

They walked the corridor to the front room and saw clothes in disarray on the floor. Rhodri was lying curled up and fully dressed on his mattress in the corner of the room. He had pulled a pillow over his head and seemed to have been in that position for some time.

"Llew," said Edward. "What are you doing there? Why aren't you ready to go?"

""Go away. Piss off. Leave me alone, you and your bloody promises. You're like everybody else; all farts and no shit. Bugger off."

"Look," said Edward, "I'm sorry we're a bit late, but we had to make arrangements for when you were away. And we've brought you some fags; you favourite Pashas."

"I don't want your bloody fags; I've got my own. And don't bother making arrangements for me. It's not worth it."

"Come on Father. Let's get you ready to go to our house by the sea. Did you find your shoes and your boots?"

"Fuck the shoes. And fuck the boots too, Madam 'Three-And-A-Bit, whatever your name is for all I care. And don't you 'Father' me Missus."

"Well you'll need them if you're going to walk on the cliff-top," said Edward. "Anna's got one more message to take then we can be off. What do you say to that?"

"You can both be off for all I care. I don't know why you came here in the first bloody place, disturbing the bloody peace. I was alright before you came with your bloody ideas and your Llew nonsense. I don't know why I listened to you, taking advantage and wanting to sit down. And you Missus, pretending to be my daughter to get your way and my money. You ought to be bloody arrested. 'Making out she's the dead, that's the charge, Officer. Lock them away to think about it, and throw away the key. I don't care.'"

Edward turned to Anna and said, "If you must go, go now and don't take too long over whatever you have to do. I'll see to this."

Anna was reluctant to leave them alone but turned and left quickly, as if, by acting more slowly she would never gather the courage to go.

"Well, that's one bloody parasite gone, thank Gods and Little Fishes. When I told her there was no money, she buggered off quick enough then: *Exodus!!!* Moses was half Egyptian, did you know that? *Exodus! Leviticus!* Whoever the hell he was when he was alive: some bloody Roman, no doubt; some Itey. '*Like a rat out of a paper bag!*' What's a woman rat called, do you know?"

"I'm sorry I don't. Mrs Rat, I suppose."

"Don't be funny with me boy bach; I'm older than you so show some respect. It's your turn next in any case."

"You mustn't talk like that, Mr Llewellyn. She is your daughter, I promise you, and she's only trying to do her best for you."

"Well, her best isn't bloody good enough, is it? Not by a long chalk. Not after all these years if what you say is true and not another bloody lie. She should have been taught better manners, that's my view. Well, she won't get anything from me, not after all these years. She can *kiss my arse and bless the revolution* before she gets a penny from me."

"Llew, this is not the behaviour of a Princeling of Wales. A young Prince should be big enough to bless people less fortunate, not curse them."

"If you think that's a curse, you've had a very sheltered life, Sonny Jim. Anyway, they should know how to behave in the presence of their Prince."

"Yes. But they haven't all been taught properly, so you can't blame them for their faults. What did God say? *'Forgive them for they know not what they do'.*"

"Jesus said that, not God; though He was God as well: *Three In One: Father, Son and Holy Ghost*; so I suppose you could say that God said it and you wouldn't be wrong. Bloody awkward that – talking to yourself. On the cross and bleeding He was from the Crown of Thorns, with Mary the Prostitute at his feet and the Romans playing dice – *Snake Eyes!* A right Frontier Town it must have been on Golgotha and no mistake; give me Jesse James and Doc, Dodge City and the OK! Corral any time; you knew where you were with them – Boot Hill more like. God was His Father, you know and what He said was, *'**Father** forgive them, for they know not what they do.'* He's our Father as well; He must have the patience of bloody Job. You'd better go back to Sunday School boyo, and learn the Bible properly."

"I'm grateful for your guidance."

"I'll tell you something else too, that not many know. This knowledge is given to very few, only the privileged, so you can count yourself blessed: the nails didn't go through His palms like they've painted it. Couldn't have done see, because His weight would have pulled them between his fingers and he would have fallen off, *arse over tip*. A right mess that would have made of the Romans, I'll be bound."

"How was He nailed then?"

"I'll tell you, and not many know this: *through His wrists!* His wrist bones stopped the nails from tearing through His fingers, see! You didn't know that now did you, you fellow-me-lad?"

"No, I certainly didn't. I'm grateful to you for explaining it to me.

Who told you the secret?"

"Father Rees; he knew a lot did Father Rees. You young people, you think you know it all; got it all from your books, you like to think. But you've only been a short time on this earth and you haven't got a fucking clue. You know very little, in fact. You're not as privileged as you like to think. Listen to your fathers, they know more than you do, with all your book learning."

"You're right there and no mistake. I'll tell you something now. Us young people could do with more of your help, you know. I'll tell you where we can start: I think you should write down all your sayings and your knowledge, so the young people will know about things. What do you think? Can we do that?"

"I don't know about that. I'm not much good at writing and spelling and things like that: the words swim about like when I look at them and I can't follow the ruler on the page. I can *say* them sure enough if I'm told them, and I remember things; I'm a good rememberer; that's easy, no problem there. Good enough for the stage my voice is; or Hollywood. It's writing that's the bugger. And I mix up my letters see. My Lady used to do it for me, but she's gone now, so not much hope left to call on."

"You won't have to do the writing. We'll sit together in the evening, you, me and Anna and you can say your sayings and Anna will write them down like your Lady used to do. I'll let you into a secret, now: Anna's good at that sort of thing, much better than me. What do you think?"

"No. No. I can't be doing with nights; nights is for making babies and mothers-to-be. My friend Richie worked nights regular for four years; miner he was but he still made three babies in that time. You'd think he wouldn't have the time or the energy. I expect it kept him going, Sunday afternoons on the sofa made of Uncut Mocquette by the fire and then a bit of a sleep to catch up. When the kids got old enough he sent them to Sunday School and made three more – got used to it I suppose. That's what he told me; he said, *'what else can you do on a Sunday afternoon?'* Not nights."

"What time is best then do you think?"

"After a good breakfast is best and before your nap."

" Right. After breakfast. Then a walk on the cliff-top to blow the cobwebs away."

"What cobwebs are you talking about? What are you going on about cobwebs and things? Have you got cobwebs? I'm not going anywhere near bloody cobwebs."

"Figure of speech. It doesn't matter."

"Why say it then if it doesn't matter? Make your bloody mind up. You've got cobwebs or you haven't got cobwebs; perhaps you've got cobwebs on the brain; have you thought about that? It's all the bloody same to me down in the cellar. If you've got cobwebs, get a cat."

"After breakfast it will be then. So we'd better be ready for when Anna comes back. We'll pack your case again shall we? Do you want my help?"

"To lift a few shirts and trousers? You must think I'm senile, boy. You go in the kitchen and make a cup of tea like a good boy. And I've put a chair there for you to sit down like I said. I'll be there in two shakes."

Edward busied himself finding the tea and boiling the kettle. The tea was brewing when Rhodri appeared. "There's milk if you want it, in the fridge. I have it black, like the Russians but you're welcome; unless it's gone off. It usually does before I finish it. My fault: I don't have it in tea and I don't eat cornflakes – cardboard it is. I keep telling Milky, 'no milk today Milky' but he still leaves it. Perhaps he's on commission for how many pints he leaves. I wouldn't put it past him. He's a friend of Winford's you know; they go dancing together; two peas in a pod. Bloody useless, both of them; two of them together wouldn't make a whole."

"I'll leave him a note, if you like."

" Do you want a Pasha?"

"No thanks, I don't smoke."

"You're missing out there boyo. Clears the tubes it does. There's only one thing better than a fag. Do you know what it is?"

"No."

"It begins with 'F' as well. Bear it in mind for the next time. But it's one after the other, mind you, not together: pay attention to the first, and you can relax with the second. Did I tell you I found my shoes and my boots?"

"No. Where were they?"

"You'll never guess. Go on. Guess."

"I have no idea."

"You give in? Under the bloody sink of all places. Now what the bloody hell were they doing there? Did they go for a walk in the night d'you think? You hear about things like that – *The Marching Boots.* Like Mickey Mouse and the buckets of water. I wouldn't like it in my house by God, thanks a lot; but it would make a great story for Christmas Eve, before *himself* came. They weren't too clean either, I admit, so I've given them a 'spit-and-polish', like in the Army; you don't want to feel ashamed.

'This is the Army Mr Brown;
You and your baby went to town.
She had you worried like never before.
But she won't worry you any more.'

Do you know that song?"

"I've heard it, yes."

"American it is. From the War. The Beverly Sisters. But that's the clean version. There's a dirty one I can't remember. Just as well. When are we off then?"

"Just as soon as Anna gets back. She won't be much longer."

"You never know with them; mind of their own; time of their own. A different clock to the rest of us, they've got. God didn't set it properly when he made them from Adam's rib; didn't have time I suppose what with everything else to make and set right and get going. Got lights on you car, have you?"

"Oh, yes; good lights."

"Damn good job if we can't get there before dark. I hope she won't be long, I'm a bit hungry. Did you bring these Welsh Cakes?"

"Yes. Straight from the Market. The best."

"I'm not too struck on Welsh Cakes if you must know. Too sweet for my tooth; they give me gip, especially the bloody raisins; stick in your teeth they do. Why can't they make plain ones for people with no good teeth? You could soften them in a cup of tea and raisins wouldn't fall out like sheep droppings. My aunty used to make them on a Mân [21] for the shop and the colliers when I was a small boy and I ate too many of them. Do you know what a Mân is?"

"Yes."

"I'll tell you anyway because the English thinks it's a man, bloody idiots. But we know it's a hot-plate, a thick one. Did you get any laver bread [12]? I enjoy that. You can keep your Welsh Cakes for me; give me laver bread any time. Taste of the sea. I'll put my shoes on now, to be ready. Put my boots in a bag, there's a good boy."

With some relief, Edward said, "I think I hear the car now."

"Better ears than I've got then. Is it her? Better late than never? Better never late!"

"I expect so." Silently, he hoped fervently that it was. The continuing, fractured conversation with Rhodri was becoming trying, and he too, was anxious to set out for home.

Anna opened the kitchen door and said, "Guess what? I'm back."

"About bloody time too" said Rhodri. "We've been sitting here with

234

our thumbs up our arses wondering if you done a bunk with this lad's car instead of getting us home before dark. Bloody miracle if we make it now."

"Father, you don't know that, so don't be so bloody awkward. There are other things I must do, apart from baby-sitting a miserable, frigging old man."

"Anna!" said Edward. "There's no need for that."

"How the hell do you know? You haven't had to justify him or your actions for the last two hours."

"No, I've just had to accommodate him."

"Don't talk over my head. 'Him's' the tomcat."

"Yes, Llew; it's wrong of us. I'm sorry; we must get weaving."

"What about her, the *Queen of the Fairies* there? Is she going to come? We could leave her behind; serve her right it would, Miss Three-And-A-Bit. If she's not sorry, I'm not coming. I don't have to you know; I can eat my own soup and smoke my own Pashas. I can't be putting up with her tantrums day – in - day out. Life's not worth living like that; better on your own."

"Father, I am sorry; the traffic was awful. But I'm here now and we can go any time you like."

"The time I liked was two hours ago, before dark."

"Yes," said Anna, "But I wanted to try to do some things. Edward will take your case and we'll lock up and go. Where are your house keys?"

"No keys."

"You must have keys, for God's sake."

"Don't take the Lords name in vain. He'll strike you dumb and where will you be then *Queen of the Fairies*?"

"Yes, Father. But we must lock up; you must have keys."

"Of course I've got keys. You can't have a house with two doors and a bell and no bloody keys; stands to reason, it does; it's like having a trousers with no braces that is."

"Where are they then?" asked Anna, while Edward smiled.

"Guess."

"Father, we haven't got time to play these games, so tell me."

"Whose fault is that then Missus, with no time? Answer me that Miss Gallivanting? Bringing bloody Welsh Cakes with bloody raisins."

"Llew, where are they?" asked Edward.

"In my boots. I always keep them there in my boots, under the sink. They're safe there. Nobody would think of looking for keys in your boots."

Edward retrieved the keys and they made to leave. As Anna locked the door, Rhodri said, "We're not going to be long, are we? I don't want to be too long. Winford won't leave my Pashas if I'm not here, see."

"We've told him to keep them for you until we call back," said Edward.

"Have we got enough to last?" asked Rhodri.

"Plenty," said Edward. "And we can always get you some more if you run out. Get in the car. Where do you want to sit? Front or back?"

"Back. Like a Prince."

As they settled in the car, Edward turned to Anna and asked, "Did you see him?

"No. He wasn't awake."

"What will you do then?"

"Go later," said Anna.

"Tell me then," said Edward.

"Yes. But later."

"What are you talking about now," asked Rhodri.

"Only what Anna wanted to talk with Lord Mostyn about. Nothing too important."

"Let's get on then if it's not important.

> *'Have some fun,*
> *Son of a gun,*
> *And pass the ammunition.'*

> *'This is the Army Mr Green*
> *We like the barracks nice and clean'".*

CHAPTER 33

THE VIEW TO THE SEA

As they crested a low hill the land ran away to the sea in the distance. There were dense areas of gorse [20] towards the edge of the cliffs which formed an effective barrier against any straying towards the edge. To the right as they looked, the land levelled out into flat fields before rising into the mountain foothills. These fields were marked out by stone walls into a manageable size for farming; sheep were grazing in the walled areas towards the cliff edge. Further inland towards the mountain, the larger fields were being harvested for their crops of wheat and barley, and the tractors and combine harvesters were still busy in the late evening light. The land then rose quickly through bracken already beginning to turn to a Rufus Red [22], to the exposed heather and bare rock that reached the summit. The road on which they had driven, became a track that curved away from the cliff edge towards the house that was set back only a short distance from the cliff. The house was low and angled away from the prevailing south-westerly winds that in winter drove the rain and sleet inland; the slate roof overhung the small upper-storey windows to an extent that the door and ground-floor windows seemed pressed into the land itself. The windows were made darker by the white-washed walls.

As they approached the house, the last of the sun flushed the western sky with gold and red. Below that sky, the land was quickly becoming darker and the cliff edge and the sea beyond it were disappearing. Even the house was becoming just a more solid darkness against the foot of the mountain.

"It's very beautiful," said Anna, "Even when it's growing dark over the sea; wild, but beautiful. I can easily understand why you sought it out."

"We're in time," said Edward. "I thought we might be too late."

"For what?"

"Wait a moment in peace. I hope we'll be privileged."

It was finally dark, then there was a flash of red-gold on the horizon before all colour and light was ended. Then the stars took their turn and showed the infinity of space and the privilege of their lives.

"Edward," said Anna.

"Yes. I couldn't speak either when I first saw it. There's a word for it of course: *dumbstruck!* Someone called this planet *Space-ship Earth* and when you see it like this, you have to agree. This Universe we live in is sometimes too much I find. That wasn't the best of the performances but each time I feel it is a great blessing and I'm grateful for it. It only happens at this time of year when they're harvesting the fields, and I would miss it greatly now if I ever went away; it tells me *where* I am, d'you see, and something of *what* I am as well. Elsewhere, I would just be *living* in my skin for a short while; but here, I'm *being*. D'you understand? Then I dismiss such Romanticism as Uneducated Mysticism and tell myself that I must get on with my life. But I would like to understand what we *are;* I can't dismiss our heritage. And I want to know what apparently less – educated people like Rhodri here, get from our Legends; what inner attraction is there to our heritage? There must be some calling. Anyway, once it's done, I wait only for the next time, next year. It's some of what keeps me here: the *balance* then, is positive. Do you understand? Religion doesn't do anything for me, but I could quite easily, become a *Mystic*." He smiled and added, "I'm already a Romantic."

"Try Philosophy then."

"No. Not that; that's very different from Mysticism."

"Yes. I can understand what you feel. When you've seen it, there must be an emptiness without it. Wherever I am now, I shall also be here at this time. *Welsh Romanticism* at its best. Is that what makes us different? Why we feel at *one* with all this? Why we cling to our History and our Legends of the Ancestors? Why we can't be alone and are easily persuaded to God?"

"Don't get carried away," said Edward. "There's a heartache in the expectation of it too, because nothing else compares: that's the Payment I suppose. When I watch, I can understand how the Ancients wrought their Gods and worshiped their attendance. It's *Surreal*; when you've seen it, there can't be any other explanation. I wait anxiously for it and when it happens I know that I'm alive again for a short while. There's also a sorrow because I am made to wait so long for the next blessing; and there's a fear that it won't come again. That will then be my time to go. Stuff and nonsense, of course, on a par with Astrology and Witchcraft; there are perfectly good physical explanations for all of it and we're scientific enough to understand it. But how did it come about? Was it inevitable? Or is it a *'Model'* we're living in? Is it *Strike One and that's your lot?* For my sanity I have to believe it to be mystical. Is that why we're Religious? For sanity's sake? Because if it isn't mystical, I'm insane."

"You must believe my love. There must be a belief."

"So it seems. So it seems. But Belief in what? There then: Man, The

Thinking Animal. And so gullible. For all our sophistication and despite my rational, scientific and atheistic mind I sometimes do need to see it as a Religious Experience. If you need another explanation of our Welsh word *hiraeth* you have it there, in a nutshell; a *Hazelnut Shell* [23] of course."

"That's not a fault, Edward. It's not the 'Religion' that matters – that's just other people's made-up word that covers many beliefs and sins and great sorrow – it's the 'experience' that can't be dismissed, because it's yours: the phenomenon exists; you're just trying to make sense of it: because we have to. Because we think - that's what we do."

"What the Psychologists call *Phenomenology* then is it? I've always hated that word, that made-up attempt at 'science': that's just jargon."

"Anyway, why can't *'science'* be a *'religion'*?" asked Anna.

"Miss Philosophy, that's dangerous! Some Scientists worship their Science as a Religion, there's no doubt about that. But fundamentally, it can't be because Science is fact; Religion is an unquestioning belief in the absence of fact …. Faith if you will: a Supposition. You can't *prove* that there's a God; you can only prove that people believe there is, d'you see? Well, file it along with 'Monatomic Gold' [24] as beyond my ken."

"What's that?"

"Monatomic Gold? To be honest, I'm not at all sure and I've not had a satisfactory explanation from my Chemist acquaintances either."

"Why mention it then?"

"Because we're talking Religion and Beliefs and Understandings. And Monatomic Gold, is to me, like them, a conundrum; and I don't like conundrums. Conundrums suggest you don't know what you're talking about with such great authority; which is very distressing and undermining."

"You undermined? Tell me more then."

"Monatomic Gold is some form of gold of course, with the Chemical Code of *Au*. It is reddish-gold in colour like that sky we saw. Some people say that Welsh Gold, that used for the rings of our Royal House, is Monatomic Gold. And it seems that there's not much of the stock left for our Royalty. That worries some of the Establishment, because it's believed that it *defines* Royalty and that it's part and parcel of the *Sang Real:* the Holy Blood or the Blood Royal. Was it *The Holy Grail - The Graal -* d'you think? Was Arthur the Custodian of it all? It would give some purpose to his Knights' wanderings. Was Merddyn (Merlin) – the Magician of the Sign of the Red Dragon - a Goldsmith? And was it why Edward 1st made his son the first English Prince of Wales? To take their Gold and usurp their Royalty? I'm weaving Tales of Old, and I shall suffer for it, no doubt."

"Never mind all that; tell me more, you're better than a Gleeman," said Anna.

"Of course there are dire predictions about what will happen to the Monarchy when it's all gone; the end of the House of Winsor perhaps? But then there are always Myths, aren't there? There must be; all woven around what folk don't understand, in order to make some sense of it – like that sky we just saw – worship it or fear it! Your father will tell you that and with greater authority than I can, I think; he doesn't recognise conundrums."

"Go on then."

"I read once that Joseph, Jesus' supposed father was not a Carpenter at all; that was a mistranslation from the original Aramaic word for Craftsman, into Greek, the so-called 'Universal Language', written a few hundred years AD; and he was not as old as he's been painted in the icons – that was the early Catholic Church's attempt to write him out of the story. He is said to have been a Guild Craftsman, rich and working in precious metals, particularly Monatomic Gold. Jesus became his apprentice, but He went off preaching instead, as kids do. The worst thing that ever happened to Him was that people started to believe what He was saying! *The words of the New Prophet: Joshua Ben Abiathar.* What *'New'* was He saying anyway? There have always been Gods – they're as old as people – take your choice. But that's by-the-by: truth or falsehood, it doesn't matter any more, or shouldn't; live your life and let others live theirs as they wish. Anyway, the point is, I raise my hand in ignorance and ask forgiveness for transgressions."

"Is there any truth in all this?"

"Who knows? Many *Believe,* but who *Knows?* Ask your father there, 'What is TRUTH?' If someone believes it, it must make it true for them, until something better comes along."

"I don't like that argument."

"No, you like absolutes; but I look for what it means. You see, *there is no Absolute Truth,* nor *Absolute* anything else for that matter, except in the *Abstract.* You can't accept that of course; you must accept an *Ideal;* for me, that's *Idiocy,* because it can't be; and you must agree with me that if you accepted my version it would avoid religious and racial conflict; yours doesn't and you share that with all the Religions of the World, more's the pity. It's like a *Theorem:* it's a *Theorem* until someone disproves it and it becomes an *Hypothesis* again; then we seek a *New Theorem* until that's disproved. It's called Progress, I believe."

"You make a case and you've read a lot."

"What else do you do aboard a ship in the doldrums, waiting for the data to come in?"

"What you're saying then, is that the *Tale of Joshua Ben Abiathar,* the true name of Jesus you say, is a Tale of Gods, Goddesses, Kings, Usurpers and Aspirers."

"Well, it would fit in with the usual reasons for *History,* wouldn't you say? History is not written about the Common Serf: he (and she) just live and die. Come, we're here and we've talked enough for now; so I'd better introduce you to the house."

They turned to Rhodri in the rear seat who was asleep with his head back and his mouth open. Anna shook him and called "Father".

He roused, and said, "Are we there yet? It's bloody dark here isn't it?"

"Yes, we're here Llew," said Edward.

"I told you it would be dark Missus with your gallivanting. *Dark as Hell with the Fire gone out*, and no lights; you'd better get the Council to put in a light or two before you break your bloody neck or something; in the circumstances; you can't sue them from the grave you know; no writing paper there! I told you we wouldn't get here in the daylight but you wouldn't listen to me, would you? Think you all know best. We left it too bloody late, as usual. It's all your fault Missus – *set out early and catch the early bus!* We could have been here ages ago if it wasn't for you."

"Well, we're here now, Father."

"Where's *here* then? Back of beyond it looks like. The other side of the *Great Divide; Across the River Styx; Back of Beyond.* Where's the town then?"

"No town," said Edward. "There's a village about two miles back."

"Two miles, you say. That's a long way to go for my Pashas."

"We can drive, if you like. Or if it's a nice day we can walk and have a sandwich in the Pub."

"What's the name of the Pub? I've got to like the name if I'm going to go in there."

"The Black Bull, is one; the Pig And Whistle is the other."

"*Two* pubs. Enough people are there then? Big village it must be then? Enough people there?"

"Used to be. It was a busy farming area here at one time; warmed by the sea. Farm labourers were thirsty people, especially at haymaking time; all that grass seed and chaff from the winnowing."

"I don't like a lot of people making a crush."

"Well, it's smaller now."

"Too quiet are they then?"

"No. Just right I think."

"Any good are they then?"

"I suppose so; I don't go there much. Anyway, they sell wet, warm, Welsh, bitter beer and dark stout, which is what people seem to want; and they'll make you a sandwich if you're hungry. They're busy in the summer too with all the trippers."

"I don't know about the waking mind; I'll have to think about that. You should have given me a bit of notice on that; I might have changed my mind. Where's the sea – side then? You said we could watch the sea and the ships. And the sands?"

"Just over there. You'll see it in the morning. It's too dark now."

"Yes. Too bloody late we are, Missus. I don't like sands; it gets in your sandwiches. I'll give that a miss thank you. Are we going in then? Or are we going to sleep in the car all night?"

"Yes, come on then. I'll get the cases from the boot. Mind your head on the lintel as you go in."

"Short people they must have been, these farmers of yours. Original Welsh, were they? The real *Cymry* [44]? They used to live in caves you know. That's why they've always been miners. Not much taken they were with the surface of the Earth; only the underground like; because of the *Caves of their Ancestors* I expect."

"It's just to keep the weather out, that's all. It's better inside."

"It had better be, otherwise I'll have a permanent crick in my neck."

Edward unlocked the door and let them in to the main room of the house. It had been changed little in appearance since the time it was built: a large fireplace took up most of one wall, with the traditional cast-iron oven on one side of the grate and a hot water tank, a 'fountain' on the other. Over it all was a substantial wooden mantle-piece, the oak blackened from the smoke of the fire over the years. The floor was of packed earth covered with flat, stone flags. The windows were small and set in the thick stone walls with deep sills; the weather was kept at bay, but at a cost of daylight. There was no doubt that the original occupiers would have lived their lives with the sun, retiring soon after sunset and rising with the dawn. Power had now been connected and Edward switched on the lights to show the rendered walls and the solid, comfortable furniture.

Anna stood at the doorway and said, "Hello, House. My name is Anna Williams and I'd like to introduce myself. I've come to live here with my husband, Edward, who you know. I hope that I am welcome."

"What the hell are you blathering on about woman? Expecting an answer from the stones are you? You'll be waiting a bloody long time for that, I can tell you; they'll be running blood before they talk to you."

242

"This is my father. He's not always so objectionable, I'm told, but I still have to see for myself if that's true. He's called by a number of names. I think his favourite is Llewellyn after the Prince; and he has taken to being called Llew. His birth name, for what it's worth is Rhodri Morgan. I hope that you'll tolerate him while he's on holiday with us. I will try to get him to behave himself in your presence."

"Don't be so bloody stupid, girl. I swear to God you've gone doolali in the car. Too much driving around isn't good for women: it upsets their constitution."

"Father, be good enough to say 'Hello' to the house."

"Stuff and bloody nonsense. Are you always like this? It must be living hell to live with you. Is it always so cold in this house?"

"I'll switch the heating on," said Edward. "It won't take long to warm up."

"In the kitchen, is it, the heater?"

"Yes. Oil central heating. There was no point wasting it while I was away."

"Quite right; save your money while you can; you'll find yourself a bit 'short' soon enough if you have to go two miles for a biscuit. Any food in the kitchen is there?"

"We've brought some. Are you hungry?"

"Fading away."

"It's too late to do any cooking but we've got some fresh bread from this morning in the market, ham, cheese and pickles. How about that?"

"Nothing hot for the old bones? I'm sorry I came now. I've got some nice soup at home – *Cockaleakie*. You shouldn't have persuaded me."

"A Ploughman's with a good strong cup of tea will be fine," said Anna. "Stop complaining, or we'll send you straight home without anything."

"I'd be warm there with some warm soup inside me, at least."

"There's a glass of beer if you'd like it," said Edward.

"What beer is it? I've got to know what beer it is before I can drink it."

"Felinfoel Ales. From Llanelli."

"Know what they call that beer? *'Feelin' Foul from Sospan Fach'* that's what; take that home with you; but it's not bad if you can afford it like. *Rhymney Ales – the Best In Wales* is alright too; but I've found *'Brains'* is best for me over the years; more up top like. In the kitchen is it? With the heater? I don't like warm beer; it gives me gas."

"It's in the pantry, so it will be cold. I'll get it for us."

"I don't like beer that's too cold; it gives me cramps in the stomach.

243

I think I'll stick to tea."

Anna followed Edward to the pantry. Edward reset the heating and Anna rested in his arms. "I like your house, husband," she said.

"Our house," he replied. "Don't be too heavy on your father. Let him come to terms with the changes in his own time. It can't be easy for him."

"I know; it's not easy for any of us. I suppose we all need some time."

Anna laid out the food on the kitchen table and brought Rhodri to a chair at its head. "There, father. Lord of the Manor."

"Where do you do your cooking, then?" asked Rhodri. "You haven't got any gas."

"There, on the Rayburn. It's oil-fired."

"Oil-fired, is it? New-fangled posh. Does it make nice apple tart? That's the test. I like a good, thick apple tart once in a while. With runny honey and thick cream. I don't suppose you've got any?"

"Not at the moment, but we'll see what we can do tomorrow."

"I'll have a Pasha now before we start eating. It'll settle the stomach."

"Father, we've just put out the food. Can't we eat first? I thought you were hungry."

"No harm in waiting a bit. Give things an edge."

"Well don't smoke in the kitchen, it will smell all the food. Go in the sitting room or outside, if you must smoke."

"Not much chance of enjoyment here, is there? Sorry I came now. I think I'll go home tomorrow on the buses. I can do what I like then. Nobody to kick me outside when I want a Pasha."

"Come on Llew," said Edward. "Let's go and see what sort of moon we've got. It could be a harvest moon over the sea."

"Too early for a harvest moon. That only comes for the Harvest Festival."

"Well, let's see what we've got, anyway."

"Did you know that the Moon is for Water; like the Sun is for Fire?" asked Rhodri. "And She's a Goddess?"

"No, I didn't know that," said Edward. "You learn something every day."

"Only if you listen," replied Rhodri. "And Air is for Wind and gives Life on Earth."

On the seaward side of the house was a wooden seat and though the moon was not yet risen, the stars were bright in the night sky.

"This is champion," said Rhodri. "I'm glad I came now. Perhaps I can solve my Riddle here."

"What Riddle's that then Llew?"

"The one about the stars. I hope it's fine tomorrow so we can see the sea."

"The Bristol Channel."

"Not quite the Sea of Galilee, then? Second Best then but it will have to do; beggars can't be choosers in the circumstances. I'd better warn you of something before we settle down now. There may be things I'm called to do here, you never know, so it's important to know for posterity's sake and the Official Record."

"Well, we'll eat now when you've finished your fags and have an early night. Then we can be up early and walk along the cliff edge. There's a seat further along as well so we can sit as long as we like and have a talk."

"What about?"

"Anything that takes our fancy."

"We could talk about my 'sayings'."

"Of course we can, if you'd like that."

"I've been giving it some thought, see; you thought I was sleeping in the car didn't you? Be honest now. Well, I wasn't, see; I was thinking. I always think better with my eyes closed – no *distractions* then see. And I thought, it just doesn't sound right just, 'The Sayings Of Llew'. It's much better if we call it *'The Acts And Sayings Of Llew'*. Like in the New Testament."

"That sounds much better; it has more authority like that."

"Good. Let's eat then and go to bed, so we can get on with it early. Got things for breakfast have you?"

"Enough to manage I think."

Anna was waiting in the kitchen and had already served herself. Rhodri sat at the head of the table, with Edward to his right.

"That's the proper seating for breakfast sorted," said Rhodri. "I think I'll go to bed now and see you in the morning."

"I thought you said you were hungry," said Anna.

"That was then; now is now, and never the twain shall meet. Where's my room then?"

"I'll show you," said Edward.

"Don't stay up too late girl; you need your beauty sleep for your beauty and you've got a long way to go."

"Goodnight father, I'll see you in the morning. And no smoking in bed, we don't want a fire on our first night home."

"Don't fuss over me, Missus; you look after yourself; no need to worry about me."

Edward showed Rhodri the bathroom and to the second bedroom

and left him to prepare himself for bed. He left a large ashtray on a small bedside table and said 'goodnight'. When he returned to the kitchen he said to Anna, "You know, he may not seem very bright at times, but you'll be hard put to get the better of him; he's learnt what seems to matter to him. I wonder what he would have been like if he could only read properly and without that legacy of his birth."

"Oh, we're all tied to the legacy of our births, husband; the Upper Classes insist on that. The rest is hope. We spend our lives trying to find our own furrow out it; and trying to avoid the puddles. Come on, eat some of this then we'll go to bed."

CHAPTER 34

AN EARLY MORNING CALL

They were woken by heavy, persistent knocking on the house door. A strange house and an unfamiliar bed had kept Anna awake, long after Edward had fallen asleep. The dawn had already lightened the sky outside the window before she finally succumbed, and now it was still the pale, early-morning light that came through the undrawn window curtains. Edward reached for the alarm clock as Anna stirred.

"Who the hell's that at this time in the morning?" said Edward.

"What time is it?" asked Anna.

"Just gone six. Somebody must be lost or something." The hammering on the door continued. "I'd better go and see. They won't give up until they wake the whole house. You stay there and try to go back to sleep."

"Fat chance now. You'd better find out what they want and get rid of them; but take care, we're a bit remote here."

"No Gypsies or Strangers here Morwenna; the locals wouldn't put up with it. Where the Hell's my other shoe?"

"You could try under the sink," said Anna.

"Don't practice your Comedy on me, Missus. You think your father's village was insular; you should spend some time with the Farmers :-

"1. They live in penury: the weather is always a *bugger,* too wet or too dry;

"2. They change from English to Welsh the minute you walk into the pub;

"3. Five years before you're considered worth a Welsh Good Morning - *'Bore Da'* - and all they expect from you is a nod and a smile;

"4. It's another five years before they'll say to you in English, *'Good Morning';*

"5. It's only then you'll know you've *arrived;*

"6. As for the Gypsies, it would be *off the turf and over the cliff before you could say Romany!"*

Edward opened to door to two uniformed policemen the more senior of whom saluted and said, "Good morning Sir. Are you the owner of

247

this property?"

"I am, and what the hell are you doing disturbing the whole house at this time in the morning? Are you pretending to be the *Stasi* or something?"

"We should like to ask you a few questions Sir."

"Have the courtesy to identify yourselves first at least."

"I'm Sergeant Thomas and this is PC Owen of the Camarthen Police. We'd like to ask you a few questions and then we'll be on our way."

"Identification first." They showed their warrant cards and Edward said, "Well, it seems that you are who you say you are, so that's some progress. Now what is it you want?"

"Just some answers to a few questions Sir. It would be easier inside."

"No doubt you think so. It would also be easier if you disturbed the house at a more reasonable hour. You might then also have a cup of tea inside. We'll get your business over with here, then we can all get on with our day. Ask your questions."

"Very well, Sir. We have reason to believe that you have a person by the name of Rhodri Morgan staying here. Is that correct?"

"You've been watching too much television down at the Station Sergeant. The *gentleman,* not the *person,* staying here is my father-in-law; my wife is also here and *Mr* Morgan is enjoying our hospitality for a few days."

"Thank you, Sir. Are you aware that Mr Morgan is required, under a Court Order to inform his local Constabulary of his movements?"

"No, and I will tell you this for your information so that we can all be about our day: I understood from his Solicitor, or at least one working on his behalf, that it would be courteous to let his local Police Station know that he was being taken on holiday. I regret that I did not do so, for personal reasons of no concern to you, and so I am at fault. I apologise for that discourtesy. However, in answer to my specific questions on the matter and my wife's, I was not informed by the Solicitor of any Court Order, nor did I understand it to be a legal requirement. Quite the reverse in fact: we were told that there was no legal restriction on his movements in force. That has been confirmed by a third party, so it should answer your matter as well. If not, then you must show me the Court Order, or at least a copy of it, for us to be certain of the situation. If it turns out that the Solicitor and the third party, are at fault in their understanding of the situation, you must take it up with them, not me. I can give you the name of the Solicitor and his Chambers if you need them."

"That will not be necessary; we have the information we need in that respect. Just one or two more questions. The name of the third party you mentioned?"

"I don't intend to tell you that at this time."

"I see. Do you intend to holiday further afield, as it were?"

"No. None of us has any plans yet in that respect, though we may travel along the coast some days. The estuary is attractive, and there are curlews along the sandbanks to watch."

"Thank you. And how long do you expect Mr Morgan to stay with you for?"

"That is rather open-ended. As long as he wishes or until he asks to be taken home, I suppose. My wife is his only daughter and under normal circumstances he lives alone, as you no doubt know. No firm plans have been made."

"Thank you, again. I would just say that if you do travel further afield, you should let us know your intensions."

"Why?"

"We are required to keep our Records up to date, Sir."

"By whom."

"By our bosses, Sir. Just one further matter, Sir. It may be necessary to arrange for the visit of a Probation Officer sometime during his stay."

"I'm sorry to interrupt you Sergeant, but why should we expect a Probation Officer? Has he been charged with anything and failed to comply, or released on probation or bail or something?

"No Sir; it's for our Records."

"Ah, your Records again. Then we are at liberty to refuse to meet the Officer?"

"That is up to you Sir, but we would be grateful if you would please let us know when you will be returning Mr Morgan to his own residence. It will save us all unnecessary work." It was obvious that he could not resist a final quip. "And allow people lying-in to be undisturbed so early in the day. Good Morning."

Edward smiled and raised his hand as they walked to the car. He shut the door and turned to see Anna standing in the room. "What was all that about," she asked.

"Did you hear any of it?"

"Most of it. What's it all about? Why are they chasing him?"

"It seems that we should have let them know he was coming to stay here. Not our fault we didn't; we should have been told more forcefully that it was necessary. But it's sorted now."

"But why? Why do they want to know his whereabouts?"

"You know that there was some issue with his wanderings on the mountain and talking to the children a while back. They remember things like that; I expect that they're just keeping tabs. Nothing major."

"I don't believe that. They've got no right to do that, Police or no Police. He's never been charged with anything. It's persecution and I'll get to the bottom of it if it kills me."

"Leave it love. It's heavy handed, of course it is, but it's sorted, so leave it. I've told them where they stand. There's no point in going back to bed; neither of us will sleep any more, will we? So how about I cook some breakfast for us?"

"I must look in on my father; he may be upset and worried."

"Would you like me to go to him first, while you dress? It may be better man-to-man if he is worried."

"Would you? It might be easier for him."

"Get dressed then and we'll all have breakfast."

Edward knocked on Rhodri's bedroom door but there was no reply. He pushed it open and the air was thick with stale cigarette smoke. The mattress was on the floor next to the bed and the ashtray was overflowing with cigarette stubs. He opened the window to the morning air and when he turned, he saw Rhodri hiding behind the door.

"There you are. I wondered what had happened to you."

"Have they gone? The snoopers?"

"Yes, they've gone. They only came to see if you were alright here."

"I don't like them watching me. They used to do it back home 'til they stopped. I didn't open the door to them; no sir. Why should I? I don't use the door; and they're no friends of mine, Your Honour. Are you sure they've gone? Not hiding down the lane or anything, out of sight?"

"No, they've gone. Now why don't you use the bathroom and get dressed then we'll all have breakfast together before Anna goes visiting."

"Going away again is she? Bloody gallivanting again."

"Just for the day. We'll be just two blokes together with no woman to shout at us."

"Champion. Lady Muck can look after herself; show her her place in the circumstances. Where's she going then? Or is it a woman's secret?"

"To see a friend, that's all. I'll go and cook breakfast so don't be too long."

"I don't like bloody Weetabix; tastes like straw; I expect it's from the fields there. And I like the milk in my tea first, and two sugars. What else have you got to tickle my fancy in the morning?"

"There's bacon, eggs, fried tomatoes, laver-bread, and bread fried in

250

the bacon fat. How do you fancy that?"

"So long as the bacon's smoked and fried crisp, it will do for a start. And the laver-bread should have corn flour on it. And a big piece of fried bread to put the laver-bread on; and the runny egg on top of that, then pepper and vinegar."

"Right. I'll get started on it. Don't be too long."

Anna had showered and dressed and was setting the table. She had her back to Edward and her short hair was still wet. He felt a great love for her then and walked up behind her and kissed the back of her neck. She turned and kissed him full on the lips. "A bit early for canoodling isn't it husband?"

"Never."

"Well, there's another in the house, so be circumspect. How was he?"

"Hiding behind the door with the window closed and the room filled with smoke. But alright."

"Poor man. No-one should have to live like that in this day and age; it's degrading."

"Let me get at the cooker. I promised him a cooked Welsh breakfast. How about you?"

"Of course; what else is there in South Wales?"

"Cockles in batter and deep-fried crisp; now there's something else for you. The mattress was on the floor not on the bed; and he must have smoked all night because the ashtray was full."

"I wish he'd stop smoking those awful fags. They can't be good for him."

"What for? Why should he stop and be miserable? He's getting old and there's not much else left for him. I'll put up with the smoke and the ash if he gets pleasure out of it. He also wants to know where you're going."

"What did you tell him?"

"I told him you were visiting a friend for the day, and we'd be boys together. He seemed happy with that."

"A clever coot you are. You're over-frying that bacon by the way."

"No. My orders are smoked and crisp. You can have it any way you want. What about fried bread?"

"Not for me, I'll have toast."

"Make the tea, then. And he wants the milk in first and two sugars."

"God! It's like serving in a road-side caff. Any other orders? Red or brown sauce?"

Edward smiled and said, "Not yet. But don't be surprised. Vinegar though is ordered."

The breakfast was ready and being kept warm in the oven, but Rhodri had not yet made an appearance. "I'd better go and see what's happened to him," said Edward.

Rhodri was sitting on the bed frame, tying his shoelaces. "Breakfast's up and ready," said Edward, "And the tea's brewed."

"We'd better do it justice then boyo," Rhodri replied.

As they entered the kitchen, Anna said, "Good morning Father. Did you have a good night?"

"It was a night; nothing special; no worse than most nights; no better than some. When are you going to see your friend then? Soon, I hope."

"After breakfast, Father, thank you for asking. I'll be late home so you two boys will have to look after yourselves."

"Have you cooked our dinner then? We don't want to starve while you're gallivantin' again."

"There's a Shepherd's Pie in the freezer for us," said Edward.

"Proper, is it?" asked Rhodri. "Made with minced Welsh Lamb. Not from a tin I hope."

"No. Proper Lamb Mince from a local farm. I made the pie myself," said Edward.

"Good boy. And lots of carrots in it I hope. And not too much suede; and no parsnips; parsnips go mushy in potato pies; roasted is best for them. Leeks now, that's good, so long as you cook them a bit first, or they can taste a bit *raw* like. And fried onions; but shallots is better. And of course King Edward potatoes. I'm a bit partial to Shepherd's Pie with carrots and King Edward potatoes, so long as they're local grown. The Sais make Shepherd's Pie with beef you know; bloody daft that is; that's Cow Poke Pie like *Desperate Dan* in the *Beano*. Lamb = Shepherd; Cows = Cow Poke. This bacon's good. What do you think Missus?"

"A bit too salty for me, to be honest."

"Nonsense; don't know what's good for you, you don't. Salt of the Earth is important. You can't live without it, and that's a fact. You'd be alright if you had some fried bread with it to put some fat on your chest; bit skinny you are to be honest. You need fattening up a bit. I'll have a piece of toast now though, with Welsh butter on it, just to clean the plate. And is there another egg going? I always have two eggs with my fried bread and bacon. And another cup of tea and don't skimp the sugar this time. This breakfast's not too bad in the circumstances, but there's something missing. A few fried cockles now would finish it off a treat, like. Are you going off now then, girl?"

"When I've washed up and got ready."

"I'll wash up," said Rhodri, "To say 'thank you' for breakfast. I'm

252

capable; you get off on your visiting: *'Don't delay, or you'll lose the day'*, as they say. Off you go then. And be sure to come back better than you went off."

"Well, it's obvious that you can't wait to be rid of me, so I'll get my coat and be off. Behave yourselves while I'm gone."

"Why?"

"Let's just say, 'For Goodness' Sake'."

"That's a good saying that: 'For Goodness' Sake'. I must remember that one and put it in our list."

Anna kissed Edward and whispered in his ear, "There must be a way to shut him up; if you discover it, share it with me."

"Go," said Edward, "And take care on the roads."

CHAPTER 35

MEMORIES FROM THE PAST

"Gone then, now, has she?" asked Rhodri. "We can go to the other seat you told about now then can we and see if there's any ships on the sea?"

"Yes. Just let me clear the dirty dishes away."

"You can leave those 'til later. She won't know you haven't done them."

"No, but I will. It won't take a minute. You go and smoke one of your Pashas on the seat outside while I see to them; then we'll go."

Edward loaded the dishwasher and cleared the table of the butter and sauces. He lingered a little, being in no great hurry to subject himself to further questions and monologues from Rhodri; the day already seemed to stretch interminably ahead. It was quite unlike when he had been alone in the house. Then, time had passed quickly or slowly according to his mood and the weather. The hours and days had been his own to face and endure; his present and his past might intrude or not, might be imperative or subdued, give comfort or despair, but they were free for him to call or to avoid. Now, in such a short time there were others who called for his attention: Anna, even in her physical absence, remained a dominant present, and Rhodri, he realised, was a commitment he needed to shoulder. Perhaps it would be through these others that he could set himself aside and reach some peace. Indeed, it seemed that his stability would be a consequence of the care and understanding that he could summon for his woman and for this man that he had only recently come to know; though that was an exaggeration: he did not *know* the man to any degree, any more than he *knew* himself. He had read somewhere, while passing time that had seemed heavy on his hands – some doldrum period of exploration time again, no doubt – that one could not *know* oneself through joy for joy needed no analysis nor understanding; self-knowledge came only through adversity it seemed, when each had to ask, '*Why this?. What does this say of me?*' Such introspection was not new, nor unknown to him; it had become a consequence of his past that he carried with him and could not evade, though it had become easier to divert it. He still found it an easy state to fall into, though one with less and less desire, understanding or reward.

Rhodri was sat hunched on the seat with his coat pulled around him, though the morning was warm and windless for so late in the year.

Edward realised that he had been longer than he'd thought for there were several cigarette stubs ground into the gravel.

"You took your bloody time didn't you, Sailor Man? All the ships will be gone there-and-back-again if you're not careful. There'll be nothing to bloody see but the fucking sea."

"We shall look at the sea then," said Edward. "That's very relaxing in any case."

"Except when it's stormy, like in the picture of the sailors being rescued by that woman up North – wassername? *Flora MacDonald!* I don't know how she could row a boat on her own in that sea. And a bloody big boat it must have been to take all those sailor boys for a ride in it. But they could have helped on the way back I suppose: turn and turn about like. *The Cruel Sea.* Good film that.

Under neath the spreading
Chest Nut tree.

Can we go now then?"

"Yes and I think you'd better cut down on your fags or you'll run out again."

"Haven't you got any shops here at all then?"

"Yes, in the village."

"There you are then. They'll have fags."

"Yes. But they won't have Pashas I don't think. I don't know how much demand there is for them down here."

"We'll have to order them then, though I haven't got any money. We should have asked her to get some on her trip to see her friend. We made a big mistake there boyo."

"Let's walk along to the seat then."

"I think we should start our writing while she's away."

"Don't you want Anna to write your *Acts and Sayings* then?"

"I've been thinking hard and serious about that; I spent most of the night thinking about it; buggered up my sleep it did in the cold light of morning. In the end the answer is 'No'."

"Why not, for heaven's sake? She's your daughter and I'm sure she'd like to know more about you."

"She's Female, see, that's the knotty problem. And you can't change that for love nor money; we're stuck with her."

"You'll have to tell me why that's a problem; I don't understand."

"She's Female, isn't she? So she is a daughter of the Great Goddess [25] then, isn't she? Don't you know anything about God? *She* was kicked out of sight right and proper when the God of the Israelites got

255

to know about it; as Jesus said, '*I come to end the work of the Female.*' See? But *She's* always trying to worm her way back in. In any case, it won't be any business of Her's when the end comes, in the end, which won't be long now. Have you got your exercise book?"

"No, but I've got an A4 tablet."

"A tablet is it? That's better still; like Moses on the mountain. How big is it then?"

"About 100 pages. Big enough."

"Aye. You could write one letter a page: A _ B _ C like and still have some room left over. You must write it down like the Ten Commandments and keep it safe in the Ark of the Covenant in acacia wood, like it says in the Old Testament. I like the Old Testament: full of battles and trumpets and God and prophesies. Not like the New Testament; a bit wishy-washy is that: like all *THOU SHALT NOT*s, and the *Sermon on the Mountain* - boring; nothing but Him trying to make a Name for Himself and waiting for Him to die; He should have died in the first chapter; saved a lot of trouble, it would have with the Romans. Except for the Acts and the Crucifixion; they're alright; bit of blood and guts there, there is."

"Let's walk along then."

They walked down the track and turned along the cliff edge. The sea was shimmering and quiet in the sunlight and the day promised to be warm and still. The tide was out and a curlew cried from the mussel beds in the estuary in the distance.

"It's a very sad bird is that," said Rhodri. "It sounds as if it's lost something and wants to find it. Perhaps its chick's gone. What do you think?"

"More than likely at this time of year."

"Gone out to seek his Fame and Fortune I bet. Like the Warriors of Old. Sad for the mother, I suppose. But we won't have Eternal Life until She stops consorting and giving birth."

They reached the bench that faced out to sea and sat alongside each other.

"Can you get down to the sands just by here then?" asked Rhodri.

"Not here, no; it's much too high and steep; you could break your neck, trying," replied Edward.

"No sands then?"

"Only when the tide is out. When the tide is in it comes right up to the cliff and smashes onto the rocks pretty hard."

"No good for a Sunday School Trip then. Pity you can't sit on the sand with your sandwiches; it wouldn't feel like a day trip out without sand in your sandwiches. I used to enjoy that once upon a time. This doesn't feel like the seaside at all with no sand."

"Well, I'm sorry about that. You can get down to the sand if you walk along to the estuary."

"Far, is it then?"

"Pretty far; a good walk."

"Perhaps I'll do it later. No ships this morning, then?" asked Rhodri.

"It seems not. At least not yet; perhaps later."

"How much later? We can't stay here all day; I need my dinner."

"Yes, so do I. Tell me more about the Great Goddess [25] then. Who was She?"

Rhodri's voice became flat, with no texture. It was as if he was reciting a learned passage, one he had learned with difficulty.

"She has many names – every land gave Her a name. All different. It wouldn't have hurt them all to use the same bloody name for a helping hand. I can't remember them all. You know Apollo's the SUN don't you? Well She's the MOON and the Great Goddess, the Triple Goddess, the Goddess of Heaven and the White Goddess and the Great Mother. Funny how they're all in threes, isn't it? *Father, Son and Holy Ghost; Triple Goddess; New Moon, Full Moon, Old Moon.* Funny that. *Hecate* I remember because it sounds like a 'He – Cat'. She was Female so She couldn't be called a 'Tom', could She? *Hecate* then. And *Mary, His Mother,* and *Mary The Witch,* and *Mary The Egyptian* and *Martha* which is the same as Mary. Some of those were there at His Crucifixion: *The Three Marys.* Then there was *Salome,* who wanted the head of John the Baptist because he prepared the path for Jesus and his Kingdom of God; God was a man, so She couldn't have that, so they had a great fight and He kicked Her out. That's why you can't have women in the Church of God the Father. But She keeps trying all the time. But you know Her best as *Eve The Temptress* I expect, in the Garden of Eden where it all started."

"Where what started, exactly?"

"The Takeover of course: the *Rule of the Female.* That's when all the trouble started, wasn't it? Everything was peace and quiet before then; before *She* came with her wiles and graces and Her Serpent to dominate Man. That's why Christ had to come to sort things out: *'To end the rule of the Female'* as He said. But He didn't finish the job so He left it to others to see to. Bit lazy that."

"What others?"

"Well nobody's finished it yet; *Female Rules OK,* but it's not been all that long in His scheme of things, has it?"

"But who were these other people? Do we know anything about them?"

"A little bit. Or one branch of them anyway. They've become scattered over the world, like. *'The Diaspora'* they're called."

"Who were they?"

"In this land we know them as the *Mabinogi,* The Ancients [15]. Some people say they are the Long Lost Tribe Of Israel but I think they're older than that. They're the *Old People* anyway, with their children and their children's children; that's all we know."

"Where did they come from then?"

"Nobody knows but I'll let you into a secret: it could be Sumaria, so Sumarians they'd be. Doesn't help anybody much though because nobody knows where the fuck Sumaria was, is, or ever shall be Amen. Do you know what *Amen* means?"

"I think so: *So Be It?"*

"Something like that. *Moses,* the *Sun Priest* from Egypt; the *Priest of Apollo* – the half - Egyptian - was one of them you know – one of their Chiefs or Priests, and that's a fact; and that's why he made a Covenant with God for the Male; and God was happy enough to give up the fighting. Well who wouldn't be, I ask you? So in due course, Moses the Egyptian was made the Guardian of the secret name of God on Earth as well, which has been passed down. It's not told to many people."

"Do you know it?"

"Yes. But I can't say it or He will strike me down: it's the **Holy Unspeakable Name Of God** [26] .And you can't write it down either; it's why they invented the TREE ALPHABET.[27] To hide it from busy eyes."

"Give me a hint then."

"I'll tell you this, and it's as far as I'm prepared to go to save my soul: people think the secret name is *JEHOVA* but it isn't; that's the name the preachers use when they pretend to hide the real secret name. But really they don't know it really. Look, there's a ship. I didn't think we'd see one. Now there's a turn up for the books I must say. I think I'll celebrate seeing a ship with a Pasha; they're always good for celebrating. I wonder where it's going? My guess is Ilfracombe."

"Or Bristol Docks perhaps. Tell me more about the Mabinogi."

"You're not writing any of this down in the Tablet. You won't remember it all, you know."

"Tell me the whole story first and I'll write it out tonight; then I'll read it to you to see if I've got it right and you can tell me what I've got wrong and what I've left out."

"That seems a bit long-winded to me but if that's what you educated people do I won't criticise."

"It will make it much better, I promise you."

"If you say so sunshine mine."

"The Mabinogi then?" asked Edward.

"The Mabinogi: the Ancient People Of This Land. But not as old as the Cymru.[44] Do you know where they came from?"

"No."

"Don't know much do you? I'll tell you: the Black Sea first – come – first - served, then the others came from all over. I wouldn't like to swim in that sea; you'd come out covered in oil or something – like a Black Man. The Ancients who were in this land were called *The Mabinogi*. I don't know what the others were called; I expect they had their own names; in Chinese perhaps; *Chinky: The Great Chinkys*. I bet their Boss was called *Mr Woo*."

He sang.

"Oh Mr Woo, what shall I do……?"
"On The Road To Mandalay.
Where the Flying Fishes play."

"Have you seen Flying Fishes boy? Bloody funny they must be with all their feathers wet.

"There were four families of the Mabinogi here in this land a long time ago. I told you, nobody knows where they came from or why they came; they could have been The Children of Hess, but that doesn't help a bugger either see, because nobody knows where they came from either, or much about them. Or they could have been the Children of the Sea: the Children of Poseidon [19] or the Gardener – him with the fork. Hecate was *Goddess Of The Sea* in one of her forms too. That was the Mother and Son *they* worshiped, so it could have been from the Female, like they say, but I don't think it was really; I hope not anyway, we don't want the Female poking Her tits in after all this time; we'll have to put a stop to that, soon as you like. That's a Riddle And A Half, that is: who are they, and who's the Mother?

"And they didn't look like anybody who lived in this world at the time; they say that anybody could see that, if there was anybody else about like; and they were very clever and could read and write long before anybody else could. They made the first Tree Alphabet[27]. Perhaps they came in a spaceship; Aliens they'd be then; I wouldn't be surprised. They were only men at first they say and they were very pure. Then they started communicating with the Female they found here and they found it good. And that's when the rot started in and they went to the dogs, and the Female started thinking above Her place and started taking over and started calling Herself the Mother Of Earth's Children, trying to be grand. Stuff and bloody nonsense that was, but She became 'Boss Lady' anyway, the way they do in the kitchen, and the women started worshiping Her and forgetting the Lord their God.

"That's why He made them bleed and they became unclean. And it's still going on because all the Men won't stop communicating. Well, *I'm* not having any of that, I tell you, not any more now I know the damage it's done. I'm not having a woman lording it over me, no sirrie thank you very much. And I'll give you a word of advice boyo, free, gratis, for nothing and no receipt required: stop communicating. Only then will you have a chance to see Eternity; you can come along with me if you like; you'll be welcome. This sun's very hot; I think I'll take my jumper off; or do you think I'll catch a cold?"

"No, I don't think so; it's warm enough."

"Well, if you're sure certain. My Lady was always worried about me catching a cold on the chest – a weak chest I've got see, that's why I smoke – keep the bugs at bay; and always flannel next to the skin with Vapour Rub in Winter; and no baths from Guy Fawkes to St David's Day. My mother told me to be careful with my jumper. But I'll take it off for a bit, now it's nice and warm."

"You remember all this from your Lady's stories?"

"Oh yes. I'm good at remembering; reading's the bitch bugger."

"Tell me more then."

"It's not dinner time yet, is it?"

"Not yet. Go on with your history."

"History is it? Well I'll shake my leg and hope to dance. I've been speaking History all these years and I didn't know it. Well, well. The Mabinogi quarrelled among themselves as all families do – over a woman no doubt, they usually worm their way in there. So they had a King whose name was BRAN and whose tree was the Alder [10] the first in the Alphabet. Grandson of Beli he was, and blessed by the Lord Jehovah so they called him Bendigeidfran, which in the rude tongue is Bran the Blessed; some called him Jesus. But their communicating was their problem; they couldn't stop doing it see, and they got lost in the Mists of Time; like Camelot [28]. Perhaps Arthur is another name for Bran; I like to think so anyway which is why I sent my Bran to Avalon[34] on his raft; I hope he got there safe. Did you know I had a son called Bran?"

"Yes. He died as a baby though didn't he?"

"As a baby in body only; but to be recognised as a true descendant of that first Bran, King of this Island, *The Island Of The Mighty* down through Llewellyn and a King still in spirit. He would have started a new age, given the chance, and I'd have helped him; but it was not meant to be: a false dawn they call it. God can't have been ready for the Second Coming after all. Or we weren't. Us, I expect – He's got it all sorted. But he was born of Woman see, like Jesus, and they say, *'Man who is born of Woman, has but a short time to live.'* He had a short time, right enough."

"What did he die of?"

"Trying to live by the Laws of God's Son."

"What do you mean?"

"Jesus. A Jew he was. Hebrew."

"So?"

"Thick are you boyo? I didn't think so with your education and all. So he must have been circumcised, mustn't he?"

"Who?"

"Jesus, of course. Who are we talking about here, if I can ask? It's like talking to a bloody brick wall here and no mistake. Stands to reason if He wasn't to be unclean and couldn't visit the Temple in Jerusalem, and couldn't go up to Heaven to His Father."

"You'll have to explain that to me."

"You don't know much do you, Mr Education? Listen! He was born like all Men, with a foreskin and He had to be circumcised *According To The Law Of The Hebrews* and the sooner the better so it didn't hurt him too much and he didn't bleed too much through the *God's artery!* Do you know that name, *God's Artery?* It's how God goes from the MAN to the WOMAN. So God sits in Man at first, the *– Pure Form -* see? And He would stay there if there was no more communicating, and you'd live with God Forever.

"Do you know who gave us our God? Tell me now."

"No, I don't," replied Edward. "God Himself, I suppose. I've always assumed He's always been there – Eternal, I suppose; *The Ancient Of Days.*"

"Oh, He is that. But *somebody* has to tell you about Him; otherwise, how the Hell would you know the chicken from the duck? Tell me that Mr Education?"

"You're right there."

"I know. What about the other chap then; the *Mustapha?"*

"Who?"

"Here we go again: *Once More Round The Bay, Back In Time For Tea.* The other bloke from the same place: Pasha – Land?"

"Mohammed, you mean?"

"Aye, Him. Mustapha Mohammed."

"I don't know much about Religion, you'll have to ask your

261

daughter about that, but to me they've always been the Same Person. I see no difference between one Myth and the other."

"You're right there, *cime sabe*. Heads on one side, tails on the other; but the same penny. The bloke who set us straight was Bede, whoever the Hell he was; I remember the name because it sounds like 'beads', you know, small marbles like. He had his marbles alright, he did; or so they say. He was a monk or something I think; trouble – maker anyway. He told us about the *Real God – The One And Only God*. God of the Middle East He was, where the Pashas come from. Every one believed him, this bloke, who ever he was, in the end, or they'd have their heads chopped off; not much of a bloody choice was it? *Say 'yes' or you've had it!"*

"What about Jesus and Bran then?"

"Yes. The trouble was then, see, there was no Certified Circumciser around at the time and no one on-call either, not like in Israel where they're two a penny – or two a shekel there I expect."

"What did you do then?"

"I talked to my Lady about it. I shouldn't have done that because she was Female, but I didn't know that then. But worried we were see and we wanted to do things right. But that was my first mistake. I shouldn't have done it I know; better to have left him unclean until the time was right. And I shouldn't have brought in the Female, His enemy because it's a Man's secret is circumcision, and that's probably why it went wrong. Anyway, she said that the Good Book says that if there's no Circumciser available, then it's up to the Son's Father to do it as God did to Jesus because He was a Jew, and that meant me. So I had to do it see, if it was going to help him to be King of this Land again; and the Next. So I made a fire and I cleaned the knife in it, right and proper, and I cut his circumcision. That went off OK and was alright, so – far – so – good, but the bleeding wouldn't stop; so I washed him in the river but it wasn't like the River of Jordan and it still wouldn't stop: it kept pumping out. So our Lord took him away from me; he must have thought I was too bloody useless to be his Earthly Father, a right Rag – and – Bone Man. But He told me in my prayers asking forgiveness that I had to send him back from where he came from. I asked Him where that was and He said in that big, gruff voice of His, *Build Him An Ark Of Willow to divide the Waters and Send Him Across The Lake To Avalon.* But there wasn't any Willow – I wouldn't recognise it anyway – so I made it from Reeds, like Moses' basket.

"Then I thought we could try again. But the Good Lord must have cursed me well and truly because He gave us a Woman instead; His enemy. She's alive and Bran is in Avalon. She's my own curse now come back to me; I have the Curse of Hecate on me now and it's my own fault and I must carry it 'til I die. I try to tell Him I'm sorry in my prayers and it's because I didn't know enough. So I told Him I would sleep on the floor until I was forgiven, but I think He must be very angry with me because He hasn't shown me a sign yet; He hasn't told me what Sacrifice I've got to make, though I keep hoping and praying for the time to come: that will come when I can answer my Riddle I 'spect."

"What Riddle would that be, then?"

"The one I told you about – the one in the stars. I must find out where to find the Answer; it will be alright then. I've promised Him I'll try."

"Llew. Who told you all this?"

"I can't read so good, as you know, the words move about, so my Lady used to tell me about the Mabinogi; we bought an old book in Harlech market once when we had a few pennies and she read from that. Quite good she was; she changed her voice for every person; it made me laugh sometimes and it all came alive. Even the *Moch* [3] .We went to see some of the places where the Battles had been fought and things. She read it there and she made it real and she told me the spirits were still there and you could feel them if you were quiet. They were waiting to rise again on the Day of Judgement when the Lord's Trumpet will sound and all the Dead Will Awake. She told me the stories over and over, 'till I remembered them."

"What about Jesus and the River Jordan and Israel?"

"Father Rees told me all that when he came and before he went away. I told you he showed me how to read better: *'Wear sunglasses'* he said; *'then the paper won't look so white and glaring'* – but I don't know what *'glaring'* is. And he said, *'Put your finger on the word one at a time; then you'll be alright.'* He was right too; he said he'd been a bit like that too, once. I could read then, but it was slow going. Never mind, it helped me to remember things, going slow like. I read a lot now and I'm sorry all my books aren't here; they keep me going, they do. I used to get angry when the light went out and I didn't have a shilling to put in the meter; but it doesn't seem to go out anymore; perhaps it's free now, d'you think? Perhaps you could go and get the books when *She* brings the car back. He got very religious as he got older – right Baptist Chapel he was when the mood was on him. He wouldn't go to Sunday Chapel though; *Den of Iniquity* he called it; *'Charlots* they are', he said. *'I'll pray to God myself if you don't mind,'* he used to say; *'If He gets a prayer and a 'Thank You', he won't mind where it comes from'*. So he said, *'I don't need you hypocrites to take me to Heaven'*. I don't know what 'hypocrites' is, but it sounded bloody awful. I wouldn't want to be one and he was very firm about it and would rave if you didn't listen to him, so I didn't argue. He would smoke cigars, big ones, but *'No drink will pass my lips'* he said. *'It is the Devil's brew; I'll wait for the Nectar Of The Lord In Heaven'* he used to say; whatever that is when it's at home. I don't mind a little drop myself but he wouldn't have it in the house. So I got used to not having it; I never had any money for it anyway, so it was a good job.

"He used to read the Old Testament to me after breakfast, first thing; I liked that, especially the stories about Joshua and the Flight Into Egypt and the escape across the Red Sea and Moses on the mountain and all the golden idols; though where the Hell all the gold came from nobody ever mentioned to me: End Of The Rainbow, perhaps. And the Holy Land. I wish I could have been there then, with the Pillars Of Fire, and God sending thunderbolts and things; it must have been very exciting – Guy Fawkes Night every night. I expect you get used to it though after a while and all you want is Peace and Quiet.

"After dinner, I had the choice and he read the Myths and Legends of our country; Wales and the Holy Ynys Môn – Anglesey if you don't know, and the First Gorsedd. After supper he read the New Testament, very loud; that wasn't so interesting. Then we prayed and went to bed. Is it dinner-time yet?"

"In a bit."

"Do you love God, boyo?"

"I'm afraid I don't believe in God as you know Him."

"That's very bad; bad mistake is that; big mistake. Look at the wonders He performed. I shouted at Him when my father – with – no - name went away, then my mother, then Bran, then my Lady Vera; that was a mistake too, praying for the Female but I did miss her see; then Dr Will, then, oh lots of people. I think He was angry about that; you shouldn't answer back, should you? It's rude. You should ask His forgiveness and He'll forgive you and you'll be alright then; you'll get through the Gates of Heaven with St. Peter. If you don't change your mind though, when you go away you could be ringing the bell at the Pearly Gates forever and a day and it won't do you any good. All you'll get will be Gabriel's voice saying *'Stand and be recognised'* but they won't know who the hell you are see; you won't be in the Book; so you won't get in and you'll have to stand there forever and a day without a drop to drink and nothing to eat. So I'll give you a tip; free, gratis and for nothing, no receipt required: take a sandwich and some 'pop' with you when you go upstairs. But best of all, change your mind before you go away though."

"I don't think I can do that."

"I'll give you another tip then: change your mind because if God is there, He won't let you in like you are; if He isn't there like you say, it won't matter a damn anyway will it one way or the other? You're a bloody fool to take the risk in the circumstances; best to be on the safe side I always say. I wonder who you'll see there? Not everyone you expect, I bet you. I've still got to wait though. Can we go for dinner now?"

"I think so. What would you like to do? Shall we walk to the pub or what?"

"It's a bit of a walk, isn't it? Haven't you got any beer in the house? Or some cider p'r'aps? I haven't tasted cider for years."

"No cider I'm sorry, but there is some beer. What do you want to eat though?"

"You said you had some Shepherd's Pie."

"That's for tonight when Anna gets back. What about bacon and egg?"

"We had that for breakfast; it's nice but I don't want to *live* on it; I'd turn out looking like the arse end of a chicken. What else have you got?"

"Pork pie and pickles. We can eat that on our knees outside."

"A picnic is it?"

"If you like; just the two of us."

"Jesus couldn't eat pork, you know; against the Tribal Laws or something. Pity. He missed out there – it's a pity never to know the taste of crackling. Your pie is very nice I'm sure but I'd rather you bought me a cider in the pub. I've rather taken a fancy to a pint of cider now that you've mentioned it; haven't had it for years. But you'll have to buy it; I haven't got any money."

"Come on then; let's stride out."

CHAPTER 36

REMEMBRANCES

The pub bar was busy with the farm-workers who were taking a break from harvesting, slaking their thirsts and discussing whether the weather would hold until they were done and the wheat and barley safely gathered in and their wages in their pockets. Edward nodded to some of the workers and ordered a cider for Rhodri and a beer for himself. They chose a cold, home-cooked, local ham Ploughman's and sat outside in the garden overlooking the fields.

"This cider isn't bad," said Rhodri. "Local is it?"

"No. I don't think so; we don't grow apples here, I'm sorry to say; at least, not for cider."

"I didn't think so; not enough trees here. It's nice enough this, but it hasn't got *a local* flavour. Somerset it'll be then I expect, across the water; where that ship was going. It's not bad for a foreign drink though; it'll break a thirst as they say but I wouldn't want it every day; not if it's not local. What about our dinner then?"

"They'll bring it out to us when it's ready."

"Champion. Dining at the Ritz we are and no mistake. I'll have a Pasha while we're waiting, to celebrate like; two men together. You wouldn't call the Queen your Auntie now would you? I bet she wouldn't mind being here instead of all dressed up in the Palace with all the servants."

"I'm sure. But perhaps she's having a glass of cider and a Pasha as well."

"Oh, not her, not if I know her. Champers it'll be for her to drink. Have you tried Champers?"

"Yes, but not the best; much too expensive."

"She'll get it for nothing I expect. What's it like then? Good, is it?"

"Some people say so but it's too sharp for my taste."

"Me too. Too Frenchie it is; like snails and frog's legs. No, I'll stick with our cider, thank you very much and *How's Your Father*, so long as it's a strong one. She'll be having it with deer from Scotland no doubt, like that one in the picture; brought down on the train by the servants this morning. After a Gin and Cin' or two before lunch, like her mother."

"Do you think so? A bit early in the day for that isn't it?"

"Not for them lot. Good constitutions they've got. Must have, to go through the War on short rations and all."

"I'm sure you're right. You've told me about Bran; what about Anna?"

"What about her?"

"What can you tell me about her?"

"Not much. She killed her mother you know."

"What do you mean?"

"When she was born; she killed her mother. A *Life For A Life* I suppose. Still, they were both Female, so it could have been worse."

"You'll have to explain."

"This weather's a bit of alright, I must say. Just the job for a bit of a holiday; it makes me glad I decided to come in the end. I'll get brown if this lasts. You could do with a bit of colour in your cheeks as well, boyo. I wish they'd bring the food though; they're taking their time."

"I expect all the farm-workers have ordered as well, so they're probably busy. It won't be long I'm sure."

"They should get a girl from the village to help when they're rushed like this. I expect the girls could do with a bob or two to get to the City for the Saturday hop, skip and jump. Do you dance?"

"Not any more."

"I used to go to Thomas the Pop's shed with all the records from America every Saturday; 6 Pence to go in but free after 10. And all the tits you could feel for nothing – if they let you. Funny how they were different: some big, some small, some none – at – all. Then the bus home without paying. Those were the days; all gone now. What's it like in the summer here with the school on holiday and with the Miners' Fortnight [39] and visitors and all?"

"They cope, no doubt. What about Anna's mother then?"

"She went away. When your woman was born. I got her to hospital when she started the 'Curse of Hecate' but it was too late; she shouldn't have walked all that way. Middle of Winter it was and all; snowed for days in the mountains of Eryri, it did then; like the Old Winters used to be on the postcards. They were glad they saved the baby, they said. I said I didn't care much one way or the other; second best, the Female is; always has been. The Book says so, loud and clear. So I gave her away *'toot sweet'*. To Dr Will and Dr Megan. That was before he went away. And now she's back again. Better if the Lord God saved Bran in the first place, then we wouldn't have bothered; we wouldn't have fussed. But I mustn't criticise *His wonders to perform* or He'll have me down here forever as an ungrateful sod: He'll show me the *Gates of Heaven* with the *'No Entry'* sign on it. And, *'Traders Round The Back with the coal for the Fires of Hell'*. Anyway, she's my doom till He

267

sends me a sign to show He's forgiven me, which I hope He hasn't forgotten about and won't take too long about. I want to get it sorted."

"You can't blame your daughter for any of that you know; she was just a baby."

"A Female issue of a Female womb: twice condemned is that. Woman she is and Woman she was, baby or no baby, and Woman she'll always be till the World turns in its grave. So don't you forget it, sunshine."

"You must stop thinking like that. It's wrong but more than that, it's dangerous; for you too. Man and Woman make a new life together. And she is your daughter; you made her so you owe her your love and care. She's of your blood, for want of a better word, and you're all she has."

"What about you then? She's got you hasn't she? You take over for a spell; I'll let you – be bloody grateful really – get her off my hands; I don't want no woman around me any more. Or are you seeing her for what she is too? You'd save yourself trouble in the long run, I must say. Well, she must plough her own path, like her mother did."

"Who was her mother? Can you tell me? Ah, here's our lunch. Tuck in."

"This ham's got a nice bit of fat on it. Local, is it?"

"Yes. Well, not far away; the pig farm at Moch Du a bit further up North. Eat up while you tell me about Anna's mother."

"Nice crusty bread too. Bake it here, do they?"

"In the village."

"Better than that plastic stuff in a bag that keeps for a fortnight but doesn't taste of shit-all. I'll just have a Pasha before I eat; it settles the stomach see. Especially with a cider to wash it down."

"I thought you said you're hungry."

"Yes, I am. But a Pasha first is best. I always have a Pasha before I eat anything; I fancy it more then. *Pipe Of Peace* when you're eating with the natives like. You're a native so you can be Sitting Bull, since you're sitting there and I'll be Davy Crocket *Born on a mountain top in Tennessee,* wherever the Hell that is in God's own world."

"What about her mother?"

"Whose mother are we talking about now then? Davy Crocket's?"

"Anna's; your daughter's mother."

"Vera, you mean? My Lady? Don't know much about her really. I met her first on the pavement in Cardiff; going home from work, I was, pushing a pram."

"You were pushing a pram?"

"Don't be bloody daft; what would I be doing pushing a bloody pram in the middle of Cardiff? *She* was pushing a pram with a baby in it; or not really a baby, more like a …. What comes after a baby?"

"A child?"

"Well not really a child; more something in between. There's a name I don't remember. I thought you would though, you being educated and that. But there you go, you're always surprised in life. Anyway, I thought to myself, 'Aye, aye, that looks a bit of alright and how's your father'."

"Did you talk to her then?"

"Not then, no; it doesn't do to be too forward. She had a baby – an in- between - so she must have had a man and they must have been communicating, mustn't they? I wouldn't want to interfere with that. No siree."

"Did she live near your work?"

"In Saint Mary Street in the middle of Cardiff? Don't be bloody daft – only big shops there; and a couple of pubs for the Rugby International. No, she lived with her mother down the Docks; where that ship went you said. *Bute Street* or somewhere. I went travelling a bit after that for a change, back to where Father Rees used to live and where I went to school and where all the children were, so I didn't see her again 'til the *thingamajig* was older."

"Toddler."

"What's that then, toddler?"

"Between a baby and a child; the word you were looking for?"

"No, I wasn't looking for that word; that's nothing like the word I was looking for; different word altogether. I've never heard of that word before; are you sure it's a proper word? You haven't just made it up have you? To show me up? Little Girl is what I was after."

"What was the baby's name? Come on, eat up; this ham's good, and the pickles."

"I'll just have another Pasha first; I don't feel so hungry now. I wouldn't mind another cider though."

"Just half a pint then; I think you've had enough already."

"Just to go with the fag see."

"Well eat something while I get it."

Edward brought him his half-a-pint of cider and noticed that he hadn't touched his Ploughman's lunch.

"You haven't eaten a thing and you've smoked two fags."

"Three; I thought you wouldn't notice."

" Come on, eat some of it; it'll waste otherwise. It's very good."

"I don't want to spoil my supper of your Shepherd's Pie. Not after you went to the trouble to make it."

"That won't be for a long time yet. Eat some of this ham and bread; it's very good."

"We'll take it home for tea later, then."

"What about your Lady and the Little Girl? What happened next?"

"The *thingamajig* went away and I didn't see it again."

"Did you know its name?"

"Dawn, my Lady said it was called; like a new day. In the fashion then it was."

"What about the Father?"

"Oh, Sailor Boy'd gone away a long time ago; before the baby came. He had some funny disease or other; from his time on the ships I expect; you get some funny disease on ships, especially in Pirate-Land where he was. Very dangerous there it is. Some sort of growth, my Lady said it was, and I think he passed it on to *it* as well, so in the end it went away as well. I think perhaps my Lady caught it as well. So I'll tell her – your Lady Muck as is – not to have any, or we'll all go away. Pity my Lady went away; she didn't do no harm to nobody – she had her bit of fun that's all; you can't begrudge someone of a bit of fun, now can you? Life's not a *bowl of cherries.* And my Bran, God's Son sent to Earth in Hope. I hope they're all together in Paradise now and they're not suffering because of my fault. But there you go; that's Life for you: *In the midst of Life we are in Death.* No doubt about that; too bloody true; no mistake there. I've smoked my last Pasha. Where's the village shop then?"

"A bit further on."

"Can we go and try and get some more?"

"It'll mean a long walk back to the house, but yes, we can go. I don't think they'll have Pashas though."

"Well something strong 'till you go and shop properly. And we can take a taxi back in style. I can't walk there and all the way back again; it's much too far; did you know I can't walk far? Did I tell you? Well, I can't. Bad feet see. So don't take advantage; you shouldn't have let her take the car all day and expect us to walk. It's all too bloody far is this. Will they have a taxi?"

"Yes. Or some car at least. Aren't you going to eat any of that? It's a waste of money and good food."

"If you think it's that good, you have it. Or take it home like I said. You should keep chickens so you could give the leftovers to them. And you'll have fresh eggs every day for breakfast. I didn't think much of the egg we had this morning; it didn't taste very fresh to me. I'll pay for the fags and I'll treat you to the taxi. But you'll have to lend me the money though. My money will be in the post back home. I'll pay you back when I get home. Come on then; I'm dying for a smoke. We'll leave the dishes for the servants to see to."

They walked the further half-mile into the village and the village stores. The doorbell on a spring above the door of the Grocer's rang as Edward opened it and the shopkeeper appeared from the store room behind the counter.

"*Prynawn Da* Mr Williams," he said. "Good afternoon. It's a lovely day."

"It is indeed; we don't get enough of these, especially this time of year. But they'll have got the harvest in before the rain, at least."

"That's true enough, but our Welsh rain keeps the grass green and the milk sweet, as they say. What can I do for you, then?"

"This is my father-in-law, Mr Morgan, who's staying a few days."

"Good afternoon Mr Morgan; you've chosen a lovely harvest-time to visit I must say. Have you come far?"

"Not far, no."

"Well have a nice vacation. You've got married then Mr Williams? Congratulations and Commiserations to the lovely lady-wife. Was it her I saw in your car early this morning?"

"That's right; she's gone visiting for the day. Mr Morgan here has run out of his cigarettes and we wondered if you had any of his favourites. He smokes Turkish called Pashas."

"No, none of those, sorry. No call for them round here; round here they all smoke Virginia; like the Americans Mr Morgan. I could order them for you for next week if you like. Come to mind now, I have got some packs of Turkish ones called Camels tucked away somewhere for the summer crowd who used to want them; didn't sell them this year – not the same old crowd as used to be - they're not very fresh, but they're still in their packets, so they'll be alright. But I'll let you have them half-price, in case. They say they're good, but I don't smoke them; they're strong anyway."

"I think well take some packets of those; they'll keep him going, at least. Four packs will do I think. And some matches. And put it on my bill will you please?"

"Certainly; a pleasure I'm sure. Is there anything else I can do for you?"

"Yes. Is Idris around?"

"Yes. He's in the cellar making up tomorrow's deliveries. I'll give him a shout now."

"Thanks. We'd just like a lift back to the house in the van. Walking in and out is a bit too far for my father-in-law."

"No trouble at all. Walking's hard when you're not used to it Mr

Morgan, for sure. I'll get him to bring the van round to the front for you; he'll be glad to get out in the fresh air, I'm sure and away from the cellar. One of you will have to sit in the back though or all squeeze tight in the front seat."

"That's alright; it's not really that far. Thanks for your help. We'll wait outside in the sun and let you get on with your orders. Goodbye for now. And again, thank you."

"A pleasure. Just let me know if you need the lad again. Goodbye, Mr Morgan. Enjoy the rest of your holiday."

Rhodri nodded and walked quickly outside. They stood in the full sun and waited for the van.

"Chatty bugger that one," said Rhodri. "You could wait days for your fags, and no mistake; you could die gasping on the pavement here; *so near yet so far*."

It was a short drive back to the house and when Edward thanked Idris for his trouble he was told that it was a help anyway, allowing him to deliver some of his orders ahead of time. He turned the van and drove, too fast, in a dust-cloud down the unmade track to the next farm. Rhodri sat himself on the bench-seat outside the house and opened his pack of cigarettes. He lit his first cigarette and drew hard on it. He burst into a coughing fit so prolonged that Edward had to pummel him on his back. When he had recovered he said, *"Beelzebub!"*

"Are you alright? Do you want some water or anything?"

"No water. You know what they say, *'Fish fuck in water'*. I'm not used to these Camels that's all. Straight from the desert they taste: dry camel dung. Bloody Hell! Not as good as Pashas but I suppose they'll have to do since you haven't got any of my favourites. I'll get used to them I expect, soon enough."

"Look, I've got some work I need to do. Will you be alright here for an hour or two?"

"Where else can I go without the car, tell me that."

"I'm sorry but there's nothing I can do about that."

"Where's your work then. How are you going to get there without the car?"

"I'm not going anywhere; I'll be in the study on the computer."

"Computer is it? What's that then?"

"It's a machine a bit like a typewriter, so that you can write and draw with it and it's linked to the telephone so you can send your writing over the phone to anywhere in the world in no time at all. And they can send their answers back to you."

"Like the Post Office then, with their letters."

"A bit like that, yes, but there's no paper and no stamps to buy and no Postman."

"Sounds like magic to me. Does it do spelling?"

"Yes. If your spelling is wrong, it will put it right for you."

"Better than me then. Spelling's the bugger. It must be big to carry all those messages."

"No, it's quite small; about the size of a school bag. Would you like to see it?"

"Where is it then?"

"In the study at the back. Do you want to see it?"

"Is it safe? It won't break down or anything?"

"No, it's quite safe as long as you're sensible."

"Perhaps later on. I feel like a good walk now. I think I'll go up to the ferns like I used to at home. I like the smell of ferns, especially when they're turning. No children around here are there?"

"No."

"That's alright then. No trouble. I'll go for a walk; you get on making your computer. I'll see you later. Perhaps the Missus will be back by then and we can have the Shepherds Pie."

"Well, don't take too long; come back before it starts to get dark; the mountain is very rough in places and you could easily stumble and fall."

"Oh, don't worry about me boyo. I was born on a mountain and went up and down it every day, sometimes three times."

"I know, but that was a long time ago; you're a bit older now."

"You don't forget how to climb a mountain. It's like riding a bike; you don't forget; you're like an elephant."

"Alright. But be careful. And don't smoke too much up there; smell the air from the sea instead."

CHAPTER 37

PREMONITIONS

The afternoon was drawing to a close when Edward rose from his desk. There was significant material from his Head Office, and he would need to set aside some hours in due course, to consider his response. For now, he set the printer to produce large copies of the maps and sonar charts; they would take time to print but that needed no supervision. He came outside the house to look up at the mountain. He could see no sign of Rhodri but that was not unexpected: the bracken colour was now a darker Rufus Red and going over, but it was still dense enough to hide anyone sitting within its confines and becoming intoxicated by its earthy smell. It was foolish to be worried about Rhodri's safety – he was indeed a creature of the mountain-side and he could come to little harm, despite Edward's earlier polemic. He sat on the outside seat and turned his face to the sun. There was still a great deal of warmth in it, even that late in the day and the late time of year; he could enjoy the sun, for the winter would not be long away. He soon drifted into reverie. When he had originally bought this isolated croft it was in the mood of embattled withdrawal and he could not at that time, have afforded himself such periods of stillness, for they triggered memories of his loss, and battles with his loneliness. Slowly, and determinedly, it seemed a truce had been called and he had come to accept the tragic loss of one he had loved as indeed a tragedy but one that was now confined, along with memories of ecstasy and happiness: while acknowledging the loss, he also acknowledged his blessing. Indeed, at times recently, he felt that he was playing truant from the real business of his life and that he should seek a return to his career, but there was still a residual fear of that degree of commitment and he hid in the excuse of 'in due course'.

It was in this period of daydreaming that Rhodri turned the corner of the house and sang:

> "'*Lazybones, sitting in the sun;*
>   *Got to get your day's work done.*'"

"Ah, you're back in good time then."
"I left my other Camels here at the Oasis."
"You don't mean that you've smoked a pack already?"

"There was a lot to see, see: I watched them Combines for a while, and the sheep, and then there were two boats going in opposite directions. It looked as if they would crash into each other but they didn't; that was quite exciting and I thought we'd have to 'phone the Navy or something to rescue the poor buggers, but it was alrighty; they weren't damaged or anything I could see."

"You really are smoking too much, you know."

"Too much for what? I couldn't see the car; I kept looking for that as well, in between building the Dolmen [29]. I had to steal some big stones from the field walls for that. Is she back yet?"

"No. 'She', your daughter Anna 'phoned; she's staying the night there and will be back tomorrow afternoon."

"She's keeping the car then? So we can't be driving to the pub tonight again?"

"No. In any case, I think you've had enough to drink for one day."

"Enough for what? It's not like it's night yet and I have to get up for a pee or two; I wouldn't know where to go in the dark anyway; time enough for that yet. 'Look for the silver lining'; we'll have the Shepherd's Pie to ourselves tonight, so we can make pigs of ourselves if it's big enough. Is diner nearly ready? I'm quite hungry now."

"I've turned the oven on but it will take a while yet to warm up and cook through."

"Get my Camels for me then will you? You remember where you put them do you?"

"Yes; I'll get them, but go steady or you'll be out of them again."

"I'll go steady, 'cos we still haven't got a car and I don't fancy another walk into that village of yours. It's too far to go just for a fag; especially when they haven't got any Pashas, only this Camel rubbish. And I don't want to face that chatty bugger in the shop again so soon. It would be different if we were going to the pub as well of course."

Edward brought him his cigarettes and they sat together on the seat. Rhodri lit his cigarette.

"These are not too bad once you get used to them, I suppose. Better than nothing anyway. Perhaps I'll change to them from the Pashas, just for a change like, while I'm here; see how it goes. I wouldn't want them all the time though; they taste foreign if you know what I mean; dried Camel dung from the desert like. But they're not too bad, once you get used to them; better than nothing, any way."

They sat quietly as the sun lost its heat and drifted towards the western sea. Edward said, "I wonder if we shall have a sunset tonight?"

"We get a sunset every night boyo. Didn't they teach you anything in that special school?"

"No, I mean a special sunset. They haven't finished the harvesting yet and the clouds are low, so we could have another special one."

"I don't want any special ones thank you very much; I like to know it's coming back again tomorrow."

"There's no fear of that; it'll be back in its right place again tomorrow morning. Look, those low clouds are beginning to go pink."

"I don't want to see that. I think we should go in now."

"No. I want to see this; good for the soul."

"No. I don't like it. It's not good for you; you don't know what it'll do."

The sky went into a repeat of the previous evening's display of colours. Rhodri became more and more agitated and failed to contain himself. "Turn away, boy, turn your face away. I'm warning you for your own good."

"No, look at it. It's beautiful."

"No. Close your eyes! The Lord is coming and you mustn't look at him; that's instant death. This is God's Chariot: *The Fire That Burns But Doesn't Eat* [30]. It's the Burning Bush. Hide your eyes."

"It's just a beautiful sunset; look, don't be afraid."

"No it isn't; it's a sign; another sign. It goes widdershins across the sky; that's how we know it's God's Chariot. He's the only One who can go widdershins, so that proves it."

"It's a sunset Rhodri. It happens every day."

"No, come inside where we'll be safe."

"When this is done. Look at it; it's such a privilege."

But Rhodri had gone into the house and shut the door. Edward waited until the horizon was dark then followed Rhodri into the house.

"You should have waited to see the end of it," Edward said.

"No fear. That was a sign, that was; another one for me and I saw it coming at last. You should have hid your eyes. I told you; I don't want to be responsible for you."

"It was a sunset; it happens at the end of every day. And at harvest-time here it's beautiful like this every year. I look forward to it."

"You must be the Messenger that brings it if you see it every year and you're still here."

"I'm no Messenger; I'm Edward, your son-in-law just like I was this afternoon. And there's nothing to be afraid of."

"You say what you like, I know different; I know the real truth, because I've been told and I've been watching out for the signs, one – by – one – by – one – by – one: four '*Ones*'. It's my sign, and you brought it; I've been waiting for someone to bring it, and it's you; I didn't expect you. But I haven't had all the signs yet; there's still one

276

more to come."

"What are your signs then? Tell me."

"Do you know the elements?"

"The chemistry elements do you mean?"

"I don't know about that. I don't know any chemicals."

"What elements do you mean then?"

"The ones you have in every land; the ones from Babylon."

"You mean the Greek elements?"

"Aye, they had them there too; they had every bloody thing, them; like the frigging Romans. There are four of them see. Do you know them?"

"Yes, I do."

"Prove it then; say them. It'll protect us from the Wrath Of God."

"Earth, Air, Fire, Water."

"That's it. But you'll have to say them in the Old Language. Do you know that? I could do it, but you're the Messenger. Do you know them in Welsh?"

"Yes: *Tir; Ayr; Tân, Dwr.* "

"That's right. See, it's gone away now; we're protected. How many letters are there in each of the words?"

"Three."

"Yes and how many words?"

"Four."

"That's right. So you see?"

"See what?"

"Jesus Wept! Forgive me Jesus, but he's a bloody trial and a half is this one; I don't know how he got his Education. Three letters each and four words: how many does that make altogether?"

"Twelve."

"God grant us small mercies. Please ask him as a favour please Jesus. Twelve. Now do you see?"

"No."

"What does twelve remind you of? God it's hard work this. The teachers must have been Saints to cope with you."

"The twelve Disciples?"

" *'God's wonders to perform'*. That's why He had to have twelve of them, see? You can see it obvious when you know the old names: one for each month of the year - *one month for each Disciple* (a different God in the original like, before *they* came along) and a tree for every one of them (and Bran – The Alder was First): *three* for the *Trinity* (whatever that is); *Four* for weeks in a month for the *Four Stations of the Cross*; and *Seven* Gods *for* the *Seven Days of the Week*. See?

That's what the numbers mean. It's easy when you think about it; obvious when you know. See Jesus? You get your reward in the end. God's power wouldn't work otherwise and He couldn't then send his Chariot when Jesus called for it in Egypt [31]."

"I see. But what have the trees got to do with it?"

"If you knew your Legends and learned your Tales of the Mabinogi, you'd know that. What do trees remind you of?"

"Very tall plants?"

"Tall trees with no branches?"

"Give in."

"Pillars! For God's sake. So, Seven Trees is Seven Pillars! What does that say?"

"Seven Pillars Of Wisdom [32]*."*

"We've got there at last! The Seven Trees are for Wisdom. She used to be *Hecate* but the *Virgin* took over the job: a *Takeover In Heaven. **Wisdom**"* he shouted.

"I know the trees 'cos they spell the secret name of God, but I must have something wrong somewhere because He hasn't granted me Wisdom yet. Perhaps when I have the last sign it will all be clear. Then I must do what He calls me to do, so I can get Wisdom and be like other people who understand things. Like you, *Cime Sabe,* but better."

"What are the trees then? What's His name?"

"The First Tree is the Alder, which is Bran, like I've told you. I mustn't tell you His name; you must find out for yourself but you'll never bloody get near there if you don't believe in Him. You must glory Him or you'll be a lost soul."

"I see that."

"I must pray to Him now and thank him; I will ask Him to forgive you your trespasses too."

"Dinner will be ready now."

"I must pray like Jesus in the Wilderness. I must ask Him what to do. I will ask Him for the last sign."

"Eat first, then pray."

"No, it's better to pray on an empty stomach- the *Fasting* they call it. I mustn't wait. That will only make Him worse."

"You must eat; you didn't have anything at lunchtime. Have something now."

"You're trying to stop me praying. Perhaps you're the Devil in disguise. *Get thee behind me!* Leave me alone. *Forty Days and Forty Nights.* It's God's food I want. *Manna From Heaven.*"

Rhodri went quickly to his bedroom and Edward heard the door shut very firmly. He looked to see whether his material from the

Company had been fully downloaded and printed, but the large, detailed A3 maps were still unfinished.

Strangely, he felt at a loose end and found himself hoping that Rhodri's prayers would be perfunctory. Unusually he had a need for company and another voice. He took a book from his shelves and sat in the light of a standard lamp to read, but his attention drifted and focused on who this person, his father-in-law, was: he began to wonder about the seeming confusion of Rhodri's knowledge and understanding of the social and religious world he lived in: a mish – mash. Songs and Sayings indeed, but with meanings he understood. His understanding was self-centred and often simplistic in the extreme: events, fictional, mythological, actual and personal were not separately characterised and classified, but had been unified into an unique credo; he clung tenaciously and uncritically to the biblical and mythological explanations he had been given or had divined, so as to impose some sort of referential structure on his intellectual boundaries within which he could live out his life. Edward could sympathise with, and even laud, the mental strength of that escape from a trance, from the recollection of his own distress. But that was not all; there was much more: there was no doubt that, though his knowledge had been gained mainly through others' repetition and his absorption of the information related to him, there was also little doubt that, within those limitations, he exercised a prodigious feat of memory and a significant degree of what many would recognise as academic synthesis. There was danger, of course, in that if his beliefs (which were largely unsupported, false maybe, questionable often, but sometimes illuminating and certainly jealously protected) were challenged with rational and realistic arguments and proof, that challenge would devastate his carefully - built protective barriers. That, in turn, would release behaviour that would be unpredictable and uncontrollable and from which as a consequence, he could very possibly not recover. Edward had erected his own barriers for protection, and though the barriers would be as different as the personalities who erected them, he had come to expect their existence in anyone who showed any degree of awareness: you protected yourself with whatever intellectual barriers you could find, if you sought an understanding of yourself: barriers built for sanity's sake! As Anna had said, with more understanding than Edward had realised: *'I hate the certainties of this world.'* Now he could have completed it for her: *for they breach the barriers of my mind.* Rhodri had breached his barriers and shown how fragile they were. So he was fearful for himself, and for Rhodri.

Edward walked into the kitchen and took the Shepherd's Pie from the oven and set the table. Rhodri showed no sign of appearing and Edward walked to the bedroom door and knocked. There was no reply so he called out for Rhodri. There was still no reply, so he listened carefully at the door and made out a low muttering. He called again and said that the dinner was on the table and ready to eat.

Rhodri shouted, "Go way! I'm saying my prayers. I don't want the food. You're disturbing me."

"It will be cold, if you don't come now."

"That doesn't matter to me. I'm seeking a Covenant that's more important that your food. Go away and leave me alone with my Father."

"Come and eat; then you can come back to your prayers."

Rhodri's voice rose to a shout. "I will curse you if you don't leave me to my prayers."

Edward felt that to persist would upset Rhodri too much, so he returned to the kitchen. He drank spirits only sparingly now: it had been a refuge he had depended on when he had first taken this house and, many times, it had been the only way to sleep. But he had come to realise that it was a false escape that clouded reality and eased his pain of loss for a while but which aggravated it on waking and which only produced the need for another oblivion. Now, as he sat alone at the kitchen table, he craved the harlot taste of a malt whisky. He had not conquered his dependency it seemed but had merely set it temporarily aside. He took a bottle and a glass from the dresser cupboard and poured himself a large measure, then returned the bottle to the cupboard. He added no water and sipped the whisky slowly, intending only to finish the glass before eating alone. He served himself from the pie dish and started to eat but the food tasted dry and unappetising; he pushed his plate aside. He retrieved the whisky and poured himself another large glass. He sat with his head in his hands and drained his glass in two swallows. The house was still and there was no sound from Rhodri's bedroom. He took the bottle and his glass to his own room and lay on the bed to continue drinking. He did not know when he fell asleep, but he was woken by the empty bottle falling to the floor. He was still fully dressed and his mouth was parched and his head ached; he barely made it to the toilet to urinate and had as little control over the process as any alcoholic in any underpass in any deprived area of any City. He sat on the toilet seat and sobbed over this self-inflicted despair; it was not yet at an end.

He could not return to his bed and went and sat on the seat outside. The night was warm and still; it was also moonless now, which only served to strengthen the stars and show the Milky Way clear in the

South West. It was the kind of night that had often given him a feeling of contentment as he had emerged from his trauma: the world had been shown to be stable again. Now he had expected that there would be nothing to see on the poet's 'sloe-black sea' but a ship with its night-lights on its mast was passing from West to East which reminded him of Rhodri's use of the word 'widdershins'; it made him wonder again at the life he knew so little about and how the man had come to know and remember such a word.

He sat until the light of dawn touched the Eastern sky and his thoughts, real and wishful, drifted, random and unstructured, until they became indistinguishable from his memories. He waited until the sun had fully risen and was about to return inside, when Rhodri appeared at the door and sat beside him.

"You've risen early," said Edward.

"Not as early as you 'Creature of the Night'," replied Rhodri.

"I couldn't sleep, so I came to see the dawn over the sea. You missed it but there was nothing very spectacular about it this morning."

"It didn't need to be, did it? I got God's message last night alright, loud and clear – *Wilco, Over and Out* – like and you were the Messenger. Do you know what that is?"

"What what is?"

"Messenger. Pay attention, boy. You're half – a – bloody – sleep."

"I think so but it's a bit early in the day for Questions and Answers."

"Not as early as in the Summer."

"I'm sure that you're going to tell me anyway."

"Messenger means Angel and Angel means Messenger; the Angel Gabriel was Abiathar Priest, the Chief Messenger and only came down on special occasions, like God's Anniversary; like unto Mary the Mother of Jesus. In the Book, when it says, '*And the Angel of the Lord came down*' it means that there was a Messenger with a message for the people, though why they couldn't say it strait up I don't know. It's not like 'Dove', which is opposite: that takes a spirit *up* to God. In any case I've prayed to Him already, so nothing lost."

"You're content now then, are you?"

"Not yet, but we're getting there; I know about my doom now and what my temptations will be. It makes it a bit easier when you know the message from God and you get a clear conscience. Have you been blessed like that?"

"Not yet. It looks like I'm not as lucky as you are."

"That's because you don't believe in God and the Power of the Lord, see. I warned you about that, didn't I? If you changed your mind there, you'd know what to do and you'd be more peaceful in yourself.

So it's your own silly fault. You can't blame anybody else for it boyo, just yourself. Change your mind and you'll sleep better at night. But I asked Him to forgive your trespasses for Charity in any case. *For Goodness's Sake.* It can't do any harm, I thought."

"Thank you. And will He?"

"He said He'd have a think about it, but He was a bit busy at the moment, what with the harvests and all, and the Harvest Suppers and his Birthday coming up. And the grain in Egypt is not as good as it should be He said."

"Well, I'm grateful for small mercies."

"Don't mock Him. They mocked Jesus in the Temple and look where that got them."

"Where was that?"

"*Armageddon. When The Dead Shall Arise And Be Judged.*"

"I don't think that's happened yet, has it?"

"Not in a big way, so's you'd notice: that's pencilled in for after the Second Coming, which won't be long now I've been told. But it's happening all the time, only individual like: face your own ending Fair-and-Square; Face-the-Facts on your own when He calls."

"Well, it will solve all our problems when it does come I suppose. I'm going in now for another hour or two. I think you should as well; you can't have slept much."

"I didn't sleep at all; I prayed on my knees all night till He told me it was alright to sleep on the bed again because I'd had His message; but I'm not tired; my Soul was with My Lord. I think I'll go for a walk now the sun's up."

"I expect the haymakers will be up and about already."

"Bugger the hay; it's the stones I'm worried about."

"Well, take care and don't be too long. We'll have breakfast in a bit."

"I fancy some Shepherd's Pie now. Put some hairs on your chest before the Winter comes. It must get pretty damn cold here in Wintertime; bit of a wind I shouldn't wonder. No snow though I expect; too near the sea for that I would say in the circumstances. Still, no sitting outside then, I bet; snuggle down with a blanket more like. And a big fire up the chimney. You go and fix the Shepherd's Pie and I'll see you later."

"A lie down first, then I'll see to it. But don't wander too far."

Rhodri walked slowly away along the cliff path before turning in towards the fields and the rise of the mountain. As he did so, he disturbed the Herring and Black-headed gulls that had roosted for the period of darkness on ledges of the cliffs. They rose, screaming and wheeling in the up-draught of air from the sea. Soon they would fly along the coast to the returning fishing boats in the harbour and on to the broad estuary. There they would spend the morning harassing the fishermen as they unloaded their catch, and the Cockle-women as they sieved the estuarine mud and sand for cockles and razor-shells; there, other women with their leather aprons would scrabble over the rocks for the mussels. They would load each into sacks for the daily city market. The birds would then fly inland to the cereal fields and return in the late afternoon when they would noisily settle down for the evening, to repeat the whole process the next day. Edward's day had been governed by their activity when he had first settled there and he had regularly cursed them when they had disturbed him so early in the day, when his sleep had only come with the sunrise; he had even come to welcome a morning south-westerly squall in preference to their cries. Now, he found that he woke early only when, for some reason, they were silent. Then, he would wait anxiously for their cries, and would rest only when they returned.

He turned into the house and went into his pantry for a fresh bottle of whisky. In the bedroom, he poured himself a glass and lay, tired but sleepless on his bed.

CHAPTER 38

FULFILMENT OF A PROMISE

Edward woke when the sun was well risen but he was not rested; his sleep had been the sleep of the drunk and comatose, not of the physically weary, nor of the mentally exhausted. His mouth was furred and his head was thick with the consequences of alcohol; he had not washed nor shaved for more than 24 hours and the clothes he was wearing were the clothes he had worn before Anna had left on her visit to Lord Mostyn; it would not do to welcome her home later in the day in such a state. For himself, he felt no compulsion to acknowledge a new day by indulging in personal hygiene and wearing clean clothes seemed of little purpose. He did not believe that Rhodri would be aware of whether he had washed or changed his clothes. But it was no way to welcome the return of his wife; it would distress Anna, and that would not be forgivable..

He rose laboriously and made his way to the bathroom and turned on the shower. When it ran hot he stood under the stream and let the room fill with steam. The tension in his muscles eased quickly but his mind cleared only slowly and as it did so, the memories of his time of exploration on the other side of the world intruded again, as it often did, and his ignorance of the site of the grave of his first love dominated his thinking – that seemed a never-ending burden. So he turned the shower to 'cold' and stood beneath it until the physical sensations became dominant. He turned off the water and towelled himself dry. He wiped the condensation from the mirror and lathered his face for shaving. The astringent after-shave lotion was welcome and when he had cleaned his teeth he had to admit to himself that there were advantages to such rituals. He dressed and went into the kitchen. Rhodri was sitting at the table. His clothes were wet and his hair was plastered to his head. There must have been a storm while he had been walking and while Edward had been asleep. Rhodri was hunched over a plate of Shepherd's Pie and was eating purposefully. Edward looked at the pie dish and saw that it was empty.

"I'm sorry," said Edward, "But I forgot to warm that up for you."

"Not to worry, Captain Cook," replied Rhodri. "It's OK. Very nice really; pity there's no more gravy though; it's a bit dry for my taste; nothing to soak a bit of bread in."

"I think you should get out of those wet clothes or you'll catch your death. It must have been a heavy downpour," said Edward.

"Yes, it was. I was up in my clearing in the ferns when it started and I didn't get back in time. No lightning though; and no thunder, so that was a blessing. I don't like thunder. It's like all the old Gods quarrelling is that. Like all Hell's broken loose."

"Well go and get changed; have a bath if you're cold, there's plenty of hot water. I'll make some tea."

"A beer would be better to wash this down; and a bit of bread to clean the plate and save the washing-up."

"There's no fresh bread and it's a bit early for beer. You can have some toast if you're still hungry, and a cup of tea when you've changed."

"Alright then, if you say so. What are we going to do today then? I could do with some more of those Camel fags. Alright them are; I might stick with those; while I'm here like."

"You haven't smoked them all already have you?"

"I was thinking on the mountain and when I'm thinking, I concentrate, and I lose track; I finished the packet, see, so I started back and that's when the rain came. Now I'm down to the last packet which won't last. I'll need some more before dinner. I don't want to go in to see that Chatty Bugger. Can we get that chap from the shop to bring some?"

"He'll be busy delivering his groceries today I expect. Anna might bring you some of your Pashas when she comes home, if you can last that long."

"Don't know about that; it'll be a terrible deprive. When's she back then?"

"Sometime this afternoon I think."

"That's a long time to go without a smoke. Anyway, I've taken a fancy to these Camels of yours and she doesn't know about those. Perhaps you can phone the shop and see if he can bring some more."

"I'll see. Now get out of those wet clothes while I make some tea."

While the kettle boiled, Edward looked out at the rain clouds moving swiftly away to the East. Behind them, the sky was blue and there were no dark clouds to the West; there would be no more rain that day. He made the tea and telephoned the Grocer's shop while it brewed. As he had known, the van was already out with the deliveries and would not be back until lunchtime. Rhodri soon appeared again in dry clothes, but too quickly to have bathed.

"That was quick," said Edward. "Did you have a bath?"

"No. I didn't want to use up your fresh water; limited it must be, here in the back of beyond. Changing is enough for now. Did you get my fags?"

"No. Idris is out with the deliveries so he can't bring them. You'll have to wait."

"When's she back then?"

"I don't know; maybe this afternoon."

"That's a terrible long time to wait; I don't think I can last that long. *'Man cannot live by bread alone.'*"

"Well, we can walk in again if you want to, but there will be no lift back."

"Oh, I don't know if I can do that. It's my feet see; they don't like roads at all; they swell up something awful if I walk too far. Perhaps you could phone your missus; tell her to come a bit earlier and to get Camels instead of Pashas."

"No, I won't do that; she'll be home when she's ready."

"Too bad that. Haven't they got a phone then, this place she's visiting?"

"Yes, there's a phone but I don't want her disturbed. She'll be back when she's ready."

"Makes no difference in the long run if she's disturbed or not. It's all a tinker's toss in the long run. Better she looked after her family first all these years, so they don't go without fags in their old age. *'Charity begins at home',* you tell her."

"That's enough of that. I won't have you talk like that."

Rhodri was silent for a while and drank his tea. Then he said, "Perhaps you can walk to get them for me. It's not too far for you; I expect you do it nearly every day when you want something for yourself, in the circumstances; you living out here in the back of beyond like this, with no shops. Too bloody far it is for me, all this way from the shop; I couldn't live out here in the back of beyond with nothing but the shite-hawks to talk to; wouldn't do for me at all; I like a bit of company, me. Stuck out here with nothing to do all day: no sands to build sandcastles, and nowhere to go and no shops and no bloody fags; and none of my books either to look at and recite. And you don't know what's on the television day and night. It's enough to drive you doolaly in the circumstances, and no mistake. No wonder you're a funny bugger with your *computer* going all day and all night, disturbing people's prayers when they're trying to save you from yourself. You need a few more people round here; that's a fact. Get a shop a bit nearer than those miles – build your own bloody shop for a change; you've got plenty of space here. Serve yourself what you want then. And your Visitors, God willing. Wouldn't be short of fags then. Nor cider either."

"Rhodri. Now stop this tantrum."

"*Tantrum* is it? Whatever that is when it's at home. You'll see the light one of these days boyo, make no mistake; then you'll know who really loves you:

Jesus loves you
This I know
For the Bible tells me so.

You'll see the *Face of Jesus* one of these days, and all those you've loved will appear from the Earth before you and scream, '*Unbeliever! Set us free! Armageddon!'* with their shouting and wailing and gnashing of teeth. Just you wait and see."

"Rhodri! Stop it. Now. There's no call for this. If you want your fags, there's a walk to the village. If you won't do that, then you'll have to do without. Now I'm going to do some work. You can sit and look at the sea or the mountain."

"Oh, don't worry about me, sunshine mine. Just think of all your loved ones calling to you from the damp dark."

"Rhodri ! I won't stand for this !"

"Calling your name – whatever it is – over and over."

"Rhodri ! Now shut up or you go straight home, shoes and all, right now."

"Oh, I can look after myself, see if I can't. Catch a bus, I can. That's nothing new to me. I'll have fags there in any case, if Winford's remembered, the lazy bugger. I'll do things in my own time and no thanks to you, your Granny, or your uncles, wherever they are. It's no skin off my nose if you'd rather talk to your computer than me. That won't answer you back, any rate; and it won't ask you to get it some fags either, you'll be pleased to know."

"Rhodri. This is pointless. You can have your fags if you'll walk into the village; you can put them on my bill with the last lot; or, you can wait until your daughter comes home and we have the car. That's the choice. You decide."

"Bloody Hobson's bloody Choice isn't it? No smokes or no smokes. And I have to face that chatty bugger on my own as well."

"I'm going to work. You can sit or you can walk; either will suit me fine."

"What about my 'sayings' then? You haven't mentioned those lately have you? Got me here in the back - of - beyond with no fags under false pretences you have. I wouldn't have come if I'd known you were lying about it. I'd be better off at home; plenty of Pashas there, at least."

"For God's sake, you're driving me up the wall with your fags. I've told you what you can do. There's no magic we can do. Go walking or something; take your mind off it. Go and see if they've finished harvesting the fields; look at the sheep. When you come back we'll do some of your sayings; how's that?"

"Don't put yourself out for me *boi bach*; it was your stupid bloody idea in the first place; I wouldn't have thought about it but for you. But I'll be alright; there's nothing much on the sea anyway; bloody boring it is, like all this back – of - beyond. I'll go and have a talk with the sheep; at least they'll say *'baa'* back."

Rhodri walked away towards the cliff path with a bowed head and Edward went to his study. The printing was done and he took the large prints to his map table. He poured himself a whisky and soon became engrossed in the lines and echoes of the sonar transects of the sea bed laid down aeons ago on the other side of the world, and he searched for clues to the petroleum seams that the present millennium world demanded for its survival. The immensity of time since the death of the sea creatures in their uncountable millions had occurred and their remains subjected to the heat and pressures of the Earth, was unimaginable on the human scale; he felt that we lived only momentarily and this realisation always put his personal problems into perspective. When he had returned to his survey ship after the disappearance and presumed death of his fiancé Jacqueline and her parents, his only escape had been to immerse himself in his work and the glimpse it gave into the immensity of time. He envied those astrophysicists whose minds could encompass such immensity and who were not cowed by it; and he envied the journeys they could make. He would like to know too, how this intelligent ape called Man, who could conceive of eternity, could equally deal with the parochial problems of living out their allotted time on Earth.

He had been reading his maps through a viewfinder and his eyes were tired and his back was aching from sitting on a stool, and hunched over the table. He had been regularly replenishing his glass without registering that he had been doing so. Even now, he was only drawn back from his structural thoughts by the sound of the window regularly moving in its frame. He looked up, expecting rain that he had failed to notice while his powerful map light was switched on, but there was no rain, just the anticyclonic wind from the South-West. However, he saw that he had been at work for longer than he had thought, and there was no sign nor sound of Rhodri. Anna had not returned and had not telephoned with information about her movements. He assumed that she was therefore on the way home. He switched off his lights and went in search of Rhodri. When he stepped outside he realised that the wind was even stronger than he had thought and he became concerned for Rhodri's safety. He looked along the cliff edge and saw him making his way back from wherever he had spent his time. As he reached the house he sat heavily on the seat, as if exhausted.

Edward said, "I'm sorry I was so long; I didn't realise the time had gone so quickly."

"Don't you bother with me."

"No, I'm really sorry. I was looking at the sea in Australia and I completely lost track of the time."

"Australia is it? That's a long way across the sea. It'll be hot there now, I expect."

"Hotter than here with this wind I'm sure. Come inside."

"In a bit. I'll just have a think first."

"A think about what?"

"What I saw along over by there by the cliff."

"What did you see?"

"The cliff's collapsed into the sea."

"I'm not surprised with this shore wind; it happens more in the Winter gales, but it's not unusual at this time of year with a big wind. But I didn't think this wind was strong enough. The erosion will take this house with it in the end, I'm sure; it will all collapse into the sea. But not for a while yet, I don't think. Not in our time, unless it gets to be much rougher than it is now. So stay away from the edge, like I told you."

"Well, Poseidon,[19] God of the Sea, and his mucker Neptune, him with the Garden Fork, won't be very happy about it I don't think, buggering up his tidy sea. There were big waves against the rocks too; perhaps they were his because he was angry, losing his sea like that, like there was a war on: Earth against Water like, I wouldn't be surprised; and I saw the sea glowing green and yellow. He was calling to me and trying to tell me what he wanted."

"No. It was just very small creatures in the sea giving off light as they hit the rocks. It can happen when you're swimming under water without goggles and they hit your eyes; the sea looks like that sunset we saw last night. It's called bioluminescence."

"What's that then, when it's at home?"

"When the small creatures hit something they send out light. They are the animals and plants that when they die, they fall to the sea bed; then, other stuff, like rock and sand falls on top of them and presses hard; if the earth is very hot, it turns into petroleum that gives us petrol for the cars, grease for our engines and tar for our roads. Think how many small creatures that you can't even see with the naked eye must have fallen to the bottom of the ancient seas to produce all our oil. More even than the stars in the sky."

"What did you call this light?"

"Bioluminescence: *bio* meaning living things and *luminescence* meaning lighting up."

"You can call it what you like with your fancy words boy; you can *Think Your Thinks* as much as you like. *I* know it was another secret message for me telling me to get on with it."

"Get on with what?"

"With what I got to do. I told you I'd have to do things here."

"What do you have to do then?"

"Not sure yet; but the Earth and the Sea must be involved somehow, I think; stands to reason; it was a battle with *Fire* and *Water,* because they've been fighting from the beginning. It's another bloody Riddle I've got to answer – as if I haven't got enough of them already. I wish He'd tell me plain, then I could get on with it to His satisfaction. I know I've got to do something. That's why you were chosen as the Angel, God's Messenger, to bring me here to this place in the back – of - beyond. To do it, whatever it is. I must think about what He wants. It would be easier with Camels but beggars can't be choosers I suppose; not when your Messenger won't look after you. It's worse than being a fucking Caravan in the Desert is this back – of – beyond . At least I could roll my own with Sun-dried Camel Shit and leaves if I was there: *Rudolph Valentino from the Valleys!* Lovely colour it was; it made you want to jump in."

"It's a good job you didn't; I told you, it's pretty rough and deep along there."

"Oh, I won't go in 'till I'm satisfied there's nowhere else and it's the End Of Time."

"Come on inside then; there's some Oxtail Soup we can have; or some French Onion if you prefer."

"No Frenchie stuff thanks. I hope the Oxtail is from around here. Local is best, always."

CHAPTER 39

AN ITERATION OF THE PAST

Edward was glad to get indoors from the wind. While not at all cold, it was uncomfortable to sit in its path and he was reminded of the constant wind aboard ship that often led to irritability among the crew. He opened the tins of soup and put the saucepan on the cooker to warm.

"Any bread to go with this soup then?" asked Rhodri.

"Only what you had yesterday; it'll be alright toasted."

"I like a bit of toast with plenty of Welsh butter. Not sure about it with soup though. Crusty bread is best with soup, I think."

"Well there isn't any. I'll show you a trick with Oxtail: you put your toast in the soup then you cover it with Parmesan cheese, then lots of pepper. It tastes good."

"Any butter on it? I can't eat it without local butter."

"You can have butter as well as the cheese if you want it, but it doesn't need it."

"I'll decide if it needs it or not in my experience. Is it going to be long? I'm starving. What's this cheese then when it's at home? Not Caerphilly is it? Not local like?"

"No. It's Italian and quite strong."

"*Eyetie* stuff it is then? Greasy I expect. They're very greasy, the Eyeties; worse than the Frenchies there they are, and that's going some, *save my skin and a pound of poo.* Caerphilly would be better, like with apple tart. Best cheese in the world Caerphilly is; not many cheeses you can eat on its own or with apple tart."

"You can have Caerphilly if you want it, there's some in the 'fridge."

"In the 'fridge? Too cold it'll be then p'raps, but we could *'suck it and see'* I suppose."

"Now then, shall I serve it up?"

"What's for supper tonight then?"

"You haven't had your lunch yet."

"You can't be too careful; it could be your last meal on earth, like the condemned man's last wish: *'one more Camel before I go, your Honour.'*"

"There's a chicken casserole with carrots, leaks, onions and mushrooms; and you can have a baked potato with it if you tell me early enough so I can put it in the oven in good time. Think you'll

291

enjoy that?"

"I like a bit of chicken fresh from the oven, especially the skin; and the Parson's Nose."

"This is the legs and wings in a nice gravy."

"Like a *cawl* [33] is it? Puts hairs on your chest when you need it, *cawl* does; good for the winter, it is, and no mistake. I don't like mushrooms though. Do you know where they grow best?"

"No, but I'm sure you're going to tell me."

"In a cow-field with dung. Not healthy is that. You don't want to eat no dung mushrooms, and that's a fact. Dangerous, they are, in the circumstances."

"I'll take them out before we eat then. Now, do you want your soup or not?"

"I think I'll have a bath first; I feel a bit chilly like; the wind's got into my bones, so it has, and no mistake. Or perhaps it's because I took my jumper off before; your bloody fault that was. A Camel would help I expect; clear the chest, like. I don't know how you can live here with that wind all the time and no bloody shops; it would drive me bloody mad, so it would. Sinbad or Barnacle Bill would be glad of it though, I expect, to escape.

I'm Sinbad the Sailor Man,
I come from the Isle of Man.

Who's that knocking at my Door
Asked the fair young Maiden?

It's only me
From over the Sea
Said Barnacle Bill the Sailor."

"Have your bath then, but don't take too long."

Edward sat at the table and listened to the running water in the bathroom. He was becoming increasingly irritated by his father – in – law and his demands; it was time his wife returned and took some of the weight of care. He rose and poured himself another whisky and realised that he was little different from Rhodri: the soup was ready and he had turned the gas off; there was no reason not to eat alone, as he always did; but the whisky was more imperative, and the food could wait. This behaviour was the simple consequence of his decision to live alone in a remote house rather than with his family. He had feared the well-meant, but personally-destructive intrusion of others into his own timetable and the solitude he sought. He had come to understand what his father had faced when his wife and the mother of his two children had died. He too, had been isolated in his grief and wanted no intrusion by others; but he'd had two children to care for and for a man like his father their welfare would have had to come first. So he had forced himself to rally and to continue.

Edward had also come to appreciate his isolation and welcomed no intrusion by others. He had not forgotten his love for Jacqueline, but time had passed, and with it had come the softening of the pain of the loss of his Love and of his Child. So he had welcomed his awareness of Anna as a cautious return to stability. When he had met her again and had come to know her prognosis, he had felt the need to commit himself to her. But he also knew a resentment of her intrusion into his isolated life; the isolation that he craved. Now, that carefully established singularity had been invaded, not only by a woman who was not Jacqueline, but also by this strange man who was an enigma and whom he did not know nor understand. He was her father and the effort to know him should be hers, not his. It was too demanding of him and he was too uncertain of himself for that purpose. It made him angry that it had been assumed that he would welcome the role of nursemaid. And he could only lay it at her door; she who had postponed any responsibility for the father she had professed to want to know.

Edward's fragile safety was threatened and his solitude was breached. He was reverting once more to the solace of alcohol. It looked now as if his *need* for Anna was to act as her *Comforter*, and was purely a displacement of his own need. Now, with her absence of only a day, he could not sustain the pretence of that other need; with this man's intrusion on his isolation, he could not engage. It seemed salutary that it was her estranged father who had shown him the reality of his state of mind and the emptiness of his heart.

He could not face the soup he had warmed and would do as he always did when the dark mood threatened: he would work on his charts; Rhodri must be left to fend for himself. He went to the bathroom and knocked on the door.

"Rhodri? I'm going to do some more work before your daughter comes home. You lunch is on the table, though you'll have to warm the soup up again. Can you do that?"

There was no reply to his call.

"Rhodri? Did you hear me? Are you alright in there?"

"Don't you worry none about me Sunny Jim. I'm alright. You look at your big books if you don't want my company; it's no hard shit for me boyo, fags or no fags."

"Right then, I'll see you in a bit."

He took his whisky and glass into his study and sat in a chair. He fought the temptation to sleep and again laid out his charts. It was difficult to focus on the data and he felt his eyes close until he noticed a discontinuity in the stratigraphy that might suggest a hydrocarbon trap sealed below an impermeable cap rock. The indications were that this was an oil field, but its extent was not immediately clear and without that information, there was no way of knowing whether it was commercially exploitable. He heard Rhodri moving around in the kitchen, but he could not now be distracted. There was no room on the map table for all the sonar maps, and he laid them out in sequence on the floor. There was still some ambiguity associated with the data, but that was not unusual following early exploration: the strata of the different densities of rock were continuous over a number of maps, which could indicate a sizeable field, but it was not clear whether the porosity of the underlying rock stratum was consistent with what would be needed for such an accumulation. There would need to be a more detailed scan of the sea bed with more focused beams before that question could be answered. There was also the possibility that this field, if such it was, encroached on the identified reserves of other companies also exploring the area. Nevertheless, and with many provisos, it was an indication that should not be ignored.

He had no thought now of Rhodri nor even of the return of Anna; he felt the excitement he always experienced when faced with an intellectual challenge to which he needed to find an answer. The problem became an abstraction, located and existing only within the confines of his mind and did not necessarily, at this stage, occupy a physical world. The fact that the data related to a part of the world he would always associate with great loss was also set aside. Such a schizophrenic focus was what had sustained him when he had returned to his survey ship after his search for Jacqueline and he had exhausted himself in his work; his sorrow was that his distance from immediate reality had not been sustained and he had returned home, thinking his life ended. This present euphoria too, would pass but now, almost despite himself, he reached hungrily for the intellectual prizes that would be another success. He made a record of the map coordinates and the additional scans and data that he would need and made a telephone call to the London Office of his company. The person he sought was not available and he left his message asking for a return call as soon as possible. He then cleared his table and started on a draft of his report: it would be sent electronically initially, and followed by a fuller report in the next few days.

It was while he was engrossed in the details of his first report that he heard a car approach. He was tempted to ignore it as disturbing his train of thought, but since it could only be Anna, and he had no idea of Rhodri's whereabouts, he went to the front door of the cottage. As he walked through the kitchen, he saw that the soup had been warmed and eaten, along with a considerable portion of the cheese but the gas ring on the cooker was still lit. He turned it off, and was disproportionately angry with such cavalier concern for both safety and cost. He contained his anger and opened the cottage door. It was an unfamiliar car from which a lady was emerging complete with a buff folder to which she referred as she approached.

"Mr Williams? Hello. My name's Jean Davies; I work for the Social Services in this County and we've been asked to touch base with you?"

"Good afternoon, Miss Davies? Who asked you to 'touch base' as you say? Was it the Police?"

"Now why would you jump to such a conclusion so early in our meeting, I wonder?"

"Because I can see no reason why the Social Services would make the trek out here, unless it related to a matter that the Police have already taken an unnecessary interest in."

"We are not the Police, Mr Williams. We do support their activities when we consider their actions justified, but equally often we obstruct them; which I don't need to tell you pisses them off something awful."

Edward could not suppress a laugh and said, "That's very refreshing and I apologise for my truculence. You'll understand the reasons why, no doubt. I apologise again and I hope that you'll forgive me if I patronise you and say that I think you'll go far in your chosen career."

"Oh, I intend to Mr Williams."

"I don't doubt it. Now can I ask that we start again? How can I help you?"

Miss Davies also smiled and said, "Fine. No doubt we should have telephoned you first; black mark! But it's true, we have been asked to make contact with you, concerning Mr Morgan, who we believe is staying with you. Is he here?"

"He's staying here, yes. With myself and my wife who is his daughter."

"I have not been told that he had a daughter; there's nothing in this file about a daughter."

Edward thought that someone back at the office would be called to task for such an omission.

"She was adopted as a baby by Dr Will and Dr Megan Griffiths, née

Phillips. You may look them up and update your records if you wish."

"Both medical doctors were they?"

"No. Dr Megan Griffiths, was, is indeed, a Paediatrician but no longer practicing full time; Dr Will Griffiths was an academic at the University and held the first Lord Thomas Fellowship while also engaged with the Safe Haven Trust; he died some years ago. But we shouldn't stand here in the wind; do come in. Can I offer you some tea; or coffee?"

"Tea would be very nice, thank you. No milk, no sugar. I know the Safe Haven Trust of course and something of its history but I was not aware of the connection."

Edward made the tea and said, "No earthly reason why you should; and the surnames are pretty common in the Principality, wouldn't you say? My father- in- law is staying with us, but it seems he's not here at the moment. He's obviously had his lunch of soup and cheese, but it looks like he's gone walkabout again. He has a habit of doing that, especially when his meal is on the table."

"Where has he gone, do you know?"

"One of two places; either along the cliff walk to watch even more of the land falling into the sea, or up the mountain to the bracken and heather to watch the harvesting in the fields. I don't know which. I've been working and he left while I was busy."

"Is it safe for him to be wandering around like that?"

"Miss Davies, he grew up in a house higher up a mountain than here; I have more confidence in him wandering alone on a mountain than I have in myself. He'll be safe enough and he'll come back when he's ready; probably when he sees his daughter's car and expects some more cigarettes; he's been complaining that he's out of them and claims unjustified deprivation."

"Well, would you mind if I asked you a few questions for our records?"

"If I may ask you one first? Why?"

"We have been asked to look after his welfare during his stay with you and we need to be sure that we would act appropriately should the need occur."

"A very textbook response. Now tell me really why and by whom."

"Someone, and I'm sorry but I don't have the authority to name the peer, has asked us to '*simply keep a weather eye out for him, but with a minimum of intrusion.*' As I've said, there is some concern by another about his welfare. I know no more than that I assure you."

"I say again Miss Davies, I predict a successful career. Now what do you want of me?"

"Is Mr Morgan's move here to live with you and his daughter a permanent arrangement?"

"It was not something that my wife and I initially discussed and certainly not with Mr Morgan. It was difficult enough persuading him to come at all and any suggestion of anything other than a pretence of a short holiday by the sea would most certainly have been counterproductive. No doubt we shall have to face the question of duration in due course – the house is quite small for three adults – but there's no pressure."

"You say that it was difficult to persuade him to come and stay. Can you say why that was?"

"It's a tangled web, but if you know anything of the Valleys, not greatly unusual. The story is hear-say and from many sources I'm afraid, but it's on good authority. He was born to a young married couple in a mining village, but the husband, according to an older generation, was not the father. He, the father, that is, was also of the village and had become someone of note. As such he was able to exercise some influence over Rhodri's young life – but always at a sufficient distance to be unseen and ostensibly uninvolved. There was a further complication: his mother had a difficult birth with complications – I'm not able to be more specific, I'm not a medic - but, apparently, he was anoxic for some minutes. He was revived but at a cost: he was inevitably intellectually damaged and has remained so all his life. I don't mean that he's retarded in the sense of stupidity; on the contrary, he can be quite sharp if there's an interest he seeks to pursue; and he is – *focussed* – I think is the word. He has a considerable ability to remember the spoken word and stories he has been told; he knows a great deal, for instance, about the old myths and legends of Wales; he knows his Bible but prefers the Old to the New Testament; and you will try to deceive him at your peril."

"What happened to him then?"

"There's not much more I know; you could ask his daughter, but I would prefer it if you didn't; she's already torn over his life. The family moved from the village to the City's docklands hoping to start afresh, but it wasn't long before he lost his parents: the husband disappeared and the mother died. The biological father was not to be seen, so he lived as best he could, in Dickensian terms as an urchin, or a vagrant, I suppose. Dr Will Griffiths had known him at school and came across him living rough. He gave him a home in his flat until Rhodri again disappeared with a girl he had befriended. They played the itinerant travellers through North Wales and had two children: a boy, who died – the circumstances don't matter now – and a girl who is now my wife.

That's it."

"But I understand he lived in a significant house alone, before you brought him here."

"Yes. His biological father turned up again – again I don't know the details – and made a home, of a kind, for them both. He died a few years back, and Rhodri was left alone in the large house."

"Was that when he was known to seek out the young children and had a restraining order imposed?"

"*Believed to* not known to; I don't believe he sought them out; they sought him, more like: a baiting game. In any case, they confined him to his house, alone. You will know the dates; to me they are immaterial beside the personal disaster. If he could frame the question, Rhodri would ask, 'Will you cast the first stone?' But he can't do that."

"Thank you for telling me all this. It must have been difficult."

"Yes. But timely and strangely cathartic too; but that's not for your file."

"I'm sorry to have missed Mr Morgan. I have more than I need to satisfy the individual and I don't think I shall need to bother you again. But if there's anything we can do, please promise to call me on the number on the card. And can I wish you well?"

"Thank you. And I wish you the future you seek."

Miss Davies of the Social Services started her car and drove away along the road towards the city.

CHAPTER 40

FURTHER UNDERSTANDING

As the car drove away, Edward turned to re-enter the house. The wind was abating and rain clouds were forming on the western horizon, banking up as a dark, sharp front, promising a squall later if it did not soon disperse. Rhodri appeared around the side of the house.

"Has she gone then?"

"Yes. What are you doing round there?"

"Are you sure she's gone? She's not coming back is she?"

"Not unless we ask her to. Why are you hiding?"

"I heard what you said to her. Family business is that. She shouldn't be poking her nose in where it's not wanted."

"She came because she wanted to know if you were alright, that's all."

"None of her bloody business. Bloody Busybodies will be the death of me, you mark my words."

"I'm afraid it is her business. She's been asked to keep an eye on you, and she came to check that you were here and safe. Nothing more than that."

"That's enough to be going on with, any rate. Who asked her to poke her nose in where it's not wanted then?"

"I don't know. Perhaps somebody from your place told her you'd left."

"Bloody Busybodies; Nosy Parkers they are, all of them."

"Yes. Well, she's gone now. Do you want a cup of tea?"

"Any cake going?"

"No."

"No Fruit Cake with currants and sultanas and cherries?"

"No cake. Just tea."

"No sponge cake?"

"Just tea."

"No Welsh Cakes with raisons in?"

"No, just bloody tea! Do you want it?"

"Not much good on its own but it will have to do I suppose; tea that tastes of iodine, no cake and no fags to make smoke signals with either; funny bloody holiday. I always have fruit cake and Caerphilly when Winford, the bugger, delivers. You could cook a cake in that funny cooker you got. Did you phone the shop?" asked Rhodri.

"No. You'll just have to wait. *'Everything comes to him who waits,'* they say."

"Unless the poor bugger dies gasping or starving first; without a decent fag to puff or a drop of cider to break his thirst."

"There's no danger of that at the moment," said Edward. "So, do you want a cup of tea, or not?"

"Alright then but it had better be quick because I want to see about the sheep."

Edward boiled the kettle and replenished the teapot. He poured two mugs and said, "What about the sheep?"

"Horses they should be by rights – White Horses - but I don't suppose it matters just for once. Bit stewed is this tea. Is it fresh?"

"Fresh enough. What about the sheep?"

"Gone, haven't they? No sign of the bleaters as I could see. Gone, along with the Combines."

"The harvesters have probably finished here and they've gone on to another farm. Can't leave them idle, they cost too much to rent."

"They wouldn't take the sheep with them though would they? What's happened to them, I ask you? Perhaps the rustlers have got 'em and they're lamb steaks and mutton chops in the market by now; quick turnaround."

"I don't think so, somehow. They're probably hiding in the lea of the walls. They do that when there's a wind or rain."

"Don't be daft. Thick as two short planks sheep are. Daft. They'll stand in the middle of the field in a snow-storm, thinking the sun is melting. I've seen them do it on the mountains."

"No, they'll hide as best they can till it blows over."

"I bet you they're not hiding. I think there's a car coming, and about time."

Edward looked out of the window and saw the delivery van.

"Is it her?"

"No, it's Idris in the shop van."

Edward went outside as the van drew up. He talked to Idris for a short while and saw him drive away, then returned to the kitchen.

"Idris has made a special journey out here for you. His father told him you didn't have any fags, and he's brought you some."

"How many?"

"Four packets. It's all they had in the shop 'til their delivery tomorrow."

"That's not much; it won't last 'till tonight will that. They should have put in an order last week. Slipshod I call that."

"Well, you've got some to be going on with, so you can start to smoke yourself to death again."

"Give them to me then."

"You can have one pack at a time. That way they might last a little bit longer."

"I've got to ask you for a fag every time I want one?"

"When you've finished the packet, you can ask me for more. That's fair isn't it?"

"No, bloody *terrorism Grade 1*, that is – *Murder in the First Degree*. Taking advantage of somebody who can't walk to the shop because of his bad feet. It's like asking to go for a piss in Baby's Class. Cruelty, it is, and that's a fact. You shouldn't be allowed out."

"It's for your own good; it will keep you going until Anna brings the car back."

"When's that going to be then, in a month of Sundays?"

"I don't suppose it will be long now. If she was going to be late, she'd have phoned."

"If she's not going to be long, you might as well give me all the fags. Save trouble later."

"No. We'll do as I said. Now, do you want a baked potato with your chicken for dinner?"

"Only if they're local."

"They're from the shop but I think they get them from Africa; best quality Zulu."

"That's alright then. That'll stop them from starving; till tomorrow anyway; it gives them a bit more time."

"Right. If you're going to smoke that whole packet, you can sit outside. I'll turn on the oven, so don't touch it, it will be hot. I'm going to finish my report. Do you want to see the computer?"

"Later on perhaps, I don't feel in the mood for a computer at the moment. I expect it will wait. I'll go and prove you wrong about the sheep. If I win my bet, you'll have to give me another packet of fags."

"Well, come back if it starts to rain; it doesn't look too good out there. And don't be too long anyway."

"Oh, don't you worry about me *Cime Sabe*. Gene Autry's got nothing on me with his *'Hey Ho Silver'*."

"Wasn't that *Roy Rogers?* "

"No. *Trigger* that was. He used to sing you know."

"Who? *Trigger*?

"Do you enjoy being daft? *Trigger* was a bloody horse. He couldn't sing for toffee; neigh, neigh. No, Roy Rogers and the Sons Of The Pioneers. "

"Right. I'll see you in a while then."

"'Adios Amigos'."

Rhodri left the kitchen and Edward watched him stride away with the gait of one who had lived all his life on a mountain. It was distinctly different from the walk of someone who had never faced the demands of an extended incline day after day. There were two ways to walk up a mountain: one was virtually on all fours, using the legs for propulsion and the arms and hands for balance and grip on the short plant growth, but this was draining and the muscles were unused to the more primitive means of mobility. The other seemed more demanding of energy and even more tiring: there was a more powerful thrust of the legs and the torso was not bent into a slouch, nor forward to counteract the slope of the earth, but was held perpendicularly to the hips with the legs working; the head was held proud and the arms were still at the sides. It was far more efficient, though for most, it would have been difficult to see why: one could compare it to a military bearing but it was for a greater purpose than drill. And it was not usually so obvious; it was seen most clearly when the hill walker considered himself unobserved. In the presence of others, there was a tendency to hide the discipline as if it broadcast too clearly a more lowly origin in the same way that once, a tanned skin, now so desirable, was an indication of someone who was exposed to the elements, rather than cosseted and sheltered from the sun; such people carried the acronym P.O.S.H. lightly, though most would not have known its origin from the time of the great East Indies liners carrying the defenders of the Queen's Commonwealth and their families to their duties; they would not have recognised Port Out, Starboard Home as the 'in status' to avoid exposure to the 'merciless' oriental sun. Edward would not worry about the welfare of his father-in-law on the mountain; there, at least, he was in no danger.

Edward went to his study and turned on his computer then settled to drafting his report. He marked the possible oil location and set it out in grid numbers. He estimated the probabilities of the existence of the field and its size, and outlined the additional surveys necessary to confirm or disprove its existence. The cost-benefit analysis would be calculated by others but only after the additional information had been gathered. At this stage the financial risk was great and the investment in the search by the exploration company could, as often as not, come to nought as to success. If the former, the team would cut their losses and move to a new location and start again, with hope of greater reward; if the latter, the field would be registered, Governments would be involved, international water sectors agreed, and partnerships for exploitation would be formed in boardrooms of multinational companies across the world. For Edward, his involvement with this particular field would end, but he would always be able to say, 'I found that.'

He addressed his report to the company and pressed 'send'; there was no more that he could do now, but wait for others' decisions. He realised that he had completed his work without the crutch of additional alcohol: it was always so; when engrossed in research or analysis everything fell away except his immediate concern. Now, however, he would toast the completion with another whisky, but this time with a 20-year old Islay malt that he kept for only such an occasion. He sat in an armchair and the sleepless night he had endured, the completion of a job, and the ease brought on by the whisky made him sleep.

He was woken by heavy rain against the window: the squall had arrived. He wondered if Rhodri had returned before its arrival. He would have been happy to have stayed cocooned in the chair and in a self-satisfied mood, and it was with reluctance that he shut down the computer and walked to the kitchen. Rhodri was sitting at the table gazing into space.

"You got back before the rain then?" said Edward.

"By the skin of my teeth," Rhodri replied. "I wouldn't like to be out in that."

"No. I hope Anna's not to long; the roads are not too good when they're wet."

"I don't know what's happened to the sheep. No proof they're alive so I claim the bet: one packet of fags. Pay up."

"You can't have finished the one you had surely?"

"Why not? There's only twenty in a packet so they don't last forever."

"No, but more than four hours. Here, and take it easy with them."

"*Easy come, easy go.*"

"So it seems."

Edward scrubbed three large potatoes in the sink and pricked them with a fork. He put them and the casserole in the oven.

"How long will they take then?"

"A couple of hours. We can eat at half-past-seven if Anna's home."

"That's a long time to wait. A lot of palaver these big Zulu potatoes are it seems to me; mash would have been quicker."

"You'll like them with butter on when they're done."

"And a bit of parsley."

"What's on the TV then? Any cowboy films? What about *Rawhide?*"

Boom ber uppom boom.
Roll along Covered Wagon
Roll along."

"I don't know. I don't watch in the afternoons."

"Haven't you got the Radio Times then? That would tell you what's on."

"No, I don't get that."

"Daft, that is; having a telly and don't know the programmes. What time is it now?"

"Five."

"Oh it'll be Jackanory or something then."

"Is that still on?"

"Only sometimes. It's not very interesting, but it's better than nothing; better than looking at yourself in the mirror anyhow: *mirror, mirror on the wall*; drive you mad that."

"Turn it on and see then."

"I don't think I'll bother. It'd be alright if we had some cake to eat like. I like a bit of cake for tea; some Madera's nice in the afternoon, or anything, so long as there's no raisins in it."

It was with considerable relief that Edward heard the car outside. Anna came quickly into the kitchen and said, "What a storm. The roads were awash. That's why I'm a bit late; nothing was moving much." She crossed to Edward and kissed him. "Hello Father; I hope you've been behaving yourself."

"You can't do much else stuck out here in the back – of – bloody - beyond in the pissing rain with no car to go for a cider or two; even the bloody sheep have legged it. It'd be alright if we joined the fishes in the 'Deep Blue Sea'. Did you bring any fags from your gallivanting?"

"Yes. Enough to last you a day or two. Here you are; your Pashas."

"Oh, Pashas is it? I don't smoke those any more."

"Why not? You've always smoked them."

"Not always; I haven't always smoked, see; not as a baby I didn't. You've got it all wrong there Woman. Think again."

"Well, I'm sorry; I wasn't to know you've given them up."

"Not given them up, just changed them for something better. I'm entitled to change, aren't I? Even a monkey can change his spots, so they say. No, Camels it is now; much better for the lungs."

"Well you'll have Pashas or nothing until we shop again."

Edward was smiling and had turned away from Anna. Rhodri was making for the door, lighting a cigarette.

Anna asked, "Has he been like this the whole time?"

"Pretty well," said Edward.

"Like what?" asked Rhodri. "What are you complaining now Missus? Complain, complain, complain. You haven't been back two minutes and you're sticking your oar in between me and him. We were alright before you came back. You should go away more often, if you ask me."

"Father, you will stop that right now. We brought you here because we wanted to, not for constant argument. We don't have to put up with that."

"More bloody peaceful it would be and all. We can look after ourselves, make no mistake."

"Stop it I said, or you're straight back home, right this minute."

"You just shut your gob, *Hecate,* or I'll put an end to it and no mistake. Your time is past: *The Works Of The Female Is Ended.* And it's no good trying to hang on, because we know your game, we've been told in no uncertain terms: the sooner Woman stops dropping babies the better world it will be."

"What are you talking about now? Have you been listening to stories again? Is that it?"

"Stories, shmories. Truth or Dare it is: your time is ended; I've seen all the signs here on this Earth. The only question now is *'when'*?"

"Father, I can't talk to you like this. Go and smoke your fags, Camels or whatever, and cool down.

"It's raining cats-and- dogs out there. Send your father to his grave early you will, no doubt, so you can have your own way. But I'm not going before my time, no chance. And don't expect any money; there isn't any."

Edward walked to the door with his arm around Rhodri's shoulders. "Let's have look outside."

The rain had stopped and the dark clouds had passed to the East. The temperature had risen with its passing and it promised to be a balmy evening. "It's stopped. Come on, I'll walk a little way with you."

They walked to a monologue from Rhodri about the need to curtail the activity of the Female if there was to be peace and the proper worship of 'The Lord Your God.' They had walked only a distance of a hundred yards or so, and Rhodri had already smoked three cigarettes.

"There won't be any peace and no Resurrection To The Face Of God until they've been told their place on Earth, which is to serve Man."

"You may be right, but perhaps we can stop talking about it for a while, until Anna feels like home again. That would be an act of compassion on your part."

"What's that then, when it's at home? This comprassion."

"Compassion. It can mean a sorrow and sympathy for others."

"Like Jesus who took on the Sorrows of the World?"

"Exactly. He understood their failures."

"He did that, and no mistake, but it was a bit easier for Him, then, because there wasn't so many people then, in His time on Earth. He was a bit of a wimp though at times. It would have been easier for Him if He'd had a stronger character. A bit more like his great-great-grandfather David, and his Army of the Hebrews. Salome tried to carry on the cruelty with, *'Bring me the head of John the Baptist'* and all that, but Jesus thought of another way to serve God His Father, and good for Him."

"Yes indeed, but there's still a great deal of evil in the world, I'm afraid."

"Don't be afraid my boy. I'm here to help if you need me. In any case, it will all pass when Jesus comes this way again, in The Second Coming, and you believe in Him and He tells us *all* the *real* name of His Father [26]. Then, *'All will be revealed'*, as the Magician said and we will rise into Heaven to sit on the right hand of God; you too if I put in a word for you with my Father, even if you still don't believe. But you should try to change your mind on that; I really do think you should suck it and see; I think it would be best, and it can't harm in the circumstances."

"What's His *real* name then?"

"Ah. Trying to trick me you are. But it won't work; I'll tell you one thing though: it's made up of the letters of the alphabet."

"What, all of them?"

"There you go again. Don't be bloody daft; that would be a bloody story not a name. No, special ones only, named after trees."

"But I'll ask you again: Who told you it?"

"Me to know, and you to find out. I'm like Jesus though: the one they think is our Father, isn't really. The real one is somebody else. I don't know about my mother though, and I've thought a lot about that. Perhaps she was a Virgin Queen too, but I don't know. Do you know why they called the Mother of Jesus a Virgin?"

"Because in their religion, she was supposed to be I suppose."

"That's all well and good for them as *Believes* that, innit, but it would be bloody Serious Magic wouldn't it? I don't think even God could pull that one off successfully. Not with all the people watching, not to mention the sheep and the goats and the cow in the stable. They say He didn't have a belly-button but I'm sure that can't be right; how the hell did He live inside her then? He couldn't breathe, could he?"

"More Ancient Magic I suppose."

"It would have to be; and bloody Serious Magic as well – another big Riddle. They say she was called a *Virgin* you know because no Man had *known* her, in the Bible sense, which the *Holy Rollers* say is true *(Clap Hands And Sing To God)*. But it can't be like that see, because then you got to explain about His *older* brothers and sister – there's a Riddle. Where did they come from when they arrived? Where was Joseph when the lights went out I ask you? Sleeping in the woodshed? No. She was called a *Virgin* because she'd been a Temple Maiden, and they had to be Virgins, called *Vestal Virgins* in the care of the Chief Priest – I forget his name, but he would go up and become an Angel when he died; he'd been promised that by the sages, if he behaved himself with the Virgins. Not all of them did, you can bet: old Caiaphus was thought to be a bit of a fly-by-night by all accounts. I wouldn't mind a dose of that myself."

"How do you remember the name *Vestal Virgins*?"

"Oh, that's easy: there are matches called *Swan Vestas*; good they are, strike first time, even in the wind."

"Who told you about the Vestal Virgins?"

"Oh, Father Rees was a dab hand with those stories; all about *'He Lay With Her And There Was Issue'*, and that."

"Rhodri, I think we should turn back now. Anna's just come home and I'd like to talk to her. Besides, I want to check on our dinner in the oven."

"You go back then. It's nice and warm now. I'll take my jumper off and have a Camel looking at the sea. No bloody ships again though; it's not exactly bloody rush hour out there, is it? You go on; I'll catch you up, no doubt."

"Well, be careful of the path, and don't go anywhere near where it's fallen away."

"Oh, don't you worry about me boyo; you think of yourself."

Edward left him facing out to sea, his face set in a determined scowl and purposefully drawing the smoke from the cigarette. There was no doubt that a few more cigarettes would be smoked before Rhodri returned to the house.

CHAPTER 41

A DAY'S CLOSURE

In the kitchen Anna embraced him and they stood for some seconds before breaking apart. Anna said, "Edward, what is it?"

"What do you mean?"

"You're cold, and you've been avoiding my eyes since I came home."

"You're imagining things. Let me check our dinner."

"There you go again. It's as if you don't want to be with me; you're finding excuses to keep your distance. Is it me, or has my father been too difficult?"

"It's nothing; it will pass now you're home."

"There is something then. Tell me what it is."

"It's of no consequence. Leave it."

"No; that way it'll fester. Talk to me. Is it my father? Has he been very difficult?"

"I don't know about 'difficult'. 'Trying', perhaps would be more accurate. I tried to get close to him and as far as he's concerned I think I succeeded. He talked to me like someone in the family would a child."

"But you don't think so? Why?"

"I don't understand him: one minute he's almost brilliant; the next minute he's a child. He's too much of an enigma and that makes me more uncomfortable."

"You're just like your father: you must understand someone before you can relate to them. It's not necessary, you know."

"Perhaps I am too much my father's son as you say but it is true for me; I find it difficult to relate to anyone otherwise. Tell me what Lord Albert Mostyn had to say."

"Yes, but you first. We've been more than 24 hours apart; you must have something to tell me, even if it's only 'love'."

"There's that, as you know. Alright, here's a résumé: you know the Police called and I sent them away with a flea in their ear, if a collective noun can be said to have *an* ear."

"They haven't been back, have they?"

"No. Just listen. We had a visit from the Social Services; a rather nice young lady; I use the word *young* advisedly; younger than us, anyway. I suppose we're at an age where officialdom will become increasingly younger than us."

"Edward. You're prevaricating and it's irritating. Tell me what she wanted."

"Yes. She was doing her job but she was understanding of the, what shall I say? *The threat of officialdom.*"

"She impressed then. What was she, Sociologist or Social Scientist?"

"There's a difference? I don't know; I didn't ask."

"There is a difference; people dismiss it, but I think it matters. In short, it's an attitude of mind, but this isn't the time to discuss it. Tell me what she wanted."

"She had come, she said, to check on your father's welfare."

"Was my father here?"

"No. I thought he was on the mountain but it turned out that he was hiding behind the house. Somehow he overheard our conversation; how much, I don't know and I don't think it did any harm."

"Why should it? What did you talk about?"

"Your father of course; it was why she'd come. I told her something of your father's history; as much as I knew of it anyway. For the rest, I told her she should talk to you."

"Pity you didn't say that in the first place and sent her packing. Pity you told her anything at all about him. You had no right; he's not your blood and his life is not yours to recount."

"Pity you weren't here '*in the first place*' then, instead of doing your own thing; it would have saved me the trouble of trying to protect your father, avoid too much exposure and of responding to a pretty firm request from *someone* via the Social Services, to consider his welfare: it's unlikely to be the Police."

"Did she show any authority for her request? Did you even ask to see it? Who is this *someone* anyway? What evidence is there that any of this is true? You'll believe anything anyone tells you if they say they're from some quango or other. You're very gullible at times."

"I'll take no more agitation from you: your father's here, you decided to bring him, then you left him to me to see to while you fulfilled some ethereal promise you once made, probably while wallowing in a fit of paternal depravation. So look to your own acts for judgement."

"He is my father and this is the only thing I've ever done for him."

"It's not so much then, is it?"

"I'm trying to make amends; it's not easy."

"I know, and I understand that. But you understand me also: I'm not a child to be castigated on my actions; I do as I believe the situation requires; I make judgements and I hope they're right, but if there are consequences of what I do, I'll face them if they arise; if you don't like that, then be here to handle things yourself. I don't expect unprovoked criticism from you or anyone else; not now, not ever. And especially not in this house."

"I'm sorry. I'm wrong, but I hope you'll understand it is for the right reason. Can we set this aside? Is there any more? You mentioned someone who had been in touch with the Social Services. Were you told who?"

"There's no reason to prolong it. No, I do not know who that *someone* is, though she dropped a hint about a peer, so I could make a guess, I suppose."

"No need. I know who it is."

"You do? Who?"

"Lord Mostyn, I'm sure."

"But why? It's all too much in the past for him surely."

"No. For some reason, this particular part of his life is important to him; I don't know why. I'll tell you what I've learnt, shall I? But I don't want to be interrupted by my father; that could be too *raw*."

"He'll not be back yet: he knows that dinner – or supper as he calls it – is later and he has a packet of cigarettes, so he'll stay away until he smokes more than is good for him. The only question is whether he has enough matches. So tell me your news; you can stop if he does turn up and finish later."

"Alright. First, Lord Mostyn. The man is ageing so quickly; he seems much older than when I saw him last. In just a few weeks he has come to look like a very old man: a sunken face, parchment skin, very dark brown raised freckles that look as if they will burst into cancer as you watch, a poor shave, a stick and a very hesitant walk; he's still as crotchety as ever and gives you information only very reluctantly and then only if he thinks it will ease *his* conscience to do so; he is not concerned about any conscience you may have; though I also think that his conscience doesn't matter to him as much as it used to. He seemed like a man who had unloaded most of his concerns and now wants nothing more to do with them. I think he's seeing an end, so I'm glad I went. I can't imagine how anyone worked for him; he must have had a devoted team and inspired something in them to achieve what he achieved from being a 'Valley Boy' as he keeps reminding you."

"Not that much of a 'Valley Boy' I think," replied Edward. "My grandmother told me stories about that family as I grew up, I can't think why: but they had a substantial estate at the top end, of the valley; and there were extensive sand and gravel pits," replied Edward.

"A bit different then," said Anna. "In any case, there's a case of his wines in the car that comes with a message: 'The last gift I promise I shall fulfil for your Father Will and Mother Megan, though it's probably you and this new husband of yours who'll enjoy them now,' he said. 'There'll be no more, the vineyard is sold now.' He also said, 'And don't ever forget who your father and mother really were'. I wasn't sure who he meant for a while, but it became clear that he meant Will and Megan, though why he had to make a point of it, I don't know. It was only when I asked him about Rhodri Morgan that he seemed to shift into another state; all he said for a while was 'Ah, *the foundling.*' Then he said, *'He also needs our care and we must be sure of his welfare; another promise I made'.* I asked him what he meant by that – *a promise to whom?* But he wouldn't elaborate more than, *'Suffer little children the consequences of their fathers'.*

"Then he went off on one of his homilies; he said, 'You know Philosopher, there's a fallacy abroad that says that the greatest care must be lavished on the newborn and the child. But the *child* persists into old age – the Russians and the Catholic Church are right about that.'"

"I asked him again what he meant, and to stop talking in riddles: tell it all, or tell noting," I said.

"He smiled at me and replied, *'Give me the child and I will give you the man.* Escape from the Commies, or the Popes is difficult, but some make it. Just note that in the man, the need for care is more purposefully hidden until Old Age appears, suddenly it seems. It must be so, lest he is said to be *weak in character* or some such nonsense. You see, the Child has a strong grip on life, because he's not seen anything of it yet; in the Old, that grip weakens because he's seen too much of it. When we are young, we don't heed the greater call for benevolence and care from the old, though the call is loud and clear.'

"When I spent time with him before, this habit irritated me and I didn't listen to him; I wish I had. Anyway, you can see now why I think that he is the driver of the attention on Rhodri."

"I can see that it's probable, yes. What I don't understand is *why* after all these years."

"Nor do I. And I don't think we shall ever know the full truth of it. He certainly won't tell us now, nor will anyone else. Do you know, this time he made me think about Rhodri, my father, the one he called the 'Foundling', and his passion for *Stories and Legends*. Did he get that from *his* father? Of course, I never met the old Councillor Rees, Rhodri's biological father; he must have been able to string a few sentences together."

"Some, I'm sure," said Edward.

"But he was before my time and yours and I only know anything of him from what I've heard," said Anna.

She smiled and reached for Edward's hand, "But if someone suggested to me, that from his rhetoric and his eclectic mind alone, Lord Mostyn would make a good candidate for the role of Ancestor, I wouldn't find it hard to believe."

"Don't read too much into that; it's a trick our Ancient Tribe learns at the breast for safety's sake. It's an ancient Celtic trait – the trick, not the erudition; that comes later, if you're lucky: you're expected to be something of a performer, one way or another, breaking into song or rhyme at the least provocation, especially, and particularly, with a beer in hand - and people don't forgive you if you don't; you 'wrong foot' them you see and they're uncomfortable with that – you're not living up to their prejudices. You've not been exposed to it much, but it's the local version of the 'gift of the gab'; you find it in markets everywhere. It's why I can stand for hours in a London market, just listening.

"Here, it makes Druids and Eisteddfod Bards of some of us, instead of barrow-boys, Costermongers or Pearly Kings; those of us who understand the intricacies of the Welsh Cynghanedd, the meter, at least. It's conceded that we don't all play the Welsh Harp though that is considered a failure on our part too - rather like being a soccer player and not a rugby player; but it's too damned heavy to lug about. So others become opera singers whose voices are supposed to soar to the Heavens; or they drink too much at Rugby games against the ancient foe – England - and sing lustily but unfortunately, out of tune. But nobody minds."

"You're none of those."

"No; nor are most of those born under the sign of Merlin's Red Dragon."

"You do have a turn of phrase, though."

"Affectation love, pure affectation; dear to the heart of a Conquered Race of course and exercised blatantly to ensure self-preservation; think of Scheherazade; or if that's too much, a puppy with its legs in the air and its belly exposed; the sign of surrender, our Behaviourists say. Rather like a woman being loved actually, though the thought hadn't occurred to me before."

Anna hit his hand hard against the table and said "I shall never let you have me in the missionary position ever again; you've ruined it. Now I shall always think of the poor puppy trying to save itself, and laugh."

"No, seriously though, it's stereotyping and like all stereotypes, not at all accurate, nor true and never desirable; though useful to hide behind on occasions, which is what I suspect, with the rhetorical ability you say he affects, is what our Lordship does: he hides behind tales as we all do. It's getting dark and the dinner's more than ready I suspect. Is there more?"

"Yes."

"Then pause. I'd better see what your father's up to."

Edward walked out of the kitchen and breathed the warmer air that had come behind the rain. It was clear now, and calm, so there could be coastal fog tomorrow, without a wind. He looked first at the path and only then noticed Rhodri sitting on the seat.

"There you are. I'm glad you're back."

There were a number of cigarette buts in the gravel.

"Have you been back long?"

"Long enough. There's no sign of the sheep still, so I came back."

"You should have come in; no need to sit out here."

"You were taking secrets, I could tell; so I didn't want to interrupt."

"You should have come in."

"Well I didn't did I? Not bloody wanted, me. 'Surplus to requirements', me. It's all the bloody Woman's fault; we were OK before *she* came back with her bloody airs and graces. You go back there, if you want to risk it; I'll stay here."

"No, come on. Dinner will be ready now; come and have some chicken and baked potatoes. It's ready now."

"Half past seven is it? Supper time."

"Yes. Come on in and eat with us."

"I don't feel very hungry at the moment; not for chicken and potatoes anyway. Chicken and shop chips would be alright but we can't have those in the back – of - beyond. All I want is a packet of my fags and I'll go to my room and you can make babies as much as you like. Just give me some Camels to puff."

"We're down to the last packet of those. You'll have to go back to Pashas after that."

"I suppose I'll have to. Where's the Camels then?"

"Inside. Come and get them."

"No. You bring them here for me, there's a good boy. And open the front door. I'll just have another puff or two then go to my room without disturbing the love birds."

"Come in; Anna will want you in."

"Bugger off I told you. Just open the front door so I can go to my bedroom; that can't be too bloody difficult, even for you. Go and eat your supper with the Goddess if you want to risk it but don't expect me to come and save you. I saved myself – that's one save and that's all

313

you're allowed – no more savings."

"If you're in this mood, I'll open the door and you can please yourself. I'll leave your dinner on a plate in the oven so you can have it when you're hungry. Don't stay out here too long."

"Don't you worry about me boyo, I can look after myself when the time comes, see if I can't. And I know what the sheep mean, too; I been sitting here thinking about it – *the sheep in the fold.* Just bring me my bloody fags and piss off to her in there. That's not too much to ask, peace and quiet when you're not wanted."

Edward returned inside and went to unlock the front door of the cottage. He went to the kitchen where Anna had set the table, and said, "He wants his cigarettes; this pack is the last of this lot; he's chain-smoking them but I can't get him to cut them down."

"Where is he?" asked Anna.

"Outside on the seat. He won't come in for dinner; he says he's not hungry for chicken and potatoes, but wouldn't mind shop chips."

"I'll talk to him and try and make him see sense."

"I don't think that will help; you'd best leave him alone. He'll come in when he wants to and he'll eat when he wants; it's what he does, it seems. Getting him agitated will only make him worse; leave him. I'll just take him these and then we'll eat."

They ate their dinner largely in silence; talk was desultory at best until Anna said, "You've spent some time with him now and you probably know him better than I do. In any case, I don't think he would unburden himself to a woman, even though she is his daughter; tell me your thinking."

"Are you sure? I can't be just *'nice'* about him you realise; are you ready for that?"

"You like to understand people, as you've said; well I should like to understand something of my father. And I know that no-one is as white as whitewash."

"If he was here, he'd probably sing that to you:

Whiter than the whitewash on the wall.
You can wash me in the water
That you washed your dirty daughter in
And I shall be whiter than the whitewash on the wall
On the Wall,
On the Wall.

Repeat *ad nauseam,* diminishing as you march away."

"What's that song?" she asked. "I don't think I know it."

"First World War Vintage Reality; what the Soldiers made up into song to show themselves there was a meaning, and hope, behind all the carnage and the mud in the Trenches that stretched from the Atlantic to the Rhine, before the Soldiers were given a Poppy for their efforts and told to go and die for somebody else's Credo; as the Servant Class has always been expected to die, in truth: in the mud, acknowledging their betters and being grateful. The songs were a bit different from the War Poets' contributions, but just as enduring, more so perhaps, and more immediate and just as real."

"Alright, enough of that sort of blaming; I don't suppose we'd be any different; *Reality* is all a matter of context, anyway. Tell me about my father."

"I've rehearsed some of this already to myself, so forgive me if some of what I say seems glib, it's not meant to be.

"If you allowed me only a one sentence summary I should say: 'He's a clever man locked in limitations not of his own making'. As I told Miss Davies of the Social Services, without the problems surrounding his birth, I believe he would have made some mark in life; intellectually more than practically I would say; he'd be happier in a library than excavating burial sites or chasing new species in a jungle, though he'd take pleasure from that too, and think it all relevant. He asked about his books, by the way. He's a strong character; he's had to be. He's clever, very focussed, and surprisingly knowledgeable within his interests; how much so I can't say, I'm not his examiner, and he knows more than I do. But where I do know something of his interests, I see that his understanding is just slightly wrong; not much, but enough to be concerning. When you consider that all of this has been accumulated from hours of difficult reading and from being told the tales over and again, by others, who in any case, would have had their own slant on things, his knowledge is quite remarkable, and mostly remarkably coherent.

"He certainly seems authoritative on the Myths and Legends of Ancient Wales and he also has a selective Biblical knowledge, principally of the Old Testament it seems. But they all seem time-condensed; conflated, if you like; they all seem to run in concert rather than sequentially – and that includes his own life. He feels that there are important Riddles whose meanings are hidden from him, and which he must solve to understand the Ancient Gods and give them their rightful place, and so End the Rule of the Female Forever: I would say that he believes that to be *his quest*. It makes me a little concerned if he doesn't answer some of his Riddles.

"However, less Psychotic, he has taken the strongly-held views of others as Truth – which we know, is very easy to do - and he's internalised it all; as a result, he is totally uncritical in his beliefs: they have become more of a *fixation* than interesting *knowledge per se*. And since he uses his own peculiar understanding of this knowledge to order his decisions and structure his life – as we all do – and to name his children even, he wonders whether his Real Life is a *Mission,* a *Quest* that he must fulfil – as many of us do, in fact; to help, as it were. There is a danger both to himself and to others, there.

"Other than all that, he likes to have his own way and often sulks when he doesn't get it. He is also very astute, and can be manipulative: I have stopped and wondered at times, to what extent he's purposely misleading us and laughing to himself at *our* naivety; it's the kind of trick he'd enjoy.

"That's a potted pen-portrait of your father for you then; it's not much and even I wouldn't take any of it as gospel truth."

"It's enough. I must say. You seem to have given considerable thought to it; you must have spent all your time criticising my father. I would have thought that you could have found better things to do with this sharp, analytical mind of yours when you had all that time on your hands."

"I told you that you might not like what I would say to you, though I see no reason to raise your hackles. I have not criticised him; I wouldn't have the temerity, but I have tried to know and understand him, which is what you should have been doing. I've also told you already that I make up my own mind about things; that goes for people too; and I won't lie; I may stay silent, but I won't lie – neither to myself nor to others."

"Upright but without a shred of compassion," said Anna.

"If you don't want to know the way I am, what I think, don't ask for my mind. I have tried to be objective and it might surprise you to know that although he can be difficult and often infuriating, when it comes down to it, I like him: he's forthright, yes; irritating, yes; child-like sometimes; but I believe he's honest with himself, as he sees it; and for me, that means a great deal, and I applaud it. I tell you, there's much about him that I *know* and acknowledge; and more than I know of you. And I'll tell you something else, daughter: I believe that in himself, if he's left alone, he's happy enough, because Happiness is a state of mind that you must strive for. You must accept the disappointments of reaching too far and work through them to reach it; and God knows he's done that. I wouldn't call him a Happy Man now, but I think he has known Happiness. I envy him that. But he also *fears* himself, and I can relate to that.

"Now, contrary to what you think I've been doing all day, while your father has been walking the hills, I have been doing some stratigraphic analysis for the Company which I have sent to Head Office. They may have replied already, so I shall be in the study for a while. Then, well, we'll see."

Edward walked to the study and switched on his computer. While it was uploading his programmes, he poured himself a generous measure of whisky and drank it quickly. He poured another to which he added water. He was not pleased with the way he had talked to Anna who was having to face a father she had never known; he knew it had been an attack more directed at himself than at her: he had been shown that among the excuses he had gathered to himself to cope with his own life, one thing had been lost, set aside as inconvenient: that was honesty, When he had said that he wouldn't lie to himself, it was an aspiration, not a fact; he had lied to himself since the loss of Jacqueline when his way of trying to cope with that emptiness was to reject any thought of it; to shut-down that period of his life. Now, incongruously, it was this man, lost in many ways, that had drawn him to face himself. This deeper understanding of himself was a two-edged sword: he now understood his behaviour a little more but the knowledge diminished his character. Neither did his realisation help to show him the road he should take. From his viewpoint, the bridge to Anna had been shaken already and he should not hurt her more, but the options were clear: continue, but constantly guard your tongue; break away and never again need to guard your tongue – become again a singularity. Simplistic, but a profoundly consequential choice after so short a time.

He accessed his e-mails, hoping that there would be a need to respond to requests, taking his mind away from worrying at his personal decisions. His Head Office had replied, but only to acknowledge the receipt of his analysis. There was no relief there.

"Damn the curse of introspection."

He drained his drink and walked back to the kitchen.

CHAPTER 42

THE DECISION

Anna had unloaded the car, had taken her case into the bedroom and had cleared the table of the dinner dishes. The gift case of wine from Lord Mostyn sat on the table. Anna had her back to Edward as she washed the casserole dish with its rim of hardened sauce and those implements not dish-washer proof.

Edward said, "We'd best get some fresh fish tomorrow, to do justice to this wine we've been given."

"Yes," said Anna. "It would be a shame not to do justice to it after the effort they've made. Did you get a response from the Company?"

"Just an acknowledgement; I didn't really expect anything else so soon."

He walked to her and put his arms around her as she looked out of the kitchen window. "Come for a walk along the path. It's warm enough now the wind's dropped."

"It'll be too dark coming back."

"We'll take a torch in case."

The light was on in Rhodri's bedroom as he pulled the door to. There was no moon and though the air was warm, it was still and there was a dampness that could be fog by morning. They followed the cliff path with the help of a powerful torch.

"Does my father know about this torch?"

"I don't think so; at least he hasn't asked about it and I haven't offered it because I wouldn't like him to wander in the dark however good he is on the mountain."

"Keep it well hidden then or he'll surely find it."

They walked in silence for a while until Edward said, "I'm sorry. When I mentioned a response to my report, I used it simply as an excuse because I felt a quarrel coming on. Forgive me."

"You were right about that; but then you usually are, aren't you? You have so much confidence in yourself that you won't even contemplate being in the wrong – another of the world's Certainties – not *fearful* at all. I find that difficult to cope with; and I'm not used to being bested in an argument. And worst of all, you don't smirk; it would be easier if you did, so I could damn you to Hell, have a blazing row and have it over with. This way, it simmers."

"It needn't," replied Edward.

"True, it needn't and for most people we come across, it doesn't. But they seem to be less analytical and far less self-critical than we spend our time being. We're not built that way, you and I; and we've been given far too much *Education*; so we say it's not true for us. We spend half our time taking the blame for our actions and the deficiencies of other people, and the other half shifting it on to someone else, along with the guilt. What an outcome of all that *Education*: you're too damned sure of yourself and I'm too calculating. Not a good balance in a marriage."

"You're very wrong."

"About what?"

"All of it; but about me in particular."

"I don't think so."

"Oh yes, you're more wrong than I think you'll ever know. Time for Confession, again," said Edward. "It's all a veneer: a fear of doubt: *fearful* most certainly, always. Take time to talk to my father sometime; you'll have a different assessment of me from him."

"I take what I see, not what others tell me. Isn't that your credo too?"

"As I've told you. I hope that your vision is less clouded than your father's; and less clear than mine."

Edward was walking on the cliff side of the path and stumbled on a tussock of grass. Anna pulled on his arm and said, "Don't go that way. You're still worth more than that to people, you know. Some will miss you."

"Well, it is good to know that some may give me a thought. You didn't finish telling me what Mostyn told you."

"No. What he said grieved me, and it could well be, no, certainly is, why I've been more snappy than my usual self; you'll accept that analysis, will you? Opinionated, but not snappy? That's *Education* for you: it teaches you Criticism but not how to Behave. I'm unsure too, whether I should even tell you this; it might be better left unsaid and forgotten."

"It won't be forgotten now though will it? Certainly not by you, and I shall always wonder what was so necessary for you *not* to tell me."

"You're right; again, sage. *'For peace of mind, one must say less and listen more'*. Who said that?"

"Apart from you, no-one I know could be as astute."

"Now you're making fun of me; but that's better than criticism. Alright. You know that the Social Services and the Police have been – what's the phrase? – 'keeping an eye on' – my father and have trailed him to this house. Of course you do, you dealt with them. Well, when the Police visited you dispatched them with bad grace but they left a reminder that they could well return should any *'activities'* come to their attention; the lady from the Social Services, you say, seemed to have gone about her business with rather better grace. Nevertheless, I don't think that we should write her off the radar either."

"What's this preamble leading to?"

"Be patient. You know, of the rumours if not of the facts, that these two institutions have been monitoring his activities for some years; of course you do; we came across it when we first went to his village. Let me recap: not to put too fine a point on it, he was suspected, on the basis of gossip, that he was being *'over-friendly'* with the young children, boys more than girls it seems. I understand that now, I think."

"Tell me it then."

"Patience! I'll come to it. In any case, people thought that was somewhat unhealthy in a grown man even though it's not unusual in a closed, somewhat *insular* society as we've been told he lived in. It all came to a head, apparently, when one of the young girls, not yet even a teenager, told her mother that Mr Rhodri had told them how babies were made. The fact that he had done only what any proper parent should have done was neither here nor there. Of course you'd also expect such prudery in a rural Welsh village: 'oh yes, *animals do it,* but not people; we're not *animals*'. As a result, he became listed as a potential paedophile on the Police books, on no evidence of any child molestation at all. They knew that of course and thought that the most appropriate action to take would be to *'just keep an eye on him and see where he goes* then send a file to the Social Services; pass it onto them and see what they think. There, it was noted but no overt action was taken other than an occasional visit under the guise of a concern about his welfare. That, as you know, is still the order of the day. There's another thing though: no action of any kind was taken by either of them until after Councillor Rees had died and my father was living on his own in that house. Don't you find that strange?" asked Anna.

"Not in the least. I understand that Councillor Rees had something of a reputation in those parts; he would not have brooked any unsubstantiated accusation from the Police, the Social Services or anyone else for that matter, once he had acknowledged Rhodri to be his illegitimate son. And they would not have been keen to draw attention to unsubstantiated rumours and tittle-tattle either; too many forms to fill. So it's not so strange that it was quietly set aside."

"I can see that," said Anna.

"Look, this fog is getting thicker; shall we turn back?"

"Not yet; there's more. There's a seat along here you said? Let's sit there while I finish this. I can't tell you it in the house – it will linger there; here, the wind can take it."

"Come on then. It's just a little further. But it can't be for long or we'll be soaked; you don't realise how thick this sea fog can get. Worse than rain it can be because it *seeps*," said Edward

"There's not much more. Here we are. It turns out that all these supposed paedophilic activities had no basis at all; just a hysterical mother seeking attention. It never had been worth anybody's time; it was a false trail entirely."

"Then why the interest? Why still the interest? Why is it still going on?"

"While my father and his 'Lady' as he called her, were wandering about in Mid- and North Wales seeking the land of the Mabinogi, she became pregnant, as you know. The pregnancy itself was not a problem; they both, but my father in particular, was overjoyed at the thought of a son – which he was convinced it would be."

"And was. He called it Bendigeidfran."

"Right. The problem was not the pregnancy but the birth. They were not registered with a GP, nor a hospital; so she gave birth in their tent and his 'Lady' lost a great deal of blood. She recovered but was careful, they both must have been, not to conceive again too quickly – not until me, in fact, when she – I must call her Mother, not 'she' nor 'Lady', though I know nothing about her – when she died giving me life. Is that a *Sacrifice*? You could argue that it was. What must a man feel about such a Sacrifice? Can you tell me?"

"Yes, something of it. Sorrow, of course, and mostly; great and enduring I have no doubt; great love that doesn't diminish with living as others do; gratitude for the supreme Sacrifice; but anger also to be called on to pay the debt for a new life. And there is great and persistent anger at the child who lives, and jealousy too for its life. Perhaps that last one, most of all, to our shame. But the strength of each depends on the person and their beliefs."

"You know of this, don't you?"

"I know it. But you've not finished."

"Bendigeidfran. 'Bran The Blessed', my brother, then. He died soon after birth; how, I've not been told; I don't think even Mostyn knows, though he knows a great deal. But the Police learned, from my father I suppose, that he had died and been put on a raft of reeds and sent over a lake, or *Llyn* in Welsh, to Arthur in Avalon[34]."

"Not reeds," said Edward. "Willow is more correct."

"Never mind that. They don't know which of those lakes, neither was the body of my brother recovered. At first, the Police dismissed the

321

account as the troubled, fanciful rantings of a not too bright man. But when Father Will, and I know now, Lord Mostyn, became involved, the Police were forced to acknowledge a missing person. Apparently, also, my father described – according to the Police Report at least – *a biblical procedure* – that he had been called upon to do and carried out as befitted the descendant of a Prince of Wales. But the *'Lord God, Blessed Be His Name'*, according to my father, had decided to take his Son into Heaven anyway. I know no more of that, but I suspect that Mostyn does. I don't know if anyone else does, but whatever act my father performed, resulted in the death of my brother. So, it seems that there was a clear case of infanticide – rather stronger than suspected paedophilia, wouldn't you say? And that's why there is still an interest in his 'welfare'. No case can be brought against him because his story is his, no registration of birth, no body, no proof, no confirmation and the mother dead. There then. Now you know it all and you can understand why they keep watching him. And here endeth the *Tale of a Princely Line in the Land of the Mighty*. Not yet worthy of a Legend to itself, but shows promise, wouldn't you agree? "

"Anna, I'm sorry that you had to face this alone. I didn't understand."

"We must all face things alone in the end."

"Yes. But be sure it's only when we must; for the rest, take comfort from someone, if you can," replied Edward.

Edward could have told her the procedure that her father had performed on her brother, but he hesitated because he believed that it would serve no purpose; it would only produce greater distress. Silence was the easier and the more compassionate act. But though silence was easier, compassion was more problematic: the silence of compassion was to whose benefit? Would Anna wonder for the remainder of her life how her father had killed her brother? *Why* had he killed her brother? Would the absence of any understandable motive produce a greater distress than the truth? With her present understanding, her father had killed her brother and it would be difficult for her to be compassionate towards him without knowing why. Could she ever be compassionate and forgiving? His motive had not been the death of the child, but the reverse: his elevation, profoundly wrong though his apparent instruction had been. Left to himself, would he have even contemplated the circumcision of his son? Edward was reminded of the command, *'Look to the living, let the dead look after their own.'*

"Come on now then, let's get back," said Anna.

"No" Edward said, "I must finish this for you. I must tell you how your brother died; staying silent is not an option for me on this. I'm sorry, I have no doubt it will distress you, but silence this time would be wrong, I believe."

"How do you know what happened? Wasn't it just the death of a newborn?"

"No. Your father told me what really happened."

"Then tell me for God's sake."

"It will sound like Genesis and truly Heretical, the sort of thing the Cathars [35] were persecuted for and I've added a little of what I know to fill some gaps.

"Your brother, Bran, was born successfully, though your Mother, whose name was Vera by the way, lost a lot of blood. Understand, this was a time when your Father had seriously taken to the Religion of his People – meaning the Mabinogi and the Princes. He truly believed that Bran was blessed by God The Father, a *Bendigeid*, a Blessed, and that he was a descendant of the Kings of the Mabinogi through Abraham and King David and Jesus; then the Merovingians [35] and the Princes of Wales which, of course meant that he, Rhodri, or your mother, Vera, was of noble birth too; or both of them were: another *Joseph and Mary* and the *Child* would bring the *Second Coming*. According to Vera, being noble, there was a ritual that had to be performed in order to secure the child's dedication to the God of his Fathers and of the Israelites."

"Baptism?" asked Anna.

"No. Some other ritual."

"What is it then? What did he do?"

"Let me tell you it in my way, please; it's not easy."

"That makes it worse."

"Yes, I know. But it's the only way I can tell you; and I'm paraphrasing this anyway – Rhodri was not as coherent. Vera told him that there was a ritual to be performed on this young King – To – Be that would be pleasing to his Father in Heaven; he should know what every male child in God's Chosen People had to undergo."

"No! You can't mean he circumcised his own son?"

"Yes. They believed, your Father totally, your Mother, at least as instigator, that it was Bran's destiny to lead his people and that he would have to be circumcised. Later of course, he would also have to be ritually lamed like Jesus[36], in order to do so. There was no Rabbi, and no hospital, so you mother told him that he would have to perform the act himself and that God had called on him to do it. On your father's assurance, the act itself was carried out, but the bleeding could not be stopped. So your brother died."

Anna was now silent, and her tears ran over her cheeks and fell to the top of her dress where the wet patch slowly spread. She had clasped her hands tightly in her lap and Edward released them and took one into his own hand. She did not object; neither did she show the need for comfort.

Eventually she said, "My father did kill my brother then. Is that the end of it?"

"Almost," replied Edward.

"Finish it then."

"Your father did build a raft (of reeds he said, because there was no willow and he didn't know what it looked like anyway) 'as he was instructed by the Lord' he said and floated it out onto the lake to reach Arthur in Avalon [34]. That's it."

Anna was silent again for a while, then said, "There was infanticide then; my father did kill my brother. The Police were not wrong."

"No. But they would not have understood the motive. That had taken a number of years to germinate, and was as much a consequence of Vera's urging as his own desire and the perceived promise of his son as a new Prophet. Its resolution was as much the consequence of others' tales of Mystery and Legend as his understanding of the ancient Romances and Tragedies. And your father could never have understood the Police form of Justice. So it's as well that the lake was never identified."

"Do we know where it might be?"

"Snowdonia, certainly; and my guess would be *Llyn y Morynion* [37]; it's important in the Tales. He said it was deep with reeds around its shore; and they used to visit Bala; and that lake fits the bill; but it could be any one of a number; there's no knowing which."

"I should go there and pay my respects to my brother."

"You can't know where he is. You would be better leaving it; make no pilgrimage," said Edward.

"No doubt; that's one view of it. But then the questions linger, don't they, if you have no sense of *place,* no sense of the *land where they lie?* Questions like, 'Where is he?' 'Does he rest?' You should know of that need."

"One likes to know where they rest; you're right. Strangely, that helps you to rest," said Edward in a barely audible voice. "Without knowing that, they might as well not have lived; and your imagination will persist in playing its tricks. You do owe them that acknowledgement at least."

"It's for *your own* benefit then? The homage is a *selfish* act?"

"Mostly, I fear it is; like any Religion, a matter of saving your own sanity. It's why the Monks recite their prayers four times a day to save

324

their souls," replied Edward. "The dead can't know you're there after all."

"So you say Edward, so you say; but that's a *belief* too, and pragmatic, and no different from any other *faith*. But I agree, the *precise* location of the body is not important, but the land where it lies is: we need that vision to call on if we need to. The body doesn't matter any more; it's soon gone anyway. But we must know the land. It matters because it's where you see their *Spirit* – that sense of place. And you carry that with you: it's called *Memory,* but that's just a different word, more acceptably secular. And then it only matters to you: there is no *Spirit* for others."

"Just a *'Thanks for the Memory'* then," replied Edward. "Is that all it is?"

"I suppose it's more than others have," said Anna. "He is amongst the lakes of his Ancestors – and mine; and yours. And perhaps with Arthur too, if we care to believe a little of the darkness, as we must; it's all that matters in the end: the Tales we leave. Do you see the need for my pilgrimage now?"

"Yes. But only for the 'Spirit', not for the body."

"Indeed" said Anna. "It's *we* that feel a need to raise a hand; to say 'Goodbye'. So, one last *Farewell* then, in a place that we will know. So that we can remember."

"Yes. For memory's sake then," said Edward, thinking not of a Lake, but of a jungle clearing and the hot, humid sun.

"Yes. Another Land, a Lake, or here on a cliff: it's where you choose it to be. As for my father, in my eyes he's condemned himself. He cannot expect redemption from me: there is a payment he must make before that. He must go"

"You're too harsh on him; show compassion."

"No. I can have no compassion. He murdered my brother – a Child who would be a Man - that is the ultimate Heresy: it's not just against *God's Law* or *The Commandments* of Moses; it's greater than that, it's against *Life's Law*: you need a damn good reason to end it. I sought my Father out, but not for this. And he got rid of me as soon as he could, as well. No, I can have no compassion: I cannot any more feel a debt to him for my life; he's had no part in it in any real sense I now know; and I condemn him to Hell for taking away the life of another, my brother. It's time we took him home and left him to his doom. My debt is paid; I tried; he can claim no more from me now; there's nothing more I want to give in any case; and his debt is still outstanding. Is there any more I should know?"

"Only that he despises the Female, *The Great Goddess In All Her*

Forms, as he says, and that our God won the battle and our true belief is Patriarchal not Matriarchal; he's terribly confused about Gods and Goddesses. I'd like to say that there's no harm in it but you can see that wouldn't be true."

"I can see that; and it explains his attitude to me. He must go; he *must go* before he does any more damage. He must be made to realise, that Life matters; he must be told of his guilt: he must be made to understand that *Murder* is the greatest *Heresy* whether you believe in a God or a Goddess, or nothing: you cannot, you must not, deny *Life*. I must put a final end to it. Damn Religion; Damn Myths; Damn Legends. They should be left in the nursery where they belong."

"But they don't belong there, do they? They're too much a core of our understanding to be left in the nursery. Come now then, we must get in from this fog. We're wet, we need some dry clothes and a warm drink."

CHAPTER 43

CONSIDERATIONS

They hurried back to the house and were glad of the shelter from the thickening fog. Rhodri was not to be seen but he had been in the kitchen and had eaten his dinner. His plate and cutlery had been left on the draining board and there were a number of cigarette stubs in a saucer on the table. The air was thick with smoke from the cigarettes and there was an acrid smell. Edward opened the kitchen window which looked out to the sea and the advancing fog.

"It's the fog or the fags. Which do you prefer?" he asked.

"The fog until it's easier to breathe," replied Anna.

"I agree," said Edward. "Would you like tea or coffee or a drink?"

"Not coffee, it'll keep me too awake, and I'm tired. So tea please."

Edward set the kettle to boil and poured himself a whisky.

"There are decisions to be made at last; it's time now," said Anna. "I can't put them off any longer. Decisions about him and about me."

"Yes, I understand," replied Edward. "But perhaps not tonight; 'sleep on it first, then the answer may be clear.' There's truth in that."

"I expect so; but it can also give you a bad night without solving anything."

"True, but be optimistic. You needn't rush anything; take a day, tomorrow, and spend some time with him; get him to talk about your mother."

"No. That's too much of a risk for me at this time; you see, I can't put it beyond him to have arranged for her death as well; or at least not made any effort to prevent it. He's demented, but he knows what he's doing; he knows what he's responsible for: an *End to the Rule of the Female*. I can't tolerate him any more; he doesn't deserve any consideration.

"Who were they anyway? Just two people who came together and fornicated. I just wonder now, whether Mother Megan knew any of this; and if it was why she was so adamant that I shouldn't pursue him. It would be like her to protect me, and the rest of her brood. My father Will would have put a stop to it; and told us 'why'."

"Go with him tomorrow; get him to show you where the cliff has fallen away or the view from where he sits in the ferns."

"We shall have to hope for the fog to clear for those. As for the rest, I'll admit it needs resolving. But if he starts on his damned cigarettes again, I tell you, I refuse to be responsible for my actions."

"I think I can probably guarantee that he will. I'll go into the City and do some shopping while you take your walk; that will probably get him off your back a little; it might shut him up at least. Try to enjoy the walk with him; he can be quite interesting if you get him going on the Legends."

"For your sake then; though I don't know how successful I shall be; it might all be for the worse. He doesn't want to know me and I'm tiring of him. But for you, and for being a good referee, I'll try once more before I finish with him. But I won't accept any nonsense from him. I don't want to battle him, nor his convictions. But I'll show him the strength of the Goddess; then, well, we'll see."

"Just try; another day won't be too difficult."

"We'll see; but I want him taken home and away from me, and soon so that we can have a short while together, just the two of us before we must get back to London. We've grown up together and I should like to think about those times. You see, my decision is pressing on me too much and I'm not sure of the way out for me; and I'm getting tired as they said I would. So I must come to a decision, and there's not much time."

"I understand that, love, but the fewer problems there are, the easier it will be for us to face. You must see that."

"Oh yes, I see that, but more imperative are the practicalities of achieving it. I regret my decision to bring him here now; we should have been alone here in this house for the first time, and under those skies too. Then we could have made them ours."

"You did what you understood to be your duty and that's laudable."

"If I'm honest, that's not all of it; or even most of it. True, I wanted to know who my father was, what sort of person he was; what I was lumbered with. I was being selfish again."

"Well, that's understandable. But, we do have to accept them, because we can't change our ancestry."

"No. But we *can* and *do* judge them."

"Not too harshly then. Be compassionate; he has preyed for forgiveness. We know only a little of others' lives and we certainly know too little of his; we don't even know what's driven him; and only a little of how he has faced his world, other than his escape to the Legends of this land. We must think about you, too; we'll take him home whenever you say; but let's leave him peacefully. Just try this for me, if not for him."

"I've said, for your sake, I will. But just one more day. I brought him with us for any number of reasons as I've told you: because he's my father and I owe him; he is an old man and he was left alone; he was being persecuted, or so I thought; and he shouldn't be left to live out his years alone and under siege; but mostly as I've said, for purely selfish reasons; and here's another one: I thought he would take my mind off what I must do about myself. I see now, that it doesn't work like that: one issue doesn't cancel another out. I should have known that of course; I did know that; but it's human nature to hope that it does, isn't it? Now, I know that most of all *he owes me* for killing my brother. I condemn him for that and surely there must be a price he has to pay. But I hadn't known that when in the end I funked it and left him to you to look after."

"Yes."

"Well, my life is not that important, except to you and a few others. But I'm glad I've seen your place and I should like to be alone here for another sky."

"Yes, again. It might help."

Anna went to the bedroom while Edward washed Rhodri's plate and their tea mugs then followed Anna who came to nestle in his arms.

She said, "Do you know Edward, despite all we've had to face, you and I, it is so much easier for us now: we are *not* alone. My father Will was very wrong: we each have sought for someone to hold; as humans do. Surely, it's the way of living that matters, not the death. So we cannot take another's life; because it matters, whatever the circumstances. You don't deserve your own life otherwise; how much does he deserve a life, when he's taken another's? He must be made to see that."

"Yes, he must. A life must be lived, and I've come to realise that you can't escape from your life by hiding yourself in a remote cottage overlooking the sea. Your life has to be lived; it is not outside of you; you have to live it within your skin, and often that's damned hard to take."

"My lover, my husband, hold me close; I need you; I'm becoming frightened of the darkness ahead; it's intruding."

"No need to be; not yet, at least."

"Not with you, like this. Not ever with you like this; but there are *other* times aren't there, on your own in the dark, when the fear comes; when there is a need; an ache. And it's why Religion has that *grip:* when the Darkness threatens, you are grateful for the Myth of God to call upon, to help out; to tell you it's not the end as you thought, but just a 'crossing over'. You learn it as a child and it sticks. We are a fearful species."

"Yes; but that's only our inadequacies," said Edward. "If we are to survive, it is an advantage to be fearful. And believing that there is a

Higher State gives courage and reinforces Religious belief, so it's a circular construct: *there is Another who's better at this, who will Comfort you, and who will give you Peace – or a Heaven of A Thousand Virgins if you prefer.* It's what Wars are made of: for all the death and devastation, they are a search for Universal Peace that only your One True God can give you."

"It also externalises and provides a form of comfort," said Anna.

"I know that as well, and there's no harm in that," replied Edward.

"Is it different in the light of day?"

"For some I suppose; for others it seems to endure."

"Yes. And for you?"

"Not for me. I came to understand it as only a prop on which to hang my grief, to renounce my despair and avoid any responsibility for myself; to put it all in the hands of Another to sort out. I found that I couldn't do that; but that is a fault of my own belief, as your father has told me several times. And you should know, right or wrong, I envy those who live in their certainties. In any case, how will we know who is right? How can we know the truth of it? Each one of us must decide for him- or herself what the truth is for them, at that time. There is no other way."

"That seems a very bleak prospect; isn't Truth really absolute then?"

"Oh no, Philosopher. Truth is whatever you want it to be at the time: you only have to look at Christianity and the Gospellers and the Popes to see that it's just another Construct of the human mind; a Legend; an Intellectualisation of Practice, that's all. It's a *'Making Sense Of Things'*, and in your heart you know it," said Edward. "Absolute Truth! That's a fallacy; and Religious Truth an even greater one – a Construct, as I say. Truth is entirely Relative, and Cultural. In the West: God and Christianity is the One Truth; in the Middle East: Allah, Mohammed and Islam is the One Truth; in the East: how about Hinduism, Buddhism, Confucianism, and more, as the One Truth; each one the One Path To Enlightenment. Take your pick then, and make a Crusade for it; or fight to the death for it: make War! When people say *'God's Truth'* I have to ask, *'Whose God? Which One?'*"

"Is it easier to accept the Myth, then, and not to think? That choice is not given to all of us."

"No, that's true and it troubles many people. Your father surprised me with his analysis of Religious Belief."

"You surprise me; what did he say?"

"We shouldn't be surprised – he's a very astute and rational man; he knows more than he can express. It could be where you get your Logic from. He despaired of my unbelief and wanted to convert me back to

Christianity, which I continued to deny. He said, *'For someone with Education, you're a pretty daft bloke; if you want to go to Heaven, you've got to believe in Him or you'll be standing at the Pearly Gates for ever, if He exists as our God; if He doesn't, there's nothing lost in any case is there? Stands to reason you should believe then. And you're a bloody fool if you don't. '"*

"I wouldn't have thought he was that sharp."

"Nor did I; but *sharp* he most certainly is. It's the sort of thing that makes him such an ambivalent character. So here I am and I must admit to being a 'bloody fool' for the sake of intellectual honesty – the most dangerous of excuses."

There was no reply from Anna, and they were silent. After a short while, her breathing became regular and deep. Despite her personal and paternal problems, she was asleep and the problems seemed successfully consigned to the next day. Edward wished that he, too, could drift into unawareness as easily. But he knew that he would be awake for some time yet. He thought again of his longing for solitude and was sorrowful for Anna who had to face her illness and the prospect of its treatment complete with the uncertainty. As her husband there was a duty as well as a responsibility to provide all the support that she would undoubtedly need; he would need to persuade her that there could be little further delay before she should be admitted for the start of her treatment. However, he also knew that whatever support he could give was entirely peripheral to the *fact* of her struggle: that reality she *would* have to face alone. Also, he was unsure how far he could be involved without breaching his own uncertain defences. But there was no escape in turning away: that would only create guilt of another order. He lay awake until the pale light of a foggy dawn showed through the curtains and he realised that once again he would have to face a new day without the escape of sleep.

He rose quietly so as not to disturb Anna and made his way to the study. His computer showed that there were e-mail messages waiting to be opened. He poured himself a drink and opened his mailbox. There was a lengthy message with attachments from his Head Office. He was grateful that his morning could be devoted to his response and that he could escape the need to consider the problems of others.

CHAPTER 44

RESOLUTION

He noted the message and the data that had been sent to him and, at first, thought that he would immediately start work on them: he was keen to know to what extent his predictions and assumptions about the oil field would be upheld but his enthusiasm waned as quickly as it had waxed. In any case he realised that the noise of the printer was likely to wake Rhodri who was sleeping in the next room and he preferred avoiding that confrontation so early in the morning. Anna, too, might be woken by an unfamiliar noise. He poured himself another drink and fell asleep in the chair.

He was not asleep for long before he heard Rhodri moving about and making his way to the bathroom. There was no sound of running water, so it was unlikely that he was running a bath for himself, nor would he be taking a shower. Edward felt too weary to rise and continued to doze in the chair. Again, it was not long before he heard Rhodri making his way outside, no doubt to smoke his early ration of cigarettes. Edward had left his watch and his clock in the bedroom so he had no idea of the time; the noises of Rhodri's movements gave no indication of the time either: it was as likely to be noon as daybreak when he stirred. He drew back the curtains. The morning light was bright and there was a rainbow over the sea. It seemed the fog had lifted somewhat, but there was no wind so it continued to provide a low ceiling while the sun was still vanquished and there was no indication of the sort of day it would be. Edward guessed that the time was about seven thirty or eight o'clock and decided to take a shower himself. When he walked into the bedroom, Anna was awake and held out her arms for an embrace. Edward kissed her and she did not release her arms from about his neck.

"You smell of whisky. You've not been drinking this early in the morning, surely," she said.

"I didn't sleep at all, so it's just a continuation of yesterday to me, and late in the day. I've been up some time looking at my mail. I find that a little dram starts me off well, that's all."

"You'll get to be worse than my father with his cigarettes. You mustn't let it get a hold."

"No, I won't let it do that."

"What time is it?" asked Anna.

"Good Lord, it's much later than I thought; it's nine fifteen. No wonder your father has started on his daily crusade to smoke for Wales. He'll be wanting his breakfast and so do I. I'll get started while you shower, but don't rush."

Edward finished dressing and went to set the table and to start cooking breakfast. Having got to know Rhodri's vagaries, he first went outside and saw Rhodri sitting on the bench seat looking out to sea.

"Back – of – Bloody – Beyond is this and no mistake. Even the bloody ships avoid it. Not even Fog Horns in the Night to give a bit of interest in cold blood. *HOOO HOOO.* I'll be glad to get home and watch *Road Runner. BEEP BEEP.* And to get away from the influence of the Female."

"Are you ready for your breakfast?" asked Edward.

"Too bloody right I am; I thought you were never getting up. Been starving all night I've been."

"You ate the Shepherd's Pie though?"

"Too bloody right, and a good job too; I'd have been dead and gone with starvation by now if I hadn't. What's for breakfast then?"

"What would you like? How about a boiled egg?"

"That's not much to keep a grown man going, one fucking egg. What I'd like is a nice piece of fresh smoked haddock. They're better than kippers; not so many bones. Yes, smoked haddock I fancy."

"Well you'll have to keep fancying it; I haven't got any."

"No haddock? And you living with the sea in the front garden? You could practically fish for the bloody fish from here; rod and line and sinker and a bit of bait is all you need. Those Zulu potatoes would make good bait. Fresh every morning it would be then; champion. You'd have to smoke it though. I could do that with my fags; help you along like. Or you could fry it like in the Fish and Chip shop."

"You can have a boiled *fresh* egg or *local* bacon and egg and fried bread. Or you can just have toast. Which do you want?"

"Not much bloody choice, is it? It will have to be bacon and egg again I suppose; get to look like the arse end of a chicken or a pig at this rate and no mistake. I could do with some more fags as well. I'm not walking to the shop though with my bad feet – you'll have to go now she's brought the car back. Talk to the Chatty Bugger about a constant supply of Camels. Where is She then? Still here is She?"

"Yes, she's having her shower. I'll go and get your fags after breakfast and you can talk to your daughter; go for a walk with her."

"Too bloody dangerous is that; best to leave the Goddess out of it all, it seems to me. Safer that way: then I won't be beholden to no Goddess and her ilk; Trouble in Heaven that is, you can be sure. Any road, in the circumstances, I don't know if I could stomach her all the time it takes to walk there and back. She'll want to know what I've been doing as well so that she can tell me to stop it, whatever it is."

"Tell her then. Tell her about the Mabinogi; she'll enjoy that. Now you stay here while I do the breakfast. I'll call you when it's ready."

"No trouble sunshine mine; but don't be too long about it or what you'll find is a pile of clothes and a skelington here when you come back. Then you'd be up before the cops and no mistake. *Guilty, Your Honour. Lock him up and throw away the key.* Count of Monte Christo you'd be, and serve you right, starving old people to death."

"It will take as long as it takes. And I hope you'll eat it when it's ready, not two hours later."

"Is *She* going to eat it with us?"

"Certainly. Anna needs her breakfast like the rest of us."

"Perhaps I'll go for the second sitting then, like in school. You couldn't have 'seconds' with the first sitting because there was a second sitting; but you could have 'seconds' with the second sitting because there was no third sitting; if there were any seconds to be had; if the bloody Prefects hadn't eaten it all. I'll have the 'second sitting' and leave you alone like."

"You'll eat with us or not at all. And if you don't, there'll be no fags later either."

"Bloody bully you are. I don't like eating with women. Too *la-di-dah* they are. Puts you off your food, it does."

"You'll eat with us and like it; I'm not cooking breakfast twice. And try and be pleasant for a change; I know you find it difficult, but try for once. I'll call you when it's ready, so don't go sloping off like your usual trick. Remember, breakfast or no cigarettes."

Edward went to the kitchen and started to cook the breakfast. While the bacon was cooking he set the table for the three of them and boiled the kettle for tea. Anna appeared and asked, "Can I do anything?"

"I haven't got any fruit juice but there are some oranges in the fridge. You could squeeze some of those. Then make the tea while I fry the eggs. I'll call him in while the bread is frying."

Edward walked outside but Rhodri had evidently wandered off as there was no sign of him either on the seat or on the cliff path. Edward was infuriated and called his name. On his second call, Rhodri appeared from the back of the house.

"There you are. What the hell are you hiding around there for? Breakfast is ready, so come in."

"I think I'll just have another fag first; just to give an appetite like. You start the breakfast and I'll catch you up."

"No you bloody well won't. You'll come in now when it's ready. Just for once, do as you're bloody well told."

"Oh, swearing now is it? Got your goat have I?"

"Yes. Now come on in and sit down at the table and behave yourself. You're worse than a child."

"Pushed around like nobody's bloody business; I'm older than you, so show some respec'. I'll go home tomorrow, I will; see to myself and no mistake. Won't be short of fags then; they'll have piled up while I've been away in this Holiday Home By The Sea With No Ships; so I'll have to do justice to them and I'll have to say 'thank you' to Winford for keeping them for me. I'm looking forward to that – the smokes, not Winford. He can kiss my arse and hope to dance the night away. Nice boy though when he behaves himself with my fags."

"Come on. Your food's on the table. Come and eat it."

Rhodri walked ahead of Edward into the kitchen; Anna was already sitting after serving the breakfast. She poured Rhodri a mug of tea. "There you are Father, eat up while it's hot."

"What's this tea then?" Rhodri asked. "Not like yesterday's tea is it?"

"Yes," said Edward. "Like yesterday's tea. It's called Earl Grey."

"I didn't like that much; it tasted like medicine to me. No, give me Typhoo any time. You can make it Strong as Hell, Black as Coal and Sweet as Sick and it tastes bloody marvellous; not like this Virgin's Water you're giving me."

"It's what all the *crachach* drink in Berkeley Square," said Edward.

"The bloody *crachach* are welcome to it, wherever the Hell that is when it's at home."

"Where the '*Nightingale sings in Berkeley Square*'.

"Well they're welcome to it – Nightingale and all - and I wish they'd keep all of it to themselves and all."

"Eat," said Anna, "And stop your damned complaining. Have a glass of water if you don't like the tea."

"Oh, you've got a voice then Woman! Just keep it to yourself and remember your manners in this man's house. You watch who you're talking to. A little drop of beer would go down a treat with this; or cider like; take away the salt of the bacon it would."

"It's too early for that," said Edward. "I'll get some cider when I go to the shop and you can have it when you come back from your walk with Anna."

"Going for a walk then are we? Wonders will never cease. I can't walk far mind. It's because of my feet Missus; in fact they're so bloody bad this morning I don't think I can walk at all really. Haven't you got any laver - bread [12] to go with this salty bacon then? It's not the same without laver - bread from the Gower. The Sais don't like it you know – fried seaweed - but they'll eat Frenchie frogs and snails by the ton. Bloody mad they must be across the border; they don't know Good Food when it's given to them. But they came from Germany or somewhere anyway, so what can you expect? I ask you? Bloody daft lot.

"Good job we won the War or we'd be eating nothing but bloody Sausages and Pickled Cabbage all day, every bloody day until the cows come home. I wonder what a Laver-Bread Sausage would taste like. Bloody Krauts – they don't know any better – the War I expect, no proper food – only boiled sausage and vinegar cabbage with a bit of black bread thrown in, for luck. The King's Uncle was the *Kaiser* you know, once upon a time. They're not true blood like us; just bloody mongrels they are make no mistake.

"So, I tell you now, Woman, that it will only be a short walk because my legs will give out because of my feet. Just down the path a bit and back for a ride on a Camel, that's all. And if I say 'that's enough', don't bloody argue or you'll be standing on the cliff on your own like the woman with the torch.

"Is there any more of this excuse for tea in the pot?"

"A short walk will be a pleasure with you dear Father. You can tell me about the Welsh Gods and Goddesses."

"Don't come all *hoity – toity* with me little lady; I've got some years on you, so show a little respect. There was a time when I'd have put you across my knee for that. Pity that's died out as well; didn't do any harm now and then and did a lot of good sometimes with the fly – by - nights. This tea's better when it's been standing a bit."

"A short walk then Llew," said Edward. "It'll give me time to get your fags and some beer, cider and laver - bread for tomorrow. You two go for a walk now; I'll just clear the table and go into the market for some *fresh, local* food."

"No bloody *Pice ar y mân* with currants or raisons, or you can take the bloody lot straight back where they came from. I was awake all night with my teeth after the last lot you brought."

"Right. Plain ones only."

"But with sugar on mind!"

"Right. We'll sit outside if the fog's cleared by then, and have a drink before lunch, how's that?. Would you like your smoked haddock for lunch?"

"No, I've gone off that idea; breakfast that is really. Some *Sewin* now, Sea trout to you Missus, would be OK. Better still though, some nice *cawl* would go down a treat in the fog; keep it out of the bones, see."

"Well, proper *cawl* takes some preparing 'cos you need to boil the shinbone slowly for a few hours to get all the marrow out. I could get one for tomorrow though, if you'd like that."

"How the Hell do I know what I'd like for tomorrow? That's like seeing into the future is that."

"Come on Father; let's get our coats for a walk and let Edward go shopping for us."

"Well, alright; but only a short one mind; my feet aren't too good just now. Just to the seat perhaps and have a fag before coming back. You'd better get off then, Sonny Jim, or we'll be back before you and starving to death."

Edward watched them walk away towards the path with Anna insisting on looping her arm through Rhodri's while he seemed to make every effort to disentangle himself from her hold. A soft wind had come from the sea and the overnight fog was blowing away and the sky was clear. Blue smoke was rising from the far field that had produced the cereal crops over the summer. Edward watched the drift and shapes of the smoke as it was carried away into the high hills; it was clear now, why the sheep had been moved from their grazing; they would be moved back to the fields when the clearing had been done. The burnt embers would be ploughed back into the soil to help with the fertilising of the fields for the winter crops, perhaps root crops like turnips or kale. Edward walked to the car and drove towards the main market in the City. He would enjoy an hour or two away from Rhodri and browsing amongst the stalls where no-one would bother him; with luck there would be a sea bass on the fish counter alongside the laver - bread, cockles, mussels and samphire from the marshes; and a good half-leg of marsh hogget on the meat stall; and warm, freshly-cooked Welsh Cakes besides the crusty batch bread. He was in no hurry to complete the shopping and took some tea and a home-baked cake before returning home.

CHAPTER 45

THE RETURN HOME

He took a leisurely detour back towards the house, past the old Castle and the Gardens and across the heath-land. As he crested the hill near home, he saw two cars parked in the forecourt. He hurried the last mile and drew up next to a Police Car. He was angry that they had taken little enough time before returning in their pursuit of Rhodri. His anger turned to puzzlement however when he recognised that the second car was that belonging to Miss Davies of the Social Services. He made his way towards the door of the house when a different Police Sergeant appeared.

"Good afternoon Sir," he said. "Are you Mr Williams, the owner of this property?"

"I am, and what the devil are you doing wandering about in my house again? Where is my wife and father-in-law?"

"I'm sorry, Sir, but I have some bad news. Perhaps we should go inside."

"What bad news do you carry? Tell me here and now."

"I really think we should go inside, Sir."

"Just tell me here and now and get off my property."

"Alright, Sir, if you insist. There's been a bad accident. Two people have fallen off the cliff path and been found on the rocks down below. One was a lady and the other an older gentleman."

"Are they alright? Where are they? Are they in the house; is that why you were in there?"

"I'm afraid not, Sir. By the time the Coastal Service got to them, they had both been in the tide for some time. The Doctor was lowered down to them from the helicopter, there's no other easy way down, as you no doubt know, but he pronounced them dead at the scene. Arrangements are now being made to take them to the Infirmary."

Edward staggered against the wall of the house and fell to the ground. A Police Constable helped him rise as Miss Davies appeared in the doorway. They supported him and walked him into the kitchen. Miss Davies poured him a hot mug of tea but he could not focus on it. He turned to her and asked, as if already knowing the answer, "Is it my wife and father-in-law?"

"Yes, we believe so," she replied.

"We will have to ask you to identify them in due course, Sir."

"Not now, Sergeant," said Miss Davies. "There'll be time enough for your routine pursuits when we've finished here. At the moment what we need is some consideration, not intrusion."

"There are steps that must be followed, Miss, in an unexplained death."

"Yes, I know, and will be when it is time. Mr Williams, drink your tea; it might help with the shock of all this."

Edward took hold of her hand and said, "Assuming the lady is Anna, her full name is *Morwena: Morwena of the Fairies* [1]. We've known each other Forever. Her father said this was our Second Life – you're allowed three, you know: *Three* plays a big part in our lives, you'll see: *Triple Goddess – Mother, Wife and Layer-out of Fallen Man; Father, Son and Holy Ghost.* In the First Life we were called Benlli, Prince of Powys and Morwenna of the Fairies (or Saint Morwenna). That's all nonsense of course, but we've known each other for .... a long time anyway; ever since our childhood in fact, when our families were close; when we used to play together – in the school holidays, mostly. In the end now, because of the lives we'd lived, we found that we needed each other. Each of us thought that we needed the different strength of the other, so we wed. But we've not been married any time at all you know – no time to judge it. She insisted that there were new family lives to build: she planned everything though I must wish that she'd given this a miss. Now, all the girls I have loved are gone and all because of my lack of care. There must be a curse I don't know about; perhaps the same one that took Bendigeidfran as Rhodri said: not made worthy of the God; not worthy of the Goddess either come to that; I've certainly not worshiped Her enough, though I've loved Her children deeply.

"He knows more than he can say you know, does Rhodri: he knows this land of ours and why it is; and I believe him more than any of the so-called Preachers - the Tellers of Tales – who tell tales to children, but know nothing of our Ancestors or how we came to be: nothing, either in Truth or Falsehood. Perhaps he was a Prophet in his own time and land: the local Guru that nobody wanted to know or understand. How many have we missed because we didn't trouble to understand? Do you know? Perhaps his Riddle will solve it all. And here's a Story: people who stutter, stutter because they are made to think about what they say, lest they speak the Secrets of God.

"And now the Gorse[20] has flowered on my land again as it did for all those we were.

"Do you know that Jesus was only an itinerant preacher who was causing trouble by His Mysticism and Magic, just like Merlin (proper name Merddyn), or Prospero. The latest in the long line from the time of King David? But He liked to think that He had a direct line to God, His Father In Heaven: *A Grand Delusion*, so no different or more peculiar than Rhodri in that case; same delusion. So if you're going to have a Delusion, make sure it's a Grand one: Rhodri thought he knew God's purpose as well, and His Name. Didn't do Jesus much good: He was murdered like so many others before Him and, no doubt, after Him too. It didn't matter much to the Romans when it was only *a little local Religion* problem a *Sectual Problem* – the Essenes were always Laying Down The Law. It was only when He turned it into a Social Structure and Way-of-Life For The Children Of God that it stirred them up. Why was Rhodri dismissed and Jesus became a Religion? It's a perilous business, this Religion."

"Mr Williams; Mr Williams? Stop now. Listen to me," said Miss Davies. "Is there anyone you would like us to call? Someone who can come to you? And be with you? Your father perhaps?"

"Yes. I hope Llew finished his Riddle before he went away. I shall have to check up on that."

"Mr Williams, where is your father's telephone number? What about your wife's family?"

"Same number: my father Charles Williams and her mother Megan Griffiths. *They live in sin together you know – the First Enlightened Generation* – I wonder why, since there have always been Ceremonies? They're in love for all that; I think; anyway, they've also known each other for years too, though that doesn't guarantee anything of course, as we see. She's not Anna's real mother, who was *The Lady* – his *Goddess* I suppose, whoever the hell she was when she was at home; Mother to a dead son too: *Mother, Bride and Layer-out of Fallen Man* who waits all his life by every Man's graveside. She was from the Docklands and was married before, to a Pirate of the Caribbean, another Morgan of the Maine who sailed against the wind, he said; you'll want to find all that out I suppose, to be tidy. Funny how the curse spreads, isn't it? *Geometrical Progression.* Like the Black Death, though the Medics understand that now, after the event; *always* after the event. Someone once said, 'Wouldn't it be so much tidier and easier if we could live in hindsight?' But I don't think so; no *sorrow* there of course, you could cut that out completely; but no *joy* either to balance the party; a pretty bland sort of life it would be. A bit like Paradise, I suppose, or Heaven. Where's the point in that?"

"Mr Williams, please, where is the number to call them?"

"In the book by the phone."

Miss Davies tried to rise, but Edward clasped her hand more securely so that she indicated to the Sergeant that he should telephone.

It was clear that it was not a duty he wished to perform; nevertheless, as senior officer present, it was a duty and he went to look for the telephone.

"You said that Rhodri was trying to solve a riddle and what it meant? What riddle was that Mr Williams?" asked Miss Davies.

"He was a Riddler, was our Rhodri; we talked of the *Riddle of the Elements* first; he solved that; to his own satisfaction anyway. It gave you Power, he said. He wanted it all to come together, which it did for him in the End I suppose."

"I was never much good in Chemistry," she said.

"No, no, I made the same mistake. Not those Elements; there's more than four of those in any case. The *Four Elements* found in all nations: *Earth, Air, Fire, and Water;* or in our own language: Tir, Air, Tân, Dwr. Perhaps we shouldn't call them *Elements,* it leads to confusion. They are more of a *Belief System.* Controlled and fought over by the Ancients, and it hasn't stopped yet. Why do you think there are still wars? The Battle for Religious Supremacy, mostly; or something in the guise of. Think about it: there have been more deaths and more destruction in the name of Religion than any other reason. The *Battle of the Trees* [38] in the Legends, was a battle for Religious Supremacy through the control of the Alphabet and therefore the knowledge of the *Name of God.* Did you know that? No, nor did I 'till Rhodri told me. The *NAME* seemed to be important to them. A bit like Christ and Mohammed today in fact.

"Rhodri didn't explain his quest really, not so you could pin him down, except *To End The Work Of The Female As Jesus Said.* And he didn't tell me the real name of God either: *'Too secret, it's concealed'* he said and perhaps he was right. I wouldn't want to be a guard of it anyway, in the circumstances; I've got enough responsibility already, thank you very much and how's your father if he's at home. Dear God, it's so easy to fall into his vernacular; let me be saved from that and from his delusions at least."

"This tea's gone cold; shall I make you another?"

"Bugger tea; bugger Earl Grey that tastes of drugs, whatever the *crachach* say. What I want is a drop of whisky."

"I don't think that's a good idea at the moment."

"You're entitled to your opinion, of course Milady but allow me mine: it's my life and for me how I treat it, what remains of it; and I know what I'm prepared to pay for *that;* it was never valued as more than a pittance anyway; and that valuation was for others, certainly not for me; so I'll live it as *I* please now, for the rest of the road."

"Why do medics hang on to *your* life as if there was no tomorrow to get to? I can understand it for themselves of course – no-one likes it when the Darkness calls; but I don't understand their passion for other people's lives; they must value them highly. Anna did, Life I mean and I planned a debate with her about it. They assume too much, these medical people: Playing at God!

"I suppose that's why I could never be a medic: I don't value life too highly, or much at all; it would be better if there was less of it around.

"However, if you can forgive this rant as the vomiting of an empty man, I would be grateful if you would pour me a scotch; my hand is very shaky and my eyes are clouded. It's in the cupboard in the study. Pour the good one if you know which it is. And have one yourself."

Miss Davies went to pour him a whisky. She returned with a half-filled tumbler and said, "Was there another Riddle then?"

"Yes: *'Where to find Olwyn.'* It seemed to matter a great deal to him."

"Did he solve it?"

"I don't think so," said Edward. "He never told me at least; I don't think he'd solved it. I didn't pay too much attention. Perhaps I should have done; perhaps it would help me now."

Edward took the whisky from her and drank. "You've watered this down," he said. "You don't do that to a 20-year old malt. And I don't need you to rule my life; I'm perfectly capable of seeing it to the end alone. Bring me the bottle."

He rose and poured the watered whisky into the sink. Miss Davies returned with the bottle of malt whisky. There was little else she could do without aggravating Edward's precarious hold.

"I expect you think that this verbal diarrhoea is an escapist ruse – my attempt at the dismissal of tragic occurrences. Well, you're entirely right. I shall take this bottle to my bed and leave you and PC Plod to organise the wake. *'Goodnight and Farewell Blodeuedd* [42] *and may your God watch over you."*

CHAPTER 46

REPRISE

It was early the next morning, soon after daybreak, when he was sufficiently awake to attempt to rise. He had woken several times during the night and each time had poured himself a large measure of whisky while trying to ignore the reality of the previous day. After several attempts he finally succeeded and passed into an alcoholic suspension that he remembered living through following the loss of Jacqueline; eventually that too passed and he fell into a dreamless sleep. He woke now, only because of the need to urinate and he cursed the demands of his physiology. He made his way to the bathroom and heard someone in the kitchen. For a moment, the previous day was a bad dream, and Anna was alive and preparing breakfast; in a moment she would call that it was ready and he would need to collect Rhodri from the seat where he would be smoking yet another cigarette. Then, reality intruded and he sat on the toilet and cried. After a while, his sobbing abated and the question that he had avoided since he had been told of the death of Anna and her father could be ignored no longer. He dramatised his words; that way they were easier to bear: *'For whom, in truth, are my tears shed?'* There was a sympathy for the death of his father – in – law and an acknowledgement of the fact that he would now, never understand Rhodri's obsession with the legends and poetic tales of the land of their birth; there was deep sorrow for the loss of his wife, but if he honestly faced himself, he could not deny that the commitment he had made and the contract he had entered into with her, on her insistence, as his father had guessed, had become an ambivalent desire. He had found that he had not escaped the trauma of the loss of his first love after all, nor the manner of it, nor the imperative of his escape into solitude; and, through no action on his part, the death of Anna had resolved the ambiguity he had faced during the night when she had been away. Now, no action was needed for him to regress to his singular existence for as long as he desired. There would be a cost: the canker of his present guilt would never leave, but it would be his to recognise and accept or face for as long as it could be tolerated. He would find ways to fill his time: there was always the work he could do, and he could ask for more to fill his days and nights; and he could read, perhaps following the paths taken by Rhodri, and immerse himself in the ancient past in order to avoid the imminent future. He could stay in this house of sorrow and guilt to watch the changes of the Earth, the Sky and the Sea and the burning of the Land and mark, each time, the Elements that Rhodri knew and what they meant to him. That would be some sort of completion and there was no timescale that he needed to set for himself.

He could not bring himself to take off yesterday's clothes and take a shower, but he would shave. He tried to rouse himself by washing his face in cold water and to an extent that did work. He ran hot water into the bowl and soaped his face and shaved. He then walked into the kitchen and saw Miss Davies sitting at the table nursing a mug of tea.

"You're up," she said. "I've just made some fresh tea. Would you like a cup?"

Edward shook his head and said, "Have you been here all night?"

"Yes. The Sergeant, who's name is also Davies by the way, but no relation, wanted to bring in a Constable but I thought it best to stay at least until you woke; I guessed that you wouldn't have liked another stranger in the house at present; he saw the sense of it in the end. Did you sleep? Are you rested?"

"I slept eventually, but no, I'm not rested; I shall have to wait for that. I must apologise to you for yesterday – I talked too much, and out of turn. I'm sorry to have inflicted it on you."

"You were traumatised, that's all. There's no need to apologise for that; I would have been more concerned it you were silent."

"That will come soon enough. Did they reach my father and Anna's mother?"

"Yes. They should be here soon. Also, your father said that they would see to the necessary proceedings before coming here."

"That's good of him; but he's had some experience of it, and it's what fathers are for, don't you think?"

"Try not to be flippant, it will hurt them. It will be very stressful for Dr Griffiths and your father but it should not take long. I understand that Dr Griffiths is a Doctor of Medicine so she will have seen a number of deaths; but I don't think it's the same when it's one of your own."

"I'm damn sure it's not, but they've both been through it before. You must be very tired if you've been here all night. You should get off home now and catch up on sleep. I shall lie down myself until the family arrive; there is no need for you to stay."

"Oh, the Police were very adamant that you should not be left alone here. Now that you're up, I am to telephone them and they'll send a relief; I'll wait for that or your father, then I'll go."

"What are you all concerned about? That I'll take my own life too?

344

Settle it all? I shan't do that; I'm too much of a masochist, or too cowardly, and too week a character for that. You're not to be concerned on that score. Also, there are others that need to be told, but a little delay won't matter much to them now, so I'll talk to my father and Megan first. So you telephone and get off. I may not see you again before you leave so please accept my thanks for your care, for listening and for staying. It did help."

Edward rose and walked toward the bedroom. "Just one more thing," he said, "for completion only: how did you and the Police get to hear about it?"

"There was a ploughman turning the soil over in the fields who saw some people walking on the path. When he'd come to the end of the furrow and turned about, they were no longer there and had not turned back. He went to the cliff edge, then 'phoned the Police from your 'phone."

Edward nodded and said, "*Thank the Good Lord God for the toilers of the field,* then; *Consider the Lilies of the field,*" and closed the door. Instead of going to the bedroom where he knew that he would not sleep, he poured himself another whisky and took the glass and the bottle to the study, and sat in his chair. He knew only too well the pattern of behaviour this loss would provoke, and what he would need to face now and what to face when others, for all their love and sorrow, had departed. He had heard that Anna's step-father, Megan's husband Will, had fundamentally believed that however you live, when death comes, you die alone. Now, Edward could not deny such a fundamental axiom either; he could not deny his understanding of the singularity of one's life: the conundrum was that occasionally, you reached out to another or to a place. He could not follow Rhodri and embrace a loving God who would welcome you to an eternal, pastoral Eden, a Heaven with no evil, or a Valhalla of warriors; not even a *Brigadoon* in which to rest for a while in transit: there was no reprieve and no escape from oblivion. He wished it were otherwise; he could understand the powerful and emotional draw of prayer and the myth of the *afterlife*. He understood too, the rather flippant dismissal of the Deity shown by non-believers: *if there is no God, it will be necessary to invent one for the sake of terminal self - indulgence.* That was never difficult: people have always made Myths of what they don't understand. But one thing he did know: you had no right to deny others their own certainties.

He rested his head on the back of the chair and his tears ran over his cheeks and down into his shirt collar. The first stage of grief had arrived along with the memories, the sense of loss and the emptiness. It would be followed by fatalism: the realisation that there was nothing he could do about any of it; then would come self-pity, and then despair, both old adversaries, before he could emerge on the other side to restructure his remaining time.

He had eventually fallen asleep and his whisky glass had fallen from his hand and the dregs were staining the carpet. He did not know how long he slept, but his neck and shoulders were aching from being in an uncomfortable position for so long. He heard voices from outside the room and realised that they had been the cause of his waking. He saw Miss Davies' car driving away as he walked to the kitchen. There, his Father and Megan were now standing about as if, after long and difficult hours they were unsure of what to do. They turned as Edward entered the room and his father opened his arms to embrace his son. Edward returned the embrace and realised that Megan was being excluded; he brought her into the embrace and they stood locked together for some time. It was Edward who broke the embrace and moved away.

"Thank you both for coming so quickly. You must be hungry and tired; would you like some breakfast? I can rustle up some bacon and eggs if you'd like." He turned to his father and added, "And there's some laver-bread I think."

"No," said Megan. "We'll just stick with the tea for the moment"

"Or there's coffee if you'd prefer," said Edward.

"Tea's fine," said his father. "I'll pour you one; it'll help"

"Yes, thanks." Edward walked to the window that looked out to sea. "It's a long time since I first came here and had my first cup of tea looking out to sea; no, it's longer than in time, or it seems so. I should have asked you down often. I'm sorry now that I didn't: you should have known the place before this happened. It was so peaceful though with the cries of the gulls and the curlews in the morning; and the skies were so big, I didn't want to share it; I was too afraid it would diminish it and I'd have to close myself down again – somewhere else. Of course it wouldn't have been like that; I realise that now. So all I can say is I'm sorry you missed out on it. Anna didn't get to know it either, nor Rhodri; so I'm sorry for them too."

"Edward," said Charles, "That doesn't matter now. You did what you thought was best for you at the time, what you believed you needed."

"Yes. But I was wrong d'you see. You don't need to be alone to be solitary, nor solitary to be alone: one doesn't feed the other, I've found. On the contrary, you can be most solitary and alone when you're surrounded by happy people – you know of that, Father; and you too Megan: we live in a *subtractive* world. But this is no time for the analysis of the human condition. You must be tired after your journey; would you like to rest for a while? I can strip the bed, if you'd like to lie down."

"No, we're alright," said Charles. "Perhaps a walk and fresh air will blow the cobwebs away."

You've got cobwebs then? Get a cat!

"Will you come with us?" asked Charles.

"Not at the moment" said Edward. "It's been a rather broken night for me too. You have your walk, I'll just lie for a while. But take care along the cliff; the earth is falling away in places.

Upsetting his tidy sea!

"There's some food in the 'fridge if you get hungry; I bought it yesterday for our supper. It would be a pity to waste it."

"You try and sleep then," said Charles. "We'll just take a short walk, then we'll make some lunch for us all."

Some fried cockles would go down a treat.
And a bit of bread to clean the plate and save the washing-u p.

"Yes," said Edward. "Then we'll have to get in touch with other people: family first of course, and always; then others like Lord Mostyn; he'll be devastated; he became very fond of her in a short time and she only saw him a few days ago. I'm sure there are others we should tell, like Rhoderick, who's been so good. You'll have to start a list. And have you sorted out the formalities? The Police Sergeant was very pressing."

"It's done for now. Go to bed; we'll talk more later."

Edward made his way to the study and retrieved his bottle of whisky and glass. As he walked to his bed, he smiled and thought to himself, 'The child goes to bed with his bottle'.

CHAPTER 47

THE RESOLVE

Charles and Megan walked arm in arm along the path away from the house until they came to the seat. They sat quietly for a while and looked out to sea. What looked like a large container ship, or a tanker, edged its way along the horizon away from the land and it would soon seem never to have been as the low cloud ceiling moved to shut out the sun. The sound of a tractor, a long field away, rose and fell as it ploughed towards them, then away from them. A dog barked insistently and sharply from inland before being silenced by a shepherd's shout; there was a bleating of sheep as they were being driven back to their pasture; seagulls hawked and fought over the newly-turned earth of the field and their rewards, then wheeled out over the shore; a kestrel hovered on the sea-wind, acutely sighted, silent, unmoving but for the angle of the spread of its tail; a sad curlew called away at the estuary but they knew not the significance of that – that was Edward's tale.

"Life goes on then," said Megan between her tears.

"It seems," replied Charles.

"As if nothing of any great importance has happened. Is each of us so insignificant? Is that why we make Myths of our Ancestors and of their Lives? To remember them? To know that they too have been for a short while? To know that there were things that mattered to them too? So we weave stories about them. Without the Myths and the Legends, who will ever know that they lived, loved, hated and felt sorrow? As we do. And without a Story, who will know of Us in turn? Not of Great Events; not of Kings and Conquerors; not of Gods and Religions – that's History for the classroom - but of Us? And who will know that we too have lived for a short while? And Tried? Don't we merit a footnote then? Don't we deserve a Tale or two? Who will write a Legend for Us?"

"Was that Will's Credo in the end?" asked Charles.

"I came to think so; it's why he thought Politics important. He once said to me, 'our Politics and Government is a record of Our struggle; it's the only true record we have.' He also reminded me that 'the more things change, the more they stay the same'. That's too abstract for me: I don't want the *Truth* of it – leave that in Libraries; I would prefer to be remembered in a Tale told over a fire in the cold of a Winter's night, with other frightened people about me. And I think Anna did too. But tell me Charles, you know more about these things than I do: is that also why we must seek a Religion, and a Greater God? Because of how insignificant we really are? And we'd like *Someone* greater than ourselves, to know we lived and tried. And we are desperate for a higher opinion of ourselves: *Man, above and beyond the Animals of the Earth*. Is that all there is to it? Our Ego?"

"What about your God then?" asked Charles. "If you believe His omnipotence, He must know that He's taken a son and a daughter to Himself."

"Oh yes. But I can't believe we created Him and that's all there is to it: it's too *stark*. Neither am I so naïve as to think that He worries too much about our loss. It's a condition, and an inevitability of the Life that He gave us and there are more important matters that need His attention. It could have been a dreadful accident I suppose."

"Why suppose otherwise?" asked Charles.

"I don't know. But I've thought of Rhodri's desperate life and what she was like: deterministic; strong, and self-contained; dominating but not domineering; and with her own agenda; and I wonder, *'Who led and who followed?'*"

"There's no future in going down that road."

"I know. But I can't avoid it. It seems that he believed in the Ancient Mythology of this land; it was a Religion to him, a Gospel Truth; and like a Religion, it took over his world. It was dangerous: it consumed him."

"You don't know any of that," said Chares.

"I know what Anna told me and she wouldn't have made tales of that. But I didn't see this coming; I didn't know the extent to which he acted out the Myths."

"It was his Reality I suppose; daily life was the trial he had to overcome," said Charles.

"Yes. And it helps nobody to speculate about it. You're right, I know that, and in due course I will agree with you. But at the moment, I'm looking for answers not dismissals."

They were silent for a while and Megan continued to weep silently as she looked out to a sea that had settled to a glassy sheen. Charles broke the silence by saying, "Do you know, when I was a child my parents sometimes took me on walks over the clifftops on the miners' holiday fortnight: that last surviving expression of Lammas.[39] It wasn't often, there wasn't the money for that. My father loved it, probably because he was a coal-miner and spent most of his life underground. He used to say than when the sea was like this, the *'glassy sea'* he used to call it, a heavy squall was not far away. *'Doldrums first, then storm'*. It looks like it's been the other way about this time."

"Yes," said Megan. "What will we do about Edward?"

"Whatever he needs. Megan, I hope that you won't take this amiss, but I must say it: he has suffered two devastating blows – three, because he was old enough to understand when his mother Elizabeth died - and I don't know how he will find a way back once more. I must do whatever is needed. I must go to my son and give him whatever help he needs; what I can, even at a cost to myself, if that is what is necessary; what I cannot do is walk out on him. But what grieves me more than any personal sacrifice I must make for my son – your father's Duty of Care - is what this must also do to you, and what it may do to us. I hope and prey you will understand."

"No, I don't – there's my loss too, you know. Well, in time, perhaps I will, but not now; not now." Megan broke into a heart-rending sobbing which she fought to overcome. "This is a bigger ending than I ever thought: I've lost a husband, a daughter, her father and now a dear, dear man that has always been in my heart. No, I don't understand."

"You've not lost me; I'm not going that easily! Love is not an easy emotion, is it? It brings sadness as much as joy – the *hiraeth* again; the old Welsh wordsmiths understood our hearts. This may be for a short time only, until I am sure of him. I hope that we understand that this is not another loss but a pause – a Samaritan act if you like. Will you understand it as that, at least?"

"I will wait; but not without a promise; I can't put my life on hold any more. You use words like Will used to do, and I can't argue; I couldn't with him and I can't with you. So promise me, that as soon as you can, you will come back to me?"

"There is no need to ask that of me; I promise now – before God as our ancestors used to say - that I will. I would not wish to face the future without the thought of you either; it would be worthless. So trust me, I will call for you; but my son is in more danger now and needs his father."

"I must know where you'll be."

"I will tell you. We may stay here for a while, the two of us, if that is what he wants. Or we shall move to some other place, but I will tell you. Now we should go back and call on the family."

"Yes, I need my other children about me. Being the older generation is a bugger, isn't it? But it helps if you have them near."

They turned and walked slowly back to the house; it seemed strange that it had not changed in any way. Edward was in the kitchen as they had left him, with his head held in his hands.

"Shall I make some coffee?" asked his father.

"No; not yet," replied Edward. "I've been thinking, while you were walking the cliff path, what a metaphor that was at the moment: emptiness on one side, an escarpment on the other. I want to talk to you, tell you what I've decided. And I want you to listen, please, and know that my mind is made up. You must not argue. Will you do that?"

Charles said, "We can't possibly agree until we know what you intend to say. That's unreasonable. We should at least, discuss the matter."

Megan said, "Edward, let us help each other."

"I don't intend that we shouldn't." He turned to his father and said, "That really would be unreasonable, again, and would break us apart. I don't intend that should happen; I love you too much to let that happen; and I mean all of you, Megan. But we must be given our own way of dealing with our tragedies; we've been through these losses before, each of us, so we know something of how to cope; but you must accept that we each cope in our different ways – you *must* accept that, if we're all going to come through it. I know what your intentions are, father. I could write your scene for you and not even the words would be far out. But you must *let go of me if I'm to cope*. Like last time. You and Megan must help each other. I'm different, you know that; I'm more insular; I exercise it as the way I cope: I seek peace through solitude. You must cling to what you have and go your way."

"The three of us should be together to face this," said Megan. "We can't leave you alone to face it."

"My thinking, while you were walking, was terribly selfish and I'll tell you what it amounted to. To get through it, I need a drink. I have a good whisky Dad; Megan, I can open a bottle of Lord Mostyn's Loire wine in the 'fridge. Will that do?"

"Never mind the drink," said Charles. "That's a false crutch; just put things aside and stay with us."

"That wouldn't work you know; it would prolong it. You see, I know myself and what ails me. If you won't join me, I shall drink alone: save me from that, at least."

Edward rose and brought the glasses and drinks to the table. He poured himself a good measure of whisky and said, "Pour yourselves what you'd like. Dad, I know that what I want to say will distress you and you'll refuse to accept it. But you must, otherwise we shall become estranged and that will add to our sorrow. At least, listen to what I have to say.

"In the short term there's not much I can do anyway. There will be a Coroner's Inquest; we can expect that. I have no doubt that the Police will also be involved, and, probably the Social Services. That will extend the process and much background will be placed in the public domain. I think that Rhoderick, your Editor friend will be circumspect and kind, but there will be prurient interests for some that will make life hard for the rest of us. All that can't be soon, but we need to make ourselves ready for it. In the meantime, you could stay in the Hotel or go home."

"We'll go home, if you'll come with us," said Charles.

"Yes," said Megan, "Come with us. At least you could rest there."

"Thank you for your care, but that's not the way for me; it will only make it harder."

"You're being contrary, Edward. You can have your own room and come and go as you please; you won't have to do anything you don't want to. What's to object?"

"The walks on the Heath? No, it's the feelings of others, isn't it? No, I couldn't deal with that as well. So, no, I'll not come with you now; later will be different perhaps."

"What will you do, then," asked Megan.

"You'll only add another worry for us," said Charles.

Edward gave a wry smile and said, "I know. But you don't need to worry. I shall get one of these new mobile telephones that I've so far avoided and 'phone you each evening; I promise to carry my phonebook with me at all times. In any case it won't be for long in the first instance. I'll be back for the *'Proceedings'* and we'll take if from there, when all the family are gathered."

"But what will you do now? Where will you go?" asked Charles.

"Not far. I shall shut down this house for a while and drive over my country. I've just realised that I don't actually know it too well. I shall visit the lakes of Snowdonia, especially *Llyn y Morynion*.[37]. I have a farewell to say for somebody. Then, perhaps I'll try to find why Rhodri got caught up with North Wales. I might even look at his house and his library – did you know he had one? But I won't be more than a day's drive away, at any time.

"So now comes the difficult bit. I want you to leave and go back to the Hotel tonight and go home tomorrow. We'll have to use your phone number for contacts, in the first instance. Please arrange that with the Police before you leave. I shall go somewhere tomorrow or the next day – another debt to pay - and telephone you to let you know where I am. That should sort it for a while."

"Edward, this is ridiculous and unnecessary," said Charles.

Megan rested her hand on his arm and said, "No Charles, let him cope in his own way."

If they were not to quarrel there was no more to say. They sat in silence for a while, then Megan said, "Come on Charles; we need to get back to the Hotel. And we have things to attend to."

Charles embraced his son and said, "You know I'll be waiting by that 'phone every evening; you'll make my days a misery; I hope you appreciate that."

"Father, you wouldn't be happy if you didn't have something to worry about. It's no good me telling you not to; it will only make you more irritable. Talk to my sister Nia; she might be more amenable and she'll bring more pressure to bear."

Megan embraced him and said, "Be tolerant of your father and phone regularly. And don't drift; please."

"No. I shan't do that any more. And you take care too. I'll redirect my mail to you; open it, wherever it's from; there are no secrets now. After the inquest, I may go into Retreat somewhere for a while. Then I'll think what I'm going to do with myself; it's time I did that anyway; there must be something of interest for me to do."

CODA

CHAPTER 48

REVIEWAL

The Coroner's Inquest was not long delayed and Edward postponed his travelling; he closed his doors and drew his curtains.

Two doors then? Who needs two bloody doors? One to come in and one to go out for the crachach I suppose.

The delay was so short that not many of either family were able to attend. The findings were not unexpected; the cause of death of Rhodri Morgan and Morwena Griffiths, Father and Daughter was given as *Misadventure.* Edward had written to Lord Mostyn of the deaths while waiting for the Inquest, and then, after a few days, pressed himself to fulfil the promise he had made though now wished that he could avoid.

He made the journey to Creigiai, The Safe Haven Trust house, as he had been asked to do. He had found His Lordship bedridden and very aged and his attention to what Edward related to him was intermittent as he periodically seemed to drift to the edge of sleep. He also showed extended periods of apnoea from which he roused himself only when Edward paused in his narrative. Consequently, Edward was unsure of how much of his report was heard and understood. Eventually, he prepared to make his farewell; the visit had been a courtesy, and there was no purpose in prolonging it. At this imminent departure, Lord Mostyn again roused himself and said, "Let's talk a little of the living then; *Let the Dead Look After Its Own*; I should like to know the end of the Saga before I too have to go. What will you do with yourself now then lad?"

Edward replied, "I'm in limbo rather and I need time to consider what my options are; I need to relate again, and soon I think, for any sanity. So I thought I'd go into Retreat for a while; take some time over it."

"Where will you go? To your house on the cliff-top?"

"No, I can't go back there just yet; the Old Man and His Daughter speak to me too loudly of the sea, and the sky, just now."

Poseidon and his friend with the Garden Fork

"Somewhere else, I think."

357

"That I understand. But you should make some decisions quickly. Following bereavement is about the only time that a hasty decision is the correct one. Do you have anything in mind?"

"Some vague ideas, that's all. Nothing concrete; I find I can't rise to that just yet."

"Tell me then; but slowly and one at a time; don't rush me."

"I knew Morwenna for many years as you probably know, but I should like to know something more of my father – in – law and his devotion to our past: I am a Geologist after all, so I claim a legitimate interest in the Past. It's just a different time scale, that's all," he said with a smile. "That will do for a start," said Edward.

Lord Mostyn said, "The Doctor who attended at the initial *Misadventure* - useful word – told me that he was most certain that Morwenna, you wife, outlived her father. I was most insistent on that, and he agreed that the *young* outlast the *old*. So you realise then," said Lord Mostyn, "That the *Foundling's* house and its contents will now be yours? I understand, *from information received,* shall we say, that there is a significant library in that field at the house. Rees built it up for Rhodri's, and his own interests. It would, *again, I understand,* get you more than started on that quest if you wish it. It would also ease your journey, I have no doubt."

"I had not thought that far ahead yet," said Edward.

"Don't stop thinking! It's the first step to idiocy!"

"Thank you for your warning."

"And don't be flippant, that's the first step to mediocrity! I warned Morwena against that character failure a few times, though she seemed wedded to it, which was, shall we say, *unbecoming* of her. However, if that Library is of interest, I will do what I can, in her memory and that of Rhodri *Rees*, to ease your search. I only ask that if once you have done your reading and you have no further use for the old books that have been collected with care, time and money, that you donate them to our University Library here."

"I will promise you that gladly," said Edward.

"Between me and God."

"I'm sorry?"

Lord Mostyn chuckled and said, "You used an ancient, mythological form of words, but you didn't finish it. You said *'I will promise you that gladly'*. The characters of the Mabinogi, used to say *'Between me and God, I promise you gladly'*. A *devout* promise then, but I leave you to seek it out in your new Library. I have a feeling, that you will keep the books to yourself once you start reading them; they do tend to bind you in; but that would be a shame, don't you think? In any case, that donation need not separate you from them; you shall always, as the donor, have immediate access to them; as well as others related to the matters."

"I shall think on your advice, My Lord."

Lord Mostyn laughed until a cough made him breathe with difficulty. He then continued, "I wish we had more time to talk, as I did with Anna, freely in the end when we had finished taking the measure of each other. But you and I, we are not blessed with Time, so we must take some risks. I've been debating with myself while you've been thinking that I have been asleep, about whether you would be amenable to exercising a pursuit I have in mind. I'm sorry about this rigmarole of self-protective language; it has always come upon me when I've been uncertain; which is precisely the time when you must cut the flannel, as the Americans say, and state your purpose with clarity and certainty if you want your own way, which is what we all want, in the end."

"Then, be clear and certain," replied Edward.

"Ah yes, but it's sometimes the '*nigger in the woodpile*' you see, if that phrase is still acceptable in this Politically Correct Age. Those who make it their life's work to pursue such transgressions will get rid of all our literary *short cuts* all too soon; then they'll attack the beauty of the phraseology; and our use of language will become too *bland*, too *pedestrian* altogether. But it is marginally better than *'the black in the jungle'* I think you'll agree, or have I mistaken your turn of mind?"

Edward chuckled and said, "I can quite understand why Anna said that she so much enjoyed your *conversations.*"

"Did she say that? How very kind of her."

"Yes. She said that you spoke in *soliloquies* which was often irritating, but that they were worth listening to; and she wished that she'd made a bit more of an effort."

"How very kind. But she was by nature, kind; troubled but kind."

"Don't get too carried away; she also said that you used the ploy very effectively as camouflage and protection."

"How perceptive of her. I will ignore the *New Pedants* for now then. I will make you a proposal, which of course, may be rebuffed and dismissed out of hand, but somehow I think not; that is the risk I take. I have some unfinished purposes, which I am unable to fulfil personally, because of a lack of energy and the disability of age; and I see that you are in need of a focus – so there is a possible marriage of fulfilment there. I have been debating with myself, while you've been thinking that I have been asleep, about whether you are someone who could draw these maters to an end for me. I will say this: go to your father's old family house and land. It has been, for too many years, in a dying part of our valley, his and mine. It should not be forgotten now that the coal is gone; but until now I have not talked with anyone who I could feel was able, and suitably prepared, to make something new of it. We owe that place much, your father, you, and I, and many others too, and we must not forget that."

"I don't need to visit; I did so only recently: it is in a sad state I'm afraid."

"I will tell you of my wish and desire then; it is simple and it is this: that you take an interest; look again at it; see what can be done; see what prospects there are; look to the earth, not for oil of course, as you used to do, but for a provision of what I think the people now lack."

"What would that be, then?"

"Oh, many things, of course, but they all come down in the end, to a single, difficult determination: a *sense of purpose*. Will you do that for an old man?"

"Certainly, I will. As I say, I've looked already from the Lower Road. It's very run-down and the garden is very overgrown; and the house is mostly ruined and needs rebuilding."

"I expect the pigsty is in something of a state as well. Pryderi[3] would be grateful from his grave for the attention I'm sure. But those things are easily put right with a bit of time and effort and some financial investment – and, of course my contacts. I should like you to do more than look: walk on it, pick up the soil; and walk on the mountain. See what plants are still doing well."

"The apple trees are vigorous, that I know, though they need attention. But I'm no farmer, or gardener, or plantsman."

"You'll be surprised what you are if you give it some thought. In any case, that is the risk you take. You can't be allowed to go Scott Free in this enterprise."

"It would need a great deal of work; too much perhaps."

"You say that to an old builder? That can be done and the old sty could be fixed as well to make the Mochyn comfortable; become something of a *Swineherd*. Anything else that's needed, like mains drainage or cess-pit, and a source of water is easily set in motion. No doubt you'll need electrics and a telephone. See what the old Market Garden is like; that might be the place to start in the short term. Think about it and let me know your thinking soon. We could attack it in the Spring. We could tackle it together; it could be something worthwhile. It would give me the interest I need at present; and I could see it as my *last thanks and farewell*. If you will complete my Tale for me."

"What Tale is that?"

"Why mine – little Alf Mostyn's. But you will come to know it and

360

be part of it, if you will take this on. I'm becoming maudlin but it was good of you to appear at this time; I believed someone would. Now I shall sleep for a while. I thank you for visiting me, and I hope you find some rest with this endeavour. And use that New Library of yours; stay there for a while and read. Goodbye Edward Williams."

"Goodbye My Lord. And can I thank you for all of us?"

Edward rose and walked towards the door. As he reached it, he heard Lord Mostyn say, "Who was the *Caravaneer*, I wonder? No matter now; it's water under the bridge now."

CHAPTER 49

THE CHALLENGE

After leaving Lord Mostyn, Edward drove to his father's childhood village again. This time he took the 'Old Road' carved into the mountain side. He drove slowly past the old Primary School that all the children of the village, back through many generations, and including his father, would have attended. It seemed smaller now than when he had visited his grandmother as a small boy; then he had looked at it in awe, high on the mountain, with its large yards, its confines marked by stone walls with a fall of many feet beyond and no safety net for the more ambitious of the climbing children, save the curse of the Headmaster. It overlooked the valley, its two entrances, segregated into *GIRLS* and *BOYS*. He smiled to himself: a Welsh, Nonconformist Coeducational Primary School with the sexes segregated from the age of three or four, when they were first delivered to the gates by their Mam. This Village had never seen a time of *plenty,* though the Mine Owners lived well enough in the big cities, far enough away from the source of their fortunes, while the older generations of the village knew the winter-bite of poverty. But it was, like many others, a close-knit community, and no-one starved.

Edward stopped the car and looked at the sharply-rising, potholed, partly – tarmaced road that seemed to disappear around a bend into the heart of the mountain and again he remembered his father's advice on the occasion of another visit to his old and ailing grandmother.

'It's very steep daddy.'

'Steeper still if you're riding a bike, I tell you. Now listen to me boy; if you ever come to drive here in your own car, bless you, you must engage the car's first gear before addressing the mountain. You think it's steep here, but it gets steeper and there is no opportunity to pull over to the side of the road and change to a lower gear, for the simple reason that there is no 'side of the road'! Pull over, and you're 30 or 40 feet down below. So, low gear and slow progress right from the word 'GO' that's my advice.'

Edward proceeded to do so and with a low growl the car started its slow ascent. He became more and more appreciative of his father's advice as the road became steeper and more deteriorated. The original road had not been made for motorised transport; a horse and cart for small deliveries would have been the most expected of it. Once, there had been an attempt to have the road improved for the elderly residents on its flanks, but there was no evidence that the road had ever been listed in the County Archives, and it had certainly never been adopted. Thus, the costs of any improvements would fall on the householders lining the road, none of whom had that money to spend. And so the road had been ignored and, year on year, had deteriorated further.

At last he drew on to level ground from where he could survey the valley floor: it seemed that little had changed from this perspective but only because he was now at too great a distance in the future and too far away in distance to see any detail. On the mountain across the valley the waterfalls no longer cascaded their way to the river below; there were still signs of the ravages of small drift mines, once mined for house coal and the poor warmth it gave, but now long closed and collapsed. Their testament was the guts of black slag that was still spewing from the old mouths. The two deep mines were no longer working: they were too costly to maintain and there was too little call for the hard-won, hard, glossy and clean anthracite coal. The market garden had fallen into disuse and the glass of the greenhouses no longer reflected the light. The Rugby field was still there, though the Club House had gone. Further up the river, the Grammar School seemed not to have changed at all, though he knew that it had now been designated a *Welsh School* which meant that all its teaching was done in the Welsh Language; Edward could think of no greater horror than, not only learning Science, but learning it in a language that could not boast the necessary terminology. He had once remarked to an old University friend, a linguist who had complained of Scientific Jargon, 'If you want to know what Scientific Jargon really is, try learning Science in a *Welsh School*: an ancient, beautiful, romantic, rich and lyrical language, and like the Land, made for Song, Poetry and the Magic of Merlin: but **not for Science.**'

He turned away from his contemplation of the valley and walked to what had been his father's Family Home. When his father, like the rest of his generation, had no longer returned to an empty house it had been sold, for a pittance, but the buyers had not tarried and no-one else seemed to have wanted it. It had clearly remained unoccupied for years and much of it had collapsed into rubble. But as he had seen from the 'Low Road' when he had driven to meet Anna, what seemed so long ago, the apple trees were flourishing. A new Apple Isle to cultivate, an Avalon [34] that he could, if he wished, make his own. And he realised that, appropriately, it was Friday [32]. *Venus* would welcome him then, but he was without his *Vivianne: Rhiannon: Lady of the Lake: Ruling Priestess of Avalon: Arthur's Sister*[6].

The undergrowth was flourishing also and would need a great deal of hard, physical work; but that would be welcome. Somehow the '*Wild Rhubarb*' had gone, so that would be a blessing. Lord Mostyn was right, there was a life to be made here if he wished it.

He walked back to where he had parked the car and sat on the grass of the hillside. Here, he remembered standing as a small child, holding his father's hand while an Army Bugler had played *The Last Post* [41] on a B*b* bugle which had been followed by a Four-Gun Salute fired over the valley for the benefit of the neighbours. In this particular case, the death was not sustained in war or conflict: the first-born and son of his father's neighbours had enlisted in the Army as the only alternative to work in the Coal Mines. He had been training in an Army camp in Devon, and the grenade he was to have thrown was faulty and exploded in his hand. It had blown off his arm, there was a great loss of blood and he had died. The arm was eventually found in bloody bracken, some 50 yards away; his watch was still keeping perfect time. Ever since that experience, Edward had found great difficulty in expressing his grief, particularly so in public, but also within the family: he had never attended a Commemoration, a Remembrance Service, nor stood bare headed at a Memorial Service since; and he would not parade behind a cortege in a funeral, in the way of the Welsh. That had been the first and only time that he had been made to stand for such a purpose. As he grew he made it increasingly clear that he would not participate in such a display of sublimated emotion. To him, grief was a private affair and he had grown up to realise that the only way he could cope with it was to withdraw within himself until the cut of the knife was closed. He understood that many had called him a *distant, reserved* child. He had not then, nor did he now, understand the need to so publicly acknowledge grief; it was not his way. It was said to be done in recognition of a death and for the comfort of the bereaved. He did not believe that to be entirely true: it was more for the living than in remembrance of the dead; and more a show for the neighbours than for the bereaved. His way was to withdraw to follow his own way of grieving, remembrance and celebration.

The descent to the main Village road, was more hazardous than the climb: there was less certainty in the grip of the tyres on the stony track and many times, in trying to avoid the deep potholes the car seemed to have a mind of its own and threatened to go over the edge and take the shorter way down.

As he drove away from the mountain road, he vowed that he would think some more of the word *Caravaneer* and its etymology. And through his grief, he was looking forward to the journeys he would take with his library. And there was work here he could do that would bring him back to his father and the family. But first, there were other duties to fulfil to the memory of his wife and her father; those would take him to another part of his country. There were some other places to know and Spirits to put to rest before some new work to start.

CHAPTER 50

REVIVAL

It was a long, bitter winter that followed. The land was in the grip of a hard frost from All Hallows when the first snow fell until Candlemass when the Sun gave a distant warning of its return from the Right Hand. By then, the snow was deep and drifted; it had been driven on the wind for four months. Away from the Cities, there had been little travel; in rural villages the people closed their doors and stayed in their houses and close to the fire. On the farms, the livestock had been brought down from the high pastures and into the barns and the winter feed was running low; the rams would not have covered the ewes and it would be a late, poor lambing season. There would be few calves, because the cows had not been put to the bull by the farmer. The mains water supply in many districts had failed because of frozen pipes; springs from the underground water table froze when they reached the surface and had to be heated for the clean, fresh water. The rivers had progressively frozen from the banks to the centre where a narrow, fast-flowing current persisted until it too froze against any obstruction. It was bitter.

Christmas had been a quiet, withdrawn time; neighbours had met around a fire and eaten a chicken together and drank more of the home-made wine than usual, for warmth and comfort, away from the cold strictures of the Druid Priests. On Holy Days, they knelt and prayed together at the fire grate. This practice persisted into the New Year as the stores of coal and logs for heating and stores of food diminished. It seemed there was no end to it. Then, on Saint David's Day, the 1st of March, the weather changed: the winter clouds rose; the Sun again warmed the Earth; and the mists floated along the river. The nights were still cold and clear and the stars of the Milky Way formed an arc across the darkness of the sky.

Edward had moved into Rhodri's house early, had secured provisions, and had passed the many weeks reading the mythology of his people. He had written a letter of thanks and gratitude to Lord Mostyn and said that he would work on the old house and gardens in the spring, as soon as rebuilding work could be carried out. He spent Christmas Day snowbound and alone with his books and the persistent telephone calls from the family. He read and waited for the opportunity to make his final farewells. He became engrossed in the mythology and then, when the weather turned, he became determined to make his farewells in the manner of his ancestors; their spirits and his memories need to rest. He took walks along the old railway line and cut lengths of willow withies as the children followed. Back at the house he sharpened the blade of a spokeshave, and split the wood into thin strips which he wove into osier baskets. He would visit the family house again and strip some bark from an old apple tree to line the baskets; there would be few apples after this Winter's frosts and snows, so the bark of Her tree would act as an homage to Her. In contrast, it would not be difficult at this time of year, following the Christmas festivities, to buy a Pomegranate, the fruit of Saturday, of Bran and of Jehovah; and of *Repose,* to honour Him. That would provide his Farewell in a seemly manner:

Willow	for the Division of the Waters	S
Apple	for Eve and Adam and Immortality	CC
Pomegranate	for Bran and Jehovah And Repose	F

For May - Eve, the land was warmed again for the advent of Olwen or Anna or Rhiannon; the grass was green for her 24 hounds – her hours, to run. It was the time to seek her Hawthorn blossom too – the May garland. Edward drove to Mynydd Eryri whose peaks were still covered in snow. He searched for the lake called Llyn y Morynion. It was too high and exposed for trees, and the shrubbery was low and sparse. Around the confines of the lake, the rushes were green and lush; the soft wind rippled the surface of the water and the wavelets broke gently on the low-lying edge of the land that embraced it. It was late afternoon and there was no sound to break the peace. This was truly a place made for Legends: that of the *Lady of the Lake* or of the knowing of *Morwenna of the Fairies.* Edward retrieved the four osier baskets he had made and in which he had placed some Pomegranate seeds and walked to the water's edge. He had also placed in each basket a plea he had written and he pushed them in turn out onto the lake.

My Mother Elizabeth: take these others that I have known and loved, and care for them as you would me;

Jacqueline: my darling, know these others and love them as you loved me;

Morwenna: love is not divisible, there's enough for all, so love each other;

Llew: I know your Legends a little now and I understand something of who we are and what you tried to be. And I have another message for you. I have solved your last Riddle – the Riddle of Olwyn. I have written it for you, but I must tell you, so the others know of it too.

"I'll tell you now, then, Llew, loudly, so that they hear; for you are the most in need of it: it is like questions and answers. You should change your voice for each one, as your Lady Vera used to do, for fun. Here are the Questions in *Italics – one voice;* and here are the answers in **bold, another, different voice**:

Who is it who seeks the Answers?
> **The One who saw the Questions**

Who is it who saw the Questions?
> **The One who searched**

Who is it who searched?
> **The One who sought Knowledge**

Who is it who sought Knowledge?
> **The One who sought Understanding**

Then,

Who was it who knew the Knowledge?
> **The One who plucked the Apple**

Who was it who plucked the Apple?
> **The One who knew the Trees**

Who was it who knew the Trees?
> **The Mother of God knew the Trees**

Who was it who knew the Mother of God?
> **The Grandmother Olwyn in the**
> **Caer Gwydion.**

"I will seek more from Caer Gwydion in due course I promise you; but for now, 'Let me go in Peace', if you will – I need to rest in your understanding."

He stood at the lake edge as it grew darker and the stars appeared and the Galaxy was clear in the sky. He looked for *Blodeuedd* whose name was also *Olwyn* in the Old Language.

"Edward? It's enough. It's time you got on now. Get Away."

"Edward? Come away now. Seek your Peace."

"Edward! Go!"

"Go Boi Bach. There's nothing more here to brood about."

"Yes, to each of you" he said. "And I'll greet you all again at Harvest Time at my house, when you can always share the skies with me and Olwyn. There is a Sense of Place now, under the White Track."

He turned and walked to his car. The sky was clear and the stars were bright.

'Where should Olwyn be found then?'
'Trefoil grows and flowers where she steps: so where else but in Caer Gwydion where was the Mother's milk.'

He reached the car and remembered the words of another troubled Welsh poet:

'When the bones are picked clean
And the clean bones gone
I shall have stars at elbow and foot'.

"The weather is clement at last," he thought. "So then, work can start on the old house and sty and there'll be a need for a chicken run. Then the trees need attention and the garden must be planned for next year – as you said Mother, I must get on; there is so much to do. And what about a smokery for the trout from the river? The builders might as well make one while they're there. Gooseberries, that's the thing – the sweet ones: *Espera* or *Lay Sun* will do for a start; ferment them for some wine – it tastes rather like Sancerre I'm told. We shall see. And blueberries from the mountain in the autumn. Perhaps the kids would pick them at weekends and half term for a couple of bob?

"And I must get the family down; give them each a garden fork."

'Him with the garden fork – old Neptune By The Sea, near Ilfracombe, where that ship was going. I'll smoke your fish with my Pashas, don't you worry boi bach!'

"I expect they could do with some physical labour in the circumstances."

CHAPTER 51

RESTART

Edward stayed in a small local hotel that night and the following day drove through the area of Snowdonia and Gwynnedd that the heroes and their Goddesses had travelled in the Tales of the Mabinogi and in the Arthurian Legends, especially the Tale of Culhwch and Olwen.[11] He came to understand the attraction the land had held for Rhodri as he made his way South to his arranged meeting, once again, with Lord Mostyn. He arrived at Creigiai in the late afternoon and was taken through to the Library where Lord Mostyn sat taking tea and reading some blueprints and drawings. He was far more sprightly than when Edward had visited him last, when he had appeared devoid of interest, and bed-ridden.

"Ah, there you are young man; I was beginning to despair of you ever remembering your way here; I couldn't wait any longer, so I'm afraid I started on Tea alone. They have some good crumpets today; I ordered them especially for you, so you must consider yourself truly honoured. I also told them in the kitchen that you were to be prepared a tray of Tea and Crumpets the moment that you arrived. And they were to make fresh tea for me and to add another crumpet for me, I said. Well don't stand loose there, sit down, sit down. It won't be long in coming, I'm sure – just the time it takes to toast; then you can spread them with good, salty Welsh butter and House-made Gooseberry jam, before we continue to enjoy ourselves looking at these Plans. Tell me of your journey."

"As I told you I intended, I visited *Llyn Y Morynion* [37] yesterday and said some farewells in the Old Way of our People, to some people I used to know."

"And are you more at ease now then? Have you finished your promises?"

"Yes. I think that my mind and my memories are now settled, as I was told they would be. But I still wonder why Lakes play such a part in our Legends. I hope I come to understand it. However, I do have a sense of place now for all of them. So I'm ready to move on with this next life – my Third Life according to Rhodri – that you're cleverly crafting for me."

"No, no, just making a suggestion; and for my own benefit, more than yours. You see, I would like to finally tidy up some matters as well. Here is your Tea. Pour yourself a cup and butter and jam your crumpet. I shall ramble a little while you enjoy them.

"You have very kindly said that I have given you a new opportunity to – shall we say, *re-emerge*. I thank you for your kindness but I must disabuse you of my motivations. While I hoped it would help, it was a purpose which I was greatly in need of, for I believed that I was drifting without a purpose. D'you see? This project we shall tackle together, if you agree, has given me a new focus, and a new lease of life – as I hope you have noticed and as I hope it will for you. Things that had lost their interest for me, I now face reinvigorated (well, somewhat more, positively, anyway). I'm having fun again, and as soon as you've finished your crumpets we will order a new pot of tea and press on. Is that agreeable? Good.

"You have visited the old Village, you said, and seen something of the age-related neglect that it has suffered; though you also suggested that all is not lost. Therefore, I also hope that you have done some cogitating. Forgive my occasional *floral* turn of phrase, but I still get excited by words and the pictures they make. I have taken to reading more poetry from the Library here, but it's been a disappointing exercise, frankly; most poets, past and present would have been more productively engaged doing a decent day's work.

"I was glad to receive your analysis because it made me more determined in my intention. They need a focus, your people and mine – and something to *do*. The place has been slumbering too long, a Sleeping Beauty, and it needs a *good shake* as my dear Grandmother would have said; or a Prince Charming. But there's no point to that if there is no point to that, if you follow my meaning. *We* shall give the point to it, you and I, if you agree. I have taken the liberty of having a quick professional view of the place done, and these draft plans are the result. They are fragmented still, but close enough to what we need in order to press on I think. There are also other drawbacks to our plans and they are, that many Land Searches for ownership will need to be done in due course if we are to proceed on a scale that makes it all worthwhile; for us and for them. Also there will be Planning Consents to seek if we are to build some structures. Local Authorities are far more *sticky* about these things than they use to be – it gives our Councillors a reason to live, I suppose. But there are no insurmountable difficulties, as the jargon says, because we shall be providing amenities, jobs and a marketing plan for a run-down area. I'm happy to use my reputation with Local Authorities to 'Oil the Wheels' as well.

"Have you finished your Tea? Good. No more tea, then. It's time we did this review with a glass of wine in our hands. On the off-chance we would enjoy one or two glasses, I've had a couple of bottles of one of best years from my vineyard chilled for us. Brenda, our working *major domo* will bring one about this time as I told her to.

"Spread the plans then; you'll have no problem reading them I'm sure; you'll be used to more complex pictures than this. You said that there was some considerable clearing of undergrowth to be done; that is not a problem; there will be manpower available no doubt, but it must be done carefully under your direction, so that the old, original apple trees are made safe and secure. They will be old varieties I don't doubt, so they must be preserved, not removed – seed banks and that. They can form the core of a new Orchard. The clearing is a progressive job over the short term, which raises the first problem: that of Oversight of Works. If you are agreeable, I would want to put a Works Manager in place so that we can proceed at pace. He would need somewhere to sleep possibly, so a caravan on site would be called for. You should also be regularly available, so another, a better one, for you too."

Edward said, "You'll need to do something with the access road for any of that."

"Certainly – we'll change the lay-out. We shall have to do that in any case if we're going to work it. So the road comes first; we will change its direction, I think; go the other way. And the Council must commit to it at long last; they can't be allowed to get away with it Scott Free as they are wont to do. Then, the House: larger than before, for the sake of your visitors: family and business; four or five bedrooms I think, living accommodation, your study and library, and with all facilities – water, drainage, sewerage, gas and electricity; telephones, faxes, broadband – we can't be doing things by half measures you know. You have the draft there before you; if you want to change it, now's the time. A building as a project Office; also a proper apple store and press for juice; you wanted a smokehouse you said and that, I approve; it will be interesting and it can be made to pay if we take advice and have it done properly; especially if we have a Trout Farm in a large pond on the valley floor fed by the river, with some released for the Fishermen; then the pigsty, big enough for two in the first instance, I think; more later with a Swineherd perhaps. Smoked Hams and Bacon as well as smoked and fresh fish; and how about Smoked Duck Breasts? Any sign of eels in the river? How are we doing so far?"

"You're going a little fast for me; it's all too grandiose. I can't get my head around the cost of all this."

"Leave all that for the moment; I'll come to it. And Gooseberries I insist on, to supplement the ones we have here, and good, named, sweet, productive ones. We must aim for a glut of them so that we can make some wine with the left-overs; perhaps we could bottle and sell eventually and give the French a run for their money. I wonder if any of the new grape varieties would grow on the south-facing slopes? We could try half-a-dozen and see. In any case, a small fermentation house for the gooseberry wine, which we will have to name with a suitably grand name. What is the Welsh for *Chateau*? How about Castell. I know, I know, that's Castle; but it has a ring to it. I'll bring in some of my own yeasts to see how it goes. What about **Castell Creigiai**?"

"Please, Lord Mostyn, this is becoming too much of a project for me. I would much rather potter a bit – it's all I want."

"Don't fuss yourself, that's not a bit of good. I'm having fun outlining future developments over the longer time-scale which we will need to consider. You must think ahead and plan accordingly – Apple Brandy, Marc, for instance.

"Now, the financing. I do not intend that the County Council should escape Scot Free as I've said, and the Parish Council must be involved in an advisory role from the start; it will save a lot of trouble later. Our Lawyer (the Firm that used to act for me, I think; I was happy with them) they will negotiate that and whatever other legal jiggery-pokery is required for any further land we shall need. So we need not worry greatly along those lines.

"I shall have no problem getting a builder. I shall negotiate a good price with him even if I have to offer him some longer term interest in the venture; we shall see; but he must be able to work fast, so he cannot be too small a Company. In any case, I will underwrite the costs initially, to get us off the ground.

"Now, Structure and Management. I suggest registering as a Small Business Venture, though we shall not need Venture Capital, initially at least; but we can then take advantage of any and every available Tax Allowance etc. So we shall need a good Accountancy Firm. For the Management of it, since I am underwriting, I shall be Chief Executive and Chairman. You, I think, will be the Managing Director seeing to the day-to-day success of the business.

"You will need time to think, of course, but I hope that you will agree – in general terms at least. The formalities will come in due course, and our meetings will take place here, in this Library or at the Property when it is available. So one of your Reception Rooms should double as a Board Room – perhaps the Library, as here.

"Is this of general agreement with you?"

"Enough for now please! I'm overwhelmed, I have to admit; but I can see nothing to object to. In any case you seem to be taking all the risks. So, 'Yes', in principle."

"Good. And remember *'Great Oaks From Little Acorns Grow.* We could make a mark. And the World could come to our doorstep. What are your plans concerning your family?"

"I have asked my father and Megan to visit me in my house on the headland two weeks from today so that we can visit the Project and see it as it is now; I know they will approve, if only for my sake. The rest of the family: my sister Nia and family, Megan's Richard and brood, and single Gwen, will come as soon as they are able. You see what you've done with your machinations – you've made me re-enter the World."

"Good. I approve of all that. I intend to have a decent, comfortable car made available to me when I need it, so that I can keep in touch with the progress being made and raise the roof if it's not fast enough. I might even occupy the new house first, to sort out any snaggings. In any case, I shall want fortnightly bulletins, with photos, from the builder. You may add your comments as you wish. I should like my first visit to be when your Father and Megan are there; you will make yourself available to help with my halting steps as we survey the Valley of Promise.

"I need to ask you what your plans are for tonight. I can offer you a comfortable room, dinner and breakfast here before you go back home."

"Thank you. I accept *'Gladly, between me and God."*

Lord Mostyn gave a hearty laugh and slapped his thigh. "You have not forgotten it then? Perhaps you have re-enforced it through your reading over the past months? Good. I've not had so much fun for years; it augers well for us. But I must let you must talk to others tonight to pay for your Board and Lodgings – broaden their horizons. It's all we ask of visitors! Is there anything else for now?"

"I don't think so. In any case," said Edward, "I have more than enough to digest."

"Well there is one other thing" said Lord Mostyn. "I've been keeping it for last, but if we are to set up a Small Business rather than just spend money on a personal hobby (which I've always been on guard against because of the charge of *frivolity* – like a bicycle, which I talked about with Anna, I seem to remember). Money should be made to *work!* You get more enjoyment that way.

"We shall need a Big Name then: I don't mean a *long* name – people get irritated with that – no, I mean a name of some *depth*, which intrigues and puzzles them, and keeps them *focussed*. I hope you won't mind, but I have already given it some thought and perhaps you will agree with my suggestion.

"I believed that both of us would not want to forget other souls who helped to bring us to this point – we owe them much. So I searched for a name appropriate for our Ancestors –in the language of our Ancestors – and for their Descendants (most of them anyway)."

"You intrigue me; why to them?"

"Why? For the same reasons you called on them. Let's just say: *'Them and Us, For Old Times' Sake'* and leave it at that."

'For Goodness' Sake! That's a good saying that.'

"Then what is it?"

"It is:

AILENEDIGAETH

"You know enough of your Welsh still, to know the meaning of it; most others will not, but can find out, if they're desperate enough – as they should be, of course: the Jewish People would know of it, of course, by another name. But none can know its relevance to us. If they should ask its meaning, we shall say,

It is a Riddle In Memory
It is for you to solve

"Is it agreeable?"

"It is My Lord, but somewhere, I would like something in Malay."

"It's not a problem; chose what you wish. I should like to know the reason if you feel able to tell me in due course."

"Of course. Perhaps as we sit and watch the birds reeling across the valley."

"You would like some pigeons alongside your chickens then? I approve – there should be a time set aside for contemplation too. I shall have to buy some cigars again and resurrect my chest; or change to a pipe perhaps, in memory."

APPENDIX I

NOTATION

1 *Morwenna (Saint)* : A Welsh Saint who crossed over to Cornwall (Morwenstow). Daughter of the King of Brecheiniog. She married Benlli, Prince of Powys . They lived happily and when they died and the Castle fell into the lake (*Llyn Elis)*, the gorse grew and flowered over it. Also as *Morwen of the Woodlands:* for one evening each week she returned to Fairyland.

2 *Anna:* a Moon Goddess also known as *Minerva* which is an inclusive name for the *The White Goddess* especially at harvest time; as such she is connected with the barley harvest when barley cakes were baked for a Festival. The Christian *Passover* was a Barley Harvest Festival. The month of the Barley Harvest was July 8 to August 4. Also as *Cerridwen (Caridwen):* The White Sow, the Barley Goddess who gave the name to Britain. Jehovah was the Protector of Barley, hence the breaking of bread at the Passover. The original *Jehovah of the Passover* was Dionysius who was usurped by Jehovah. To Christian Mystics she is God's Grandmother (*Olwyn* or *Olwen*).

3 *Mochyn (pl. Moch];* Pigs, or more properly, *Swine:* Names have been retained from history, e.g. Mochdref (Pig Town), site not known but c.f. Swindon, Swine Town. In the Legends, the Pigs were stolen from Pryderi, Son of Pwyll King of Pembrokeshire Annwm, by the magic of Gwydion the Ash God, on behalf of Math son of Mathonwy, King of North Wales. Gwydion and Pryderi fought a battle and Pryderi was slain. His grave is in Maentwrog in Gwynedd. A Standing Stone stands by the wall of the church. The *Swineherds* of Mythology were not to be despised: they were the Oracular Priests in the service of the Death Goddess.

4 *Ladi Wen* : (White Lady or White Goddess). She was a lovely, slender woman with a hooked nose, pale face, red lips like Rowan berries, blue eyes and long fair hair. But she could transform herself into animal form: Sow (see Cerridwen [2], Mare (see Mari Lwyd [9]) and more. A Celtic mythological apparition who was the ancient power of Fright and Lust whose embrace was Death. She was evoked to warn children of the consequences of bad behaviour; a terrifying ghost who

377

may ask for help or may offer treasure or gold in return for obedience.

5 *Will o' the Wisp:* the self-ignited flame of methane gas that hovers over bogs and marshes. It also accumulates between the stone strata underground causing explosions and fire. It has caused many coal-pit disasters, taking many lives. Called *'Firedamp'* it is the fear of all Miners, along with water.

6 d*u Lac (e.g. Lancelot du Lac:* Lancelot of the Lake.): du Lac (del Acqs) signifies a descent from the Desposynia bloodline, Lac being a Holy Paint Colour, as purple is now. Lancelot's mother was Vivianne II, the *Lady of the Lake.* She has been variously named: Nimue, Elaine, Niniane, Evienne, Niviane, Nyneve and Morgan (Morgaine) le Faye (Arthur's sister). Lancelot then, was Arthur's nephew. Vivianne II was the Ruling Priestess of Avalon (Elysian Fields, the Isle of Apple Trees, now believed to have been Glastonbury). She gave the sword Excalibur to Arthur and retrieved it when thrown into the lake by Sir Bedivere (Llaminawg) at the death of Arthur.

7 *Gwenhwyfar:* The Three Great Queens of Arthur were all named Gwenhwyfar (=*Guinevere;* Mod.Eng. *Jennifer*). The Three Great Queens in a Welsh Triad (Prose Tale) are, *Rhiannon, Branwen and Arianrhod.* They have also been said to represent the 3 – fold Demoness (White Goddess) who is *Mother, Bride and Layer Out* to Fallen Man. The Greeks worship her as *The Three Fates.*

8 *Rhiannon*: Daughter of Hefydd the Old. Earlier, as *Epona,* a Celtic Horse Goddess. Then as the Celtic *Rigantona* (Devine Queen), one of the Three Great Queens of *Arthur* then called Gwenhwyfar. She was also known as *Branwen, Arianrhod, Cerridwen, Blodeuwedd, Olwen (Olwyn), Dann and Anna,* whose castle was the *Corona Borealis.* As such she may also have been an aspect of the *White Goddess. (*see also *Gwenhwyfar* and *White Goddess).*

9 *Mari Lwyd:* (Grey Mare or Grey Mary). A Welsh midwinter tradition. A form of visiting wassail, a luck-bringing ritual where the participants follow a person dressed as a horse from house to house (including pubs) and sing at each door in the hope of food and drink. The 'Horse Dress' consists of a mare's skull fixed to a wooden post held by a person concealed under a white sheet. (c.f. 'Hobby Horse). The tradition is derived from an ancient rite for the Celtic Goddess Rhiannon (see [8]). The tradition still persists in parts of South Wales, when on New Year's Day children go from house to house to sing *Blwyddyn Newydd Dda* (Happy New Year) in hope of a monetary blessing.

10 *Bran (Bendigeidfran; Bran y Fendigeid)*: "Bran the Blessed". Bran = Raven. Son of Llyr, whose tree was the **Alder** – the first vowel of the alphabet. Other names for *Bran* are *Cronos (Odysseus)* the Alder-and-Crow Hero, *Apollo, Saturn, Aesculapius, Hercules and Jesus*. His face was artificially coloured crimson with the dye of the sacred Alder. (The *Sirens* of the *Odysseus* Myth are the *Birds of Rhiannon* who also sang in the Myth of *Bran*). He was of giant stature and had a *Cauldron of Rebirth*. His death could only be brought about by a poisoned arrow in the foot. (cf Achelles). He was also the Celtic forerunner of *Bron*, the Fisher King of later Arthurian Legend . Bran was the father of *Gwion* and was known as the Giant *Ogyr Fran* ; *Gwion*'s mother was *Cerridwen* [2] [42].

11 *Culhwch and Olwen:* Culhwch was the son of King Cilydd by his first wife Goleuddyd (Daylight). Culhwch was so named because he was found in a Swine's (Hwch's) Burrow [3].

Olwen, or Olwyn, daughter of the Giant Ysbathaden Pencawr, was also known as the Laughing Aphrodite of Welsh Legend and as Blodeuwedd, (Flower Face) [42]; the May Queen (Daughter of the Hawthorn) and always connected with the Wild Apple (Eve?); a Summer aspect of the White Goddess; *She of the White Track*, since four White Trefoils sprang up with her every step on the forest floor. *So where should she be sought but in the White Track of the Milky Way Galaxy formed from the spurt of milk from the breast of the Great Goddess Rhea? Rhea was the celestial counterpart of Olwen/Blodeuwedd..* She may also have been taken form the original source and enlisted to act as Tolkien's Ladies In White: *Luthien* in the Silmarillion, and *Arwen* in Lord of the Rings.

The Hanes Culhwch ac Olwen is the first and oldest of the Celtic Arthurian Legends; it is not collected with the four tales of the Mabinogi but occurs in the earlier original Red Book of Rhudderch. Culhwch was Arthur's cousin and he enlisted Arthur's help in finding Olwen. Arthur sends six of his finest warriors to search for her. She was receptive to Culhwch but her father the Giant Ysbathaden Pencawr ruled that she could only marry him if he completed about forty impossible tasks, one of which was to fight the terrible boar *Twrch Trwyth*. He succeeds and the Giant is killed, and so the marriage takes place.

Much of the original tale is a list of the Knights of Arthur, some 200 of them, together with their antecedents, horses and swords; and a list of the 40 or so tasks which Culhwch was to perform.

12 *Laver-bread (Bara Lawr): Porphyra umbilicalis.* An edible, littoral alga, (seaweed) found on the West coast of Wales and Scotland, East coast of Ireland, and along the coasts of Japan. A delicacy of S. Wales, shredded and eaten fried in bacon fat. In Japan it is shredded and dried and eaten as *Nori.* It has a high content of Iodine, Iron, and Vitamins B_2, A, D, and C.

13 *Gaia Theory (*1960's, James Lovelock) proposes that the organic and inorganic components of Earth have evolved as a single living, self-regulating entity. It automatically controls its systems in order to maintain its own survival.

14 *Nolle me tangere*: Literally "Do Not Cling To Me." (John 20. 17). Jesus speaking to Mary Magdalene in the garden outside the cave after His Crucifixion and Resurrection. Mary attempted to cling to Jesus but was rebuffed according to the Law, because Mary was pregnant and physical contact was forbidden. Mary Magdalene has also been identified as Sophia = Wisdom = Baphomet..

15 *Mabinogi (sometimes: Mabinogion)*: Four tales drawn from Welsh myth, legend and lore.

16 *Llew Llaw Gyffes.* One of the Three Skilful Shoemakers*: Llew:* lion; *Llaw*: hand; *Gyffes* : skilful. Son of *Arianrhod* and grandson of *Mathonwy* Lord of Gwynedd (effectively, North Wales). *Math,* son of *Mathonwy* would call him Dylan, the Divine Fish-Child, but *Arianrhod* would not name him. Then she saw him throw a missile at a small bird (?wren?) that had landed on the gunwale of the ship and struck it between the sinew of the leg and the bone. So he came upon his name. Caesar would call him *Mercury* the inventor of all the Arts. Llew Llaw Gyffes was to become a Sacred King by marriage with Blodeuwedd[42] but he had to sustain *Jacob's injury* i.e. an anterior dislocation of the hip, causing an abduction (a turning away) of the thigh, so that he would never put his sacred heel on the ground. (See also *The laming of Jesus[36]*).

17 *Penstiffs*: Colloquialism; literally, *Stiff Heads* with a meaning of Thick Heads, unpersuadable, rigid thinking.

18 *Morganwg:* A Welsh County, now known as Glamorganshire.

19 *Poseidon:* (Also for some, as Neptune; for others Neptune was his helper). God of the Sea. Son of Rhea and brother of Zeus. His wife was Amphitrite, the Sea Goddess. His tree was the Ash, the tree of Sea Power; ships were built of Ash wood because of its power to resist rotting by seawater. He ruled all sea beasts and fishes.

20 *Gorse:* In Welsh folklore is good against witches.

21 *Mân:* (with a long 'a' as in ah) A thick iron griddle plate heated over a fire and used for cooking flat, or unleavened breads, and biscuits.

22 *Rufus red:* The colour of a red beard.

23 *Hazelnut Shell:* The *Hazel (Letter C)* is the *Tree Of Wisdom.* Knowledge of the Arts and Sciences is bound up with the eating of these nuts. The Hazel tree also produced the forked stick used as a Divining Rod in the search for water.

24 *Monatomic Gold:* The Philosopher's stone. Orbitally Rearranged Monatomic Elements (ORMS). Used to produce stained-glass. The Knights Templar in the region of Languedoc used the area's alluvial gold to manufacture their Ormus Powder. They were carrying on a tradition first established by Moses when he burned the golden calf in Sinai and made a *'bread'* with it, which he gave to the Israelites.

The later Davidic Dynasty was founded on this *'bread'* made with this gold. The Karnack Priests in charge of its production settled the Therapeutate (Healers) – an ascetic Jewish sect - as the Essene Community in Southern Judea and the Edomite Dead Sea region - notably at Qumran – hence *The Dead Sea Scrolls.*

Both King David, Son of Jesse, and Jesus, a Royal Child, were born in *Bethlehem* which means 'House of Bread'. *Nazareth* did not exist at the time of Jesus; He was a *Nazarene* - a Sect of the Essene Therapeutate community.

Early practitioners of the processing were *'Master Craftsmen'* which is what Jesus' 'father', Joseph was called. (Carpenter , is a mistranslation of the original Aramaic into Greek).

It is now known that this white powder gold has the qualities attributed to it by the Therapeutate priests of Qumran: it stimulates hormonal production and enhances the immune system. It has been prescribed as a treatment for Rheumatoid Arthritis, an autoimmune disease.

25 *Great Goddess:* The Triple Goddess or The White Goddess or Fates.

26   *The Holy Unspeakable Name Of God:* Derived from 6th Century BC Jewish sources by the Pythagoreans. In four letters it can be given as *JHWH* which is a Tetragrammaton:

> *J:* The letter of new life and sovereignty.
> *H:* 1.The letter of the first day of Creation (let there be Light).
> *W:* The letter of the last day of Creation (let there be Rest).
> *H:* 2.The Brightness of God (identified with Wisdom).

It is also found in unsigned Jewish-Egyptian papyri as *IAOOUE*. The Eightfold Name Of God was *JEHUOVAO* the lofty Name which gave *Gwion* (Fion in Irish) his power: he ate of the *Salmon Of Knowledge* that had fed on the nuts fallen from the nine hazels of poetic art; he claimed to be a spiritual son of the Alder God – Bran. The *Eightfold Holy Name Of God* also served as the *Eightfold City Of Light* in which Thoth, Hermes, Mercury and Jesus the Christ were said to dwell. By utterance of the Name, the dead may be restored to life: it was in such a fashion that Jesus raised Lazarus (brother of his Queen, Mary (Martha), daughter of Cleopas) from the dead at Bethany. But there was a ransom to be paid, and Jesus said: 'I have not come to take life. Greater love hath no man than he lay down his life for a friend.' Among the Greeks and Jews the tradition was 'A Life for a Life'; and Jesus said, 'O Lord, be merciful to me on the Great Day when you call for the full ransom.' In the historical event, He was crucified, not transfixed with a sword as the Messiah was fated to be. (Was this the reason His 'death' was hastened by impalation with a sword?) This was of some importance since the God of the Hebrews, Jehuovao, cursed a crucified man and debarred him from the after-world. However, there was no reason why He could not be worshiped as a Gentile God.

27 *Tree Alphabet:* The letter of each tree, in its season, represented the alphabet by which learning was attained. The *Battle Of The Trees* (on the order of the letters) was a primitive British tradition dating from the 4th Century BC and relates to the capture of an oracular shrine (possibly Avebury) by the guessing of the letters of a God's name. It became a struggle between two rival Priesthoods in Celtic Britain for the control of National Learning, and their control was fiercely guarded for it hid the Holy Name Of God. The Seven Vowels of the Tree Alphabet, read sunwise (i.e. from East to West) form the Sacred Name: II I E U O A AA – in Latin letters, J I E V O A A. The word *Tree* in the Celtic Language meant *Anna* or *Learning.*

28 *Camelot:* Arthur's Castle. Many attempts have been made to locate it physically. A late addition to the Arthurian Legend (12 Century) it was considered (and accepted) to be Caerleon in Wales – or Carlisle or, Celliwig in Cornwall, or even Winchester, Capitol of Wessex under King Alfred, which is also home to a Medieval Round Table (a Copy). It is likely that, like most Medieval Kings, King Arthur probably used many locations for his Courts and so kept his Lords and Knights pacified.

29 *Dolmen:* A burial chamber, a 'womb' of earth consisting of a capstone supported by two (or more) uprights in which a dead hero is buried in a crouched position like a foetus in a womb awaiting rebirth. The cross-stone and pillars held consonants and the threshold held the seven vowels of the Tree Alphabet which formed the Sacred Name of God. This alphabet also served as a calendar with one post for spring, the other for autumn, the lintel for summer and the threshold for New Year's Day, or renewal, or Rebirth.

30 *The Fire That Burns And Doesn't Eat:* Actually, *The Fire That Burns But Does Not Consume.* God is a Spirit and His Ministers are a *Flaming Fire* which is the Fire that Moses (Priest to the Sun God) saw in the bush. *'When Fire descends from Heaven, then is the time to sing the Hymn of Praise.* (There is an interesting tautology associated with so-called 'Lesser Gods' when Jesus maintained that *'We do not worship the Sun but our God in the Form of the Sun').*

31 *Chariot in Egypt:* Chariot of Fire: relates to the Vision of Ezekiel and to the Four New Years in a twelvemonth: the *Autumnal Equinox,* the *Vernal Equinox, Midwinter* and *Midsummer.* Each New Year is a spoke in a wheel: *A wheeling Year Of Four Seasons,* and *Each Year Is A Wheel in a Four – Wheeled Chariot (An Olympiad* as measured by the Greeks) running from the beginning of things to the end of things.

32 *Seven Pillars Of Wisdom: The Litany of the Blessed Virgin* contains the Prayer **'Seat of Wisdom Pray For Us.** The Virgin has been represented as the Seven Pillared Temple which Wisdom (Proverbs 1X, 100) had built for Herself.

(i) They are the Seven Pillars Of Solomon's Temple and represent the Seven Holy Trees (letters) where is the *White Hind Of Wisdom*. Each Pillar is symbolised by the Seven Buds (Lights) of the Sacred Candlestick (*Menorah*) and the Seven Vowels of the Tree Alphabet (see *The Holy Unspeakable Name Of God*).

(ii) The Seven Pillars Of Wisdom are identified by Hebrew Mystics with the *Seven Days Of Creation* (Genesis I) and with the Seven Days of the Week; each day is linked to one of the Heavenly Bodies and to the Seven Sacred Trees of the Irish grove with their letters (and Hebrew alternatives):

Light	Sun	Sunday	Birch (Broom)	B
Division Of the Waters	Moon	Monday	Willow	S
Dry Land & Trees	Mars	Tuesday	Holly (Kerm Oak)	T
Heavenly Bodies & Seasons	Mercury	Wednesday	Hazel (Almond)	C
Sea Beasts & Birds	Jupiter	Thursday	Oak (Terebinth)	D
Land, Beasts Man & Woman	Venus	Friday	Apple (Quince)	CC (Q)
Repose	Saturn (Bran Jehovah)	Saturday	Alder (Pomegranate)	F

(iii) Also, each Light of the Sacred Candlestick symbolises one of Seven Doctrinal Categories (Pillars) of almost every religious belief system. They are: *The Origin and Nature of the Universe; The Nature of God; The Nature of Man; The Nature of Salvation; Dimensions of Existence; The Destiny of Man; Cycles, Ages and State of the Universe.*

384

(iv) The title is also well known from TE Lawrence's book on the First World War Arab Revolt, and much has been made of its 'mysticism'. But in this case there may be nothing mystic about it; it was a title that TEL intended for an earlier book (possibly about his digging for relics at Carchemish in modern day Syria) which was never written.

33 *Cawl:* A Welsh broth made with a marrow-bone (usually, and properly, a shin-bone of mutton) with whatever vegetables were available and cooked slowly in the stock.

34 *Avalon:* Now considered to be Glastonbury: the Isle of Apple Trees where Vivienne II: The Lady of the Lake resided [6]. The Apple Tree was the noblest tree of all and was the Tree of Immortality though Wisdom. One can speculate therefore that she was also the Christian Eve who plucked the apple for the First Adam, conferring upon him the Knowledge of Good and Evil (i.e. Wisdom) and thus Immortality. This provides an alternative understanding to the traditional Christian story of the Garden of Eden (Avalon?).

35 *Cathars /Merovingians:* The *Cathars* were a Christian religious movement with *dualistic* and *Gnostic* elements that came from the Byzantium Empire and appeared in the Languedoc region of France in the 11C at a time when the Virgin Goddess *Rhea* – Mother of Zeus – was honoured as *Mary* Mother of Jesus. The devotees were persecuted and massacred under the Inquisition because of the threat they posed to Papal Orthodoxy. They were an anti-sacerdotal community who did not believe that a propitiatory sacrifice by a priesthood was a moral, spiritual and political corruption by the Catholic Church. Their greatest *Heresy* was the rejection of the *Circumincession: The Doctrine Of The Trinity – God The Father; God The Son; God The Holy Ghost.* They adhered to *Arianism* which holds that Christ, the Son Of God did not always exist but was created by, and was therefore distinct from, God The Father. This belief was grounded in John 14. 25 and Proverbs 8. 22. The historical relatives of Jesus, including His sister Mary (Martha), His consort (Mary) and her brother Lazarus, His brothers Jose, Judah and Simeon and their descendants are known as the *Desposyni*. But there is more: In the Catharist belief Jesus and Mary Magdalene were married under the Hebrew Law and they travelled together to the S. of France after his 'resurrection' where Mary (His wife) gave birth to a Son who established the Merovingian Dynasty. As such he is said to be the ancestor of all the European Royal Families – *The Sang Real* (Blood Royal.), a contention upheld in Free Masonry.

36 *The laming of Jesus:* Jesus had seven signs of royalty: a red beard; left – handedness; a hooked nose; a pale face; sea – green eyes; forehead veins in the form of Upsilon; a white right shoulder. But He lacked the eighth sign of royalty: *the sacred thigh* shown by Abraham and his son Jacob (Genesis). This eighth sign was added at the Heel Stone: He was held with thighs divaricated and His left thigh was displaced at the hip by being leapt upon. Henceforth He would walk in a 'mincing' style, His left heel never to touch the ground.

37 *Llyn y Morynion:* A Lake in Gwynedd. Blodeuedd's maidens are said to have drowned there when pursued by Gwydion. He caught her and changed her name to Blodeuwedd which means Owl or Flowerface so that she would be forever harassed by other birds.

38 *The Battle of the Trees:* Ancient Bardic Tales signifying the Battle for Religious Supremacy and the secrets of the Alphabets. Religious Mysteries were fundamentally concerned with astronomical predictions. Jesus was born at the Winter Solstice, the birthday of the Sun at its southernmost or right-hand point. Jesus' baptism and anointing was a ceremony of Rebirth on the date of the rising of the Dog – Star (a *Bar Mitzvah)*. The Messianic Star of Isaiah's prophesy (and followed by The Three Wise Men), was the Dog – Star, the badge of the House Of David and whose Priest was Moses.

39 *Lammas:* (August 2nd). *Lugh* and *Lughmass* in Ireland. One of the four 'cross-quarter days' on which the British Witches celebrated their Sabbaths, the others being Candllemass (Feb 2nd), May Eve and All Hallows E'en, when the year died. The name has been given to the *Hiring Fairs* which took place between the Hay Harvest and the Corn Harvest (see the works of Thomas Hardy amongst others). Now it has been retained and celebrated by *Wakes Week.*

40 *Holy Spirit (Sophia = Wisdom)* was female in Hebrew. The Virgin Mary was the physical vessel in which this concept was incarnate and *Mary* to the Gnostics meant *Of The Sea.* In the *Elusian Mysteries* it is written that she gave birth to the *Devine Child, Son of the Wise One who came from the sea.* He was seated in an Osier (Willow) harvest basket, as was Moses, Taliesin, Llew Llaw Gyffes, and Romulus. Such a basket was also used as a *Manger, Cradle,* and *Winnowing Sieve.*

Hence Jesus, the Devine Child was laid in a Manger used as a cradle.

41 *The Last Post*: Used in British Army Camps to signal the end of the day. From the Dutch custom called *taptoe* which signalled the moment beer taps had to be turned off. Similar to the American *Taps* but with significant differences, not least in the music. It is incorporated into Military Funerals and Commemorations (e.g. at the Cenotaph) to symbolise the final farewell.

42 *Cerridwen:* The White Sow, the Barley Goddess; the month of the Barley Harvest was July 8 to August 4. The Passover was a 'Barley Festival' Jehovah was the Protector of Barley, the original *Jehovah of the Passover* being *Dionysius*. She gave her name to Britain.

43 *Blodeuwedd (originally Blodeuedd):* Literally, 'Flower Aspect'. A maiden originally produced by enchantment by *Gwydion* and *Math, son of Mathonwy* from the flowers of the Oak, Broom and Meadowsweet. It was also another name for *Olwen (Olwyn) the May Queen,* daughter of the Hawthorn and the laughing Aphrodite of Welsh Legend connected with the Wild Apple (Eve?); also as *Morgaine le Faye* King Arthur's sister. Renamed *Blodeuwedd (Owl)* by Gwydion.

44 *Cymru:* Now the inhabitants of Wales they were originally a wandering Black Sea Tribe known as the *Cimmerians,* the Tribe of Gomer, son of Japhet (Genesis X, 2).They were led into Britain via Spain by Hu Gadarn. There is a rich history of the wandering tribes of the Middle East who followed the ancient Trading Roots.

APPENDIX II

SOURCES

Baigent, Micheal (with Leigh, Richard and Lincoln, Henry). 1982. The Holy Blood and the Holy Grail. Jonathon Cape. London.

Bollard, John K. (Translation) 2006. The Mabinogi. (Also known as The Mabinogion). Gomer Press. Llandysul, Ceredigion.

Gardener, Laurence. 1996. Bloodline of the Holy Grail. Element. London.

Gardener, Laurence. 2005. The Magdalene Legacy. Element. London.

Gould, Steven Jay. 1997. Questioning The Millennium. Jonathan Cape. London.

Graves, Robert. 1946 King Jesus. Farrar, Straus, Giroux. New York

Graves, Robert. 1948. (Paperback 1999). The White Goddess. Faber & Faber. London

Jones, Eirwen. 1947. Folk Tales Of Wales. Thomas Nelson & Sons Ltd. London.

Korda, Michael. 2011. Hero. The Life and Legend of Lawrence of Arabia. JR Books. London.